D0042383

CALGARY PUBLIC LIBRARY

DEC - 2013

# Journey to Rainbow Island

# Journey to Rainbow Island

## Christie Hsiao

BENBELLA BOOKS, INC.

DALLAS, TX

This book is a work of fiction. Names, characters, places, and incidents are the product of the author's imagination and are used fictitiously. Any resemblance to actual events, locales, or persons, living or dead, is coincidental.

Copyright © 2013 by Christie Hsiao

All rights reserved. No part of this book may be used or reproduced in any manner whatsoever without written permission except in the case of brief quotations embodied in critical articles or reviews.

BenBella Books, Inc.
10300 N. Central Expressway
Suite #530
Dallas, TX 75231
www.benbellabooks.com
Send feedback to feedback@benbellabooks.com

Printed in the United States of America

10   9   8   7   6   5   4   3   2   1

Library of Congress Cataloging-in-Publication Data:

Hsiao, Christie.
    Journey to Rainbow Island / Christie Hsiao.
        pages cm
    Summary: When her idyllic life on Rainbow Island is destroyed by the dragon, Obsidigon, Yu-ning must embark on a dangerous journey, guided by her master teacher, Metatron, in hopes of overcoming the darkness attacking her home and also the scars of sadness marking her own heart.
    ISBN 978-1-939529-24-4 (hardback)—ISBN 978-1-939529-28-2 (electronic) [1. Fantasy. 2. Self-reliance—Fiction.  3. Adventure and adventurers—Fiction.  4. Dragons—Fiction. 5. Islands—Fiction.]  I. Title.
    PZ7.H85618Jou 2013
    [Fic]--dc23

                                                                                    2013027275

Editing by Kyle Duncan
Copyediting by Annie Gottlieb
Proofreading by Michael Fedison and Amy Zarkos
Cover and interior illustrations by Ralph Voltz, www.ralphvoltz.com
Cover design by Sarah Dombrowsky
Text design and composition by Publishers' Design and Production Services, Inc.
Printed by Bang Printing

Distributed by Perseus Distribution
www.perseusdistribution.com

To place orders through Perseus Distribution:
Tel: (800) 343-4499
Fax: (800) 351-5073
E-mail: orderentry@perseusbooks.com

Significant discounts for bulk sales are available. Please contact Glenn Yeffeth at glenn@benbellabooks.com or (214) 750-3628.

*To the light, to the children, and to all the beautiful beings in the world . . . And to the infinite love that we all are.*

# Contents

# Contents

# Contents

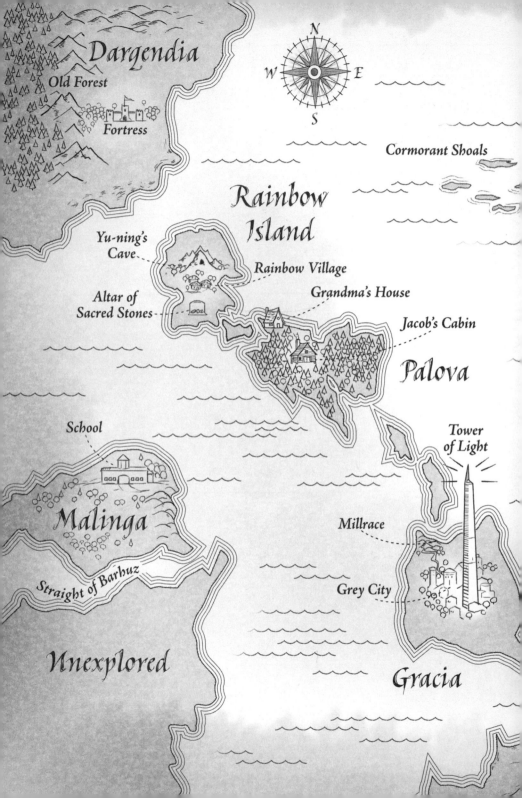

# Yu-ning's World

Obsidigon's
Lair

Baggul

Underground River

Tunzai Imperial
Palace

Cliffs
of Conundrum

The Ghost Ship

Tunzai
City

Tunzai

Caer-a-mor

Porch of
Tranquility

Farcara

Snowy
Mountain

# One

# Conjured

THOUGH IT WAS DAY, it was quite dark, with no sun in the slate grey sky. The ocean was all froth and rage. The wind and rain slammed against the waves as the elements crashed against one another with violent fury. In the distance was an enormous mass of rock—a desolate grey island alone in a vast ocean. Waves crashed against steep, treacherous cliffs. There were no beaches or bays—just walls of rock and cliff surrounding the entire island. High on a bluff, a dark opening could be seen: a cave. Inside was a strange dwelling, full of old scrolls, bones, books, and items of enchantment. It was the dwelling of a sorcerer.

Inside the cave a bent figure waved his arms about him slowly, from side to side, hands whipping to and fro, front to back, back to front. The man seemed neither young nor old, but mysteriously ageless. His eyes were pale—the color of moonlight on a cold winter's night. He was tall and thin as death, with dark robes draped across his bony shoulders.

The light of a nearby fire danced off his shaved head, his skin nearly as pale as his eyes. He was in a trance. Over a large murky pool before him, arms outstretched, he held a huge skull—the skull of a long-dead creature. Though you wouldn't know to look at it, the skull was a very rare specimen, belonging to a race of dragons long thought erased from the face of the world.

The pale-eyed sorcerer lowered the skull into the water, and immediately the dark, still surface began to roil and turn as smoke rose from the inky waters. The roiling turned to violent crashing as waves of water spouted upward; and soon, out of the angry black liquid the outline of a dark, scaled head rose slowly. A pale yellow eye appeared, followed by a long, hard-scaled neck. It was indeed a *Darq* creature—a black dragon. And it was the first of its kind to rise from dark waters in 100 years.

The man smiled, closed his eyes; his hands stopped their macabre, slow beating, and rose in front of him. His creation at last was born. The creature continued to rise from the water and stepped onto the floor of the sorcerer's dwelling, dark water pouring from its body onto the hard, smooth surface of the grotto. The sorcerer stood before the creature, took its enormous head in his hands, and whispered an indecipherable incantation into the black creature's ear. The dragon pulled back, stared into the man's eyes, and, ever so slightly, nodded its head in recognition.

The creature ambled toward the entrance of the cave and moved to the precipice of the cliff. It beat its massive leathered wings three times and took flight into the dusky sky. It rose higher and higher into the stormy elements, racing through cloud and rain. Lightning flashed intermittently, revealing rock-hard, obsidian black scales as it flew into the coming night. Its blackness merged with the ever-darkening sky, a black shadow that blended into the young, violent night.

# Two

# Home

*I*T WAS ANOTHER BEAUTIFUL DAY on Rainbow Island. The sky was soft baby blue, and plush cotton clouds darted across the azure expanse. A comfortable breeze blew as summer's mild sun pulsated gentle rays onto the Island, warming it slowly and sweetly. A brilliant, gigantic rainbow covered the sky over the Island; its seven-banded light streaked out from the Island as far as the eye could see.

Beneath the large rainbow were lush, verdant trees, mountains of green, and grasslands that rolled for miles, speckled with colorful flowers. Large morpho, hairstreak, and swallowtail butterflies skipped through the afternoon air as honeybees drank sweet nectar from voluptuous tropical blooms. The calls of resplendent quetzals echoed from the cloud forest above, while lower on the slopes military macaws, toucans, and blue-crowned trogons hunted for ripe fruit in the thick forest canopy. The Island was surrounded by pristine ocean, and a dazzling tropical reef ringed the entire Island—a beautiful band of teeming life and color.

This was paradise—the most beautiful and joyful place in the universe.

A dark-haired girl of eleven sat blissfully in the middle of a field of heliconia, plumeria, and hibiscus flowers. Her frame was petite, and her long, dark brown hair was pulled loosely into a ponytail, renegade wisps blowing across her face in the breeze. She swept the hair out of her face as she leaned over to escort a ladybug from a blade of grass onto her finger.

Her large, round brown eyes focused on the tiny creature as a smile danced across her open, beatific face. Her spirit was one with the bountiful nature that surrounded her, glowing, joyful, and luminous.

But she was not any ordinary child. This particular girl was endowed with powerful spiritual and healing gifts— abilities she had received from birth. This special place was called Rainbow Island. As with all the children of the Island, she had a purity and goodness of heart that gave strength and vibrancy to the rainbow that shined above. Though only eleven, she was the leader of all the Island children and was deeply adored by all. You see, there was nothing known of jealousy, strife, or hatred on Rainbow Island.

Her name was Yu-ning, which means love and serenity.

Yu-ning smiled happily as she basked in the splendor of her surroundings. She began each morning lying in this exact field of flowers, daily filled with the same wonderment and delight. She gently placed the ladybug upon the leaf of an orange plumeria blossom. As she did, she swept her right hand across all the flowers in front of her. A wave of warm pink light appeared and began to sparkle and spread across the entire field. Sparkling, heart-shaped pink gemstones could be seen all across the field, shimmering in the sun. These were the precious pink crystals of Rainbow Island, Yu-ning's favorite gemstones. Yu-ning looked into the distance beyond the field with excited expectation. Her eyes gleamed with joy as a huge smile spread across her face.

Across the field a cluster of happy children and animals skipped, ran, and twirled toward her. "Yu-ning, Yu-ning!" they called out, laughing as they approached. Some of the children were dripping wet, having spent the morning frolicking on the beach. Others wore garlands of flowers in their hair, and all were admiring the beautiful pink crystals. Some of the children trailed colorful pieces of silk as they ran through the field, the diaphanous material blowing above them in the breeze.

Several children bit into mangos and papayas freshly picked from surrounding trees. As they gathered to play and dance, melodious music played softly beyond the meadow. A gigantic kapok tree loomed in the distance, its full, lush leaves shining subtly in the soft sun. The base of the kapok was vast, its massive trunk branching out in many directions. The noble tree was 40 feet in diameter and rose 150 feet into the sky. As Yu-ning gazed up into its great branches, she saw a riot of life, including large, elegant bromeliads and other colorful epiphytes. The late morning sun grew warmer and they enjoyed the cool grass and shade beneath the shelter of the massive tree. Families of colorful toucans, parrots, and toucanettes landed on the outstretched branches and sang playful summer melodies to the children.

"Hello, my friends, it is such a beautiful song you are singing," Yu-ning called to a boisterous flock of red-lored parrots on the branch above.

The parrots squawked, "Hello, Yu-ning. We are singing this song for you."

"Thank you," Yu-ning laughed. "Let's all sing together."

Yu-ning and the other children produced wooden flutes, small lyres, and harps from small, colorful bags. Yu-ning sang a beautiful melody as she strummed her lyre to the tune of the parrots. As she rested her head against the trunk of the tree, a flash of rainbow colors undulated through the bark and moved upward into all of the branches. The tree too began to sing—the voice of the wind, but with words that were clear and bright.

"My rainbow tree," she sighed with reverence as she looked up into its leaves. All the children were enraptured by its magical presence. They felt the power as the tree radiated light and energy, and Yu-ning heard enchanting music playing on the other side of the great trunk. Yu-ning walked to the other side of the tree, following the gentle, sweet sounds of a flute. A handsome eleven-year-old boy with large round eyes and brown hair sat with his back against the trunk. The melody he played was sweet but sad. Yu-ning jumped happily at the sight of her best friend. "Romeo!" Yu-ning exclaimed.

Romeo looked up and smiled tenderly, lowering his flute. "Hi, Yu-ning," he sighed, his voice filled with apprehension.

Yu-ning knelt down next to him and furrowed her brow. "It's such lovely music you are playing. Why aren't you happy?" she asked.

8

"I had a dream filled with many dark faces, and one face in particular. It was large and black, with yellow, dead-looking eyes. Almost like stone," he said softly.

Yu-ning looked at him pensively, concern filling her eyes. She could see the vision. She leaned in to hug her friend and said, "Don't worry, Romeo, there's only the rainbow in the sky and beauty all around us." Together they looked up through the leaves of the kapok tree to see the clear blue sky and sunshine.

"Let's play more music. It will make you feel better," Yu-ning encouraged him.

Romeo was quiet. Yu-ning nudged him to look at the rainbow above them. "Look, Romeo, the rainbow! I'll sing a song for you. You are like that shining rainbow in the sky!"

Yu-ning opened her arms wide toward the sky. "Whatever our lessons, Romeo, always remember that only the light and color in this world matters. Come on; let's sing a song together. Let's sing a song with the birds," Yu-ning said eagerly, trying to distract her friend.

"All right ..." Romeo nodded and smiled slightly as he started to hum with Yu-ning. He picked up his flute and played his gentle tune.

"Romeo! Let's play in the tree!" Yu-ning exclaimed. "We'll make our music with the tree." Together they watched as the massive branches swept down, grabbed hold of them, and carried them high into the foliage above. Yu-ning laughed with delight as the tree pulled them higher and higher until they were sitting in the center of its vastness. Romeo looked down at all the children as they danced and sang below. Yu-ning leaned back and tucked herself into a comfortable

nook within the branches. "Let's play, Romeo." Together they played a lilting melody and smiled together as they closed their eyes and felt the coolness of the bark beneath their bodies.

Yu-ning looked up as four large leaves fluttered into her right palm. Slowly she inspected each leaf, reading each one like a book. She saw words, drawings, and little pictures etched into the green chlorophyll veins of each sheath, and nodded slowly as she thanked the tree. She looked at her friend compassionately, with a deep, knowing gaze. "It's going to be all right, Romeo. I will be here for you."

Romeo just looked at her and nodded. He asked no questions and stared out across the serene ocean. Yu-ning looked back at the leaves and whispered, "Thank you, wisdom tree." She placed the leaves gently on the branches.

"I have something for you, Romeo." She reached into her pocket and produced a particularly brilliant purple crystal heart, attached to a red silk thread, which she handed to Romeo. He held it up as soft purple light flowed out of the crystal and out from the tree. "Keep this close to your heart when you are in need of comfort, and hold it before you when you need light to guide your way."

"Thank you," he whispered as Yu-ning tied the necklace around his neck. It was identical to one that Yu-ning had around her neck, except his stone was dark lavender instead of pink. "May its light always remind you of my friendship," said Yu-ning. "Now play some music, Romeo, and let's sing with the parrots; it will make you feel better!"

A crooked smile slowly broke across his face. "All right," said Romeo. He played music on his flute and started singing, along with a chorus of three-wattled bellbirds, blue-crowned motmots, and sleek rufous-tailed jacamars in nearby trees. Afterward, the boy and girl gazed out at the Island, taking in the beautiful view.

"Race you to Rainbow Meadow!" Romeo pushed Yu-ning sideways on the branch as he raced down the tree. They descended the tree as the limbs of the kapok grabbed them and gently passed them down to lower limbs, which deposited them softly on the springy green turf. They ran across the field, leaving the other children to play near the great kapok tree.

They began to slow down as they reached a steep cliff with a narrow path that zigzagged back and forth to a higher meadow above. Romeo picked a pink plumeria blossom and handed it to Yu-ning. He reached for a yellow one, then orange, red, and blue-violet. "All the colors of the rainbow," he said tenderly, handing her the flowers with a nod of his head. "You are my closest and dearest friend, and I know I am not alone with you by my side," Romeo said softly.

Yu-ning held the aromatic bouquet in her small hand and, with her other hand, reached for Romeo's fingers. "It's going to be all right, Romeo. We're together and we'll always have each other."

"Last one to the Seven Sacred Crystals is a tortoise!" Romeo yelled as he pushed her sideways and raced to the head of the path. Yu-ning gave chase, just steps behind him as they ascended the steep trail up the side of the cliff. Many of the other Rainbow Children had followed them, along with their animal friends Leonidas the lion; Shamza the zebra; Stout and Madrigal, who were black and brown bears; Lightmere the deer; Prometheus the horse; and several members of the pink rabbit clan. But most important of all was Octavian the owl, Yu-ning's closest animal friend—her mentor in all things of nature and wildlife.

From a rock that overlooked the path, a green tree frog leapt into the air, headed right for Yu-ning. Yu-ning laughed as the frog landed on her chest, the surprise of it knocking her to the ground as she rolled over giggling. It was Magic, Yu-ning's tiny pet frog—a ball of energy and green lightning. "Hi, Magic!" called Yu-ning, scratching the frog on top of its head as it croaked with delight.

The three ran across the meadow toward a green cliff and were joined by the other Rainbow Children. Cascading waterfalls dotted the side of the steep, lush green cliffs. As they crested the cliff onto a small plateau, before them was a large, flat golden rock. On top of the rock, resting on a natural stone altar, were seven beautiful crystals, each the size of a man's forearm, each with its own beautiful, hand-crafted placeholder hewn into the top of the stone altar.

Out of the seven crystals streamed brilliant translucent lights, the source of the Island's stunning rainbow: red, green, yellow, violet, orange, indigo, and blue. The colors rose in smoke-like wisps above the stone; they intertwined and danced like the most beautiful aurora borealis, reaching well above the Island and outward across the blue sky. This was the sacred rainbow of Rainbow Island, its light going out into the world.

As Yu-ning approached, she saw an unusually tall figure standing near the rock. His hair and beard were long and white, and he was wearing a grey robe and a conical hat that was old and careworn. In his right hand was a shining yellow staff with a large quartz crystal encrusted on the top.

His eyes were filled with wisdom as he waved warmly at Yu-ning. It was Metatron, the Island's master teacher. The large rock upon which sat the Seven Sacred Crystals was surrounded by a glass-like, translucent dome, "unbreakable by any creature," said the kindly wizard to the children now standing by his side. "The first Rainbow Children found the stones in different parts of the Island and brought them together in this meadow," explained Metatron. "They were surprised and delighted to discover that the seven separate stones, when brought together, formed this beautiful prism of light—this rainbow—that has shined brightly over Rainbow Island for multiple generations."

Though the children had heard this story many times in school, they never tired of it. As long as Yu-ning could remember, in fact, she never wearied of Metatron—either sitting with him in silence, or hearing him tell his tales. After all, the wizard was the closest thing to a parent she had ever known. All she really knew was what Metatron told her: as a newborn, she had been brought to the Island by night and left on the steps of the Rainbow School, not far from the main beach. No one knew who brought her, or whether or not her birth parents were still alive. In the morning, the only sign of visitors was the track marks of a small boat that had been pulled high onto the sandy beach.

What she did know was that all the adults on Rainbow Island were wise, kind—and, well, rather mysterious. They themselves were all former Rainbow Children. Metatron was always quick to say that while all children are special, Rainbow Children possessed extraordinary and unique wisdom and spiritual sensitivity. The Island and its school had been built with the express purpose of educating Rainbow

Children, who came from all corners of the realm to live and learn from the gifted instructors.

Though many of the children had not seen their parents for years, they knew this was where they needed to be. Twice a year, on Visitors' Day, many of their parents would travel by ship to visit with their gifted children. That was always a tough day for Yu-ning, who typically sat alone, watching the other kids receive gifts and hugs from their proud parents.

"We all have light within us," said Metatron, interrupting Yu-ning's thoughts. "And everyone's light is important and different. But only when we work together, as one, does that light form a beautiful prism—like our beautiful Island's rainbow! The love flows through us, into the crystals, and out into the world. Without love, the crystals are just, well— interesting rocks." He winked as he said this to Yu-ning.

"Metatron, what do you mean that we all have light inside us?" asked Yu-ning. "Do you mean we are lit up on the inside?"

Metatron offered an easy laugh. "Well, not exactly, my dear. It is like this: our light is born of the human heart and spirit. In other words, goodness, kindness, love, and selfless-ness are an outgrowth of a person being in touch with their inner light—their inner 'spark' of humanity and love. Light is in all of us, we just need to tap into it, exercise it like a muscle, and embrace it. As we do, it is released through us."

Yu-ning pondered this and said, "But what about the rainbow and the crystals—aren't they the source of our light?" She said this as she pointed up at the beautiful display of colors shooting from the crystals at the base of the huge rainbow.

"The goodness comes *through* us, Yu-ning. Without love from our hearts, these stones are lifeless. But as we love one another, that force can flow outward," added Metatron, with a sweep of his arm toward the arc of the rainbow above them. "The light inside us becomes brighter when we share it with others. If we keep it within, it becomes extinguished—like a flame that receives no oxygen. It is always our choice alone, Yu-ning, to embrace the light and allow it to flow, or to reject it, in which case it can die. Outside forces, such as the rainbow here, can encourage the light and spread it. However, the opposite is also true: if we don't nurture the love in our hearts, we can be influenced to make unwise choices—or even to embrace evil."

Yu-ning and Romeo paused, taking in Metatron's words. He could see the looks of confusion on their faces, so he tried a different tack.

"Have you ever seen a stagnant pond?" asked Metatron.

Yu-ning and Romeo looked at each other with quizzical looks and said, "Yes."

"In order for a pond or lake to remain fresh, there must be an outflow," continued Metatron. "If all that happens is that water flows in without flowing out, that body of water will eventually stagnate and die. That is like love: unless there is outflow, a way for us to share our light, it is in danger of dying inside us."

Yu-ning looked thoughtfully at the wizard and nodded that she understood.

"Enough of my lecturing now, and follow me!" he invited, a twinkle in his eye. They walked down the same jungle path, and from this height, their entire village of bamboo huts and cottages lay below on the grassy knolls leading to the main beach. To the left was the Rainbow School. This was a school like no other, where the children were encouraged to study the subjects they chose, to create and dream and imagine, and to explore any subject that inspired them. Yu-ning's favorites were Folklore and Archery.

In her Folklore classes, she read every book she could get her hands on about the history of Rainbow Island and the world surrounding this idyllic land. She knew that for the last 100 years, as Rainbow Island thrived under the teaching of the masters and the community grew, the light of the rainbow had grown stronger. Each year the rainbow's light stretched farther out into the world, reaching islands hundreds of miles in every direction.

Yu-ning loved to spend time on the beach, because that was where she received news of the outside world. The pink dolphins of Rainbow Island were master storytellers, and on many evenings, Yu-ning and the children, along with their teachers, would gather in nearby Rainbow Cove to listen to their tales. By the light of glowing torches at the water's edge, the dolphins would swim in from the open sea and take their positions in a semicircle at the edge of the pool. The children would gather round, perched on rocks at the edge of the water, sitting on soft blankets, listening to the majestic pink creatures take turns sharing news of the outside world. Torchlight would illuminate the heads of the pink dolphins as they bobbed in the gentle waters of the cove. These gatherings were a highlight for Yu-ning, as she had never left Rainbow Island to see the world for herself.

Yu-ning also knew that before the rainbow was manifested from the seven stones, a great darkness had shrouded the world, snuffing out the love in many a man's heart. Evil came in the form of black dragons, or obsidigons, that battled against the mightiest warriors, called the Darq Renders. But the books on this subject were scarce, many having been destroyed by the terrible fires lit by the dark dragons in attacks long forgotten, or lost in the mists of aging, distant memory.

Metatron walked down the path, staff in hand, and took a turn on a seldom-used trail leading further along the side of the mountain. There, off yet a smaller, hidden path, behind thick trumpet vines, was a cave. "This way, child," Metatron said, as he used his staff to pull back the vines to reveal the entrance. Yu-ning turned to smile at Romeo, who entered behind her. Throughout the cave was an array of colorful furniture creating a relaxed, intimate atmosphere: a pink bed, red coffee table, violet sofa, green cabinets, blue drawers, and a well-stocked pantry. The entire cave was filled with beautiful shining colors.

Yu-ning saw a pink knob on the wall next to the bed. She pulled it open to reveal a large walk-in closet. Inside was a wardrobe of dazzling, colorful clothes in just her size. Yu-ning realized in that instant that this was her cave. Everything was scaled down to her size in a dreamy, cozy wonderland. She squealed with glee and plopped down onto the soft, cushiony sofa.

Metatron smiled and looked at Yu-ning with kindness in his eyes. "Yu-ning, you are old enough now to have your own space, as do all the Rainbow Children around their twelfth birthday. And now, this is your home. But don't worry, Yu-ning—you can hit my cottage with a rock from the entrance of your cave! I am always close by."

Yu-ning looked at the wizard as a bright round light floated into the room. It was like nothing Yu-ning had ever seen before. The light halted before them and hovered there. Then, materializing before their eyes, it became a man wearing a soft, white, long-sleeved shirt open at the neck, white cotton pants, and leather sandals. Magic was frightened, and as was his way when he was nervous, he jumped straight up into the air, landing on the ceiling and clinging there upside down.

Though nothing was spoken, Yu-ning heard a message in her head: "Yu-ning, I am One, your divine protector, and I am always with you. No matter what comes, I will stand with you. There is strong darkness engulfing the world, child. And you must combat it." And with that, there was a bright flash, and the man turned back into a floating white light and drifted out of the cave.

Metatron stared long at Yu-ning, compassion in his eyes. Yu-ning broke the silence by asking, "What did One mean, Master?"

"What did you hear?" asked Metatron.

"He said a darkness is covering the world, and that I will need to combat it."

Metatron showed Yu-ning an ancient book resting on the table, covered in soft, hand-tooled leather. This was a book she had never seen in the stacks of the great Rainbow Library, where she had spent many lazy afternoons. Metatron explained that as a Rainbow Child, she was now old enough to learn more about the Island's history and significance. He turned to a particular section toward the center of the book that talked of strange creatures returning 100 years after the death of the last obsidigon, when the light had grown in strength.

"Yu-ning, I have seen a darkness growing in the skies to the east, and in the sea, which has grown grey and stormy around many of our neighboring islands. Rumors abound of ships lost in storms, islands under attack, and darkness coming over the waters. And this year marks the one-hundredth anniversary of the Darq Renders' defeat of the obsidigon army. As you have learned in school, the Renders were warriors who gathered on the plains of Darqendia to defeat the obsidigons. That is what is revealed in this book, and it is that of which One spoke," said Metatron.

"This is my dream!" added Romeo. "The dream I told you about, Yu-ning."

"I'm not sure I understand," countered Yu-ning. "I have heard of the Obsidigon War, but the dark dragons were defeated, and none have been seen in the world for many years, according to what our instructors have taught us."

"What you don't know, Yu-ning, is that a sorcerer of the kind that created the first race of obsidigons is rumored to have risen out of the east. Our dolphin scouts tell us that there is disturbing news from the Imperial Palace of Tunzai: one of the royal princes stole the last obsidigon skull in existence and disappeared. Only from one of the dragon's skulls can a sorcerer conjure an obsidigon. The fear from the Floating Imperial Palace is that this sorcerer is Hobaling, grandson of the Darq wizard who helped unleash the fury of the last Obsidigon Conjuring."

"What is an *Obsidigon Conjuring*, Metatron? I don't understand," persisted Yu-ning.

"These creatures are called *Darq* because they are not natural. They are *conjured*, or crafted using dark magic, and live only to destroy and bring darkness to the world. In the dark is where they thrive and breed, and only through the light of love can they be defeated."

"When will it come, Metatron—this darkness?" inquired Yu-ning.

"We do not know, my child. And the trick is that recognizing the dark is not always easy. Sometimes, telling the difference between good and bad—light and dark—takes more than your physical senses. The key is to also measure a thing in your heart to help you tell the difference. Remember, everyone has light within their heart—only some choose to ignore it, or allow it to be extinguished. And so it's important to always lean on your friends for guidance and wisdom."

"How can we stop it . . . this sorcerer, from creating another obsidigon? Isn't there something you can do to contain it, Metatron?"

"I cannot predict its arrival or discern how it will be stopped," said the wizard. "No one knows the future. All we have is today, Yu-ning. Each day is its own page in life's mysterious book. If we try to read ahead, we lose the story."

"But Metatron . . ." said Yu-ning, before the wizard leaned down and took her face in his hands.

"It is late, the hour past midnight. Sleep, and we will talk more of these things in the morning."

And just as suddenly as he had arrived, the wise wizard was gone.

# Three

# Destruction

THE DARKNESS CAME QUICKLY.

The children of Rainbow Island, along with all the animals, were asleep. This would not have been unusual, for children and animals tend to sleep when they are tired. Particularly when the night is still, the moon a silver sliver in the southern sky, and a soft breeze blows gently from the east. That night was such a night. But this darkness—this sleep—was not normal. In fact, it was unnatural. That is to say, the evil presence that brought the darkness cast it off of itself like a sinister cloak. Whatever and whoever came in contact with the cloak fell even further into slumber. A deep, dark, dreamless sleep.

All were asleep, that is, except Romeo, Yu-ning's most trusted friend. Romeo could not stop thinking of his dark visions, and as much as he wanted to sleep, he couldn't. He tried counting pink dolphins jumping out of the sea, but even that didn't work. Finally, exhaustion overtook him and he nodded off.

Four hours later Romeo woke with a start. Something was not right. He bounded off the oversized chair upon which he had been sleeping and headed for the entrance of the cave. As he exited the small cavern, he knew for sure that something was wrong. It wasn't a sense of strong alarm—just a gnawing twinge of danger.

It was very late—well past midnight—and the slice of moon was beginning to set on the horizon. And the darkness—it was a darker dark, a deep, frightening darkness. "What is the source of this strange darkness?" Romeo asked himself as he made his way down the path toward the beach.

And then he saw the creature.

It stood at least fifteen feet tall, its wings flapping slowly as it hovered just a few feet from the ground. There, an inky silhouette against the white of the sandy beach, was what looked like an obsidigon. But could it be? They were said to be extinct—erased from the world decades ago. Its body, wings, talons, and head were angular, shining, scaled, and very black. Except for its eyes. They were a jaundiced shade of pale yellow. "This is what I saw in my dream," Romeo whispered to himself.

The obsidigon searched the beach, making sure it was not being observed. As its yellow eyes scanned the village and surrounding cliffs, Romeo ducked behind a large tree next to the path. The obsidigon—if that's what it was—began to move down the beach, searching for something. But what?

As the dragon reached the end of the shore, it ascended the cliff, heading toward Rainbow Meadow, the most sacred place on the Island. Realization hit Romeo—the dragon planned to steal the crystals!

Romeo moved with stealth up the path, keeping the dark animal in his sight. He crested the cliff that spilled down into the Sacred Meadow where the Seven Sacred Crystals were located and stopped in his tracks. The large golden stone upon which were set the Seven Sacred Crystals was directly before the dragon. Romeo watched in horror as the obsidigon brought down its huge wing, shattering the protective glass covering the seven stones. The obsidigon breathed fire, swooped up the seven crystals, and flapped its wings, ready to make its departure.

The loud crash awakened many of the children and teachers of the village, who emerged from their homes to investigate. Yu-ning awoke too and sensed danger. She retrieved her bow and quiver of arrows, which were never far from her reach. Though the Rainbow School taught the children to pursue peace and harmony with all creatures, each student was allowed to pursue a martial art. From an early age Yu-ning had exhibited a true talent for the bow.

A crowd formed along the path above the village and moved swiftly toward the crest of the cliff. Romeo appeared on the path above, an orange glow growing above the meadow behind him. "It's a dragon! A dragon has taken the sacred crystals!" he screamed. All froze in their tracks as the giant dragon appeared above, flying low and hard in their direction. A huge ball of fire erupted from its horrible jaws—Metatron stepped in front of the crowd and planted his staff firmly in the ground before him. The fireball smashed into his staff, sending sparks and flame away from the children.

"Run, everyone, back to your homes!" yelled the wizard. Yu-ning emerged, standing next to Metatron, who advanced toward the dark dragon hovering just ahead. The creature flew at Metatron, swept its wing low, and knocked the wizard off his feet. Yu-ning nocked an arrow and let it fly. The arrow hit the dragon dead center between the eyes, but skittered off the obsidian scales and fell harmlessly to the ground.

The terrible creature opened its massive jaws and spewed fire directly at Yu-ning. She dove from the path, but not quickly enough: the edge of the fireball hit her left shoulder, sending searing pain up and down her arm. Yu-ning screamed in agony as she fell into deep grass next to the path, out of the dragon's sight. She tumbled hard down the grassy cliff and landed near the edge of the beach, wounded and semiconscious.

Many of the children and instructors armed themselves with rocks and long sticks. Even Magic heaved a pebble and hit the obsidigon above one eye, causing it to flinch. Leading the charge was Romeo, ahead of the crowd by a dozen steps. The dragon descended on the unsuspecting boy as its talons grabbed hold of Romeo and carried him off the ground. As he rose higher and higher, he could only watch in despair as the dragon sent fireball after fireball upon the scattering villagers below, whose homes were now engulfed in flames.

The creature kept an iron grip on the seven crystals in one talon and Romeo in the other, as the flames engulfing Rainbow Village grew smaller and smaller. As the dragon flew ever farther away, the fires became orange dots in a sea of blackness. Romeo strained to keep his eye on the flames as the orange dots became a single speck that disappeared as the obsidigon headed eastward.

# Four

# Aftermath

THE MORNING DAWNED BLEAK AND STORMY on Rainbow Island, rain falling hard amidst flashes of lightning and thunder. The rain had started shortly after the attack of the obsidigon, sparing the village from total destruction. Even with the rains, the fires had caused massive damage; nearly half the village was either completely or partially burned. Smoke and cinder replaced the idyllic peace of just the day before.

Because the Island had never before experienced war or violence, its small medical clinic was ill equipped to handle all the wounded from the night before. All told, one of the teachers died, and three were severely wounded, including Yu-ning's master Metatron. Eleven children had been injured, some seriously. To make room for more wounded, they converted the main hall of the Rainbow School into a temporary hospital. This is where Cristobel, Yu-ning's archery instructor, was headed, to check on Yu-ning and the other children.

Cristobel had come to Rainbow Island as a child and was taught the art of the bow by her master teacher. She was tall, thin, and athletic, with lovely round eyes of deep brown to match her long hair, which she normally kept in beautiful braids. She was the best archer on the Island, and taught her students to only use a bow and arrow in self-defense, never in anger.

Cristobel walked quietly into the school hall, which at first she did not recognize. The main hall she knew was a colorful, airy room, with floor-to-ceiling white curtains, three sets of French doors on each wall, and lovely mahogany benches. But all of the hand-carved school furniture that normally adorned the room had been removed, and cots occupied most of the large space. Cristobel walked from bed to bed, visiting her pupils and her adult colleagues. Metatron was sleeping heavily, the Island's doctor standing near his bed.

"How is he, Doctor?" inquired Cristobel.

"He has suffered a severe blow to the head, and there is swelling. I won't know the extent of the damage until the swelling around his brain subsides. Until then, all we can do is keep him comfortable. He also suffered burns on his legs and torso."

"Thank you for all you are doing," added Cristobel as she moved on, visiting each of the cots down the row. At the end she saw Yu-ning's cot, and what she saw brought tears to her eyes. Yu-ning's face was swollen and bruised, and her left arm and shoulder were wrapped in bandages containing healing herbs and balm. She was asleep, but tossing fitfully in her cot.

The doctor joined Cristobel at Yu-ning's bedside and inspected the skin under her bandages. "The bruising is superficial, but the burns she sustained on her arm and shoulder are deep, and we need to make sure they don't become infected. She will make a full recovery, but this dark day will always remain with her in the form of her scars. All in all, she was fortunate. It could have been much worse." The doctor placed a reassuring hand on Cristobel's shoulder as he moved away to attend to some of the other children.

Cristobel placed her staff next to Yu-ning's bedside and sat beside her. She brushed the hair gently away from Yu-ning's face, which caused Yu-ning to shift in her bed and slowly open her eyes. "Cristobel . . . what is going on?"

"Do you not remember last night, Yu-ning? The dragon?"

Yu-ning didn't say a word, but sudden tears appeared in her eyes as she remembered the terrible events of the night before—and the abduction of Romeo. "I couldn't help Romeo, Cristobel. I was knocked down and was trying to get up to warn him to move off the path, but it was too late . . ."

"There is nothing you could have done, dear one. The dragon was too strong, and we had no way to defend ourselves," said the teacher.

"Metatron. How is my master?"

"He is unconscious right now, Yu-ning. The doctor has given him an herbal sedative to help him sleep, and his brain is still swollen. The next twenty-four hours are critical. We must hope and pray that the swelling subsides and that there is no permanent damage."

Yu-ning did not say anything else but shifted in the bed, her back now to Cristobel. The little girl reached her free hand over her shoulder, and Cristobel took ahold of it. The instructor sat quietly holding her hand until Yu-ning finally drifted off to sleep.

Yu-ning slept off and on for two days. She dreamt she was in a stone tower on a high mountain. She was caretaker of the tower, and for days upon days it rained. Try as she might, the rain kept seeping under the stones and through the roof, and no matter what she did, she could not stop the water from seeping into the tower's inner chambers. She used blankets and mops and buckets to soak up the water, but she had no place to dump the water, except out of the stone windows. But every time she threw a bucket of water out the window, it would end up trickling back down toward the base of the structure and begin seeping back in.

Finally the grey clouds covering Rainbow Island began to break, and the rainstorm blew itself out to sea. After three long days of torrential rains, the sun reappeared. But instead of bringing joy to the Island, it had the opposite effect: for the first time, the Islanders fully understood what the loss of the sacred crystals meant. There was no rainbow. And with the disappearance of the sacred rainbow came a strange, melancholy light. Not the kind of light that brings a smile to a child's face—a grey, brooding light. It was as if the Island itself were mourning the loss of the great rainbow.

Slowly, the bruising around Yu-ning's eyes and nose began to heal, and the swelling subsided. The bruises, though smaller, were nasty shades of purple and blue. And though her face did not pain her, the burns on her left arm and shoulder did. Even the strong herbal tea the doctor gave her only took the edge off the pain.

On the fifth day after the attack, Cristobel came to visit Yu-ning. "The doctor says it's fine for you to begin walking— that the exercise and fresh air will do you good. Plus, there

31

is someone who could benefit from seeing that crooked smile of yours."

Yu-ning's legs were shaky but in good working order. Her arm was bandaged and wrapped in a sling. She walked gingerly around the makeshift hospital, using Cristobel for support. They made their way to Metatron's bedside, and Yu-ning was heartened to see him awake and alert.

They sat next to the great wizard's bed. "I am so happy to see you awake, Metatron. I . . . I was so worried . . ." Yu-ning's voice broke off as she began to sob, placing her head on Metatron's chest. The wizard winced silently, as his ribs were very tender, but he did not want to let Yu-ning know. He patted her head gently and smiled for the first time in many days.

"Yu-ning, the sight of you has accelerated my healing by leaps and bounds. I feel as if I could take on the obsidigon myself, seeing you up and about. Let me see you, child. How are your burns healing?"

Yu-ning slowly removed her left arm from its sling and gently pulled back the bandages around her wound. Metatron, who was wise in the ways of natural healing, examined the wound carefully. "It looks like our good doctor is taking excellent care of you, my dear. The balm he is using is working nicely, and . . ."

Metatron stopped, transfixed as he stared at the underside of Yu-ning's left arm, just on the inside of her upper tricep. "Why, this is amazing . . ." he muttered. He turned the arm this way and that, in his excitement causing Yu-ning to wince in pain. "I'm sorry, Yu-ning. It's just that I have not seen this in several decades . . ." Again the tall wizard's voice trailed off, leaving Yu-ning and Cristobel to exchange quizzical looks.

"What it is, Master Metatron? What do you see?" queried Cristobel.

"Why, I am not 100 percent positive, but I believe something extraordinary is happening here, Cristobel. I believe we have a Darq Render in our midst."

As he said this, the old wizard and Cristobel gazed at Yu-ning in what could only be described as a new light. They were smiling at her, but there was also a sense of reverence in their looks that made her feel a little uncomfortable.

"I don't understand . . . why are you both looking at me that way?"

Metatron asked for a drink of water. Cristobel poured water from an earthen jar next to his bed and handed a ceramic mug to Metatron, who drank deeply. He handed the water back to Cristobel and with both hands smoothed the covers around himself, gathering his thoughts. "Yu-ning, do you see that birthmark on the inside of your left arm, above your elbow?"

"Yes, I've had it since I was a baby."

"Look closely at it, and tell me what you see."

"I don't see anything at all," said Yu-ning, now thoroughly puzzled.

"Exactly!" said Metatron with growing excitement. "Look at the skin all around that birthmark. It is red and burned from the attack. But the birthmark and the skin around it were not touched by the dragon's fire. Don't you see, Yu-ning? The old texts say that every Darq Render has a crescent-shaped mark on the inside of their left arm, as you do. But I never thought anything of yours—I just thought it was an ordinary birthmark. But I was wrong. The texts also tell us that the certain sign of a Darq Render is that their mark cannot be damaged or harmed by dragon's fire. That perfect and unburned skin is proof that you are, indeed, a Darq Render." The wizard had raised himself up in bed by his arms in his excitement, but now he collapsed back down, his fragile state getting the better of him.

"I honestly did not know any of the bloodline were still alive," he finally offered, as if starting in mid-thought. "The last known Darq Render disappeared into the northern wastes of Darqendia more than twenty-five years ago. Since then, I have been waiting and watching for their return, but to no avail."

Cristobel and Yu-ning helped Metatron get comfortable in his bed and poured him more water, which he accepted with gratitude. His voice dropped an octave as he gestured Yu-ning to come closer. "The only way for you to fully learn all there is to know about a Darq Render, Yu-ning, is to meet the man who knows more about them than anyone I know. Very few people still survive from the Great Obsidigon War, but one in particular can be of great help to us, I believe. His name is Balthazar, and he lives on Gracia Island in the Tower of Light. I first met him on the plains of Darqendia, immediately after the last battle against the obsidigons. I was serving behind the lines, as a healer to the wounded.

"There were hundreds of obsidigons then, and the Darq Renders were the only warriors who battled the beasts on the front lines, their light bows bringing victory over the dragon horde. If it weren't for the Darq Renders, it is uncertain whether or not we could have defeated the obsidigons."

Without being aware of it, Yu-ning was gently touching her crescent-shaped birthmark, tracing the arc of the crescent back and forth. As evening wore on, bedside lanterns went dark around the infirmary. Eventually Metatron's light glowed as a single beacon in the large hall. Long after the other patients drifted off to sleep, Yu-ning, Metatron, and Cristobel still talked about the history of the Darq Renders, their role in defeating the Great Obsidigon Horde, and what had happened to their kind since then.

Metatron told them about how the Renders once ruled Darqendia Island and prospered there in peace. Though the island was now mostly vast expanses of sand dunes and desert, the Renders had discovered diamonds and other precious stones and minerals in the hills and mined the land prosperously. They also harvested the bounty of the sea, mastering the arts of shipbuilding, fishing, and ocean trading.

When the warlocks conjured the obsidigon army, their plan was to pillage the precious stones of Darqendia for their own. Thankfully, many of Darqendia's surrounding neighbors came to their aid, and with the Darq Renders leading the army, the obsidigons and their warlock masters were defeated.

"Each Darq Render bares the mark of the crescent moon, as you do, Yu-ning," said Metatron. "And there is this: Darq Renders have an ability to understand the obsidigon and to fight it more effectively than other clans or races. That is why that mark on your arm is so significant— you may have inborn abilities against these dragons that the rest of us do not possess," added Metatron, looking intensely at Yu-ning. She felt a little nauseous and couldn't quite take in all that her master was saying!

"But no one knows just exactly how the Darq Renders were able to slay the dragons," Metatron continued. "Legend says that all earthly weapons are ineffective against the beasts. And we have no surviving texts or firsthand accounts

35

of the Darq Renders' methods in bringing down the obsidigons. They marched into battle as one—alone. The rest
of us—all those who did not bear the Darq Render birthmark—stayed in the rear guard, simply waiting to come to
the aid of the wounded after the battles were over. All their
history has either been lost beneath the sands of Darqendia, or destroyed in the fires wrought by the dragons' breath.
Balthazar is the one man who may still have some clues to
these hidden mysteries."

Metatron paused, a far-off look in his eye. "A rainbow
bean for your thoughts, Master," said Yu-ning.

Metatron smiled and said, "I just remembered the odd-
est thing. There we were, in the midst of war, surrounded
by darkness and destruction, but the thing that I remember
most is the colorful butterflies."

"Butterflies? What do you mean, Master?"

"After the battles, as the Darq Renders marched back
from the front lines, oftentimes great masses of butterflies
could be seen in the skies," said Metatron. "I don't know why
I just remembered that—even in war, beauty can be found,
I suppose."

Their heads filled with images of diamonds, deserts, and
dragons, Cristobel and Yu-ning sat silently next to Metatron's bed. After the wizard drifted off to sleep, Cristobel
and Yu-ning made their way back to Yu-ning's cot, where her
dinner tray had been placed earlier by one of the teachers-
turned-nurses. She said goodnight to Cristobel, nibbled a bit
at her food, but soon pushed away the tray, too overwhelmed
to eat. She reached under the bed and pulled out the careworn book Cristobel had brought earlier. She hoped it would

distract her from the terrors of the past few days and from the revelation of being a Darq Render.

As she slowly and carefully leafed through the thick pages, her eye stopped on a striking image of a dark dragon. It was an exceptional rendering of an obsidigon, which looked a good deal like the beast that had attacked Rainbow Island. Its eyes were piercing and full of malice; it seethed destruction and chaos in the angle of its wings. Its tail was raised high in the air, poised to crash down on a terrified group of Darq Renders. The warriors were frozen in terror, crouching away from the dragon, with wide, terrified eyes.

As Yu-ning carefully closed the book and slid it under her cot, she revisited the evening's revelations in her mind, floating in that in-between space where wakefulness ends and sleep begins.

# *Five*

# *Departure*

**D**AYS WENT BY, and each dawn came pale and sullen, the light of the bright tropical sun diminished by the loss of the sacred rainbow. Slowly the village was rebuilding, with many of the burned structures already cleared, fresh timber and thatch taking their place. At least the work of house building served to distract the masters, teachers, and children from the loss of their colleagues, the sacred crystals, and Romeo.

Yu ning recovered sufficiently to return to her own camp, where she was visited throughout the day by both Cristobel and many of her fellow Rainbow Children. Her burns were healing well, allowing her to remove the sling and to do small tasks, with just bandages protecting her arm and shoulder. The herbal remedies given her by the Island doctor worked remarkably, reducing the healing time of the burned skin by half. Though tender to the touch, the skin healed quickly, and the pain diminished more each day.

As she rose one morning, slowly dressing herself and eating the breakfast of eggs, toast, and mango juice that one of the teachers brought her, she heard a familiar voice at the entrance of the cave. "Hello? Are you up, Yu-ning?" It was Cristobel.

"Yes, come in. It's good to see you, Cristobel. I was just about to come down the path and visit you in the village. How are you?"

"I'm well. Very busy helping to oversee reconstruction. But this morning, we've a special visitor who would like to see you. Come outside and you will see what I am talking about."

Curiosity aroused, Yu-ning emerged from her cave into the morning light, the sun not yet hitting the entrance of her grotto. From between the great tropical trees surrounding the path, she saw a massive creature with enormous, rainbow-feathered wings; it had the head of a man, a pointy eagle nose, a magnificent white-feathered body, and two human legs. The creature's gigantic, colorful wings seemed to fill the entire sky and radiated shining, dazzling lights.

"Suparna, Suparna, it is so good to see you! It's been so long since you've visited us!"

The breathtaking creature glided to a landing before Yu-ning, lowering his body and wings before her in a sign of respect. "Suparna, your friend, at your service, Yu-ning," said the regal figure.

"At *my* service, Suparna? No, it is I who should be bowing to you, in your beauty and wisdom," said Yu-ning, bowing at the waist before Suparna.

"No, Yu-ning. You do not need to bow to me," said Suparna. "I have learned of your bloodline, Yu-ning. You are a Darq Render. I am familiar with the noble history of the Darq Render clan. I am proud to serve you."

"Suparna, I am still so confused about who I really am. But I do feel different. I don't know if it's because of how everything in my life seems to have been shattered, or because of the revelation of my identity as a Darq Render. All I know, Suparna, is that I am scared, I am confused, and I don't know what the future holds." At this, Yu-ning ran toward the magnificent bird and buried her face in the soft feathers of his chest.

Suparna looked at Yu-ning with shining eyes and enveloped the diminutive girl in his voluminous wings. "Much has happened in your life these past few fateful weeks, but I know one thing for certain: the light of love is in you, it is in me, it is in the children and teachers of this Island, and it will once again shine in the world around us. But in order for the light to shine, and for our glorious rainbow to be restored in its healing glory, we must rend—or tear—the light from the dark. Do you understand what I am saying, Yu-ning?"

"But that is not me, Suparna. I am not capable of rending light from a dragon! I am just one little girl."

Suparna drew back from Yu-ning, releasing her from his wings, and rose up before her, thunder in his eyes. "YOU ARE NOT just a little girl, Yu-ning! Light does not know *size*—even the tiniest speck of light, when it touches darkness, tears it apart!" As Suparna finished addressing Yu-ning, his eyes grew soft again, and a smile creased the corners of his beak.

"I believe you, Suparna, but I am still very scared," said Yu-ning.

"I know, my child. But we are in desperate times, and you are going to have to face those fears. News travels fast, and when I heard about the troubles on Rainbow Island, I came as quickly as I could," added Suparna. "Unfortunately, Rainbow Island is not the only part of our realm under attack. The warlock Hobaling and the obsidigon have also attacked the Imperial City of Tunzai. Even the skilled bows of the Empress's own royal guard were no match for the hard-scaled armor of the obsidigon."

A light went off in Yu-ning's mind. "Metatron told me about the rumors from Tunzai, which you have confirmed to be true. I want you to talk with Master Metatron," urged Yu-ning. "He knows of a man who has knowledge of the obsidigon."

"What man is this, Yu-ning?"

"His name is Balthazar, and he lives in the Tower of Light within the Grey City on Gracia Island."

"Balthazar? I know the man! He is an old friend, and if anyone knows Darq Render lore, it is he."

They decided to consult with Metatron, to seek his advice on what to do next. They walked together out to the edge of the path overlooking the vast expanse of the village and beach below. There she climbed atop Suparna's back and pointed him in the direction of the hospital, where Metatron was making a slow recovery.

They swooped out over the village, and for the first time in her life, Yu-ning was able to experience something she'd only dreamt about—what it's like to fly. They landed near the school hall entrance, and Yu-ning gingerly slipped from Suparna's back, careful not to bump her tender left arm.

"Wait here, Suparna, I will not be long."

Inside, the scene was markedly improved from even two weeks before: most of the children had been released from the hospital, and only four patients remained under the care of the Island's kind doctor. One of them was Metatron, whose head still ached, and whose old bones were still recovering from their encounter with the obsidigon.

The color was returning to Metatron's face, and he was able to take short walks with the aid of his staff. As Yu-ning entered the hospital, her master was sitting on the edge of his bed, fully dressed. "Hello, Yu-ning. What a nice surprise, and you are here just in time to accompany an old man on a short walk," he said with a twinkle in his eye.

She gave him a gentle hug and told him about the events of the morning. He was anxious to see Suparna, and walked slowly with Yu-ning into the morning sunshine, where he greeted the stunning bird. There was an old stone bench on the path between the school and the beach, and there the three sat to talk privately about the unfolding events of the past few days. It was a quiet, tranquil spot where Metatron often came, with an arbor framing the bench, and wisteria blooming in the spring and summer.

Suparna and Metatron knew what had to be done. In his still-fragile state, it would be difficult for Metatron to make the journey to Oracia Island to visit Balthazar. Therefore, Suparna would travel with Yu-ning to the Grey City and provide protection for her. They all knew that Balthazar was probably their best chance of finding out more about how to defeat the obsidigon, recover the sacred crystals, and rescue their friend Romeo.

"Yu-ning, the Grey City is a labyrinth of narrow streets and stone buildings—too narrow for Suparna to fly through," urged Metatron. "Therefore, he will need to fly you *over* the city to the Tower of Light. It is the tallest tower in the realm, and lies at the very center of the Grey City. It has been decades since I have visited Balthazar, so I do not know what you can expect once you arrive. The people of the Grey City were once allies of Rainbow Island, but we have lost contact with the city over the last several years. Be careful, and before you leave, I need you to ask Cristobel to bring me the crystal box in my cottage. I keep it next to my bed in the side table. She knows where it is. You will need to make ready this evening, and leave at first light."

With that the friends agreed to part ways for the day, to make ready for their journey. Yu-ning found Cristobel near the archery range, giving a lesson in the art of bow making to some of the younger Rainbow Children. Yu-ning gave Cristobel the message from Metatron; she ended the class early and left to retrieve the box for her master. Yu-ning walked back to her cave, politely declining a ride from Suparna. Something inside her wanted to walk through the village and up the familiar cliff path; deep inside she wondered when she would once again see her beloved Island.

Yu-ning spent most of the day preparing for her journey, only packing those provisions that were vital. That evening Metatron and Suparna talked deep into the night, while Yu-ning retired early to get a good night's sleep. In the morning, she double-checked her provisions and prepared to leave her cave. Once her leather backpack was ready, she called for Magic, who was hunting insects outside the entrance. The loyal frog came bouncing into the grotto as soon as he heard Yu-ning calling.

"It's time for us to go, Magic. You can hop into the outside pocket of my pack, where I've put some soft grass, and even a few crickets for you." Hearing about crickets made the frog leap for joy, bouncing like a rubber ball from floor to ceiling, and ricocheting off the walls as well.

"All right, I know you're excited, Magic. But we need to go, so hop in!" The frog jumped off a side table and gently landed in the outer pocket of Yu-ning's leather pack. She cinched the leather strap, and reminded the eccentric frog not to eat all the crickets at once. "Those may be the only crickets you get for many days, you slimy green *Hyla cinerea!*" she chided.

"Hyla-*what?*" Magic said.

"It's your scientific name, silly. Don't you ever read?" Yu-ning teased.

The frog was excited to leave Rainbow Island, as he had never before ventured from its shores. Popping his head out of the narrow opening between the strap and the side of the pocket, the frog spoke in a croaky, low voice. "I won't let that nasty dragon hurt you. If I have to, I'll plunk him in the eye again with the biggest rock I can find!"

Yu-ning smiled and said, "Magic, my friend, the pleasure of your company is enough to boost my courage — no need for any rock-throwing against a dragon a gazillion times your size!"

Yu-ning exited the cave, her backpack secure on her shoulders. She tested its weight, and adjusted the shoulder straps for maximum comfort. The straps rubbed against her left shoulder, which was tender to the touch, so she had to stop and slip a soft bandage between the large strap and her skin to relieve the pressure. As she descended the familiar hill path, she inhaled the sweet tropical air, full of the wonderful aromas of the Island—fertile earth and waterfall, of plumeria, passionflower, and orchid. Once down the hill, she made straight for the school hall, where Suparna and Metatron were awaiting her arrival.

Metatron approached and handed Yu-ning a small wooden box, which she opened. Inside was a beautiful, small round crystal orb, radiating powerful yellow light.

"This is the Light of Balthazar," said Metatron. "It was a gift given to me by Balthazar himself a century ago, after the last obsidigons were defeated on the desolate plains of Darqendia. Bring this to Balthazar, and it will prove to him that you are my student and will help you earn his trust. Treasure this light, Yu-ning, as it will guide you in times of darkness."

Yu-ning slipped the small box into her backpack and turned toward Suparna, signaling him that she was ready. A small group of children and teachers gathered, and Yu-ning said her goodbyes one by one. She received small tokens from many, including her favorite fruits, notes of encouragement, and other keepsakes that she hastily slipped into the side pockets of her pack. Many of her closest animal friends were there too, including Leonidas the lion, Shamza the zebra, Octavian the owl, and Prometheus the horse.

Finally ready, she hugged Metatron and whispered to him, too low for others to hear. "I am so afraid, Metatron. I believe that I am a Darq Render, but I don't feel like one."

The wizard closed his eyes hard, wishing that he could lift the burden from this precious little girl. "My sweet Yu-ning, there is strength in you that is yet undiscovered. But just remember that it is not violence that wins in the end, but love. *That* is your true strength, Yu-ning, and it is a weapon that will be completely foreign to your enemy. Therefore, love will be your *strongest* weapon."

He pulled back, both hands on Yu-ning's shoulders, looking straight into her eyes. He said no more words, but nonetheless let her know how much he loved her.

She turned, waved to the rest of the group, and mounted Suparna. For their journey, which would be long—covering two to three days over open ocean—the teachers fashioned a sort of saddle for Yu-ning, including a high leather back for comfort and a waist cinch to hold her true when she needed to sleep. The saddle even had straps with which to secure her backpack, placed close by for easy access. Magic rested comfortably in the top pocket, ready for the journey ahead.

Everything in order, Suparna began to beat his giant wings, slowly rising into the air. As he ascended, his rainbow-colored wings caught the morning light, and all those on the ground looked on in awe: for a brief moment, the color bands of his wings mimicked the bands of the sacred rainbow, now so sorely missed on Rainbow Island.

Metatron smiled and saw it as sign of good things to come—a glimpse of a future when the lights of the sacred rainbow would once again shine brightly over Rainbow Island, sending its light and rays of love into a world in desperate need.

# Six

# Storm

𝒴U-NING AND SUPARNA BEGAN THEIR JOURNEY flying silently over choppy, turquoise blue waters as they left Rainbow Island. The brisk breeze was out of the north, making Suparna's job easier as the two flew southward. By that afternoon, their spirits were high, as they had encountered nothing odd or out of the ordinary, and the seas had mellowed to a dead, glassy calm. They wondered if the darkness rumored to have arrived elsewhere had not yet afflicted realms further south.

Through that night Suparna flew, with Yu-ning finally nodding off to sleep as a gigantic waxing moon rose out of the north, bathing the ocean below in a haunting dark purple. The moonlight formed a trail heading southward across the water; it was almost as if its light was leading them to their destination.

As morning dawned, Yu-ning awoke to leaden skies. The seas were still deathly calm, but there was a strange feeling in the air. The sun was just a weak orb of pale yellow, veiled by a thin layer of high clouds. As they flew on that day, they came to a small chain of tiny islands—small rock outcroppings, really—which allowed Suparna to land and rest for a couple of hours. As the tide rose, however, the tiny islets began to disappear, the water rising up to Suparna's claws, the rock disappearing before their eyes. It happened so quickly it seemed almost as if the ocean was forcing the pair back into the air, cutting short Suparna's much-needed rest.

That night grew colder, with the wind picking up once again. The skies had not changed, and the cloud cover meant there would be no moon or watery moonlit trail to lead the way. Suparna, however, had an uncanny sense of direction—a gift he had been born with. And the map Metatron had given to him prior to their departure had proven to be highly accurate, even down to the exact location of the tiny islands they had rested upon earlier that day.

On the dawning of the third day, a light mist began. The mist turned to drizzle, followed by light rain, forcing Yu-ning into her slicker to keep the water from soaking her to the bone. Finally the skies completely opened up, and a heavy rain began to fall. As the rain increased, so did the wind. Then came the lightning and thunder. If it weren't for the fact that the winds were still out of the north, it might have been impossible for Suparna to continue on. As it was, however, the two forged on, into the teeth of the storm. Just when visibility seemed to be reduced to just several feet in front of them, they spotted land ahead through a break in the low clouds. It was Gracia Island, home of the Grey City and the Tower of Light.

Soon the stormy beach gave way to low hillocks and then open, flat plains with little vegetation. Mile after mile they flew, buffeted by winds that seemed to swirl and change direction with no predictable pattern. Now it was becoming quite difficult for Suparna to fly safely, as the winds began to hit him from above, causing him to drop in altitude without warning. Soon, indeed, he was forced to land, and the two had no choice but to continue on foot. They trudged forward, the ground soaked and muddy, with no discernable paths or signs of life. They crested a low hill, and on the other side they were relieved to see a narrow road leading off to the south. As they picked up the road, the way was made easier, with the hard dirt below not yet turned to mud from the rain. As the afternoon light began to fade, and with the rain having only increased in intensity, the two finally conceded that they needed to find shelter and wait out the worst of the storm.

While searching for refuge, Yu-ning spotted granite out-croppings in the distance. As they walked closer, they realized the mass of rock was actually a city, and that the various rocks were grey buildings made of stone. They had reached the Grey City. The buildings were only two and three stories tall on the outskirts, but grew taller further inside the city. The roads between the buildings were very narrow—no more than eight feet wide, too narrow for Suparna to enter.

"Now, here's a dilemma," Suparna shouted over the howling wind and rain. "I can't see far enough into the city to spot the Tower of Light, which stands at the center. And with this storm, I don't think it will be safe for me to fly you over the city. With this reduced visibility, I am concerned that the

51

local militia might mistake us for an obsidigon. I hate to say this, Yu-ning, but I think you need to press on alone. I will remain at this very spot until the rain clears sufficiently for me to make a safe sweep over the city. Wear your crystal-heart necklace outside your shirt, so that I can see its light from above. It seems that it will be the only visible color in this grey city."

Suparna was right—the winds were swirling in every direction, making a flight into the heart of the city very dangerous and even an overflight potentially deadly if they were mistaken for a dragon. "All right, Suparna, I will go in alone. But please start looking for me when the visibility improves. I don't like the look of this city. Plus, where are all the people?"

The pair stared down the empty streets from where they stood on the edge of the city. Not a soul in sight—not even a dog or cat crossed the desolate road. "Be careful, and remember your pink crystal heart . . . It will guide you to the center of the city, Yu-ning," Suparna reminded her.

With Magic's head poking out of the top of her backpack, she hefted the bag's weight onto her back. "Goodbye, Suparna. I'd better go right away, because it's probably already noon, and I don't want to get stuck in the city after dark."

With that, Yu-ning adjusted her pack, turned toward the city street, and started off down the road, leaving Suparna to huddle against the wall of a nearby house, somewhat protected from the rain under a large awning. He watched as she headed into the heart of the city, growing smaller as she seemed to blend in with the granite buildings and grey rain. At last she was swallowed up by the colorless city and the coursing rain.

Once inside the city, Yu-ning began to notice little signs of life: bits of trash on the street, a hint of light behind shuttered windows, an umbrella left on a porch. The farther she walked into the city, the harder the rain fell. Even so, as she walked on, block by block, townspeople began to emerge from houses and buildings, carrying umbrellas and wearing rain gear.

As the buildings grew taller and closer together, the smell and gritty taste of smoke from thousands of chimneys mixed with the miserable rain. She looked around and saw only dark, ominous clouds and dirty, mud-soaked streets. As she walked forward, the pollution dissipated slightly. She saw hundreds of tall stone buildings, towers, and homes before her, many jutting into the sky, all of varying heights. The colors of the city were black and dull shades of grey. Even the people who emerged into the rain wore clothes of grey and black.

People seemed to be in quite a rush—the city changed from deathly empty one minute to buzzing with activity the next. She was unable to capture the faces of the people around her, but she was anxious to make contact with someone, to feel a human connection. "Is this the Grey City? Why are you going so fast?" Yu-ning asked. Droves of people rushed back and forth on the busy streets, moving in different directions, heedless of the torrential rainstorm. No one paused, even for a moment.

All of the people wore grave, solemn expressions. They didn't speak or even acknowledge one another. Despair, hopelessness, and gloom seemed to pervade the entire city. Yu-ning was disheartened that there could be such desolation among a community of so many people. She looked at every person beseechingly, as if imploring him or her to return her gaze, but no one made eye contact; no one smiled.

Yu-ning felt desperate, so she stopped momentarily and closed her eyes, and cried to One, "Why do they walk alone? Where are their friends and family? Why is there no color in this place?"

People continued to race by, the pace brisk and unabated. Yu-ning just stood in the middle, as if caught in the vortex of the storm. The droning vibration of the city and all its sounds caused her to lose her footing as she tried to find a place to step out of the way. "Everyone, please, why are you going so fast? Please slow down. Please talk to me." One by one, she tried to reach those passing by.

"Hello?" Yu-ning said to a woman dressed in a black skirt and dark hat. The woman didn't even blink as she continued on past Yu-ning with a stern expression. "Hello . . . ?" Yu-ning said to a man all in grey. He also jetted by without looking at her.

Sniffling, she stood dejected on the high curb along the street. As she stared out at the sea of faces amidst the dreary rain, she felt dizzy and overwhelmed. She took a deep, shaky breath and continued walking down the dark street, moving with the cacophonous drone of rapid footsteps and the loud sounds of a crowded city.

Without warning, she heard a loud whirring sound behind her. She spun around to see a man standing on a flat, circular disk, holding onto some sort of steering wheel, flying toward her about three feet off the ground. She hit the deck hard as the flying disc flew over her, barely missing her head.

"Get out of the street, little girl!" shouted the man as he raced by. "Or else you'll get killed by a whirlicon!"

She stood up slowly, both amazed and terrified by what she had just seen. "How can he fly like that?" Yu-ning wondered to herself. As she dusted herself off, she could see other discs flying about the city, racing in every direction. She looked on in fascination. She could see glowing blue stones secured underneath each of the discs, dull blue light trailing from behind. She continued walking, staying out of the center of the road, blending in with the foot traffic hugging both sides of the busy street.

She searched the sky for signs of Suparna, but the cloud cover was still thick, making it difficult to see. At that moment, she heard One's voice in her mind—his words were like beams of light searing through a storm cloud. "Yu-ning, show the people the light," he said in a gentle tone. "There is always light at the center. Don't ever forget this. Trust and believe. There is always light at the center."

As she took in his words, her eyes were drawn to a bright, clean light emanating from the center of the city—piercing through the rain and smoke. "The light! It's coming from the center of the city. It's coming from that single tall tower at the center!"

As she moved forward briskly, she began to make out the upper stories of a tall glass tower, shining bright golden light from every archway and window. As Yu-ning fixed her gaze on the luminous light, she noticed that it shined straight up into the sky. Not only did the light shine up into the stormy sky, but the tower extended all the way up into the clouds and disappeared. Her eyes kept going up and up as the structure continued growing taller into the sky. It was as if it were reflecting the light of a thousand suns.

This display reminded her of Suparna's words about her pink crystal heart. Yu-ning looped her finger around the silk thread of her necklace and pulled it out from under her shirt, raising the pink gemstone before her. As she did, beams of light raced toward her from the tower, converging on the pink crystal heart. It was as if the pink crystal was a lightning rod that drew thousands of separate beams into one location.

The effect of so many light beams racing toward Yu-ning forced her to close her eyes and turn her head away, holding the crystal heart in front of her. There was a low humming sound, and the pink heart began to vibrate. Yu-ning opened her eyes, staring in amazement at the pink crystal.

She thought her mind was playing tricks on her: all the beams of light were hitting the center of the pink crystal heart, and the gem, acting as a prism, was reflecting a beautiful, shining pink path that spread before her. It was like a shimmering carpet, leading in the direction of the light tower. It took Yu-ning's breath away: it looked just as lovely and brilliant as the beloved rainbow from Rainbow Island, only smaller and all pink.

As she walked, she looked down and laughed gleefully. Bright, sparkling pink lights were casting their rays as if from a prism. The further the path extended, the more shadow it chased away. All the streets, alleys, corners, and buildings sparkled with light. Even the raindrops reflected the lights of the pink pathway, causing the air to be filled with millions of falling pink diamond raindrops. Yu-ning picked up her pace and followed the beams of light flowing from the tower.

The lights, bejeweled and glistening, led toward the majestic tower at the center of the city.

"It's a light tower to heaven. It's a cathedral of light."

She heard One's voice whisper to her, "It is the anteroom of heaven."

"The anteroom of heaven," she repeated, bedazzled and inspired.

"Look, everyone, the building at the center of your city is full of beautiful light. It's a light tower to heaven!" she said excitedly. To her amazement, many people began to walk toward her slowly, and some even began to follow her.

But one man stepped forward and said, "It's not a tower to heaven, silly girl. It's just a plain glass tower. My uncle lives in that tower, and there's nothing magical about it." Other onlookers, however, were mesmerized, both by the diamond lights flowing from the tower toward Yu-ning and by the pink pathway flowing out of the little girl's pink crystal.

"I've lived in the Grey City my entire life, and I've never seen the tower look like this—shining so bright, with such beautiful lights!" marveled a dark-haired woman in her midthirties.

On either side of the pink pathway, the city droned on in a cloud of delusion and misery. Whirliigins hummed by, and most of the pedestrians didn't give her a second glance. Yu-ning sighed woefully, but the pink lights inspired her and gave her courage. As she turned around, she now saw that about fifty people were following her.

A woman, slim and pale, said, "I know a lawyer who has offices in the tower, and have visited him there on several occasions. The tower has never been lit up like this, though. What is happening?"

"This crystal heart not only reflects light, it reflects love," Yu-ning responded. "Where I come from, our desire is to help everyone find the love that is locked inside them and set it free. The light you are seeing is strong because it is powered by love. Follow me to the Tower of Light, and we will see what the source is!"

"What is this bright shining thing?" a man said as he brought his whirlicon to a halt and stepped off of it. He removed the small blue stone from under the floating disc, placed it in his pocket, left the whirlicon behind, and joined Yu-ning. He was looking under his feet at the pink path as it extended out, connecting him to crowds of others. Those enveloped by the soft rays of pink light were drawn onto the path by some inexplicable force. Whirlicon after whirlicon slowed to a stop.

Yu-ning looked in the distance and noticed that some people still walked briskly along, oblivious to the light. And further off, whirlicons continued to race by. She noticed no pink around them. She and her followers tried to flag them down, but they wouldn't listen. Yu-ning shouted out, "All of you, please join us. We're going to the Tower of Light at the center. Your whole city can be full of light; you just have to believe."

One man paused and asked inquisitively, "What light tower?"

Yu-ning sighed gratefully and put her small hand in the man's much larger hand. "Look, sir; look at the ground beneath our feet, then follow that light." The man looked down to see a beautiful pink glow transform the ground beneath him. He looked up and saw the path stretch ahead, and the glow of light spread in all directions.

He gasped as the light of recognition emanating from him flowed out and reached several people around him. Yu-ning and the man looked at each other and smiled broadly as others walked toward them. The man was stupefied, and every feature softened on his face.

"Hey, look, do you see the light?" Yu-ning said to a woman who ignored her and walked away quickly. But as the woman rushed away, she looked up and came to an abrupt stop.

"What is it?" she asked, standing still, looking disoriented and confused.

"It is light. Follow us; it only gets brighter," Yu-ning said, leading the woman onto the pink path. The woman sighed deeply as she saw the ground transform beneath her. Yu-ning squeezed her hand tightly and smiled, before trying to gather more people from the grey heart of the city.

One by one, more people drifted over in a daze, like a scattering sea of stars amidst a sea of darkness. They saw the pinkish tinge in the air flowing around them, and they followed it toward the source at the center. They were not sure what it was, but its force was magnetic.

Yu-ning noticed an elderly man standing in the middle of the street, entranced by the pink path. A speeding whirli-con raced down the street directly toward the man and tried to go around him—but it was too late. The old man was lying in the middle of the street, blocking the path of a man who looked like a banker. The banker just stood there, doing nothing.

"Oh no!" Yu-ning said, running toward the old man. "Are you all right?" Yu-ning knelt down next to him. He was not moving, and the banker was just standing there, impatiently trying to find a way to leave. He watched Yu-ning as she leaned over the elderly man, her pink crystal necklace touching his chest. A rainbow stream of color flowed into his body, and the old man slowly opened his eyes.

The banker looked as if he had seen a ghost and dropped his satchel. He quickly took off his jacket, folded it, and helped Yu-ning place it under the old man's head. Despite the rain, all the people were coming forward to offer their coats and umbrellas. News of the miracle was spreading through the crowd, and soon everyone was repeating the story to his neighbor.

"This little girl has magical powers."

"It's a miracle."

Yu-ning and the banker helped the elderly man to his feet as others from the crowd leaned in to support them. The elderly man stood smiling; he softly thanked everyone. The crowd became very quiet, as no one had ever experienced the kind of compassion, support, and warmth flowing among all of them.

"What are those flying things, anyway?" said Yu-ning, still upset about nearly being run over herself.

"They are whirlicons. They are powered by brillantium— gems that we mine here on Gracia, which produce their own source of propulsive energy," said the banker.

"Well, they are very dangerous," Yu-ning retorted, unimpressed by magic rocks that can cause discs to fly into people.

As the elderly man dusted himself off, all those gathered looked at one another and then at a sea of pink light flowing beneath their feet. Everyone gazed in amazement at the path, which was emanating a spectacular pink glow in all directions through their once dark and dismal city.

They saw a beam of light in the distance shooting up to the sky. "That is the Tower of Light; you can all see it now!" Yu-ning called out as they continued on the pink path. "You failed to see that the light in your city has been blocked because you forgot what the light looks like. Now you all see, because you believe!"

There was a sense of reverence, humility, and peace as the growing crowd reflected on Yu-ning's words. Many were sharing the same insights with one another:

"We didn't see each other. We didn't see ourselves."

"It's within us. It has always been within us."

Some were waiting to see more—waiting for some kind of proof that this magical light could impact their lives in a positive way. As the crowd moved closer to the center and turned a corner in the direction of the tower, a sacred silence filled the air.

The crowd was in awe as they looked at the spectacular sight before them. They had reached the Tower of Light, its grandeur thrusting upward into the dark clouds above, bathed in the most heavenly light they had ever seen. Other people, who either refused to see or were not able to see, looked at the mesmerized crowd as if they were crazy. For most people in the city, the tower was void of any light.

Yu-ning's legs were tired and her left shoulder ached, but she was relieved to have reached the base of the tower. As she gazed heavenward, it seemed as if the tower was growing higher by the second. The entrance had a large archway with massive, thick doors made of frosted glass. The massive doors swung outward, and a guard stepped forward.

At that moment, a man's voice bellowed down from the sky. Yu-ning looked away from the guard upward to the top of the tower and saw a man's head—a small speck extending from a balcony thousands of feet up, it seemed. But how could she hear him when he was so far away? Or see him, for that matter?

His upper body leaned out to wave to her. "Come up!" he shouted to Yu-ning from the balcony.

Yu-ning was thrilled. "Me?" she replied, pointing to herself, still not comprehending how she could see him and hear him from what must be thousands of feet above her.

"Yes, are you Yu-ning?" It was as if he was right next to her, his voice clear and strong.

"Yes, I am Yu-ning!"

"Then come on up, we're waiting for you! And bring your new friends with you."

It was the kindest greeting she had received since arriving in the Grey City.

# Seven

# Tower

"ALL RIGHT! I'M COMING," she shouted up at the man peering down from thousands of feet above her.

As people looked on, most of them were smiling, but others looked confused, defensive, and even scared. Yu-ning and the crowd stood outside the great tower, just staring up at its beauty. "Everyone," Yu-ning yelled out to the crowd, "I am going inside, and once there, I am traveling to the top to meet the man who lives there. You are all free to join me—it is your choice."

Yu-ning turned toward the entryway below the front gate, ready to approach the guard who stood stock-still next to the main entrance. Before she could approach the guard, however, she noticed a teenage boy crouching next to the entrance of the tower. His face and clothes were dirty, and in his hands was a wooden bowl containing a few copper coins.

"Are you all right?" she asked tenderly.

"Spare some coins?" he replied feebly, looking depressed and sickly.

"Coins?" she asked curiously.

"Money," the teenage boy repeated. "Spare any coins," he said, without looking up.

"I don't have any money, but I have an apple from my island. Here," she said, extending the apple toward him. It was her last apple. "Where do you live?" She put the apple in his hand. He looked confused, not knowing whether to accept it or not.

"I don't have a home," he said, taking the apple and biting into it. It was the first thing he had eaten in two days. As he chewed, he looked at her with a vacant stare.

"Then you can come with me back to my home. I live on Rainbow Island. It is the most beautiful place in the world. I'll take you there, but first I'm going inside this tower."

"That is the tallest tower in the world," the boy said in a monotone.

"It is the anteroom of heaven!" said Yu-ning, with great enthusiasm. "Look at all the brilliant lights above us," she exclaimed as she continued to hold her pink crystal in front of her, the pink colors now shooting skyward.

"What lights?" said the boy in a dejected and forlorn manner. "I don't see any bright lights. It just looks like any ordinary tower, only taller."

Yu-ning looked at him with sorrowful eyes. "My name is Yu-ning," she said. "This is a lonely place. I can be your friend if you need a friend."

The boy just stared at her sadly. "My name is Julian."

Yu-ning smiled. "Julian, can you see the light?"

"I told you I don't see any lights," Julian replied dryly.

"No, if you look with your heart, you will see them." He looked at her as if she was speaking nonsense, but she continued, "I'm going all the way to the top of the tower. An important man is waiting for me there. He has wisdom to share—he is a great teacher. Come with me, Julian," she said persuasively.

Julian shrugged her off. "I don't know what light you are talking about. Many people live and work in this tower, but from what I know, no one lives at the top, because it keeps growing higher. Why don't you go back home to your parents? And stop bothering me with this nonsense," Julian snapped, looking very weary.

"Then you will come when you are ready," said Yu-ning. "The door is always open. Finish your apple and then you will see." She walked back toward the main gate, turning back one last time to smile at Julian. He was staring down at the apple. Quietly, most of the crowd followed behind her at a distance. She didn't notice that Julian had risen slowly and had also followed her, staying at the back of the crowd.

"Hello." Yu-ning smiled at the gate guard, who ignored her. She walked through the massive glass doors and entered an enormous atrium in the center of the tower. The glass rose hundreds of feet, forming a vast hall with the next floor of the tower perched far overhead. The color inside was bright, in stark contrast to the grey outside. The light was shining into the clear windows through intricate designs etched into the glass. It illuminated the entire space with textured shadows, as the colors danced and refracted off every surface.

"Oh, my goodness," her tiny voice squealed with glee. "It's so very tall, bright, and lovely! It's so magical."

She noticed a sentry with bushy brown hair and a black robe sitting behind an old dark desk on the left. He held a large scroll and was examining it with a furrowed brow.

"Do you work in this beautiful tower?" she asked with reverence.

"Yes, I work here; what is it you want?" he said curtly.

"This tower, it is so bright and beautiful," Yu-ning continued.

The guard looked up from his parchment. "I don't know what you are talking about. What's your name?" he asked impatiently.

"My name is Yu-ning," she said confidentally.

"Oh, yes, I see your name here. What part of the tower are you going to?" he asked.

"I'm going to the top floor," she said matter-of-factly.

"The top floor? You can't get up there; no one can get up there," he said rudely.

"Oh, we can all get up there. There's a very powerful man up there, and I'm going to meet him," she said.

"There's no one on the top floor," he responded in a curt manner. "I have served in this tower for twenty years; no one can get up there. This tower has hundreds of floors, with many businesses and private dwellings, and it keeps growing higher. But it's impossible to get to the top, because the top floor is always changing," he said in a tired tone.

"Yes, it is possible. There's a powerful man at the top of the tower. Anything is possible; we can all get up there. *I'm* going up there," Yu-ning said with determination.

"You can't go. Even if there *was* a man up there, the large sky conveyor does not work—hasn't worked for years, ever since the water stopped flowing through the millrace."

"Millrace? And what's a sky conveyor?"

"The conveyor is powered by a pulley system that operates like a mill," the sentry said, at the edge of his patience, sighing loudly. "If you must know, the water flows in through a small stream, or millrace, which forces the wheel to turn." As he spoke he made an exaggerated circular motion in the air with his finger, right in front of Yu-ning's face. "That, in turn, causes the conveyor platform to rise. But as I said, the water spring that fed the millrace dried up years ago. There are smaller sky conveyors through that arch over there," said the sentry, pointing in the opposite direction toward the far side of the atrium.

"They will take you to the first 400 floors," added the mirthless sentry. "The millraces that power them are smaller and not strong enough to get you to the top floor. The only pulley that was ever made to go to the top is the one over there," he said, pointing with his thumb back toward the broken sky conveyor. "But even when it *did* work, it wasn't always dependable, because the top floors kept growing! Do you get it, little girl?" He said this last sentence in a high, shrill voice, his face turning a fascinating shade of tomato red.

Yu-ning left the sentry and walked in the direction of the broken conveyor platform. The crowd followed dutifully. Out of the corner of her eye, she noticed that Julian had joined them, which made her smile to herself. Just as the not-so-polite sentry said, there the large mill wheel stood silent, with dust and debris covering the floor and the guardrails of a wooden platform adjacent to it. Yu-ning walked onto the center of the platform and looked up. As far as she could see, the shaft for the conveyor went up and up. Next to the platform were four enormous, thick ropes, attached to each corner of the platform—some sort of pulley system, she surmised.

Yu-ning walked to the far side of the platform and placed her hand on the huge water wheel. Large buckets were spaced about a foot apart, encircling the entire wheel, to catch the water. The buckets were full of dust and debris, and they were dry. The millrace was about five feet deep and six feet wide and ran under the wheel. It was expertly built, with fine, smooth river stones lining the bottom and the sides. Not a drop of water could be seen.

Then Yu-ning had an idea. "Excuse me," she said in a loud voice, in the direction of the crowd that had followed her inside the tower. "Where is the man who has that blue gem—the one that powers the flying disc?"

"You mean brillantium, like this?" said the man with the gem, holding up the robin's-egg-size crystal between his thumb and index finger.

"Yes!" said Yu-ning. "Can't we just use that magic gem to power the platform upward?" she said with expectation in her voice. Several of the adults sniggered, and others looked embarrassed for Yu-ning.

Julian spoke up and said, "Brillantium can only move small amounts of weight, Yu-ning. It's strong enough to power a whirlicon with a few riders, but all the brillantium in the world wouldn't be able to lift that huge platform all the way up there." Julian raised his head and pointed up toward the top of the tower, thousands of feet above.

"Use your crystal heart, Yu-ning." She heard the voice, which seemed to be just behind her left ear. Yu-ning turned around to answer the person who had spoken to her. No one was there, and the crowd of people was a good twenty feet behind her. She realized it was One, and lifted up her crystal heart necklace, thrusting it toward the platform.

As she raised the pink crystal above her head, brilliant bright lights from within the tower began showering down like gossamer waterfalls from above. The lights of the tower descended and raced directly toward the center of the pink crystal heart, and struck the crystal with a loud *thwoop!*— causing Yu-ning to stagger backward several steps. The crowd of adults around her gasped, but no one said a word.

Yu-ning regained her balance and was amazed to see that a new pink beam was flowing outward from her necklace. It was just like the one that had led her through the city in the form of the pink pathway. The pink beam moved toward the corner of the platform, down into the stone-lined millrace, and into a dark tunnel that led under the foundations of the tower—and disappeared into the darkness.

The pink light continued to flow, accelerating in speed and pouring into the tunnel, for several minutes. Yu-ning's arms started to tire from the power of the light flowing through her pink crystal heart. Eventually, much to her relief, Julian joined her on the platform, supporting her arms so she could continue to hold the pink heart aloft. Yu-ning smiled gratefully at Julian. As quickly as the beam materialized, it ceased—the pink light beam disappeared in a bright flash, and the light waterfall from above stopped flowing—as if some divine faucet from above had been turned off.

A minute later, however, came a new sensation: a low rumble, like distant thunder. The rumble grew louder and was followed by a rush of wind that raced down the length of the millrace, out from under the large dark opening where the watercourse emerged from under the foundation of the tower. The noise grew, as did the breeze, which carried the scent of water and damp earth.

"The water!" Yu-ning exclaimed, an idea popping into her head. She walked to the center of the platform, where there was a large wooden handle with a lever at the top. She guessed that squeezing the handle and pulling down on the lever would engage the pulley system and allow the platform to rise—if water was available to power the water wheel. She began fiddling with the handle to figure out how to disengage it, but it wouldn't budge.

"What is that sound?" said a middle-aged woman standing toward the front of the crowd, which had inched closer to get a better look at the platform and water wheel.

"Well, it sounds like water from far away," added the elderly gentleman who had been hit by the whirlicon. "But that's impossible! The water source has been blocked for years, ever since the avalanche."

"Avalanche? What do you mean?" asked Yu-ning.

"More than two decades ago," the elderly man said. "The water dried up after an avalanche covered the spring that powered this particular sky conveyor. There's a narrow canyon about a mile outside the city, with high rock walls on either side. The avalanche brought a ton of debris down on the waterway, and ever since then, the spring has been blocked."

As he finished his explanation, Yu-ning felt a fine mist of water on her face, carried by an ever-increasing rush of air from the direction of the loud rumbling. "I think the water is back!" yelled Yu-ning over the now-deafening roar. A wall of water exploded from the entrance where the watercourse exited the tunnel under the tower's foundation. With the first wall of water came a great rush of mud, rocks, tree roots, and other debris, picked up along the way as the water headed toward the platform—presumably from outside the city.

Yu-ning and Julian hit the deck of the platform, covering their heads to protect them from large objects. People standing just off the platform also fell flat on the ground, covering their heads for protection. The water rushed past them, and after what seemed like an eternity to Yu-ning, the water slowed, and debris was no longer hitting her body. Soaked to the bone, she opened her eyes, seeing that the water had turned clear and free of debris and was subsiding now, back into the channel of the millrace.

As the rush of water decreased and the roar of the initial flood diminished, a new sound was noticeable. It was the *thwack, thwack, thwack* of the water buckets as the old mill wheel creaked to life. As the water made contact with the water buckets, it began to push against the wheel, which creaked, gave way, and began to move. And as dirt and debris was cleared from the mill wheel, it began to turn faster and faster.

"How did you do that?" exclaimed Julian, his eyes wide with wonder.

"I held up my pink heart necklace, and the water just started flowing," answered Yu-ning. "I had faith that it could happen—and it did. I believed!"

Julian was dumbstruck and speechless. The people gathered in the atrium just to the side of the sky conveyor were very quiet, trying to understand what had just happened. Then the crowd around the platform parted, and up walked the main sentry, holding the large scroll in his hand.

"We can't have all these people within the tower, you—" he stopped in midsentence and dropped his scroll, staring in disbelief at the water wheel, which was turning strongly now, full of water. "How—how did you do that?" he said to Yu-ning.

She smiled at him and simply said, "Faith!"

The sentry quickly regained his composure, picked up the scroll, and said, "You are a strange little girl, full of surprises." He looked hard at Yu-ning, and then back at the water wheel, which was now turning rapidly, water gushing out of the buckets as it made its revolutions. The sentry's demeanor softened, as he was clearly impressed by Yu-ning's ability to bring the mill wheel back to life. "I never thought I'd see the day when that old mill would once again dance with water. But still, there are rules here in the tower, and I have a job to do. The main rule is that only those who have been granted written permission can be here. The rest of you will need to leave."

Disappointment registered on many faces, but Yu-ning had an idea. "Sir, could you start reading off the names on your scroll, please?"

As the sentry began reading the names, voices in the crowd started shouting out, "That's me!" or "I'm here." In fact, the first thirty names the sentry read were all present in the crowd. He paused, began to speak the next name, but simply shook his head, rolled up his scroll, and said, "All right, you are all allowed to enter. But if you plan to ride the conveyor, let me warn you that it has not worked in more than twenty years, and neither I nor the keeper of the tower can guarantee your safety." With that, he gave a respectful nod toward Yu-ning and started to walk away, shaking his head.

"Sir, can you please wait? I can't seem to move the control lever—it is rusty or stuck. Can you help us?"

"It's been so many years, little girl, since I have worked on a pulley," said the sentry, his tone now sympathetic. "But if it is anything like the smaller pulleys on the other side of the tower, it has a small compartment in the floor, and inside is a jar of oil. Try oiling the handle."

Sure enough, Yu-ning could see the outline of a small square compartment next to the lever on the floor of the platform. She pried loose a small ring lying flush with the wooden planks, grabbed hold of it, and gave a tug. The compartment popped open in a puff of dust; inside were a few hand tools wrapped in an oily rag and a small jar, which she removed. After opening the lid of the jar, she poured a small amount of musky-smelling oil onto the handle and base of the lever.

She gave the handle another squeeze, and to her delight, there was a satisfying *click* as the handle engaged, allowing her to lower the lever toward the ground. The platform gave a sudden lurch upward half a foot—with dust rising from underneath in brown puffs. She quickly reengaged the handle, and the platform dropped down to the floor again, releasing a second, even larger dust cloud, causing many in the crowd to cough and cover their eyes.

"Who is coming with me? Come to the top with me, everyone!" said Yu-ning in a loud voice, so the entire crowd could hear her. "You have all made it this far. Are all of you courageous enough to continue on? There are only more gifts and blessings, and you only need to trust and believe. And if you like, you can return with me to Rainbow Island."

Everyone was standing to the side of the platform, but the entire crowd moved closer to Yu-ning. She looked around, marveling at all the people she had inspired. From the elderly man who had been hit by the whirlicon to Julian, the homeless teenage boy seeking alms, they were all here. Silence fell as the crowd paused, uncertain what was being asked of them. An energy of skepticism began to circulate, and Yu-ning felt it strongly. "Come on, everyone," she said coaxingly. "What are you waiting for? Get on! We came all this way; do not give up now!"

"There's something mysterious about this platform," one man said. "It's too risky." With that, he turned on his heel and strode out of the tower. As he walked away, Yu-ning noticed many other people coming and going in the tower atrium. They were heading in the direction of the other tower sky conveyors, oblivious to the lights pouring down through the center of the tower.

Another man spoke up. "I'm not sure about this. I'm not sure about any of this."

A woman responded, "The little girl is right, we have come all this way. My life is miserable in the city, and all I do is rush, my lungs full of smoke, my days grey. What is there to lose?"

"Yes, come on, everyone, you only need to believe and have faith. And then, you can travel with me to my home. It is full of color and love—not like this grey city you live in," Yu-ning said.

"Like we're going to listen to a little girl," a young man shouted from the back of the crowd. "She's making fools out of us," he said as he turned and walked away, back toward the main gate of the tower.

Julian stepped forward. "Every word she speaks is true. I have seen her magic and I have been healed by her love. And if you don't believe me, many of you saw her heal the old man over there." Julian looked at Yu-ning and said, "Yu-ning,

I want to go to Rainbow Island. I want to know love and color." Yu-ning squeezed Julian's arm, delighted by his change of heart.

The elderly man stepped forward. "You all saw what happened to me—I shouldn't be alive. And now I stand here and I have never felt more alive. I am eighty-three years old, and I feel like I did when I was eighteen, riding with the Empress's cavalry across the countryside!"

Yu-ning nodded at Julian gratefully and continued, "What you believe becomes your reality. If you do not believe or have faith—if you only believe in darkness—then that will be your reality. Choose to believe and we can all travel to the top floor!"

"I believe you," said a mother holding the hand of her five-year-old daughter. "There has to be a better life for my daughter than in this city of misery. I want to travel to your island, little girl. The light you have shown us has given me sensations I have never experienced before."

"It's joy," said Yu-ning, smiling sweetly, her eyes beaming with love.

The elderly man and the mother impacted many people. They were moving forward one by one, pressing through the crowd, causing more and more people to come forward.

"Me too, I want to be on the top of the world!" said a postman who was still carrying his mail satchel. Several dozen people now stepped onto the platform, which was jammed with people. There seemed to be no more room.

"Come on, everyone," said Yu-ning. "You only need to believe! We can reach the top in no time," she said fervently. "Don't lose this sacred opportunity. This is your chance to reach the top!"

This final plea reached more and more people. They rushed forward onto the platform as those on board smiled warmly and patted them on the arms and shoulders, congratulating them. Everyone was feeling the vibration of excitement, nervousness, and expectation. And then something strange happened: the platform seemed to be expanding, growing to accommodate anyone who wanted to climb aboard.

Yu-ning felt the platform expanding and looked wide-eyed at those around her. "Yes, everyone. If you believe in your heart that you can ride to the top, then the platform will make room for you!" This exclamation caused a few last-minute passengers to rush onto the platform, which expanded once again to accommodate them. As she realized that no one else in the crowd was willing to come with them, Yu-ning knew it was time. She grabbed the handle on the control lever, squeezed it, heard a click, and lowered the lever. As she did, the platform again lurched upward several feet, causing many on board to yell out in alarm. Yu-ning reengaged the handle, and the platform stopped moving upward.

Just then, a young man in his early twenties came running toward the platform and leapt upward, grabbing the edge of the platform with one hand. Women on board shrieked, worried the platform would begin to rise with the man dangling below it. A boy and a woman next to the railing grabbed the man's arms and helped him climb aboard. The man was shaken, but a smile of joy lit up his face.

In the commotion, the platform began to sway as it lifted off the ground. "Easy, everyone. It's like being on a boat—we need to remain steady, and not rock one way or another. Take a deep breath, and here we go!"

# Eight

# Anteroom

**Y**U-NING SLOWLY DISENGAGED the locking mechanism on the platform, which jolted into motion once again. This time, however, the passengers remained calm and steady, and the platform began to move smoothly skyward.

Yu-ning looked out at the faces of those below—those who chose to stay behind. Some were weeping, knowing instantly once the platform left that they had made a mistake. Others were still scoffing dismissively, as if to convince one another that they were the only sensible people. A hushed silence fell over the platform. Everyone was breathless, not knowing what to expect next. They watched the faces of those below and saw bitterness, confusion, and sadness. Their attention was drawn back to Yu-ning.

She whispered reverently, "You did it, and now all you have to do is believe."

Voices called out, "I believe. I can get to the top!" Everyone on the platform was suffused with yellow, beaming light. It was shining down, covering their entire bodies.

"I don't know. I'm scared," a man said, as he nervously looked down at the growing distance below. "Oh no," he shouted. "It's too dangerous! We have to get off!"

He and a panic-stricken woman next to him started to climb over the ropes to jump off the platform, which was now about thirty feet off the ground. Yu-ning moved over to them and gently placed a hand on each of them. "Don't worry, you only need to believe and trust. Just close your eyes, and in just a few minutes we will be at the top. Everything is fine." People were taking deep breaths and bowing their heads in prayer, perhaps not even knowing they were intuitively guided to do so.

"All right," said the man, holding Yu-ning's hand. His eyes were closed and he began to feel the platform accelerating. "Oh, it's working. We are moving skyward!" he exclaimed. When others saw him, they were encouraged too. People looked up and nodded in disbelief. They were traveling ever upward, while at the same time, the platform was accelerating faster. It was as if they were flying *above* the platform, rather than simply riding it to the top floor.

Up they went, past the atrium and racing past floor after floor, the city now spreading out before them. They also noticed that the rain clouds were breaking up, as if the lights of the tower were melting them and causing the rain to dissipate. They raced ever higher, the entire city now laid out below them as the sun broke through the clouds to the west. The platform was moving so fast now that people began to have a sense that they were actually flying.

With no warning, the platform jolted to a stop, and those who had been closing their eyes throughout the journey blinked with amazement at the sight in front of them.

The platform had emerged from the enclosed glass of the main tower column and was now resting high over the city; the ropes of the pulley fell hundreds of feet downward to a small opening in the roof of the atrium, through which the platform had risen. As they looked down, it was as if the tower was still growing, and they were rising higher above the city. But the large, sturdy ropes were connected to massive beams above them—this was as high as the platform could go. They had indeed reached the top floor!

"Are we here?" several people queried.

"Is this the top?" a few others inquired.

"Yes, we are here," said Yu-ning." She took a step forward off of the platform and was standing on a white shining marble floor. Everyone else followed with reverence and trepidation. Waiting to greet them was a smiling woman, dressed in a beautiful, wispy white robe. She had plaited blonde hair, interwoven with small white daisies. Her eyes shone bright blue and reflected warmth and kindness.

"We have been expecting you. Please follow me." She walked over to Yu-ning, took her hand, and they walked in front of the others down a long, glass-lined hallway, the city visible far below, growing ever farther away, but still somehow close. All the faces that were once gripped in doubt and apprehension were lighter now, smiling and hopeful. Some closed their eyes and felt the air flowing around them. The entire hallway was infused with pure white light, and its energy and sensation were purifying and cleansing. They didn't know what they were experiencing, only that it felt heavenly.

They arrived at large, frosted glass doors, which the woman opened, beckoning them to enter. The group entered silently and with awe, for before them was the most beautiful room they had ever seen. It was wall-to-ceiling glass, stretching from the marble floors to at least 100 feet into the air. The ceiling above them was vaulted, and also pure glass, with nothing but pillowed clouds and cerulean sky above.

The room was empty except for a stately mahogany desk sitting in the very center. Behind the desk sat a dark-haired man wearing a green shirt and black coat. His hair was long and dark, as was his beard. His eyes were a vibrant blue-grey, with the focus and regality of a hawk. He had a kind face, and as the group entered, he rose from his desk, opened wide his arms, and smiled.

"Welcome, everyone . . . and you, my girl, must be Yu-ning! My name is Balthazar, and I am pleased to see you all." He strode from around the desk and reached out his hands, grasping Yu-ning's in his own. "We have much to discuss, young lady, but first things first!"

He released Yu-ning's hands and turned to address Julian and the adults who had braved the ride to the top of the tower.

"Yes, welcome, welcome," Balthazar repeated.

"Are you the only one up here?" a man from the back called out quietly.

"Yes, my assistant, Melodia, and I," Balthazar replied, nodding respectfully to his assistant standing by the door. He had an air of power and dignity that stilled everyone in the crowd, but he was warm and welcoming, so they continued with their questions.

"Why is this place called the Anteroom of Heaven?" asked a little girl standing next to her mother.

Balthazar knelt down and smiled at the little girl. "Do you believe in heaven, sweetheart?"

"Yes, I do," said the little girl sweetly.

"I do too," answered Balthazar, gently squeezing the little girl's hand. "And it is my life's mission to help other people believe in it, just as you do. To find paradise, we first must find the light. That is the first step. And that is what I help people to do."

"Oh!" exclaimed the girl. "Like the way Yu-ning showed us the pretty pink path?"

"Yes, exactly," said Balthazar. "Yu-ning simply helped you have faith to see the lights. And faith is always the first step on the journey." He turned and motioned them over to the enormous floor-to-ceiling glass windows. They gazed out the windows in astonishment: the city below them had been transformed from darkness to shimmering light. The tower seemed to be rising, growing ever taller, but they could still make out the details of the city below.

A beautiful cascade of light was spreading from the tower throughout the once grey city. The rains cleared, and life was springing up everywhere. All the streets, alleys, and once-dark corners were now repositories of light. Interspersed through the sidewalks and streets were beautiful pockets of green vibrant grass and trees. The brightness continued to spread throughout the entire city until every square foot was gleaming in the light, including the now-sparkling blue sky and late-afternoon sun.

"What is happening? Where is the light coming from?" said Julian.

"The city has been grey because no one chose to believe in the light—that is why none of you could see the light from this tower until Yu-ning had the courage to believe," explained Balthazar. "By believing, we embrace faith, and in faith, we find the power to act. And when we act—well, that is when miracles happen." Even though the sun was setting, the entire city was emblazoned by some miraculous light source. As the people watched the city transform, they began to smile and weep with joy.

"Yes, very good!" Balthazar added. "Thanks to you, this city and each of you shines with all of the light you have required for this time." As he said this, he looked far off in the distance, at something coming from outside the boundaries of the city. "Come, everyone, and see." They all followed Balthazar to the glass windows that faced north, away from the city. The light ended at the outskirts of the city, and though the moon had not yet risen, an object could clearly be seen now, with the lights of the city reflecting off it. It was flying upward, and as it grew closer, Yu-ning gave a shout of recognition.

"It's Suparna! Oh, I was wondering where he was!"

The magnificent bird looked majestic in midair, his wings spreading out wide against the dusky sky, his rainbow feathers illuminated by the shining lights of the tower. Slowly, as if by secret command, the great glass windows began to slide apart, and the night air poured in. Balthazar walked through the opening and stepped onto a large marble balcony that encircled the top floor of the tower. Yu-ning, Julian, and the group of passengers followed Balthazar outside, overcome by the brightness of the rising stars and by the beauty of the city below, bathed in beautiful light.

The crowd grew hushed as the regal figure of Suparna slowly became visible from below. His wings were making a soft *whooshing* sound as he flew up and over the balcony railing and landed softly on the marble floor nearby.

Yu-ning rushed forward and embraced him; Suparna enveloped her in his enormous wings, returning the warm embrace. "I was so scared, Suparna," said Yu-ning. "I kept looking for you in the sky as I walked through the city, but saw no sign."

"The storm was just too strong for me to successfully navigate the city," said Suparna. "Several times I tried to find you, but each time the rain and wind were too strong, and forced me back to the outskirts. I began to circle the perimeter of the metropolis and was becoming more and more worried. But then I saw a brilliant pink light shoot out from under the city—it flowed swiftly along the path of a dry watercourse, and led me into those nearby hills."

Suparna pointed with his wing to a long dark line of hills about a mile outside the city to the northeast. "I decided to follow the light, because I was fairly certain it was coming from your pink crystal heart. Because of the storm hovering over the city, I couldn't follow the light into the city, so I followed it into the hills. It led me to a large wall of debris, where the dry watercourse ended."

Suparna gestured again toward the hills, his voice husky. "Somehow, I sensed that the light was trying to tell me something—and I guessed that it had to do with the blocked canyon where the pink stream of light ended abruptly. I quickly cleared the rocks and debris, and as I did, the light kept leading me to a certain spot—like it was telling me where to dig. Finally, as I dug deeper, I released the waters of a blocked spring.

"The water rushed down the waterway, across the plain, and disappeared through a tunnel leading below the city. Slowly, the storm began to clear, and the once-grey city was filled with magnificent light—that is when I could finally see the lights of this tower, and fly here to meet you."

Yu-ning clapped and jumped. "It's another miracle! My pink crystal heart sent a beam of light under the city and out into the hills, Suparna, which guided you to the old spring. And by releasing the water, you allowed the millrace to flow once again, so it could power the sky platform that allowed all of us to come to the top! Thank you, Suparna, for believing." Yu-ning gave her feathered friend another hug and turned back toward Balthazar.

"It is very good to see you, my wise friend," Balthazar said to Suparna, stepping forward to greet his old comrade. "It's hard to believe that so many years have flowed past us in the winding course of life's river."

"It has been ages, good Balthazar, since we were last together on the barren plains of Darqendia," marveled Suparna. "But look at you! You haven't aged a bit, even though an entire century has passed since you tasted victory over that dragon horde."

The two of them walked to the far side of the balcony, leaving the rest of the group to marvel at the city lights below. Balthazar and Suparna struck a serious tone and talked for quite a while. Yu-ning could not make out what they were saying but could see that it was of great importance. The two nodded in agreement, as if a plan had been decided upon, and Balthazar walked back to speak with Yu-ning.

Balthazar said, "Do you bear the mark, child?"

"Yes—how did you know?" asked Yu-ning, startled. She slowly rolled up the sleeve on her left arm, showing the old man the bow-shaped birthmark, unharmed by the dragon's fire, and surrounded by the burned skin still in the process of healing.

He stared at it for a long time and said, "Then it is you," as if making a decision. "But you are too young—this cannot be." He seemed unsure as he stared first at Yu-ning, then at Suparna, and then walked back toward Yu-ning. "You are not yet ready to face an obisidigon. You will stay with me, and I will teach you what I can; but admittedly, we don't have as much time as is truly needed. I have months of teaching to share, and only days in which to share it!"

"Also, sir, I have this," said Yu-ning, reaching into her pack and pulling out the Light of Balthazar. "Metatron told me to show this to you."

He reached out and took the Light of Balthazar from Yu-ning's hands, holding it up to the light. "It is good to see this again, my child. I have not seen it since the day I gave it to your master. But I'm afraid this crystal orb won't protect you against an obsidigon," he said, handing it back to Yu-ning, who placed it in her pack. "However, it does have its uses," he added for good measure. "So it is settled. You will stay with me, then," said Balthazar, in the form of a statement.

Yu-ning glanced at Suparna, who slowly nodded his head, as if to confirm what Balthazar was telling her. Not wanting to fight, she accepted the fact that she would need to stay behind with Balthazar rather than return to Rainbow Island. She looked at Balthazar, and pointed at the people who had come to the tower with her. "Sir, many of these people would like to go to Rainbow Island. Is it all right for them to leave?" asked Yu-ning, her eyes wide with anticipation.

"Of course it is, Yu-ning. They are free to choose their own paths," said Balthazar, who turned toward the large crowd of adults. Many of them were anxious to leave the Grey City for the promise of a quiet, peaceful life on Rainbow Island. A few, however, had changed their minds, as they had loved ones and families in the city.

The elderly man who had been hit by the whirlicon stepped forward. "Thank you, Yu-ning, for all that you have done for me—for us," he said, as he motioned to those standing behind him. "I have decided to stay, as my children and grandchildren are here in the city." He turned to the many adults, and Julian, who had decided to leave for Rainbow Island. "I wish you all safe travels. Be safe, and be blessed."

It was decided that Suparna would transport those who wished to go to Rainbow Island, and then return for Yu-ning in several days' time. If others decided to go to Rainbow Island at any time in the future, transport would be arranged. The adults were given blankets and provisions for the journey and said goodbye to the adults who had decided to stay behind in their newly reborn, illuminated city.

Julian walked up to Yu-ning and gave her a strong hug. She could feel his tears against her forehead as he whispered, "Thank you, Yu-ning, for caring about me. I hope to see you again some day."

"You can count on it, Julian. I wish you safe travels— until we meet again."

"Make haste, everyone," said Suparna. "I want to get a good start before the sun rises and the heat of the day is upon us." With that, the travelers, starting with Julian—who took the first position atop Suparna's neck—climbed upon the great bird's back. In all, more than fifty people were able to climb aboard and find secure positions within the thick layers of feathers upon his back.

Yu-ning approached Suparna and said her goodbyes. "I will see you within seven days' time, Yu-ning. Learn well what Balthazar has to teach you."

As Suparna rose above the tower balcony, Julian and the other travelers waved to those below. In one swift motion, Suparna glided away from the tower and into the evening sky, heading north, in the direction of Rainbow Island. Within a few moments, his beautiful rainbow wings faded into the starry night.

# Nine

# Balthazar

*J*T HAD BEEN A LONG, EVENTFUL DAY, and Yu-ning was exhausted. She had flown through the night with Suparna, catching only snatches of sleep as they made their way over the ocean during the storm, before arriving at the Grey City. Then she had walked miles through the city streets during the storm, found the center, and led her fellow travelers to the top of the Tower of Light. The adrenaline that had been pushing her onward had now subsided, leaving her utterly spent.

"Come, Yu-ning," said Balthazar. "A hot meal and a comfortable bed await you. Dragoncraft can wait until morning." Yu-ning did not argue and followed Balthazar down a small corridor off the main room. There were doors on either side, and toward the end of the hallway, Balthazar led her into the last room on the left.

The room was appointed with a large bed with a down comforter and soft pillows, a closet with robes and other finely woven garments hanging inside (that seemed to be just her size), a table with two chairs, an antique desk, and a large, floor-to-ceiling window with the lights of the city shining below. On the table was a platter covered with a silver lid.

"Eat, rest. A hot bath waits just down the hall. Just let Melodia know if you need anything at all by ringing that bell." He pointed to a small silver bell on the table next to the food.

Yu-ning thanked Balthazar, who started to close the door to leave Yu-ning to her meal. "Master Balthazar?" said Yu-ning.

"Yes, Yu-ning?" he said, poking his head back through the door.

"What is going to happen?" Yu-ning said, her mind swirling with so many questions that she couldn't quite grab hold of any one in particular, so she asked the one question that was a piece of all the others.

"We are going to fight with the strongest weapon we have, Yu-ning. The strongest weapon we have *ever* had."

"And what is that weapon, Master? The bow?"

"No, Yu-ning. We will fight with *love*." Balthazar's eyes burned brightly, and it was a look that Yu-ning never forgot. Balthazar slowly closed the door, leaving Yu-ning alone with her meal and her thoughts.

That night she slept soundly and deeply. The next morning Yu-ning awakened late—well past ten—but feeling fully refreshed. She pulled back the curtains and was greeted by brilliant sunshine. The city below was washed clean by the rain and the light that now filled it. It was as if the grey and black buildings had been painted in light, transforming and renewing them.

From this height, Yu-ning could see a shining silver ribbon leading out of the city into the nearby hills. This was the old millrace, the sun reflecting off the water now running through it. It flowed from the natural spring down to the plain and into the city, where it surfaced at the water wheel at the base of the tower. It disappeared under the tower on the far side of the conveyer platform, exiting the city at the other end.

Yu-ning dressed in a clean white robe, similar to the one worn by Melodia, and placed Magic in the front pocket. "No mischief out of you today, Magic," she said to the frog, pointing her finger at his head, which was poking out of the pocket. She walked down the corridor toward Balthazar's chambers and entered the massive room, with the desk sitting empty at the center.

No one was in sight. She crossed the room and, noticing that the huge sliding glass partitions were open, stepped onto the balcony. Balthazar was sitting at a round table at the far end, sipping a steaming bowl of tea. "Good morning, Yu-ning. I trust you had a good rest," said Balthazar, as she joined him. Yu-ning assured him that she had and told him she was ready to learn.

"Good," he said, "because time is precious."

All that day they sat on the balcony, as Melodia brought manuscript upon manuscript to Balthazar. He taught Yu-ning all there was to know about the history of the obsidigons, the warlocks who created them, and the Great Obsidigon War of a century before. Midday supper came and went, and the sun began to sink lower on the horizon as the afternoon wore on.

A warm breeze blew softly across the balcony, rustling the thick brown pages of the leather-bound manuscripts that lay on the table before them. With the beautiful view, the rain-washed city below, and the safety of the tower, it was hard for Yu-ning to believe there was such a serious threat roaming the land. She felt as if she were perched atop the world, and that no sorrow, destruction, or death could reach her here. She longed for home—for the comfort of Metatron's embrace, the friendship of Romeo, and the glow of the sacred rainbow.

But all that had been shaken—though Rainbow Island had been an oasis for her throughout her entire childhood, the attack of the obsidigon, and the horror it brought, had shaken her more than she realized. The things she took for granted—the peace and tranquility of the Island, the joy of her school and her teachers, the pleasure of an afternoon swim in the beautiful bay—she missed terribly now. She shared all these thoughts and sensations with Balthazar as they gathered up the manuscripts, getting ready to retire as night drew close.

"Ah, yes. What you are experiencing, Yu-ning, is a very *adult* thing. It's called regret. As we grow older, and leave behind more and more years of living, we have more things we wish we had done differently. And that makes us sad, and causes us to long for the opportunities we missed," explained the wise teacher. "Does that make sense?"

"I think so," said Yu-ning, as she picked up leather books from the marble floor and stacked them on the round wood table. "I regret not appreciating Rainbow Island more, and I regret not being able to do more to protect Romeo."

"Yes, I understand, my child," said Balthazar, sensing the young girl's remorse. "But don't forget that life is a book. Each day is a page. Each year is a chapter. And all those chapters form separate parts—*seasons* in our life. And of course, all the chapters and parts make up the entire book that is our life. The ink on the early chapters of your life, Yu-ning, has barely dried! But still, what has been written in those pages cannot be changed. What you *can* control, however, is what is written on the page of your life *today*. That is all you have."

Yu-ning smiled thoughtfully. "That is what Metatron always says: *Each day is its own page in life's mysterious book. If we try to read ahead, we lose the story.*"

"Ah!" said Balthazar. "Your Metatron is a wise man . . . just like me!" He said this last part with a smile, and he and Yu-ning began to laugh.

Over the course of the next several days, Balthazar taught Yu-ning about the old lore: the rise of the obsidigon army a century earlier, and the defeat of that army by the Darq Renders—the bringers of light. Though she had learned bits and pieces of the story from Metatron and Suparna, Balthazar explained it in full. "Darq Renders are not killers—or destroyers. Just the opposite: they are bringers of light into dark places. For darkness and light cannot exist simultaneously. The light will always expel the darkness."

"Where did the Darq Renders come from, Balthazar? And why am I one?"

"Your kind is an ancient race, Yu-ning. The Renders once had a thriving kingdom on the island of Darqendia. They came from all over the northern islands, and over the years, they developed the birthmark you carry on your left arm. In those days—hundreds of years ago, in the days of our great-grandfathers' grandfathers—the obsidigons were more common, and made frequent attacks on your villages. Over time, your kin learned how to fight them. The bows were made of the best wood, as well as the arrow shafts. And the arrowheads were made of a gem mined only on Darqendia—a secret gem possessed only by the Renders. Even I don't know the secret of the arrowhead, Yu-ning. There is magic in those arrows—or so the legends say."

Yu-ning looked at Balthazar thoughtfully, and in a new light. For the first time in her life, she was talking with someone who understood her history and lineage.

"Yu-ning, I have lived in this tower for many years. I came here to bring the light back to this city. I have tried to reach so many, but today, when I called down to you—you were the first person to actually hear me calling! I have yearned to descend the tower and enter the streets of the city to bring the light. But that is not my role, Yu-ning. I needed just one person—just *one*—to have the necessary faith to release the light. You had the faith to do it."

"I still don't understand why it has to be me, Balthazar. The Empress has an army of warriors at her disposal. And I'm . . ." Yu-ning's voice trailed off as she gazed out over the city far below.

"Destiny. Do you understand this word, Yu-ning?"

"It means path, right?"

"Yes, it means one's path. But don't confuse destiny with destination. What I am talking about is the purpose behind the destination. This is your purpose, Yu-ning—to embrace the role of a Darq Render, and fulfill your destiny as a bringer of light into darkness. That mark on your arm is not about violence, it is about love. That arc is like a bow—or a *rain-bow*. With both, the arc points up and outward—shooting its light to the world. That is the role of a Darq Render: to extend love and to only use one's bow to fight darkness, when all other means fail. That mark means at least one of your parents was a Darq Render also, for the birthmark is only passed down through bloodline. In that history is your future—and your destiny."

Balthazar carried the wisdom not only of years but also of trials and tribulations. When he spoke, he did so with purpose. His ideas were well formed, as if he had already thought of the answers before being asked. But it was more than that: it was as if he had already lived through the questions, so that his answers came not by opinion, but by exploit. Yu-ning respected him, even though she also feared him a little.

With the day's lesson at an end, Melodia informed Balthazar and the girl that dinner was ready. Another day had come and gone, yet Yu-ning was surprised to see the sun setting in the west. It felt as if the two had been talking for just an hour, when in fact the entire day had raced by.

The following morning they had a hurried and early breakfast, as Balthazar felt a growing urgency to teach Yu-ning as much as he could, in the limited amount of time he had left. He knew Suparna would be returning soon from his trip to Rainbow Island, after safely transporting Julian and the adults to their new home. And over the past two days, a plan had crystallized in Balthazar's mind about where Suparna and Yu-ning would need to go next. And now that Balthazar had the plan, he was anxious to set it in motion.

"Yu-ning, do you know about the Darq creatures—what they are?" asked Balthazar, as Melodia cleared away the breakfast dishes from the balcony table.

"You mean the obisidigon?"

"The obisidigon is of a Darq nature—the former is born of the latter."

"I'm not sure I understand," said Yu-ning.

"Darq magic is not natural—it is not part of the natural order of things," explained Balthazar. "This is not natural darkness we are talking about—such as the daily phenomena of the setting sun and the coming of night. This is an *unnatural* darkness—one made of malevolent magic. It is a conjured and controlled darkness, manipulated for evil, to cast the world into gloom. That is Hobaling's plan. Therefore, the obsidigon is his creation, born of a *Darq* nature."

"Metatron mentioned Hobaling to me—the day before the obsidigon attacked Rainbow Island. He said that he is some sort of warlock. But why does he want to bring gloom into the world?"

Balthazar explained that Hobaling was a conjurer and warlock and a disgraced prince of the royal household. Several years back, he had seduced one of the imperial princesses, married her, and ingratiated himself into the royal court. For three years he bided his time—but his loyalty was a deception. Some months ago he had disappeared from the palace, taking something very valuable and dangerous from the catacombs beneath the royal residence: the last known obsidigon skull.

The skull was a trophy taken secretly from the battlefield of Darqendia by the Empress's grandfather, Emperor Ming, and hidden deep in the bowels of the Imperial Palace. Hobaling's grandfather, Hobanor, who lay injured and presumed dead on the battlefield, had seen the former Emperor retrieve the skull and hide it in his saddlebag. Hobanor ruled Baggul Island at the time, and raised the army of obsidigons using twisted magic. Though defeated along with the dark dragons, he knew the Emperor had taken the skull from the battlefield and told his grandson about it before he died several years later from lingering wounds that never truly healed.

"Hobaling now carries his grandfather's thirst for power and control," explained Balthazar, "and seeks to avenge Hobanor's death and restore darkness again. His blood runs deep with hatred, which was nursed by his own father, Hobacol, who disappeared years ago while hunting for obsidigon skulls on the Steppes of Darqendia. Rather than search for his lost father across the desolate plains of Darqendia, Hobaling devised a plan to infiltrate the royal family and find the skull taken secretly by Emperor Ming so many years ago. I believe, Yu-ning, that Hobaling has discovered how to use the arcane magic to conjure an obsidigon from that one skull—the same creature that attacked you and Rainbow Island."

The following day Yu-ning learned about the physical strengths and weaknesses of obsidigons, as well as the best ways to confront them. Balthazar taught her the limited knowledge that he had: Darq Render warriors use the light to penetrate their prey.

"Darq Render warriors never reveal the type of stone they use on the tips of their arrows. It is a well-guarded secret—all we know is that this special stone is found only on Darqendia. And I never got close enough to the front lines to know just how the arrows worked. The battles I saw were from far off, but they were still an amazing sight. The warriors' arrows were ablaze with what looked like white fire, Yu-ning— thousands of shafts of light streaming from a line of 1,000 archers. I do know *this* for certain: the arrows only work at the back of the neck. A Darq Render did tell me that much."

"But what is sharp enough to do that, Balthazar?" asked Yu-ning. "I know how to use a bow, but when I shot the obsidigon the night of the attack on Rainbow Island, the arrow simply bounced off its forehead."

"You will need both a Darq Render bow and the special arrows I speak of, crafted by their fletchers. But Darq Render bows and arrow shafts can no longer be crafted, I am afraid, because they are made of the wood of *Taxus baccata*."

"Taxus ba-*what?*" asked Yu-ning.

"Commonly known as the yew tree," added Balthazar. "It's a conifer—like a pine tree. But it is believed that the last of the yew trees were destroyed during the Great Obsidigon War. They once grew in the old forest on the western side of Darqendia Island; in that forest were several large stands of yew trees. But the obsidigons, knowing the danger of the yew wood, burnt the ancient forest, and from what I have been told, no yew trees still grow there."

As Balthazar spoke, Yu-ning felt sadder than she had in a very long time. She knew what the fire of an obsidigon could do—she had seen it with her own eyes, and felt it in her own body. Indeed, she need only look at the wounds on her arm and shoulder, and the scars that would permanently mark her, for such a dark reminder. But the thought of an entire army of those terrible creatures burning and destroying an entire forest full of life—it made Yu-ning very sad indeed.

Balthazar saw the sadness hanging on Yu-ning. "But Yu-ning, I have heard that at least *one* obisidigon bow yet exists, as well as a single quiver of yew arrows with the magic arrowheads."

"Where? Where can we find them?" Yu-ning implored.

"I have blue dolphin friends who live around Palova Island, to the north of us. This blue pod speaks of a reclusive hunter who lives near the center of Palova, who is rumored to be a descendant of a Darq Render bowman from the Great Obsidigon War. If the story is true, this hunter could be in possession of the last known obsidigon yew bow—called Lightcaster. When Suparna returns, you must go straight-away, and seek out this mysterious hunter."

"There is still something I don't understand, Balthazar," said Yu-ning. "Why is Hobaling doing this?"

"From what I know, Yu-ning, this hatred for the light has been a part of his family for more than 100 years. At one time, his grandfather, Hobanor, was in line to become the next ruler of the Darq Renders. But he was passed over—his royal blood was disputed by other powerful families, and in outrage he left Darqendia, bringing his entire family with him."

"Wait—are you saying that Hobaling is a Darq Render like his grandfather—like me?"

"*Was*, Yu-ning. Hobaling *was* a Darq Render. But his grandfather twisted his mind, filling it with hatred and murderous rage toward all other Darq Renders. While your ancestors were fighting the dragons and their masters, Hobaling's family was secretly aligning itself with them, promising them gold and treasures if they would help Hobanor seek revenge on the Darq Renders for withholding the throne from him. Do you see now, Yu-ning, why you are a part of this? It takes a Darq Render to understand a Darq Render. It is in your blood, Yu-ning. You are fighting one of your own—but one who has passed out of goodness and honor, and into desolation and shadow."

Yu-ning nodded, the pieces beginning to fall into place: she had been chosen by destiny to battle Hobaling, a foe born of the same race, baring the same bow-shaped birthmark. She had been chosen because she was born with the instincts and

99

gifts of a Darq Render to battle dragons that had once come against her ancestors. It was her time of reckoning, and even though it scared her more than she liked to admit, she knew there was only one path forward.

For better or worse, she needed to surrender to that destiny, and pursue it with as much courage as she could muster.

# Ten

# Hunter

Yᴜ-ɴɪɴɢ ᴡᴏᴋᴇ ᴇᴀʀʟʏ, an hour or two before dawn, and couldn't fall back to sleep. She rose, slipped on her robe, and quietly made her way through the main hall to the open windows leading to the balcony off the great tower. There before her was Suparna, sleeping with his head tucked under one massive rainbow-colored wing. "Suparna," she said excitedly in a hushed voice, just as he stirred and raised his head to see her. She embraced him and asked him about his journey back to Rainbow Island.

"All is well, Yu-ning. As well as can be expected, I should say," Suparna said. "The village is nearly rebuilt, and only two children remain hospitalized. They, like you, will carry scars the rest of their days, but they will otherwise make full recoveries."

"And how is Metatron?"

"Slow and steady progress. His staff now doubles as a cane, but his strength is returning. He will be glad to see you, Yu-ning."

"Oh, Suparna, I so miss him and my friends on the Island. When can we leave?"

Balthazar joined them on the balcony, the city below still covered in darkness, lights like diamonds twinkling from the buildings. "Hello, Suparna, and welcome back. I trust your journey was safe and uneventful," said Balthazar.

"Thankfully, yes, my friend. The journey was quiet, and the welcome was indeed warm for Julian and the other travelers upon reaching the shores of Rainbow Island. It was wonderful for the Island to think about something other than recent sad events. A huge welcome banquet was thrown in honor of the new arrivals, and it was good to see the Rainbow Children smiling again."

Balthazar welcomed Suparna into the main hall, as there was a chill in the air on the balcony, and though the bird was well insulated, Yu-ning was shivering from the damp early-morning air. Even Magic, snuggled in the soft pocket of her robe, was shivering.

Melodia moved the small table from the balcony inside, and then excused herself to fix a hot breakfast. Balthazar briefed Suparna on the events of the past few days and the progress Yu-ning had made regarding her knowledge of the Darq Renders, the obsidigon, and the history of Hobaling and his family. Suparna could see that Balthazar had grown fond of the child and had discovered how smart and wise she was beyond her years. As a Rainbow Child, Yu-ning often surprised the adults in her life, especially those who truly took the time to listen to her—as Balthazar had.

"Balthazar, now that we have completed my studies, may I return to Rainbow Island?" Yu-ning said hopefully.

"I wish it were so, Yu-ning. But you cannot return to the Island just yet. I have a very important task for you and Suparna—involving Lightcaster." As Balthazar said this, he looked at Suparna, who gave Balthazar a look of surprise.

"Lightcaster! I haven't heard that word spoken in nearly a century. What news have you of Lightcaster, Balthazar?" said Suparna, his voice animated.

"It is rumored that Lightcaster survived the Great Obsidigon War, Suparna. You need to travel straightaway to Palova Island. As I told Yu-ning, I have heard from credible sources that a hunter who lives on the island may have knowledge of Lightcaster."

An hour later Yu-ning was ready to go, with Magic in his favorite spot in the pocket of her backpack, his head poking out the top. They said their farewells to Balthazar and Melodia, and Suparna lifted off the balcony, the Grey City far below. The height took Yu-ning's breath away as they circled the top of the tower twice, waving farewell to Balthazar and Melodia, who were waving in return.

They followed the straight line of the millrace out of the city—a shining line of water below flew across the plain, and into the hills beyond. Yu-ning could see the water spring, flowing free and clear out of the canyon, as well as several mine shafts further up the ravine—she guessed this was where the city mined brillantium, the wondrous gem that powered the whirlicons that had nearly run her over.

Soon they left the hills behind and reached the ocean, which stretched out before them as far as the eye could see, with no other land in sight. They flew all that day and into

the night, headed northwest, back in the direction of Rainbow Island. "If only we were headed home, Magic," she said to her little friend, whose head was peeking over Yu-ning's shoulder from his position in her backpack.

When night fell Yu-ning scooted down in the saddle, resting her head against the soft leather, and drew a blanket from her backpack, which she wrapped tightly around her. Soon, she was asleep, dreaming of whirlicons, mill wheels, and deep, dark forests full of terrible monsters.

As dawn broke, Suparna could see a dark green line on the horizon. "Yu-ning, are you awake?" he inquired, peering over his shoulder at the sleeping girl, whose head was barely visible from the folds of the blanket enveloping her.

"Yes, Suparna, I am awake. What is it? What do you see?"

"There, Yu-ning, far on the horizon," added Suparna. "That green line—I believe that is the forest island of Palova. We will be there within two hours, I would guess." As they continued to fly northwestward, and the green band grew larger, individual trees could now be seen. Yu-ning ate a quick breakfast of dried fruit and prepared to land.

Suparna flew high over the forest, thick trees covering every inch of the island from the interior mountains to the shore, right down to the water line. He was being cautious, not wanting to fly too close to the tops of the trees, not knowing what creatures lurked within the dark canopy. They flew on with nothing but thick pine forest below, a sea of green carpet in every direction. As they flew toward the center of the island, the terrain began to rise in a gentle slope, till at the center a mountain jutted out of the sea of green pines, rising well above the forest. The mountain's peak was barren of trees, capped by a white rim of snow.

As the pair flew toward the mountain, Yu-ning spotted something brown below—just a speck in the green carpet of the forest. "I think I see a cabin!" she said to Suparna, who banked in the direction Yu-ning was pointing. Suparna circled the cabin twice, searching for a safe place to land. "Yu-ning, I think I can land in that small green meadow not too far from the cabin. Do you see it?"

"Yes, Suparna. That looks as good of a spot as any."

With that, the two descended slowly and silently, Suparna maneuvering his body vertically and beating his wings quietly in a slow descent. They touched down in the small meadow, bisected by a fast-moving, bubbling brook rushing over small rocks on its way down the mountain, seeking its course to the sea. They listened for the sounds of the forest. Nothing.

And then, "Did you hear that, Yu-ning?"

"What is it Suparna?" Yu-ning whispered. "I didn't hear a thing."

"It sounded like a roar, or a growl, like that of a lion. But I can't be sure," added Suparna.

Yu-ning carefully dismounted, and she and Suparna refreshed themselves in the cold water of the frothy stream. They strained to hear other sounds, but heard nothing more. "Suparna, I want you to stay here. I don't want to startle who-ever lives in the cabin. Just stay nearby, and I will call for you if I need help."

Without waiting for a response, Yu-ning unfastened her backpack from the cinch around Suparna's neck and took out the Light of Balthazar—the glass orb that Metatron had given her before she left Rainbow Island. "It's dark in the woods, and Metatron told me that this will be a light to me in dark places." Yu-ning coaxed Magic out of the top pocket, instructing him to stay with Suparna. She slung her pack over her right shoulder and started walking toward the tree line.

Magic hopped atop Suparna's head to get a better view of Yu-ning as she walked in the direction of the cabin. Yu-ning entered the dark woods, where the air was heavy and still. The forest floor was spongy and slightly wet, as if it had rained in the past day. A deep carpet of pine needles covered the ground as far as she could see. As she walked deeper into the woods, the light grew dim; she peered above her, and though she could see patches of blue sky in the breaks of the tall trees, no light reached the floor.

As it was still early in the morning, the sun was not yet high in the sky. Yu-ning considered removing the Light of Balthazar from her pocket, but decided against it, concerned that the light might draw attention from any unseen creatures that might be lurking. With that thought, she shivered and quickened her pace.

After several minutes the air felt slightly fresher and the light grew brighter; she could see an opening in the trees ahead. At the edge of the forest, she positioned herself behind a large tree that looked quite ancient; its limbs were gnarled and twisted. She peered from behind it at a log cabin, which stood about forty feet away. There were no windows, and no signs of activity. A lone axe was imbedded in a large, squat tree stump near the front door, as if to say, "Keep Away."

Yu-ning closed her eyes and said a quick prayer. "One, please protect me." She walked out from behind the tree, quickly but quietly crossed hard-packed dirt, and stood facing the door. She lifted her fist to knock, but stopped in midair. She closed her eyes again, and rapped on the door three times.

Nothing.

She knocked again. "Hello?" she called out timidly, and waited. No one answered. She knocked again, more firmly. "Hello . . . is anyone home?"

A spine-chilling silence fell over her, and she was eager to turn and go. Fighting the urge to flee, she knocked a fourth time as loudly as her fist could hit the door and shook out her hand, wincing from the pain. "I don't think anyone lives here."

Then she heard thunderous, booming sounds, followed by an angry bellow: "Who is it? Who's there?"

Yu-ning jumped with fear. It was a man's voice and it was hostile. "Hello, sir? Sorry to bother you. I am Yu-ning," she said, with a quiver in her voice.

The footsteps grew louder until they were directly on the other side of the door. She heard two locks unlatch, then the door swung open heavily. Standing in darkness was the figure of a tall man. She couldn't see him clearly, because the cabin appeared to be completely dark. There was silence for a moment, and then the man slammed the door.

Yu-ning realized he must not have seen her—or was he just ignoring her? She was trembling.

"Hello?" she said, knocking again. *I don't want to knock again. I don't want to visit with him,* she thought. She turned around, but there was nothing but unwelcoming, dark forest. And she knew what she had to do—what Balthazar had sent her to do.

"Hello?" she muttered helplessly. Yu-ning knocked again, and this time the door creaked open slowly. She pushed the door a little; it was damp and mossy to the touch. She poked her head inside and whispered, "Hello?"

She heard a man's gravelly voice say, "Come in if you dare!"

She took a few steps forward into the pitch black—and recoiled in terror as a terrible stench reached her nostrils. "This is not right. The smell, this place," Yu-ning whispered to herself, or perhaps to One.

In a louder voice she called out to the man, "Hello? Sir, are you there? I can't see. Where do I go?"

"Who are you?" the voice snapped.

"My name is Yu-ning," she said. "I'm sorry, but I can't see where I am going. Do you have any light? A candle, perhaps?" Yu-ning took tentative steps and noticed the floor was sticky and moist beneath her feet.

"There's no light," he responded in a flat voice.

She couldn't see him, but his voice was closer. Yu-ning stopped and said softly, "You have light. We all have light. Here," she said, reaching into her pocket and taking out the Light of Balthazar. The sphere shined so powerfully that it lit up a ten-foot radius around her. Yu-ning blinked as her eyes adjusted to the yellow light.

When she stopped blinking, the first thing she saw was an enormous bear head hanging from a hook right in front of her. She screamed at the top of her lungs "No! Oh no!" Shaking, she took a few steps back, looking down at the wet floor. "No! Oh no! It's blood! It's blood! No!" She was crying inconsolably and trembling with fear.

From where she stood, it seemed like the entire floor was covered in blood, and there were splatters of it on the wall. She took several steps forward with her sphere and found a tiny area where the floor was clear. She took a large step forward onto it, but the blood from her boots seeped out, leaving bloody footprints.

She lifted the crystal, her small arm rattling like a kite as she moved it around the room. She saw several stuffed animal heads hanging from the walls and ceiling: bear, deer, wolf, and fox. On another wall, above a steel table, a large crossbow, scores of steel cutters, knives, and blades in all different sizes hung on rusted hooks.

This gruesome sight horrified Yu-ning. "Oh no . . . all my friends." She held the crystal ball to her heart and folded into herself, wanting to disappear. For at least a minute she stood silently, terrified and uncertain of what to do. Then she took a breath, lifted the crystal again, and walked carefully into the center of the room. There was no ventilation, and it was stuffy and damp. Just in front of her she saw the shadow of the man standing in the dark corner next to another bear head.

He was tall and wide, with long, curly black hair. "Who are you and what is that?" he said angrily, referring to the glimmering crystal. "It's too bright. Get that thing out of my house!" he said with fury, walking quickly toward Yu-ning. "Answer me! Who are you? Get that thing out of my house!"

Yu-ning was still shaking, but she stood firm, trying to be brave. The hunter continued in a menacing tone, "I said, who are you?"

"I told you, I am Yu-ning. Why did you kill all these animals? Who would do such a thing?" she yelled, bursting into tears.

The hunter could see her clearly now. He was staring at her ferociously with his eyeballs popping out of his head and purple veins pulsating on his temples. He was fuming as his grip tightened around a serrated hunting knife in his huge hand. Seething through his teeth, he said, "No child has ever dared to enter my house." Yu-ning lifted the crystal orb to see him talking. "Get that yellow light out of my face!" he continued with rage.

Yu-ning held her ground. "It stays here with me. I asked you, why are so many dead animals hanging on the wall?" Yu-ning was still quivering, but she pushed past her fear. "You killed all these innocent creatures? You are responsible for this?" Yu-ning demanded an answer.

"Yes, I killed these animals!" the hunter spat back, his voice cold and unfeeling as he shielded his eyes from the crystal light.

"These animals are our friends. They are innocent. How could you?" Yu-ning was devastated.

The hunter calmed his voice and said with a quiet, cold tone, "How could I do this? I do this because I am a hunter. This is what hunters do. Do they not have hunters where you come from, little girl?" He looked wicked in his indifference as he walked over to a high counter and started using the knife to chop up animal parts.

"No, there are no hunters where I come from. We grow our food from the land—all the animals are our friends. We protect and treat each other with kindness. We are all one," said Yu-ning, resolve and emotion thick in her throat.

The hunter was not persuaded. "It's none of your business what I do. If you keep talking, I'll put you in that bag!" he said, pointing his knife at a thick, dirty burlap sack sitting on the floor near the front door.

Determined, Yu-ning continued, "Animals have spirit and heart; they have babies and families. You must stop this suffering you are causing. It is why your world is so dark."

"Well, aren't you a spirited one. You know nothing of the world, little girl, if you don't understand the role of a hunter. Animals exist to feed and clothe us." He growled as he rolled up his sleeves and continued hacking away, even more fiercely than before.

"Where I'm from, we are all nice to each other; we don't hurt each other," Yu-ning responded.

"I don't know what kind of place you are from, and I don't care," the hunter countered, continuing to chop. "You can't stop everyone from killing animals."

"You can be the example," Yu-ning persisted. "If you stop, other people will stop too. We are all here to teach each other important lessons. Come with me outside, sir, and I will show you the magic I see every day with these beautiful animals. You will see how lovely they are. Please, please come with me."

"You've worn out my patience, child. You pound on my door, insist on disturbing my morning's work, and then shine that annoying light around my house. I don't need this. I need you to leave—now!" he screamed, pointing the knife within inches of Yu-ning's face.

As he said this, Yu-ning sensed a profound loneliness in the man. Perhaps it was in his tone, or in the slump of his shoulders, or in the veiled look of his eyes—she couldn't be certain. But her anger and fear gave way to an unexpected emotion: pity. And it confused her. She just stood there, staring at him.

"Child, are you *deaf?*" the man snapped. "I have no idea why you are on Palova—I know for certain you are not an islander. And truly, I don't care. Just leave. Now!"

Yu-ning didn't flinch. Calmly she replied, "You asked me to come inside. I brought in my shining crystal light—light that you have never seen before. Why would you ask me to leave?" Yu-ning asked, in a matter-of-fact tone.

"You are an annoying one, aren't you? I have seen light, child. I see light enough when I walk out my door. I don't need your stupid light."

"No," Yu-ning countered, "you don't belong in here. This devastation doesn't belong here! The light belongs here."

Turning away from Yu-ning, and in a barely audible voice, the hunter said, "I have seen that light before, and it's done nothing for me."

"You've seen this light before? What do you mean?" queried Yu-ning, taken aback.

The hunter's voice calmed down to a gravelly whisper. "When I was a boy. After my mother died." He stopped as if he had forgotten himself. "I said get out!" he added, in a louder voice.

"I am sorry about your mother. How did she die?" asked Yu-ning, trying to coax more information from him.

"Get out and take your light with you," the hunter countered, unappeased. He was silent then. He looked dark. He was holding onto his bloody knife tightly, his back to Yu-ning, hands resting against the metal table.

"All right, I will leave. But I'm *not* taking this light with me. The Light of Balthazar remains." Yu-ning gently placed the sparkling orb on the rough-hewn floor of the cabin and made her retreat. As she backed away from the hunter, he turned around, a look of utter confusion on his face.

"What did you call it?" asked the hunter, in a startled voice.

"I'm going. It is your choice to either embrace the light, or remain in darkness. I will leave my crystal ball for you. Good-bye." Standing straight and tall, Yu-ning opened the door, and without looking back, closed it behind her, leaving the hunter alone with the Light of Balthazar.

# Eleven

# Forest

THE HUNTER SEIZED THE DOOR HANDLE, the Light of Balthazar in his right hand. He threw the door open, sunlight pouring into the cabin, momentarily blinding him as he shielded his eyes from the brightness. Yu-ning walked away from the cabin, heading back toward the tree line and the meadow beyond.

"I said I don't want this light, little girl. Here!" shouted the hunter, hurling the orb high in the air, right in her direction. The orb rose through the morning air, headed straight for Yu-ning. The hunter watched in amazement as the girl paid no mind, not even turning around to look at the approaching orb.

Instinctively, the hunter opened his mouth to shout a warning at Yu-ning. Instead, he froze: the round sphere had stopped in midair and was hovering several feet above Yu-ning. It was like a beautiful Christmas ornament hanging from the sky, attached by some invisible thread. Yu-ning turned and saw the orb suspended above her in the air. "Oh my goodness!" she exclaimed, marveling at the floating light.

She looked at the orb, and then at the hunter, who was standing in front of the cabin; he stared at the orb, and then back at Yu-ning. He looked confused, and was about to say something, but stopped. His eyes hardened once again, his look of confusion replaced by irritation. "That's a nice trick, little girl. But you can't fool me with simple illusions!" But rather than walking back into his cabin, he lingered there.

"This isn't a magic trick. I've never seen it do anything like that, hovering in the air." She looked up at the orb again, still suspended above her head; it was gently bobbing up and down, as if floating on an invisible, airy sea. "Like I said, it is the Light of Balthazar—he is the man who sent me to you."

"Balthazar," said the hunter evenly, as if he'd been asked a question and was repeating it back, considering how best to respond. Without saying anything else, the hunter turned around, walked back into the cabin, and slammed the door.

Yu-ning stood there, not sure what to do next. She stood on her tiptoes, extending her hand upward toward the Light of Balthazar, still bobbing and radiating a glittering array of soft yellow lights.

With the tip of her index finger, she touched the bottom of the orb. When she did, it immediately dropped from the air, as if someone had cut the invisible thread holding it aloft. Just in time, Yu-ning caught the sphere before it hit the ground.

She weighed the orb in her hand, looking at it in a new light. Metatron's words came back to her from the night he gave it to her: *It will guide you in times of darkness.* When Metatron told her that, she had assumed he meant it would serve as some sort of torch or lantern, helping her see at night. But now she wondered if his meaning was something entirely different. She stood for another moment, considering her next move.

Her mind made up, she walked back to the cabin and again knocked on the door. This time, however, she didn't wait for the hunter to answer, but gently opened the door herself. She found a new confidence: whether it was from the orb or from the hunter's reaction to it, she didn't know. But with boldness she held the light before her again, illuminating the interior of the cabin.

Curiously, the cabin looked different than it had even a few minutes earlier. It seemed smaller. She had lost her fear. The hunter was sitting in a large chair in the corner, staring at her with a strange, unknowing look. Yu-ning crossed the room silently, holding the Light of Balthazar in front of the man, offering it to him. He stared at her with an intensity she could not read. He just looked at her, refusing to touch the orb.

"You don't know me, and you have no right to come here and invade my home," uttered the hunter, his voice thick and deep. Before Yu-ning could respond, he added, "Is this a trick?" Though his expression was dark, a visible change had come over him—ever since she had mentioned the Light of Balthazar to him, his demeanor had changed.

"No," said Yu-ning, now completely confused. Though she was wise for someone as young as eleven, the emotions the man was eliciting were very *adult-like*, and a bit foreign to her. "I wouldn't make fun of you, sir. Honest, I don't know why the orb did that, or how it happened. You must believe me." No words were spoken for a full minute, which to Yu-ning seemed like an hour. The newfound confidence she'd discovered upon entering the cabin the second time was slowly seeping away; she felt out of her depth, unsure what to do.

"What is your name again?" the hunter said finally.

"I am Yu-ning. What's your name?"

"Jacob. At least, that is the name my master, Metatron, called me when I first came to Rainbow Island—many, many years ago. I don't remember much before that—from my life on Darqendia."

"What?" said Yu-ning in shock. "Are you saying you used to live on Rainbow Island? That is where I live, and I am also a student of Master Metatron."

"Yes, I figured as much, since you carry the Light of Balthazar—I didn't recognize it at first, though it looked very familiar. It wasn't until you mentioned its name that I knew for sure where you have come from. There is only one such orb. When I was a boy on Rainbow Island, Metatron would talk about his old friend Balthazar. Sometimes he would bring out the Light of Balthazar and show it to the Rainbow Children."

"If you knew I was from Master Metatron and Rainbow Island, why did you ask me if my visit was a trick?" asked Yu-ning.

"I have been alone for so long, and strangers are an uncommon occurrence on Palova," Jacob explained. "One can't be too careful. At first, I thought it might be some sort of trick—someone sent to harm me. But when I realized you carried the one true Light of Balthazar, I knew that your visit was no accident, nor malicious. That you were sent here for a reason."

"But how did you end up here? Are you alone?"

"I live alone, but there are others on the island. I keep to myself, though. After my mother died, I was brought to Rainbow Island," he continued. "I never knew my father, and the people of my village thought it best that the teachers of Rainbow Island take me in—along with my twin brother, Joshua. So, when I was four years old, we went to live there; Metatron became our teacher—he was the only father we ever had."

"How did your mother die?" asked Yu-ning, still in shock from these latest revelations.

"Our mother was from Darqendia," Jacob said, deflecting the question. "My father was a Darq Render. Do you know what that is?"

"Yes, I do," answered Yu-ning, but saying no more for the time being.

"Our mother had a secret, and someone found out about it. The man who found out came for my mother—but she refused to give up the secret. So this man killed her."

"And what is the secret?" said Yu-ning.

The second the words left her mouth, she wished she could bring them back. She must have blushed, because Jacob said, "It's a fair question. And it seems that today is a good day for sharing answers," he added, deciding in his mind to trust Yu-ning.

"My grandfather, like my father, was a Darq Render. He was a great archer, and fought alongside the Renders of Darqendia against the dragons that invaded our island. Though my father died in the war, my grandfather survived," added Jacob. He looked at Yu-ning, making sure she understood his story.

Jacob explained that after the war, the Darq Renders were scattered, their numbers decimated by the obsidigons and their warlock masters. Though they won the war, it all but destroyed their clans. Jacob's grandfather, Corain, was one of the only surviving Darq Renders, and his most prized possession was the bow he had carried with him as a warrior and had used against the obsidigons. Before his grandfather died, Corain had given the bow to Jacob's mother for safe-keeping. The evil warlock Hobaling feared that bow, because it was the only one remaining after the war—the only one capable of killing an obisidigon.

Though the obsidigons were destroyed, Hobaling was searching for an obisidigon skull, with the intent of creating another obsidigon army using his Darq magic. Rumor from one of his many spies must have reached him, however, that one last obisidigon bow yet existed. And so terrified was he of that bow that he hunted for it until finally his search paid off, and he tracked it to Jacob's family on Darqendia.

After Jacob's grandfather died, Jacob's mother, Calia, was left alone to raise her young sons. One night Hobaling broke into their home, confronted Calia, and demanded she give up the bow. Unwilling to tell the warlock where the bow was hidden, she was seriously wounded by the sorcerer's blade. Though Hobaling tore apart the house, he did not find the bow. The next morning, townsfolk found Calia clinging to life and the young twins hiding under a bed in a back room. Before she died, Calia told her cousin, Silas, where the bow was hidden: inside a compartment beneath the floorboards of the house.

The mother urged Silas to take the boys to Rainbow Island to be raised by the teachers, and to never tell a soul about the hidden bow—unless one of the boys were to return to claim it for his own. It was better to leave it buried and hidden from the world than to risk its being discovered again by the warlocks. Silas was the only person who knew where the bow was hidden, and he kept an eye on the house to make sure it was left undisturbed.

"And so," Jacob said, "when Joshua and I turned eighteen, we left Rainbow Island and sailed back to Darqendia to visit the home we left as children. It was then that we visited our old village and were welcomed by Silas, who by that time was a very old man. He took us to our old house and led us inside. He told us about my mother's death, and then showed us the secret compartment hewn into the floorboards of our home. And buried within was my grandfather's bow and his quiver of arrows."

Jacob paused, gathering his thoughts. "Silas urged us to stay, but it was too painful for us; we wanted nothing to do with Darqendia and all its sad memories. So we left again, traveling for nearly a year as first mates on a merchant ship called the *Paragon*. One day the *Paragon* docked in one of the bays here on Palova, and without saying a word to anyone other than Jacob, I took the few possessions I owned, including my grandfather's bow, and slipped off the ship late one night, never to return to life at sea. I was weary of the ocean, and just wanted to be alone. Joshua remained on the ship, but agreed to return to Palova within a year's time. That was twenty-one years ago . . ."

A silence hung between the girl and the hunter, and neither spoke for a while. Yu-ning sensed great sorrow in Jacob, but she didn't know what to say. She had never had a brother of her own, though she knew how sad she would feel if she weren't able to see her friends on Rainbow Island for so long. That made her think of Romeo, and tears came to her eyes.

"In my heart I know Joshua is safe, and I am sure that one day I will see him again," Jacob said, breaking the silence. "I just don't know where he is now."

Yu-ning collected herself and had another thought. "Are you . . . are you a Darq Render, Jacob?"

"No, I am not. Neither is my brother. Though my father and grandfather bore the mark, we do not. My mother was not a Darq Render, and we took after her kin," added Jacob. He looked at Yu-ning with a sharper gaze. "How do you know about Darq Renders, Yu-ning? Few folk speak of the old bloodlines these days." Yu-ning didn't say anything but slowly rolled up her left sleeve, revealing the new red scar on her arm and the large, undisturbed bow-shaped birthmark in the center. It had been years since Jacob had seen the Darq Render mark.

"I was sent by Master Balthazar," said Yu-ning. "He believed that the bow still exists, and that it might be found here on Palova. There is a growing darkness in the land, Jacob, and Hobaling, the man who killed your mother, has successfully conjured another obsidigon. So far, we only know of the one, but there might be more. We just don't know."

Jacob looked concerned. "If Balthazar and folk as far as the Grey City have heard rumors of the bow, it means the enemy will soon hear the rumors as well. The bow is no longer safe here, Yu-ning. You must take it for safekeeping and seek the protection of those who can help you use it against the obsidigon."

With that, Jacob rose and disappeared into a back room. In a moment, he returned carrying the most beautiful bow Yu-ning had ever seen. It seemed twice as large as her Rainbow

Island bow and was made of a beautiful blond wood, polished to a fine sheen. Jacob handed the bow to her, and she whispered, "Lightcaster."

"Yes, this is Lightcaster—the last remaining obsidigon bow. With it, a Darq Render wields something strong enough to stop an obsidigon. *You* are a Darq Render, Yu-ning—which means you have the ability to wield this bow. If, of course, you have the proper missiles."

"Missiles? Oh, you mean the special arrows?" queried Yu-ning. "Don't you have the arrows for the bow?"

"No, I don't. My brother, Joshua, took the quiver and arrows, and I kept the bow. We each wanted something of our old life by which to remember our family. When we parted ways that night on the *Paragon*, little did we know that we wouldn't see each other for two decades . . ."

Yu-ning asked how she might be able to track down Joshua, but Jacob did not know. "Yu-ning, these past two decades have been sad ones for me. I have become more and more isolated on this island—in this cabin," he said, sweeping his hand outward at all the trophy heads on the walls. "I typically only come out at night to hunt, and rarely see the light of day. I have so many dark memories . . . so many years of killing. It seems it's all I know any longer." Remorse hung on Jacob with great weight.

Tears of both surprise and joy sprung to Yu-ning's eyes. She had truly doubted if the light would still be able to reach this troubled soul. "It isn't all you have ever known. You remember the light—when you were a boy. Your mother was in the light; you saw the light—and not just this orb here," Yu-ning said, holding the Light of Balthazar in front of Jacob. "I can take you to the light you once shared with your mother and your brother. You can leave all this darkness behind."

Jacob cowered, looking weak and vulnerable. "You would forgive me? You would let me walk with you back to the light?"

Yu-ning nodded. "Though I came here looking for Lightcaster, I believe there's another reason why I came, and why you were supposed to see the Light of Balthazar again. And, there's nothing to forgive. Yes, you can come with me."

Jacob was doubtful. "But didn't you say that I need your crystal orb to see?"

"You won't need my orb if you stay in the light and choose love over hate," Yu-ning replied in a comforting voice.

Jacob looked at Yu-ning, truly wanting to believe her. Slowly he rose from his chair, and the two walked toward the door of the cabin. Yu-ning placed the Light of Balthazar back into her robe, slipped Lightcaster around her shoulder, and left the cabin. Jacob turned to look back into his house and stood just inside the doorframe. He shook his head. "I . . . I can't leave. I have work to do here." His voice and demeanor became slightly defensive.

"That's not work," Yu-ning said, pointing back into the cabin full of dead animals. "That's just death. If you come, you will see," Yu-ning urged.

"No, I can't go," the hunter insisted, still standing just inside the door of the cabin.

"There is nothing in your house for you anymore, Jacob. It is darkness and pain." Yu-ning stood on the patchy grass that ringed the clearing of Jacob's cabin. The air was fresh, and a soft breeze was blowing. The fragrance of honeysuckle filled the air. She breathed in deeply and smiled. "Jacob," she said, trying to appeal to him. "It is so beautiful here, and only twenty feet beyond your cabin door the air is pure, clean, and fresh. Come outside," she said, extending her hand.

At that moment, Yu-ning heard a shuffling and chuffing nearby. "I know that sound . . ." said Yu-ning as she turned around to confirm her hopes.

It was Leonidas, her lion friend from Rainbow Island. He emerged from the forest and walked toward Yu-ning, head held high, looking very regal. He began to play his flute. "Leonidas! Oh, Leonidas. Hello! I'm so happy to see you. Such lovely music; I should have known," she said with joy. "But how did you get here?"

"Hello, Yu-ning. It's wonderful to see you." Leonidas smiled, holding his flute. "It's not an overly long journey from Rainbow Island to Palova—especially if you ask the pink dolphins nicely," added the lion, chuckling. The pink dolphins of Rainbow Island were a helpful source of transportation for anyone wanting to travel to nearby islands—and as large as the dolphins were, even a lion could ride comfortably atop one's back. "I come here often, Yu-ning, to visit my kin. I was walking nearby and heard the sound of voices. What a pleasant surprise it is to find you here," exclaimed Leonidas.

Yu-ning reached for his mane and snuggled his large furry cheeks, scratching him behind his ears. After they rubbed noses and laughed, Yu-ning looked over toward the cabin, and though the door was ajar, she couldn't see Jacob. "Jacob, my lion friend is here; come out and meet him!" Yu-ning called out loudly, while still scratching and cuddling her friend.

The hunter stood back in the darkness of the cabin and said, "There's no lion here, Yu-ning. The lions live deep in the forest, away from people."

"You heard his music," Yu-ning continued. "He was playing his flute. Come outside and you will see." Yu-ning nodded and winked at Leonidas, who stood proud and protective at her side.

Jacob retorted, "There is no lion!" Leonidas lifted his flute and began to play another soft, sweet melody. Jacob paused once again, utterly surprised for the second time that day, for he remembered a tune like this from his childhood. He peeked from the doorway and his eyes strained to focus in the distance. He squinted and saw Leonidas playing the flute next to Yu-ning.

"There's a lion!" he said, turning back to retrieve his crossbow from above the steel table. He emerged from the cabin with his weapon, nocked an arrow, and took aim at Leonidas. His arms, however, were shaking, as he could see that the lion held a flute.

"Jacob, stop!" shouted Yu-ning. "It was Leonidas who was playing the beautiful melody that calls you. He is my friend, and he is playing beautiful music for *you*." Jacob seemed not to be listening as his finger started to squeeze back on the crossbow trigger.

"No, stop! Please don't hurt Leonidas! He's my friend!" She stood in front of the lion, extending her arms to protect him. Leonidas pulled Yu-ning softly aside with his teeth on her collar, and stood to face the hunter some thirty feet away. His eyes were without fear as he looked directly into Jacob's lethal gaze. Leonidas began to play his flute again, with Jacob's crossbow pointed directly at his head.

Yu-ning hugged Leonidas, calling out to Jacob, "Leonidas won't hurt you, so please don't hurt him. He is our friend."

Time seemed to pause as Jacob's gaze was frozen on the fantastic scene of a lion playing a flute. Then, calmly and slowly, he lowered his weapon. It was almost as if he remembered something long forgotten. "I had forgotten that animals could play music. But now it's coming back to me—from when I was a very young boy on Rainbow Island," Jacob murmured.

Leonidas nodded, acknowledging that he was one of the animals that had played for Jacob when he was a lad. The tune he was playing was one that Jacob had forgotten, but which had reawakened memories of a long-ago, happier time.

"You don't need to bring anything," Yu-ning called out reassuringly. "Just come with us. We have everything you need."

Jacob gripped the crossbow in his left hand, but his hold on it was different, less certain. It was like a foreign object rather than a familiar killing tool. He slowly walked away from the cabin.

"You can trust us. You won't need your weapon; Leonidas won't hurt you," Yu-ning called out reassuringly. The hunter looked uncertain as he walked toward them. He stared again in disbelief at the peaceful, flute-playing lion, but refused to lay down his crossbow.

Cold beads of sweat formed on his forehead and rolled down his temples. He was ten feet away from them when Leonidas smiled and produced a handful of colorful, shining beans, seemingly from thin air. He held out the beans with his large, furry paw and offered them to Yu-ning.

"Thank you, Leonidas," Yu-ning said as she took a handful. She instantly felt the light and magic from the beans. Leonidas smiled as he walked toward Jacob, who immediately stepped back, holding the crossbow tight in his trembling hand.

Leonidas called out, "Hello, my friend. I can play music for you anytime you like. Don't worry; I won't hurt you. Here, take some magical beans and allow them to grow in your heart. You will then know how to use them."

Leonidas set some beans on the ground in front of Jacob, who was sweating profusely. Yu-ning slowly approached him, placed her hand on his forearm, and gently reached for his crossbow. As the hunter stared at the beans, without realizing it he released his grip on the weapon.

Yu-ning took it and placed it by a tree. "Don't worry," Yu-ning whispered, "Leonidas won't hurt you."

The hunter nodded slightly and leaned down to pick up seven beans. He held the shining beans in his hand, amazed. Lights danced and vibrated in his palm. Jacob looked at Yu-ning, his eyes wide. "I had forgotten that lions could play music," he said.

Leonidas walked up to the hunter and said, "We only roar to protect ourselves. We never want to hurt you; please don't hurt us anymore. We only want to share this place with you."

The hunter stood in silence, shocked by Leonidas's warm gesture and greeting. The lion gazed into the hunter's eyes. "You are safe now. Walk in the light. Only choose the light." Leonidas ambled over to Yu-ning and rubbed her face with his.

"He's safe now," he said to Yu-ning. "I will see you soon. I am off to visit my cousins!"

Yu-ning threw her arms around Leonidas's mane before he ambled off into the forest. "Goodbye, Leonidas!" Yu-ning said, waving after him.

Jacob stood in disbelief, and Yu-ning gently took his hand. "Let's go to the forest. Come, but not with that," said Yu-ning, nodding toward the crossbow.

"Let's just bring this," he said, stopping. He reached for the crossbow that Yu-ning had set by the tree. As he did, Yu-ning placed herself between him and the bow, and just shook her head from side to side. Then she reached out her hand, and he reluctantly took it again. Together they walked into the forest.

"This way," Yu-ning said sweetly, smiling at Jacob. He looked down at her and a small smile formed on his lips.

It was the first time he had smiled in years.

# Twelve

# Cottage

THEY VENTURED INTO THE FOREST, back in the direction of where she had left Suparna. And as they walked, all kinds of animals materialized to greet Yu-ning. Rabbits, birds, squirrels, chipmunks, frogs, lizards, insects, and even snakes approached her joyfully. All creatures great and small were celebrating her as she ventured through the forest.

"It's Yu-ning, it's Yu-ning!" the birds chirped with excitement. Yu-ning was very happy and she greeted everyone, though she wasn't quite certain how they all knew her, since she'd never before been to Palova! She inquired about this mystery. "Leonidas and other friends from Rainbow Island have told us about you, Yu-ning!" the animals explained. "Your love and care precedes you!"

Jacob couldn't believe his eyes and ears and had difficulty shifting his customary reaction toward animals. As they continued walking into the forest, they noticed blood and animal footprints on a dirt path, leading away from the meadow where she'd landed earlier that day. She hesitated, but decided they needed to follow the footprints and blood drippings, which led them deeper into the woods. Jacob stopped. "I don't think we should go any further. Who knows what the blood is from, and I don't have my weapons with me. It's dangerous; we should head back," he said.

Yu-ning shook her head. "Maybe someone is hurt and needs our help. Come on, let's go," she said firmly. Jacob nodded as they continued to follow the footprints and blood, which led them down a steep ravine. At the bottom, a rushing stream tumbled through, most likely the same stream where she had refreshed herself that morning. They forded the stream across a thick mossy log and climbed up the far side of the ravine. Once they exited the dell, the path weaved along the edge of a cliff, and eventually led through a dense thicket to a large stone cave. As they quietly approached the entrance of the cave, they heard talking.

They crept closer to the entrance and saw two bears inside, one black and one brown, talking to each other. They looked like Yu-ning's Rainbow Island friends Stout and Madrigal, but they were different bears. Yu-ning wondered if they were related to her bear friends. The black bear was hurt; his leg was bleeding, and the brown bear was helping him with the wound. It became clear that the brown bear was a female and the black bear was her mate.

She was licking his wounds and spoke softly to him. "Oh, darling. Are you in pain? Why do they want to hurt us? We are just trying to take care of our family." Just beyond them was a soft bed of leaves where three cubs were sound asleep.

"I wish they would stop hurting us," the black bear replied, cringing in pain. "Our clan is dwindling; the death is senseless."

Jacob hung his head as he listened to their conversation. He whispered to Yu-ning, "I've killed many bears. I'm probably responsible for the suffering in this family."

Yu-ning looked at him with eyes full with tears. She reached for his hand and said, "It's never too late, Jacob. You can help protect the animals from this moment forward." Jacob was quiet as they backed away from the cave. He saw Yu-ning pull out several fruits and nuts from her pack to leave at the entrance. She continued to pull more and more food out of her backpack, smiling at Jacob, who looked at her in fascination.

"Bears eat a lot." She smiled. "This is food from the Tower of Light, where I've just come from. It will help the black bear heal, and there will be plenty for the cubs."

Yu-ning and Jacob backed away from the cave, leaving a full harvest of fruits and nuts behind them. Jacob paused and turned. He put his hand in his pocket and pulled out the magical beans that Leonidas had given to him. He carefully placed them next to the fruits and nuts. They continued down the path.

In front of them as they headed back down the path, they saw a deer—a large brown buck—standing on the right side of the hill, looking at them. Yu-ning had never seen this deer before. His body was beige with brown spots, and he had a huge rack of antlers, from which yellow rays of light were shining. It was clear he was not a normal deer.

Wherever he stood, the path lit up. He looked very alert and wise. A small fawn walked out of the trees, and a doe

133

walked out from behind a large bush. They snuggled and frolicked as the buck above kept watch. The fawn began to nurse as the doe ate grass and looked up at the buck, smiling.

"Look at that beautiful family," Yu-ning said. Jacob nodded reflectively. He was filled with regret and remorse. "It's all right, Jacob. You will see many things that will leave you questioning the life you've lived. This is what is supposed to happen. Surrender the guilt, and commit to your transformation. There is so much you can do to make up for the suffering you caused. Let that be your inspiration."

The beautiful buck spotted Yu-ning and bounded down the hill. "Hi, deer!" Yu-ning cried out happily, placing her cheek on his large nose.

"Jacob, you don't need to fear him," Yu-ning said.

The buck looked at Jacob with an all-knowing gaze. "I've known you for my entire lifetime," said the buck. "I lost my parents, a brother, two sisters, and many friends to your killing. A lot of joy and freedom have been robbed from us as you have hunted our forest. You have caused tremendous suffering."

The deer paused and looked to the horizon. "I can also feel all the regret and shame within you now. We have Yu-ning to thank for that. Listen to her. Make the change now. Make your life matter now. Pray for all the souls you have taken, and ask for forgiveness. Let your path be sacred now, and remember to respect everyone; all life, large and small," he said solemnly. "There will be others, and you will need to reach them. Help awaken them as you are awakening," the beautiful buck continued.

Jacob's shoulders caved in as he began to shake and sob uncontrollably, the floodgates finally breaking. "I'm so sorry. What have I done? I am so very sorry." His huge body was broken and woebegone. Yu-ning hugged him as the deer family looked on quietly.

After several minutes of silence, the buck said, "I want to take both of you to a special place."

Yu-ning nodded with excitement in her eyes. Jacob nodded as well and said, "But it is getting dark, and I don't know the route to get back home."

The buck replied, "Maybe after you see and experience this place, you won't want to go back."

Yu-ning's eyes opened wide as she nodded at the majestic animal. She pulled on Jacob's arm. "Yes, come on, let's go with him," she said convincingly.

The buck smiled. "We must go now if you want to see this special place." He waited a moment for Yu-ning and Jacob to follow and galloped down the path.

"Yes, we want to see. Let's go now!" Yu-ning pulled on Jacob's sleeve as she skipped after the buck. They moved down the path briskly and continued on for quite a while. Jacob and Yu-ning watched the deer descend to a small stream for a drink of water, and they both sat down for a minute to rest in a thick grove of trees. Beyond the trees she saw that the dense forest gave way to a wide-open, grassy space.

They were near a seaside cliff. The air was fresh, and baby blue sky unfolded for miles above them as the sun sank toward the western horizon, a huge ball of orange bathing the cliff in soft light. Below them was a white sand beach onto which the pristine waters were cresting and breaking.

The ocean was sublime. "The sand is so white, clean, and soft," Yu-ning said dreamily.

Jacob walked over and peered through the trees out into the vast expanse of sea. He was overwhelmed by the beauty and shook his head. "I knew this was here, but I've never cared to really see the ocean like this. I lived in the darkness of my cabin and only came out at night to hunt. I never thought about how beautiful it is," he said remorsefully.

The buck reminded them that they had to get going before it got darker. Yu-ning and Jacob nodded and walked back on the path through the forest. Green leafy poplar trees jutted above them, mixing in with tall stands of pine. It would be dark soon, and there was a gentle chill in the air. As the sun began to sink, Yu-ning produced the Light of Balthazar, which illuminated the path and made it easier to negotiate.

They once again met up with the stream, which flowed over small rocks and stones down the path next to them; the crystal clear water reflected the last of the day's light. They followed the buck across the stream as the path reappeared on the other side. Beautiful purple flowers bloomed atop squat, waxy green bushes under a ceiling of vibrant green poplar and birch trees on each side of the path. It was a colorful display, and Jacob could hardly believe this was the same forest he hunted in night after night.

As they continued walking, the sunset and night came quickly. Even with the Light of Balthazar now in her hand, Yu-ning remarked that it was getting harder to see beyond the path. All of a sudden bright white lights sliced through the green leafy trees, so bright that it was hard for them to open their eyes. Jacob and Yu-ning had to stop and let their eyes adjust. The buck waited patiently to guide them further.

The forest path was lit up in bright, shining lights, and before them was a quaint cobblestone and wood house. The house was small, with three short steps leading up to a wide porch and bright white door. A simple love-seat swing sat on one side, and potted pink jasmine grew abundantly up a trellis on the other side. In front of the jasmine were two rocking chairs.

The windows were sparkling clean, refracting the light from the house. The steep roof was made of thick thatch with a sparkling white chimney. In front of the house was a beautiful garden of wildflowers, twice the size of the actual house. The home was lovely and absolutely eccentric. The buck smiled. "This is your destination; go on now. I must leave you. Remember your lessons, Jacob, and stay in the light." The deer bounded into the forest, leaving Yu-ning and Jacob on the edge of a dozen questions.

"Thank you! Goodbye!" Yu-ning waved happily.

"Wait!" Jacob called. "How do we get back?"

"Don't worry about that now," Yu-ning said. "Follow your intuition and don't plan for your future before you know your present. Remember what the deer said— you may not even want to go back." Yu-ning yanked Jacob's sleeve down toward the cobblestone walkway and through the gate in the white picket fence that surrounded the house. Yu-ning was beside herself with excitement. "Here we are, Jacob! Wow, it is so colorful." Jacob was silent. He just stared at the house with wide eyes. Though he had seen this cottage from a distance, he had always hurried by, never taking the time to approach it or its occupants.

"Your house could be like this if you choose. Come on, let's go inside," Yu-ning said, skipping to the door. Jacob stood motionless. "Come on, Jacob," Yu-ning said as she pulled his sleeve again. He and Yu-ning continued up the steps and stood in front of the clean white door. Yu-ning looked at Jacob and said, "You knock. Let's see what happens!" Jacob paused for a moment and knocked three times.

They heard shuffling inside and sounds of someone approaching the door slowly. An old woman opened the door. She looked quite old, her silver-white hair tied in a small bun at the back of her head. She was slightly hunched, wearing a simple green long-sleeved shirt and red pants. She smiled and looked loving and kind. "Hello, my dears," she said, filled with warmth and affection. "Welcome, welcome. Come on in, my darlings," she added, smiling ear to ear.

Yu-ning lunged toward her and hugged her. "Thank you, Grandma," she said excitedly.

Jacob whispered into her ear, "You know her? Is this your grandmother?"

"She's like my grandmother—everyone calls her Grandma. She and Grandpa come to visit the children on Rainbow Island, and always bring us gifts when they come! But this is the first time I've been to their house." With that, Yu-ning entered the house, filled with wonderment and curiosity. The house was old-fashioned and charming. It was everything you would expect of an elderly couple's home, but inside, the house was saturated with color. Every single thing in the house was a rainbow of colors. The table, cabinets, desk, bed, chairs, closet, sofa, shelves, and every other piece of furniture were each a different color.

The fragrance of freshly baked cookies wafted through the air, and hot chocolate bubbled on the potbelly stove. On the counter next to the hot chocolate was a brimming bowl of white, thick cream. Jacob stood at the door, not knowing what to do. He had never seen such a spectacle and was overwhelmed by all the miraculous events he had witnessed that day. "Jacob, come inside," Yu-ning coaxed.

"Yes, dear, we welcome you," Grandma said kindly. "You are welcome in our home," she continued.

"Thank you," Jacob whispered shyly as he took two more steps inside, shutting the door silently and waiting by it.

Yu-ning was in a reverie. "Grandma, your home is so beautiful and colorful. It is just like my cave!" Yu-ning pulled out a chair to sit down. "Everything smells so sweet. Like candies and cookies! Ah, I'm so hungry, Grandma!" Yu-ning sighed and collapsed into an orange chair with pink legs at the kitchen table, which was bright red.

Grandma laughed. Jacob smiled and looked around. Quietly, he said, "The house looks so simple from the outside; you would never expect such a world of color on the inside."

"Yes, but not everything is what it seems on the outside, is it, Jacob?" Grandma asked softly. She was filled with the wisdom of many years. Jacob just stared, standing by the door like a still board.

Yu-ning was swinging her legs back and forth. "You live here, Grandma?" Yu-ning asked, as she looked around in sheer delight.

"Yes, I live here with my husband." She smiled and pointed into the living room at the center of the house. On a purple sofa sat an old man wearing glasses and reading a book. He had silver hair, a white moustache, and a neatly trimmed beard. He looked into the kitchen and nodded at Grandma as he rose and walked over to join them.

Grandma pulled out a dark blue chair with light blue legs and gestured for him to sit across from Yu-ning. He was holding a big colorful mug of softly steaming tea.

"Grandpa!" Yu-ning said happily.

"Hello, sweetheart. Welcome." He smiled at Yu-ning as his eyes twinkled with light. "And welcome to your friend here. Jacob, is it?" Grandpa said kindly, looking toward the entryway. Jacob nodded uncomfortably and lifted his hand to greet Grandpa. "Come here, son. Sit with us."

Awkwardly, Jacob walked over to a purple chair with green legs and sat down next to Yu-ning. He looked around in amazement at the beautiful, unusual house. "Your home is so nice. I've never seen a home like this. How long have you two lived here?"

Grandpa sipped his tea as he reflected on the house and the years he had spent here with his beloved. "We have lived here nearly seventy-seven years—since we finished building most of the house. We had our eye on this land since we found each other at fifteen; our families were refugees after the Great Obsidigon War destroyed our village on Malinga Island. Many of the families lived a nomadic life, sailing from island to island, seeking a new home—somewhere quiet and far from the reminders of the war. So we decided to marry, and settle here on Palova. We started building this house when we were eighteen. We are both nearly 100 years old and we have spent every day together."

"You are from Malinga?" asked Jacob. "I am from Darqendia. Well, I mean, I was. My mother and father are long dead, and I have lived on the other side of the island for about twenty years."

"So we are both refugees in our own way, aren't we, Jacob?" said Grandpa.

"Yes, I suppose we are . . ." Jacob answered. "I have walked by your cottage many times late at night, but I have never seen the lights. I had heard that an elderly couple lived on the far side of the island, but I never took the time to come visit you. I am sorry we haven't met before now . . ." his voice trailed off.

"Well," said Grandpa, "we are meeting now, which is a great thing."

Grandpa reached over to hold Grandma's hand. He smiled and said, "She is as beautiful to me now as the first day I laid my eyes on her, dancing in this magical forest with all the animals. We began to meet in the forest every day and to speak with the animals. We fell in love right away. When we were sixteen, we planned to build our home in this beautiful forest, and we started the day we turned eighteen. Both sets of our parents died long ago, of course, and the few relatives we had either are dead, or moved on to other islands long ago."

He explained how he and Grandma built the house from the ground up, all by themselves. "We made every piece of furniture in it together. We painted everything. It took us ten years to completely finish, and each year since we have made additions and have continued to cultivate our home, like our garden of wildflowers. We live here among the animals, forest, and sea. It is our heaven. We have had a blessed, blessed life."

Tears came to Jacob's eyes. "You have been here this entire time, and yet I have only known darkness. I don't have any friends. I've caused only pain in my life."

Grandpa looked Jacob in the eyes. "We have been waiting for you, Jacob. We have known of you for as long as you have lived in these forests. We first saw the crimes you committed many years ago, and we vowed to live here and shelter this sacred forest and all the animals in it as best we could. We saved many animals from your barbarism, but so many we lost. We made peace long ago, knowing it was the path you'd chosen, and all of the blessed animals that you killed submitted to the fate of being taken by you.

"They all gave their lives for the gift of your transformation—they sacrificed themselves and their families for your rebirth. They are to be thanked, honored, and revered for the light you have found now. You can never go back to that darkness, and you must spend every moment of your life from this day forward making up for the senseless destruction. Do you want to know our secret of eight decades of bliss together? Do you know why our lives are so filled with brightness and color? Well, it's very simple: we do everything with love. With love everything is possible. Love keeps everything together."

Grandpa stopped as tears flowed down his cheeks. Grandma walked over to the table and leaned over to embrace him. As they hugged, Jacob looked at them wistfully. "I hope one day I will have what you have," he said sadly. "I will do as you say. I will devote every day of my life to making restitution. I will create a world in which I give back to all the animals. I will revere this forest and all its blessings."

Grandma looked at Jacob and placed her right hand over his. "This is your new home, Jacob. Grandpa and I won't be here forever. You are meant to take over this home and continue our mission. You can have anything you want in life if you only keep love in your heart. Find your life's love, and together build a community and make the world a brighter place."

"You can make so many friends and have a beautiful life like Grandma and Grandpa!" Yu-ning said, filled with excitement.

Jacob looked down at the red tabletop. Tears continued to flow. "Right now? I can have this all right now? What about my punishment? I am guilty of such horrible acts. How can I be worthy of living in this world of color and love?" he asked, weeping freely.

"It will take some time for your heart to heal and for you to find forgiveness within yourself," Grandpa said, nodding with understanding. "There are no punishments, only sacred lessons. You are a beloved child and the moment you accept that truth and honor yourself, your life of color and bright-ness will begin. This is your work."

"Just like that?" Jacob asked in disbelief.

"Just like that," Yu-ning, Grandma, and Grandpa said in unison.

"But I am all alone," Jacob said, filled with regret.

"No longer. You have all of us! And you can go out and share your love with everyone you meet, and you will never feel lonely. You will see how beautiful your life can be when you share your love," Grandpa said, smiling.

"You will never return to that dark cabin," Yu-ning said. "It no longer exists. The light will transform it into a beautiful field in which the animals can roam safely. There is only this moment now and every moment to follow, and all of those moments are filled with color." Yu-ning's words were powerful, and Jacob's eyes and heart were wide open to receive them.

Grandma exclaimed, "Oh, I just remembered, I made hot cocoa and freshly baked chocolate chip cookies. Would you all like to have some?" She rose and started for the kitchen, her cheeks round and rosy from the fire. It was hard to believe she was almost 100 years old; in the light of the fire she looked like a young girl.

Yu-ning clapped. "Oooh, hot chocolate and warm chocolate chip cookies. My favorite! Thank you, Grandma, thank you!" she said, as she followed Grandma to the kitchen to help with the cookies and cocoa. When everyone had their fill of cookies, Jacob poured a little more cocoa into each of their mugs. Grandma and Grandpa walked to the living room to sit, bringing their mugs with them and gesturing for Yu-ning and Jacob to follow.

In the living room, Yu-ning saw a short pink and purple cabinet with flowers painted on each side. Next to it was a large colorful console with a thick photo album on top. "Oh, wow! It's a rainbow book!" Yu-ning exclaimed with excitement.

Grandma and Grandpa nodded together. In an animated tone, Grandma said, "Oh, yes! Those pictures are of our adventures together in our younger days. You can look through it if you wish," she said.

Yu-ning opened the photo album carefully and started to turn the pages very slowly, and then returned to the first page, savoring each image. On the first page was a black and white photograph of the young couple holding hands in the back of the garden. They were planting trees and flowers and looked to be about twenty years old.

"Come see this!" Yu-ning said to Jacob, who walked over to Yu-ning and stood next to her, looking at the picture.

Page after page showed their life together. There were images of the two of them atop a mountain peak; laughing in the ocean; smiling by a cave with a black and brown bear; climbing a tall green mountain; feeding each other exotic fruit on a tropical island; sitting under a waterfall; making food in their kitchen; Grandpa giving Grandma a bouquet of tulips in a field.

The photos were numerous, and the album glowed with bright lights as she turned the pages. Jacob stood next to her, and they were both deeply moved. "You will have a life like this with your love one day," Yu-ning whispered only to Jacob, smiling up at him.

"You saved my life, Yu-ning," Jacob managed, thickness gathering in his throat.

Grandma approached, her arms wrapped around two bright, shining books. She gave a pink one to Yu-ning and a yellow one to Jacob.

"They are photo albums!" Yu-ning cried out, hugging hers to her chest. She and Jacob opened the albums. The pages were illuminated but blank.

"These are for your new lives; you can put anything inside," Grandpa said lovingly. "Make your life; make it beautiful and make it colorful. It is our gift to you."

"Thank you so much, Grandma and Grandpa. I will make it beautiful and colorful!" Yu-ning said, squeezing the pink photo album to her chest.

"I can't thank you enough for giving me another chance," Jacob said quietly. "I will make my new life colorful. I will build a new home." He looked wistful and vulnerable.

"You *are* home," Grandpa said.

"This is your home," Grandma added.

Tears filled Jacob's eyes. "How can I ever thank you?"

"You will thank us by making your life matter and by filling it with love and color," Grandma said.

In that moment there was a loud rushing sound, like beating wings, just outside the cottage. Yu-ning gasped, ran to the front door, and quickly opened it. There before her was Suparna, who had landed in the small yard between the cottage, the forest, and the cliffs overlooking the sea. And hopping down from his back was Magic, smiling broadly and leaping thirty feet into the air, excited to see Yu-ning safe and sound. "Hello, Suparna! I am sorry I never returned to tell you where I went after I left you in the meadow this morning."

"That's all right, Yu-ning. Magic and I decided to fly over the forest, and I was keeping my eye on you from a distance," said Suparna, winking at her as a sly smile formed at the corners of his beak.

"Suparna, wait until you see what I have!" she said, hurrying back into the cabin to retrieve Lightcaster from where she had placed it along with her backpack when they arrived.

"Is that the bow, Yu-ning? Let me see it." Yu-ning walked to Suparna and reverently placed Lightcaster at the great bird's feet. Suparna gazed at the bow in amazement and said, "It is a beautiful bow, even after all these years—you can see that it yet has power within it."

Yu-ning pondered this thoughtfully as the elderly couple emerged from the cottage, smiling and waving at Suparna. "It's wonderful to see you again, Suparna. It's been a long time," said Grandpa.

"You know Suparna?" said Yu-ning, turning toward Grandpa.

"Yes, my dear. Suparna has been a good friend to us over the years," answered Grandma.

"And you must be the hunter," Suparna said, turning his gaze toward Jacob.

"Yes—I am Jacob. You probably don't remember me, Suparna, but I grew up on Rainbow Island. I left when I turned eighteen. That was more than twenty years ago, though . . ." Jacob's voice trailed off, his mind filled with distant memories.

Suparna nodded at Jacob. "It is very good to see you again, Jacob. It's been many years." Suparna shifted his attention back to Lightcaster. "But I have not seen Lightcaster in many decades. I knew its owner." As Suparna said this, he looked again at Jacob. "If this is Lightcaster, and you have had it all these years," Suparna said, "then you must be Corain's grandson . . ."

"Yes, Corain was my grandfather . . . how did you know?" said Jacob, amazed.

"I knew many of the Darq Renders and was a scout for the Darq Render army. Your grandfather was legendary, Jacob. He was known as the greatest archer in Darqendia. All those years you spent as a child on Rainbow Island, but I never knew you were Corain's kin. This day is most certainly full of surprises," he added. With that, Suparna bowed solemnly toward Jacob, in honor of the hunter's grandfather.

Suparna turned toward Yu-ning, with Magic on her shoulder. "Night is upon us, Yu-ning, and there is much to do. I am afraid we must leave now and return to Rainbow Island with Lightcaster. Metatron will be anxious to see you, and to hear about the events of these past weeks."

Yu-ning hugged Grandma and Grandpa and thanked them for their help. She turned to Jacob, whose eyes sparkled; he gave Yu-ning a long, strong hug. "I can never repay you, Yu-ning," he whispered in her ear. "You believed in a stranger, and that stranger is now your friend for life. If you ever need anything, you know where to find me."

"Won't you come back with us, Jacob? I know that Metatron would love to see you again after all these years."

"No, Yu-ning, not now. My place is here—it's time that I started to give back to Palova, as I have taken much from it over these past years. But I promise to visit you someday soon," Jacob added.

She walked to Suparna, placed Magic gently inside the outer pocket of her backpack, lashed it to the harness, and tied Lightcaster crossways behind the saddle. "Goodbye, everyone!" croaked Magic, who smiled from ear to ear.

As Suparna, Yu-ning, and Magic lifted off from the grassy knoll next to the cabin, the moon began to rise over the ocean. Its light cast a beam across the glassy sea, which Suparna followed into the night—a gleaming beacon that led them safely back to the familiar shores of Rainbow Island.

# Thirteen

# Baggul

THE WARLOCK RAN HIS HAND ALONG the top of the razor-sharp wing of the obsidigon. The hard obsidian scales made a *click click click* sound as they hit against one another under the sweep of the warlock's bony fingers. The dragon lowered its enormous head in submission at the touch of its master. "You have done very, very well, my friend," said Hobaling, continuing to stroke along the top of the creature's scales.

It was dusk, and the wind and rain that had earlier been swirling around Baggul Island had eased considerably. As the winds died, the cold rain turned to silent drizzle, falling straight from the sky—a quiet, muffled mist clothing the island in a grey shroud. The sea was dark grey, blending seamlessly with the granite rocks jutting from the sea like long, thin fingers grasping upward. The sea cliffs revealed no signs of life—no trees or grass, just the orange glow of a single fire flickering from a cave high above the desolate waters.

Christie Hsiao

150

Inside Hobaling's grotto, the conjurer stood before the obsidigon, admiring his creation by the light of the large fire blazing near the entrance of the cavern. The past several days had been fruitful. The dragon had successfully attacked villages on many islands, including Rainbow Island, which had suffered the most of all. It was more than Hobaling had hoped for: he had thought the Seven Sacred Crystals would be heavily guarded, and was shocked to learn that the dragon had only had to break through the protective glass to reach the large, gleaming gems. But even better, the obsidigon was able to bring back another prize: the boy.

"I sense the light in that boy, which means that his companions from Rainbow Island will come for him," Hobaling said. "And when they do, we will kill them all—and destroy the light's best chance of defeating us." The warlock understood that without the crystals the rainbow could not exist and that the power of light and love would slowly drain from Rainbow Island and the world; and as the light faded, Darq power—and Hobaling—would rise.

The dragon opened and closed its massive jaws and shook its head, causing the scales to click together—the sound of sea pebbles tumbling against one another. The obsidigon slowly walked away from Hobaling to the far end of the cave. As the cavern receded into the mountain, it narrowed to a tight passage. At the end of the passage was a heavy, rusted metal gate with massive bars, secured with a heavy chain and ancient lock. Inside was the boy. The obisidigon pressed its head against the bars to peer inside, turning its head, one yellow eye scanning the darkness for signs of life.

Behind the gate, the tunnel made a sharp left turn and opened up into a huge, cavernous hall. When Hobaling had

151

thrown him in this prison, Romeo had stumbled, half conscious, deeper into the cave, away from the gated entrance, and collapsed from exhaustion. He now slept in a corner of the cave where a bed of sand had collected over the years, making the hard floor of the alcove at least a bit more tolerable.

Finally, Romeo awakened.

Blackness.

He felt around him. Under the thin layer of sand all was hard, cold rock. Though his mind was foggy, he remembered being placed in some sort of cave or cavernous dungeon. There was no light at all; even when he held his hand an inch from his face, he could see nothing.

He did not know where he was, but he did remember how he had gotten here. The beast had snatched him from Rainbow Island too quickly for him to react or flee. The trip had been like a nightmare. He felt his neck and shoulders, remembering the pain—excruciating pain from the talons of the dark beast.

He shuddered, remembering the ugly dragon, and stared into the dark. As he lay there, listening to the sounds of the cave, he could just make out the far-off but distinct sound of trickling water. He tried to stand but felt wobbly on his feet. How long had it been since he had eaten? It was pitch black in every direction.

In the distance, however, it seemed there was a slight flicker of light. He started walking toward the speck of light but he could not see at all, and the ground was rocky and slick with moisture. His head collided with a stalactite, and before he knew it, he was on the ground again.

All went completely black.

And then he was out of the cave, with warm sun on his face. A glowing light hovered above him, just overhead, and then transformed into a shimmering man dressed all in white. It was One, whom Romeo had first seen in Yu-ning's cave, just before he was kidnapped! It was a bright day, and he could feel the sweet breeze and smell the Island's tropical aromas. He was on Rainbow Island.

"Romeo, can you hear me?" One was standing in front of him, radiating light in brilliant, pulsating rays. The white sand beach was just beyond One, and the gentle, clear turquoise waters of Rainbow Cove beyond that.

"Yes, One, I can hear you. Where am I?"

"You are in the lair of the obsidigon and his master, in a place called Baggul Island."

"What am I doing here?" said Romeo.

"Listen carefully to what I am about to tell you, Romeo," said One, the light pulsating so brightly that Romeo had to shield his eyes from its intensity. "You have no earthly power that can defeat the obsidigon."

"Then how can I escape, One?" cried Romeo.

"By using your light, Romeo. The light within your heart is not an earthly element, but a divine one. The obsidigon, who is made only of hatred, cannot comprehend this light, because he does not possess it. For a century the obsidigons were not seen on the face of the earth. But the warlock who kidnapped you was able to conjure this creature from the last remaining skull known to humankind."

"But why would they want to steal the Seven Sacred Crystals?" Romeo asked.

"Because greed and lust for power are ominous forces,

and left unchecked, they can bring chaos to the entire world. Hobaling once lived in an idyllic empire ruled by a beautiful, benevolent Empress. But he was thirsty for power, and knew that the only way to defeat the Empress was to use a force thought dead and gone to humankind—the Darq power of the obsidigon. Hobaling heard rumors that the last known obsidigon skull was kept in a secret hall in the Imperial Palace of the realm. He went so far as to seduce a daughter of the royal court to marry him, so he could gain entrance to the Imperial Palace.

"Hobaling was patient," added One. "He waited, biding his time, and earned the trust of the imperial court. For three years he played the role of a loyal member of the court, slowly gaining access to the most private and secret parts of the palace—places where even some members of the royal family had never been. Late at night he would enter the hidden catacombs and passages under the palace, searching and searching for his prize."

"And he was searching for the last obsidigon skull?" asked Romeo.

"Yes, Romeo. The Empress's grandfather, Emperor Ming, secretly took it from the battlefield, after the Emperor's army defeated the obsidigons in the last battle of the Great Obsidigon War. And though Hobaling did not know for certain that the Emperor had brought the skull back to the palace, he had a strong feeling that he had. And so he devised a plan to infiltrate the royal household and find the skull."

"But why did the Empress's grandfather take the skull in the first place?" Romeo asked.

"The ego of man," said One. "The skull was a tempting trophy for a triumphant emperor—a memento to treasure in secret, and a reminder of the Emperor's crowning victory. So the Emperor returned with the skull hidden in his private luggage, and kept it hidden in a dark room deep in the catacombs below the Imperial Palace at Tunzai."

"But how could an army of mere men defeat such powerful creatures?" asked Romeo.

"Ah, now that is where the story turns, Romeo. These were no mere men. Well, yes, they were flesh and blood, just like you, but they had something that the obsidigon horde did not comprehend."

"What was that, One?"

"The light of eternal love, Romeo; the light that dwells in each one of us, and is there to guide and empower us—*if* we are able and willing to let the light shine. It was the divine lights of 10,000 warriors that destroyed the obsidigon army, and forever rid the world of their sickening darkness."

"But if Hobaling has the obsidigon, why did he also need to steal the sacred crystals of Rainbow Island?" Romeo said.

"Greed is a deceptive mistress, Romeo. Hobaling was seduced by the power he held in his hands and wanted even more power. So he stole something of which he has no understanding: the Seven Sacred Crystals. He thinks that by capturing the crystals, he will be able to kill the light and subdue all the kingdoms of the world. And the crystals *are* powerful, Romeo. They are more powerful than most humans know. Placed in the wrong hands, their pure energy can be manipulated in terrible, deadly ways. That is why the obsidigon kidnapped you, Romeo."

"I don't understand, One. Why would he kidnap me? I am not powerful."

"My dear boy, you *are* powerful."

"But how, One? What is my power?"

"Your power, Romeo, is revealed by—"

There was a loud screech—a horrible, unearthly scream louder and more disturbing than anything Romeo had ever heard. He realized he was awake. Blackness again. No more One.

Had it all been a dream?

Romeo's head pounded from where he had hit it on the stalactite of the cave. He lifted his hand to feel his head and realized that he could actually see his hand! As he peered into the gloaming of the dank cave, he could make out—just barely—the floor, littered with rocks, mineral deposits, and sharp stalagmites. And in the distance, some 300 feet away, he could see a small keyhole of light—an exit from the cave.

Dizzy, but able to stand, he was determined to make it to the mouth of the cave before the light faded. He carefully made his way across the cave floor, and, in the weak light, was now able to see the enormity of his subterranean prison. The cave was at least 200 feet high and 100 feet wide.

In the distance, behind him, he again noted the sound of water. He decided to follow the sound, as his need for water was stronger than his need for light. As he walked, the sound of the water grew louder, leading him downward, toward the middle of the cavernous hall. At the bottom was a small stream that ran downhill from where he stood, deeper into the bowels of the cave. He knelt down and drank deeply of the icy cold water, and rubbed it on his throbbing forehead, which was painful to the touch.

He stood up without any dizziness, feeling refreshed from the spring water, and headed back up the gentle incline in the direction of the light. Ahead of him the cave entrance was getting closer, and he realized the brightness he was seeing was sunlight. As he approached the light source, he saw that it was coming from around a bend in the cave tunnel. He was now about fifty feet away from the place where the tunnel turned and where the light was streaming in. As he approached the turn, intent on peeking around the corner to discover the source of the light, a foul, disturbing odor hit him like an avalanche. So strong was the smell that he had to concentrate just not to lose whatever food was left in his stomach. How many days had he been in this cave, anyway?

Slowly he crept near the bend in the tunnel, and as he did, the light seemed to fade again. He peered around the corner, and his heart sank as he saw that a gate blocked the tunnel about ten feet away. He turned the corner and quietly crept up to the bars of the gate; peering down the tunnel, he saw that a large black rock blocked the exit to the cave.

But now the rock was moving. And as it moved, light burst through from the outside world, blinding Romeo. After days of lying in the dark, his eyes adjusted slowly; finally, as he blinked desperately to see what was before him, he recognized a large shape: there, scuttling down the tunnel toward him, light streaming in from behind, was the obsidian-gon, whose skin resembled black obsidian rock, but with fine, sharp scales.

Romeo pulled back, confident the creature had not spotted him. He began to retreat backward, putting distance between himself and the gate, the stench of the creature approaching swiftly from the other side. As he backed up, his heel hit a flat rock, which skidded across the floor and hit the wall of the tunnel. The sound reverberated throughout the cave, echoing momentarily. Romeo froze, closed his eyes, and hoped the foul monster had not taken notice.

Though Romeo had backed around the corner so the gate was no longer in his line of sight, he could see the long shadow of the obsidigon dancing before him on the opposite wall of the cave, growing larger as the creature approached. *Is the gate locked?* Romeo wondered. And then he had a strange thought: *I'd rather be locked in here than face that disgusting beast!*

He paused, standing still. Then he noticed that the light had faded. Was the sun setting, or was the dragon again blocking the light from coming in through the tunnel? Curiosity in an eleven-year-old boy is a powerful force, and Romeo was no exception. He couldn't resist the temptation to peek around the corner and see what was what. He quietly approached the spot where the cave bent right, and peered around the corner. As he did, there was a flash of movement, and the shadows danced again on the wall. There in front of him the dragon moved swiftly, its neck whipping around as the massive head turned back toward the gate. The dragon's jaundiced left eye was staring right at him.

Romeo was so startled that he stumbled backward and began to run back into the large chamber of the cave, no longer concerned about the noise he was making. As he ran, he heard the terrible call of the obsidigon, the sound so piercing it forced him to his knees, his hands shoved against his ears in a vain attempt to block out the shrill screech.

*Well, there's no escape in that direction,* he said to himself, shaken by his confrontation with the dragon. As he retreated further into the darkness, his mood seemed to darken along with the fading light of the distant tunnel. He was utterly alone, and was now beginning to wonder if One's visit had been real, or just a fevered dream—meaning nothing.

Sensing the boy was gone, the obisidigon left the gate and made its way back to the main chamber. Hobaling was standing over the same dark pool of water where he had conjured the obsidigon. "I see you were having a bit of fun with the boy, yes?" Hobaling said, cackling at the dragon. The obsidigon only smiled, revealing his sharp, bloodstained teeth, his yellow eyes shining with recognition.

Hobaling turned back to the pool of water, staring into its black depths. "We will finish what my grandfather and the last Great Obsidigon Horde failed to do—light and dark cannot exist together—as the light fades, our destiny and strength grows, and the Darq powers will reign," the warlock exclaimed.

"We must spread the darkness not only through the air, but also through the sea," he told the obsidigon. He bent down at the edge of the pool and placed various elements into the water—bits of dried animal flesh, hoofs, roots, and bones—as he began to recite an ancient incantation. He took a long, curved knife (the very blade that had killed Jacob's mother many years before) and removed three scales from the back of the obsidigon. He tossed them into the water, one by one, and as he did, the water began to boil.

Hobaling scooped out a large bowl of the dark boiling liquid, exited the cave, and descended a long, narrow set of stone steps carved into the face of the cliff. The staircase wound down hundreds of feet to a large flat rock just above the raging sea. There, with the waves crashing about him, he knelt down, closed his eyes, mumbled indecipherable words, and slowly poured the black liquid from the large bowl into the frothy waves below. As he did, a dark circle of water began to spread outward from where the liquid fell into the sea, like drops of black ink falling into a basin of water.

Under the water, various fish began to writhe and transform into twisted, evil creatures, their teeth growing long and sharp, and their eyes turning yellow. The dark pool of water began to expand and move slowly away from the sea cliffs, out toward the open ocean.

The circle of water seemed alive as it moved as one away from the island. The transformed creatures—barracuda, sharks, and other fast-swimming fish—could be seen darting out of the Darq pool, their silhouettes just below the surface, swimming north, south, east, and west, as if on a mission.

From his rocky ledge just above the crashing waves, the warlock stood and screamed in a high, haunting voice, "Yes, Darq hunters, seek out and destroy creatures of light. Go now!"

# Fourteen

# Lightcaster

YU-NING AND SUPARNA flew most of the night to get back to Rainbow Island. A shining full moon bathed them in shimmering light, and they encountered no trouble. Suparna was aided in flight by a gentle wind at his back, which was a welcome relief after all the flying he had done the past few weeks.

The first hints of dawn were breaking as the majestic bird, along with a sleeping Yu-ning and Magic, approached Rainbow Island. From far away, in the early morning light, the Island looked perfect and undisturbed. It wasn't until the trio flew into Rainbow Cove that the telltale signs of the obsidigon's attack could still be seen. Though most of the village was rebuilt, there were ugly scorch marks upon the earth, and dark scars on the hillsides where the forest had burned from the dragon's fire.

As they landed on the beach, Yu-ning removed her pack and the great bow, Lightcaster, and headed straight for the school hall/hospital in search of Metatron. She found him awake, sitting up in bed eating his breakfast. She hugged him sweetly and perched herself on the edge of his cot.

"It is indeed very good to see you again, Yu-ning," said Metatron, smiling at the dark-eyed girl. "You and Suparna have been in my prayers, and it is a great relief to know that you are safe and sound." Yu-ning felt as if she had been gone for months and months, even though it had only been two weeks since she had left for the Tower of Light and the Grey City. So much had transpired, and she didn't know where to begin.

"I see you have brought something back from your travels?" asked Metatron, pointing at Lightcaster. Yu-ning looked at the bow, running her hand along the finely carved surface and tracing along the inscription etched into the inner curve of the bow.

"May I see the bow, Yu-ning?" asked Metatron. Yu-ning handed Lightcaster to him, and he examined it carefully for several minutes. It was a magnificent artifact—like none that Metatron had ever seen. "I knew many of the Darq Render archers, but this is the finest bow I have ever seen," marveled the wizard. He tested its weight and read the inscription on the inside:

*Strike sure, strike bright.*
*Strike with stealth, strike with might.*
*Rend the darkness, bring the light,*
*Invite the day, or fade as night*

Yu-ning asked the meaning of the inscription, and Metatron said, "'Rend the darkness, bring the light' refers to the light in all of us, Yu-ning. I cannot discern the rest—Darq Render ways are well-guarded secrets, and there is very little known about the power of their bows and arrows, or what magic lies within. But what I do know is that the bow and the arrow are useless against an obsidigon unless used together. Do you have the arrows, Yu-ning?"

"No, Master, I don't," Yu-ning said. "The man who gave me the bow, a hunter named Jacob from Palova Island, says that his brother has the arrows. The problem is that he and his brother parted ways twenty years ago, and he doesn't know where his brother lives."

"Jacob," repeated Metatron. "We once had a Rainbow Child here on the Island named Jacob. What is his brother's name?"

"Joshua. And that is the same Jacob—both brothers once lived here on Rainbow Island."

"Yes, I remember them very well," Metatron recollected. "They were sad boys who had suffered a terrible ordeal. I believe they lost both their parents and were brought here by ship from Darqendia. Set off on their own when they came of age."

"Yes, that's right, Master. The one I met has guarded Lightcaster all these years. After he and Joshua left Rainbow Island, they traveled back to Darqendia to their old village and retrieved the bow and the quiver of arrows. But then Jacob stayed on Palova, keeping Lightcaster, while Joshua went back to sea on a merchant ship and kept the arrows. And Jacob hasn't seen him since—that was more than twenty years ago."

"Then we need to find Joshua, Yu-ning," concluded Metatron. "Does Jacob have any clues as to where his brother might have gone?"

"No, none," replied Yu-ning.

Metatron and Yu-ning talked for a long time and eventually took their conversation outside onto the shaded veranda surrounding the school hall. Metatron moved slowly, using his sturdy staff for support. It was a perfect Rainbow Island day, the sun shining warmly, white puffy clouds dotting the sky, and a lovely warm breeze blowing. When they moved outside, Suparna joined them, and they discussed what steps needed to be taken to track down the long-lost brother, Joshua.

"There is no way of knowing where he is, Metatron," offered Suparna. "All we know is that when they left here they went back to Darqendia, to their old village. A close relative showed them where Lightcaster was hidden, and then they left again on a merchant ship. From there, they traveled throughout the islands until the night that Jacob decided to stay on Palova. That is all we know."

"It seems to me that we need to go back to the beginning, so we might pursue a successful end," mused Metatron.

"What do you mean, my friend?" asked Suparna.

"We need to go to Darqendia, and see if Joshua ever returned to his boyhood home. Even if he is not there, perhaps he has visited, and someone in his old village will know where he lives now."

Suparna looked thoughtful, considering Metatron's logic. He nodded in agreement, and both he and the wizard looked at Yu-ning, who was rubbing her left arm where her scars were healing. Though the wound was not as painful as even a week before, the arm still caused her pain.

"Yu-ning, I need to send you out again—with Suparna. I wish I could take on this task myself, but I am still quite weak," said Metatron. He nodded at Suparna, who took his leave so that Yu-ning and her master could be alone. It was now late in the day, and Yu-ning felt very, very tired.

"I don't want to leave you, Metatron. I am frightened, and my arm hurts me still."

"I am sorry it has come to this, Yu-ning," said the wizard with love in his eyes, removing a wisp of hair from Yu-ning's face and tucking it behind her ear. "This is your path to follow, Yu-ning, and I think that has been confirmed to you, as it has to me. In another place and another time, others older, stronger, or more experienced might have been chosen for this task. But today, for this time, and this task, it comes to you."

Yu-ning nodded sadly, not wanting to face the full force of Metatron's words. She knew he was right, but wished with all her heart he wasn't. The two sat quietly for a while, the soft breeze blowing across the veranda. It was so peaceful that Yu-ning just rested in the tranquility of the moment, almost able to forget all the unsettling problems of the world.

After Yu-ning shared a quiet meal with Suparna and Metatron, Suparna flew back up the hillside, depositing Yu-ning, her backpack, and Magic on the trail in front of the cave.

"Magic, I am so glad you are here with me—because I feel so alone right now."

"I won't leave you, Yu-ning," croaked Magic. "I will always have your back." Magic jumped onto her shoulder, and Yu-ning scratched his head with her finger and smiled. They entered the cave together and took comfort in the cozy surroundings. That night Yu-ning tossed and turned, but finally drifted off to sleep from sheer exhaustion. When she did sleep, she rested deeply and soundly, and woke feeling calm and refreshed.

She made her way down to the school hall, ate breakfast with Metatron, and readied herself for the trip to Darqendia. As she and Suparna walked down to the beach, she saw many friends coming out of the village and the nearby meadow to say goodbye. It made her feel sad. She turned to Suparna and said, "If we don't go now, Suparna, I don't know if I ever will. To Darqendia."

"To Darqendia," Suparna responded, as the two left the jungle path for the soft sand of the idyllic beach.

All her friends came out to see her off, including her bear friends, Stout and Madrigal, Shamza the zebra, Lightmere the deer, Octavian the owl, Prometheus the horse, many of the Rainbow Children, and most of the teachers from the school, including Cristobel.

"Yu-ning," said Cristobel, as she approached. She pointed at the bow, Lightcaster, slung over Yu-ning's back. "Remember to keep your arm straight and your eye steady. You know how to shoot, Yu-ning. Remember your training, and you will shoot true," Cristobel said in an encouraging tone. Yu-ning thanked her and gave her a hug.

From out of the crowd came Julian, looking healthy and handsome. His short time on Rainbow Island had already transformed him for the better. As he approached her, he produced an apple from his pocket, holding it in front of her. "Yu-ning, you once gave me an apple—a small act of kindness that opened my heart to a brand-new life. Take this apple, and remember that you have friends who believe in you."

Tears filled Yu-ning's eyes as the two friends hugged. "Thank you, Julian. I hope to see you soon." The mood was solemn, as all who gathered had a sense that Yu-ning's mission was very important—not just for Rainbow Island, but for all the islands of their once-peaceful realm. One by one, each animal, child, and adult approached Yu-ning, some bowing before her, some giving hugs, and others offering small gifts.

Octavian flew forward, landing on a tree branch next to Yu-ning. "This seedpod is from the great kapok tree," he said, producing a brown four-inch pod from under his wing. "Remember that within this pod are tiny seeds—all the elements needed to create a mighty tree. You have that strength in you too, Yu-ning. You might be small like these seeds, but you are also mighty like the kapok."

Yu-ning was moved and stroked Octavian's feathery cheek. "Thank you, my wise friend. I will carry this in my satchel next to my water flask, so whenever I take a drink, I will remember your words."

Yu-ning mounted Suparna and waved goodbye to all the people and creatures she loved most in the world. Suparna ascended swiftly with the morning breeze, rising high above Rainbow Cove, as the farewell party grew smaller on the sliver of beach below them. As Suparna turned north and began to fly in the direction of Darqendia, Yu-ning strained to keep her friends in view. Soon they were out of sight, and Yu-ning could no longer see the village, or even the great kapok tree.

"One, I am too afraid to do this for myself," she whispered quietly. "So give me the courage to do this for those who love and believe in me." She tightened the harness around her waist, double-checked to make sure her pack was lashed securely to the back of the saddle, adjusted the leather cords that secured Lightcaster, and turned her gaze toward the northern realms. As she glanced over her shoulder one last time, she watched as Rainbow Island receded behind her, disappearing on the shimmering horizon.

# Fifteen

# Darqendia

THE LARGE ISLAND OF DARQENDIA had not always been such a desolate place.

But now, wind and heat blasted the land for most of the year. Sandstorms raged across the island, and food and water were precious resources. The rains that had once been so common had all but disappeared, turning the island into a virtual desert. Most of the clans had left Darqendia long ago for more temperate islands, in search of dependable sources of water. They left behind a lonely path [illegible] of abandoned villages, now scattered across the desert like skeletons—wells long dry, buildings collapsed and bleached white by the intense sun and unrelenting winds.

The island was divided by a long mountain range covering the western side of the island, running north to south. The Steppes, a vast area of flat, treeless land straddling the northern quarter of the island, had been the site of the last great obisidigon battle, where Suparna, Balthazar, Metatron, and the Darq Render army had come against the obsidigons and their overlords.

In days past, plentiful rains in the lush western mountains had produced a healthy watershed, with many streams and rivers bringing life to the plains on the eastern side of Darqendia. But after the end of the Great Obsidigon War, the health of the land began to falter. With the war came the destruction of vast tracts of forest—fodder to feed the war machines. And with the destruction of most of the forests came a decrease in rainfall, which eventually led to the evaporation of all but the largest rivers.

With few rivers to support them, the villages of the eastern plains were forced to dig deep wells to tap into the aquifers far beneath the soil. For several decades the underground sources of water were sufficient to sustain their farms and mining operations. But the aquifers began to drop, and it became increasingly difficult to dig wells deep enough to access the water. Many clans were forced to abandon land their forefathers had worked for centuries. Life as these hardworking farmers and miners had known it for generations came to an end. Thus, they quietly sailed out of the eastern bays in search of new, more suitable lands.

Only small outposts of stiff-necked settlers remained, there to harvest the minerals buried beneath the desert, or to mine the diamonds and precious metals found in the western mountains. But settlements were few and far between and were located almost exclusively along the foot of the mountains, where mining deposits were the richest and water more plentiful. On the eastern shore, however, the desert that once only occupied the very center of the island had slowly crept all the way to the sea. Sand dunes now kissed beaches where green fields and farms once thrived.

It was toward this desolate eastern shore that Suparna and Yu-ning now flew in search of Jacob and Joshua's boyhood village. It was where the twins' mother had died and where Silas, their mother's cousin, had guarded Lightcaster until the boys came to reclaim it two decades ago.

Metatron had drawn a map for Suparna and Yu-ning before they departed Rainbow Island, showing the village to be about three hours north of the southern horn of Darqendia, along the eastern shore of the island. The fact that they were looking for a coastal village at least eliminated the need for Suparna to venture inland, across the trackless desert where the island was most inhospitable. But truly, they didn't know what to expect—or whether or not the village was even still there.

Suparna flew hard most of the night, and just as he picked up the scent of earth on the early morning wind, he spotted a long brown slice of land in the distance. He met the coast on the southernmost tip of Darqendia and followed it north. The heat rose with the sun, as an offshore breeze blew hot and strong.

Suparna recalled Metatron's instructions: "When you see a large citadel—a fortress made of sandstone—you will know you are there. That is the old southern garrison of the Darq Renders, a staging point in their war against the obsidigons."

Just when he and Yu-ning were starting to feel the full effects of the intense sun, they saw what looked like an old castle, about a quarter mile from a protected bay. "There! Suparna, do you see it?" yelled Yu-ning, the hot wind blowing through her hair as she pointed to her left, inland from the coast.

"Yes, Yu-ning, I see it. Hold on, we are going in," said Suparna, as he banked and turned inland. To be safe, he maintained his altitude, now high above the turquoise waters of the sheltered bay. They made a wide sweep of the surrounding area, searching for signs of life. Beyond a high bank of sand dunes hugging the beach, the terrain gave way to flat, sandy desert, dotted with scrub brush. They flew over the large desert fortress, whose walls and squat, turreted towers were still in good shape. They saw no one.

"There, Suparna!" said Yu-ning, pointing further inland. Past the citadel, another quarter mile away, were some buildings and houses. Suparna descended, alighting on the soft desert sand next to what looked like an old stone-rimmed well. Yu-ning dismounted, instructing Magic to stay in her backpack, which she left strapped to her saddle. She peered over the edge of the well and was disappointed to see it filled with sand and bricks. She felt thirsty and took a draw from her water skin before putting it back in the pocket of her pack. When she did, she noticed the seedpod Octavian had given her the day before, resting next to Julian's apple.

The town was abandoned, with no signs of life. The roofs of the houses were collapsed or missing altogether. The larger buildings—a barn, an inn, and a school—had fallen inward, with very little remaining other than broken walls and bleached timber.

As she walked back to rejoin Suparna, she noticed another house in the distance. This one had an intact roof and walls. To her surprise, the front door of the house opened, and a tall, gaunt man dressed in a dirty robe strode out, slamming the front door behind him. He did not notice Yu-ning as she crouched behind the well. Catching her drift, Suparna furtively slipped behind a broken wall.

The man was heading for the old fortress, kicking up dust as he crossed the desert toward the main gate. Yu-ning approached Suparna behind the wall and told him she was going to follow the man. Suparna would keep his distance until the man went inside and then take to the sky, keeping watch from above.

Yu-ning crossed the desert behind the man, crouching behind low bushes so as not to be seen. The man kept his head down, his stride long and his demeanor serious. He walked up to the main gate of the fortress, which was large and heavy, with two enormous doors. She saw the man walk to the side of the gate, where there was a smaller door through a narrow arch. Shoulders hunched, his energy dark and heavy, the man pulled out a large ring of keys and unlocked several bolts on the ancient door.

Yu-ning quickly ran on her tiptoes toward the main gate, crouching down behind some wooden barrels. The man was so preoccupied with the last large bolt that he didn't notice the dark-haired girl behind him. He pulled the door open with a loud grunt, and Yu-ning noticed there was a second large, heavy door, just past the first, that the man now began to unlock.

Like a mouse, she quickly darted through the first door. The vestibule was dark, and Yu-ning concealed herself between two sandstone columns. She watched as the man swung open the second door, then casually swung it shut as he walked into a passage in front of him. Quickly, Yu-ning slipped through the second door and moved into the space beyond.

She followed the man down the dark passageway, which ended at a large courtyard near the center of the fortress. He walked across the courtyard, with an old, dry fountain in the center, and approached another wooden door on the other side. After unlocking that door, he swung it shut behind him. Again, Yu-ning used her speed and stealth to just squeeze through as the door closed behind her. The man disappeared around a near corner; she waited a moment before moving, to make sure she didn't get too close.

As she stood in the passageway, she could hear sounds of tools and hammering. She walked to the edge of the passage and peered around the corner. There on the floor below were hundreds of children sitting at long wooden tables, working with tools. She was startled to see so many children in such a desolate place, especially in the middle of an abandoned fortress.

The room that housed the children was large, with a high ceiling. There was a narrow stairway on the opposite side of the hall, with stone steps leading up to a third floor and down to the first. She watched the tall man climb the stairs to the third floor and open a door into a room with a large window, which afforded him a view of the entire work area where the children were seated.

The children appeared to be making toys. Other than the sounds of woodworking tools, it was completely silent. Yu-ning estimated about 500 children were sitting and working at tables, assembling wooden toy parts. They looked sad and exhausted, their eyes hollow, showing signs of anxiety and weariness. The man emerged from his office; he seemed to be coming out to observe the children. Narrowly escaping the man's notice, Yu-ning scrambled behind a rough, paint-stained drop cloth hanging on the wall.

She watched the man look down at the children, systematically scanning from row to row. He gave a perfunctory nod and walked back to his office, which was dimly lit. He sat down again and peered through the window at the children for a brief moment before resuming his work.

Deep concern swept over Yu-ning as she peeked out from the drop cloth. She searched for the nearest stairway to the work area below and found it to her left. She swiftly descended the stone steps as quietly as was possible. She kicked a small block of wood on the last step and noticed many of the children jump in fear.

When they looked up to see a strange girl in their midst, expressions of astonishment could be seen all down the rows before the children quickly looked back down and continued with their work. It was clear they were terrified to be caught looking at the stranger rather than at their work. Yu-ning walked over to a boy who looked to be about nine years old, but who was small for his age. His eyes were downcast and sunken in despair.

"Hello, my name is Yu-ning, what is your name?" Yu-ning asked.

The boy looked around nervously and whispered, "Caspar." He quickly looked back down at the workbench, hoping this strange intruder would leave.

"Hi, Caspar. What are you making?" Yu-ning continued.

"A rocking horse," Caspar said with a hollow look.

"A rocking horse! How fun. Are you making it to play with later?" Yu-ning asked with a smile.

175

Caspar looked up at Yu-ning, confusion in his eyes. She noticed that his clothes were threadbare and his hands were dirty. His socks were mismatched and his shoes were falling apart. He was shivering.

"These toys are not for me," he said.

"Why not?" Yu-ning asked.

"We work here. They make us work . . . Please go away. I'm going to get in trouble if he catches us," Caspar whispered loudly.

Yu-ning was confused by his answer. "You should be outside playing. You don't need to be in here if you don't want. You should be at school."

Caspar's eyes grew wide. "I want to go outside. I want to go to school. We sleep here and wake up here. We never go outside. I think I've been here for three years."

A five-year-old girl with blonde hair sitting next to Caspar said, "We work all day, and we don't have much food to eat."

"My name is Yu-ning. I can take you out of here. Come leave with me. Come outside."

Another girl who looked to be about Yu-ning's age chimed in. "Hi, Yu-ning. I'm Anne. I don't want to be here, and I'm hungry and cold." Even though it was hot outside the fortress, here in this enclosed hall there was a distinct chill in the air.

Voice after voice spoke up. "Me too, I go to sleep hungry every night. I want to leave this place," a little boy said.

"I don't want to be here either. He keeps us locked in here . . . it's so cold. We never see the sun," another little girl's voice called out.

Yu-ning was angry to hear what the man was doing to them. She listened to every little voice and nodded in support. "Come on, everyone. Let's go outside! This is no place for you!"

"We can't leave," a boy called out. "He locks us in. You can't open the doors."

"Who is the man?" Yu-ning asked.

Caspar pointed up to the window on the third level. His hand was shaking and his voice was trembling. "The man up there. He watches us. He is scary and mean. He would hurt us if he saw us leave."

"Oh no, he's looking down at us!" Anne called out, her face petrified. Instantly, all the children bowed their heads and began working again.

"Don't worry. I will take all of you outside," Yu-ning continued.

"He's coming. He's coming. He's coming this way. Back to work!" Caspar called out in a hushed tone.

Yu-ning looked up to catch the gaze of the tall, slender man. His eyes were cold and black. His dark, oily hair was pulled back to a sleek sheen. His eyes fixed on Yu-ning as he exited his office and negotiated the narrow set of stairs to the factory floor. As he moved, he held a long wooden stick in his hand and was hitting it against the stone steps; the noise was jarring and unsettling.

Yu-ning was also intimidated, but she tried to comfort the children. "Don't worry, everyone. I will go talk to him. I will be right back." She stiffened her spine as she walked over to the steps to meet the man.

"Oh no . . . don't go," Caspar called out. "He is very mean and scary; he will hurt you."

"What do you mean, Caspar?" Yu-ning asked.

*"He'll take you to the monsters . . ."*

# Sixteen

# Factory

"**D**ON'T WORRY," Yu-ning said to Caspar, shaking her head. "I don't think there are monsters—and he won't be able to hurt us. There are more of us! Wait for me here, and I will go talk to him."

The man noticed Yu-ning walking toward him, and his face shriveled up with anger. His pace quickened. The hall was huge and it took time to walk from the upstairs office to the children's work area two floors below. As he approached, there was fury in his cold, sinister eyes. "What are you doing standing up!" he shouted loudly at Yu-ning. He didn't distinguish her from the other children, and just viewed her as an errant worker.

"Oh, sir," Caspar piped up in a small, timid voice. "She was just picking up that wooden piece on the stair; no need to be upset."

"You, shut your mouth! I'm not talking to you. Get back to work!" the man screamed spitefully at Caspar.

He turned to Yu-ning. "Why aren't you working? Go sit down and start working now!"

"I'm Yu-ning, and I'm not here to work. No one is here to work."

"What?" the man bellowed. "You *are* here to work; *everyone* is here to work. What quadrant are you in? Where are you supposed to be?" the man demanded.

"Quadrant? I'm from Rainbow Island. No one forces us to work on my Island, especially the children," Yu-ning said.

"What quadrant are you in?" the man repeated, his shrill voice reverberating throughout the large hall. The children observed this exchange in silence as they cowered in their chairs.

"I am from a place called Rainbow Island, and . . ."

The man didn't wait for Yu-ning to finish but grabbed her by the collar. "I have no time for your jokes. You're going to the dungeon!"

"I'm not making jokes," she countered. "I'm from Rainbow Island. We all love and help each other and the work we do is fun," Yu-ning said fearlessly.

"You *are* going to the dungeon!" the man shouted, but with what Yu-ning detected as just a hint of uncertainty in his voice. You see, he often threatened to take those who disobeyed to the bowels of the fortress, where he said there was a dungeon. But he never did, because no one ever disobeyed, and he didn't want to lose a worker.

Caspar tried to grab her arm and whispered fearfully, "Yu-ning, sit down."

The man was furious; he picked up his stick and pointed it one inch from Yu-ning's face. "Go sit down and work now!"

Yu-ning slapped the stick away from her face with such force that it slipped out of the man's hand. He looked aghast as the entire room of children gasped in shock. "I said I am not here to work. Why are you keeping the children inside? What kind of person would do this? These children have been here for most of their lives," Yu-ning said with anguish.

The man had never encountered such disobedience from any child, and was both baffled and enraged that Yu-ning wasn't succumbing to his threats. He pressed his lips together tightly and seethed through his teeth, "No one is going anywhere. You will finish a day's work, go downstairs to sleep, come up again in the morning, and do it all over again!"

Yu-ning continued to shake her head, defying his every word. "Everyone is hungry, exhausted, and sad here. This is a dark, miserable place, and you have created these conditions. What could be worth this degree of despair you are creating?" Yu-ning asked with sincerity.

Yu-ning's resistance overcame the man. "Sit down and start working. I have no time to discuss all this. This shipment will make me a lot of gold. Go sit down and work!"

Yu-ning nodded and said, "Ah, gold. It's all for gold?"

The man looked almost amused. "Of course it's all for gold, you stupid child."

"But how can you enjoy gold when you are surrounded by such misery?" countered Yu-ning. "There is no abundance here, just despair and scarcity. There is no color and no heart. Everyone has a heart. Where is yours?"

The man was flummoxed. "What are you saying? We are all here to gain power and control. Everyone is here to make gold. That's what everyone is here to do! That's why—"

"We are NOT here to get control," Yu-ning interrupted. "We are here to give love. The only role gold has to play is to bring greater joy and generosity. Where I come from, we don't need gold, and we certainly don't use money to hurt each other. We would never try to find happiness through the misery of others, which is what is happening here."

"You're just a child. What do you know? Money and power are what everyone is here for; that is what's most important!" said the man. "I can't help them. I don't even make enough money for myself! There are over 500 children here. That is too many hungry kids. I can't feed them. I have other important things to do!"

"Whose problem are they, then? You are the one who is responsible for them. You've taken them away from their parents and relatives!"

The man shook his head, denying Yu-ning's accusations. "No, that is not true. I am not responsible for how they got here. Many came from the master school on Malinga Island— the ones who did not live up to the school's standards. They do the work, and at the end of the day get one cup of broth. Everything is in order. I fill my quotas." The man nodded emphatically, as if to absolve himself of any wrongdoing.

"You see all this misery and suffering every day and pretend as if you don't," she said. "And that's because you don't see that suffering in yourself. You stay in this dark factory all day, monitoring and threatening these poor children. You lock them up at night, go home to a life that is void of any light, and you come back and do it all again the next day. Why?" said Yu-ning, with passion in her voice.

"I don't have time for your nonsense!" the man continued. "You have already delayed this workday by an hour, and that will reduce my profits. I am expecting a ship to arrive in the cove within five days, and I must have the shipment completed by then. Otherwise, it is another three weeks before the next ship arrives. Sit down and start working now, or I will beat you," he seethed.

Yu-ning continued to shake her head. "No. I'm not here to work. It is blood money you make, and no one here should have to do your bidding!"

"Yeah, he only cares about gold," a little boy in the center of the room called out anonymously. "He doesn't care about anyone else. Yu-ning is right; there are more of us!"

Yu-ning could see that the man was terrified to lose his power. He turned to Yu-ning and hissed, "Stop trying to rally them. They are all here to work. You are here to work too!"

He grabbed his stick and aimed it two inches from a little boy's face. "You! Tell her that!" The little boy immediately began to tremble and stutter.

Yu-ning lunged for the stick, pushed it away from the little boy, and grabbed it out of the man's hands. She broke the thinnest point in half, throwing it to the ground. "No. Your work is play; your play is work!" she said to the little boy. "Come on, everyone; come with me outside. You don't need to be here!" Yu-ning said, gesticulating widely with her arms to gather everyone up and toward the stairs.

The man pulled up a wooden crate, set it on its side, and grabbed Yu-ning, forcing her to sit down. "Now, work. Make this toy!"

Yu-ning's fire was stoked and she held her ground like a warrior. "I am not sitting down and I am not making your toys!"

All the factory children watched in disbelief. Caspar

produced a handkerchief and furtively tucked it into Yu-ning's palm. She looked down at him and smiled, wiping her cheeks.

"I said sit down and work!" the man roared, his arm cocked above Yu-ning as if to strike her. Yu-ning instinctively crouched and winced, bracing for the blow. The effect on the children was immediate; many began to cry.

"One," Yu-ning called out, whimpering. "One." She continued to call for One until she heard him say, "Yu-ning, remember you have power in you." Yu-ning felt the power in her and stood up firmly, squaring her shoulders to face the man. Yu-ning kicked the wooden crate and reached into her shirt for her crystal heart necklace. Bright pink light began to flow around the room like a floodlight. It was so bright that the man let go of her arm to cover his eyes.

"What is that? My eyes!" he said, bending over and covering his eyes. The light was mesmerizing to the children. Some reached up to touch the rays dancing around the room, while others left their seats to follow the light currents. "If you do not get back to work this instant, I will lock you all in the dungeon!" bellowed the man, afraid that his control over the children was beginning to slip.

Yu-ning looked eagerly to the children. "You will have to bring all of us to the dungeon, and you won't be able to do that, will you?"

Caspar stopped working and looked up at Yu-ning. The man pointed at Caspar and screamed angrily, "You! Keep working!"

Caspar was scared and quickly looked down and continued working. Yu-ning said, "Look at me, everyone. There are more of us, and you don't need to be scared. You don't know it now, but this is your last day here—I'll take you to my Island. There is so much love and you can do anything you want there," Yu-ning implored.

"The door is locked. We can't get out," Caspar whispered to her, looking afraid.

"Don't worry, I will ask him to give us the key," Yu-ning said with conviction, loud enough so the man could hear. At this, the man started laughing cynically.

Caspar pulled Yu-ning by the wrist, filled with concern. "No, Yu-ning. You need to stop. He is going to lock you in the dungeon."

"Don't worry," Yu-ning said firmly. Yu-ning removed her pink crystal and set it down on the table in front of Caspar. The lights continued to pulsate around the room, sending light waves in every direction. The man couldn't bear to look at the crystal. Yu-ning stood by it, holding out her hand. "Please give me the key. I'm taking everyone outside," she said plainly.

The man chortled with antagonism. "What? You think I'm just going to listen to you and give you the key? I'm going to my chamber, and when I come back you all better be sitting down working, otherwise you will all be locked downarois menrdlyht." With that he walked to the stairs and back to his office, fleeing the lights shining from the pink crystal. He looked back out of the corner of his eye and the lights seared his sight. As he climbed the stairs, he shouted, "Back to work, or else you will all suffer a punishment you will never forget." As he said this, though, he wondered if this final threat would take hold. The experience with Yu-ning and her crystal left him shaken and unsure of himself, but he refused to show any signs of weakness.

Yu-ning turned away from him and eagerly toward the children. When the man was far enough away, she continued urgently, "Come on, everyone, let's go outside!"

Caspar looked up and saw the man enter his office and shut the door. He looked back at Yu-ning and said, "But the door is locked. There's no way out."

Yu-ning walked over and held his hand. "Don't worry, Caspar. We can do it together." She glanced up from Caspar and looked out at the rows of children. "We can all do it together," she said, her voice rising as she gazed out over 500 faces, many looking up at her with expectation and dismay. Many other children were still looking down at the pile of work in front of them. They knew they would not make their quota for the day, and that would bring its own punishment. There would be no broth for any of them, and they were already famished. And it was only noon.

"There is no way we can push the tall, heavy door," Caspar said with concern. "It's locked, Yu-ning."

"You have to trust me, Caspar," Yu-ning replied emphatically. She walked to the front of the hall and stood on a chair so everyone could see her. She had the pink crystal heart in her hand again and held it aloft as it softly glowed with warm pink lights. All the children gasped in amazement and stared with open mouths. Caspar looked at her with wonderment as Yu-ning offered the gem to him.

"Caspar, here—this crystal heart is for you. It is from my heart to yours," Yu-ning said sweetly, holding the pink crystal heart in her open palms, its silk red cord dangling below. Caspar was deeply moved as he looked at the shining pink crystal heart, and held his palms open for Yu-ning to place it there.

"My heart feels so warm. It has been so long since I felt this. The last time was when I was in my mother's arms." Caspar wept softly, looking at the crystal heart, holding it reverently.

"Yes," Yu-ning said, "I see your heart. It is so beautiful, just like this pink crystal heart." With that she turned to the others and called out, "I see everyone's heart. All of you have beautiful hearts waiting to be lit up once again like Caspar's. We are all powerful. We are even more powerful together. Stand up with me and believe. This is not your life; this is not your destiny."

Caspar was smiling, holding the crystal heart with gratitude. "Thank you, Yu-ning. Thank you. It is vibrating with light. It is magic."

"Let's share it with everyone here," Yu-ning said.

"But there are 500 of us, and we only have one crystal heart," Caspar said.

Yu-ning walked over to Caspar and placed her hands over the crystal heart in his palms. "For all of those who believe, we will be able to generate more hearts from that magic." She glanced a few chairs down and said, "Anne, do you believe?" Anne rose as Yu-ning nodded for her to come over and place her open palms on theirs. The three of them cupped the crystal heart in their palms.

Anne whispered, "I believe." She removed her hands to reveal a second crystal heart. She lifted it into her hand and held it up for the others to see.

Everyone gasped in astonishment.

# Seventeen

# Hearts

"**J**F TWO PEOPLE BELIEVE in our crystal heart, it will become two hearts," Yu-ning announced softly. "If three people believe, there will be three hearts. If four people believe, there will be four hearts. Now, if we have twenty people who believe, there will be *forty* hearts. This is the magic of the crystals. If forty people believe, there will be eighty hearts. And on it will go! All you have to do is believe, just like Caspar and Anne."

Slowly children began walking over to Anne and Caspar, until all the children formed a circle around more and more crystal hearts overflowing like a fountain. The rhythm of the room flowed in a beautiful, undulating circular pattern, pink light emanating from the center and filling the entire space, until all the children had produced thousands of crystal hearts together. Yu-ning was at the center, handing out a crystal heart to each child until everyone was fastening a luminous crystal heart around his or her neck with a beautiful red silk cord.

"The man will see our beautiful shining crystal hearts, and he will unlock the door," a little boy said.

"I see him. He's walking over to the window," another girl cried out. Yu-ning saw the man scanning the room; as he took in what was happening, he became instantly horrified by the sight before him. All the children were hand in hand in a spiral around the factory floor; pink lights flowed from the center of the circle, where a mountain of crystal hearts was rising toward the ceiling. The man's rage grew until he banged on the glass in a state of fury.

Yu-ning saw some of the children grow nervous, trying to conceal their crystal hearts. "Let it shine," Yu-ning instructed ardently. "You don't need to put it away. You don't need to hide it."

"Oh no . . . he is coming this way, he looks so angry. I'm scared," exclaimed a small boy.

The man stormed out of his office and down the passageway toward the stairs. He paused at the top and shielded his eyes from the light pouring out from the hearts of each child. He bounded down the stairs toward the children, who braced themselves, tightening their grip on the hands of the children next to them.

"What is that around your necks? They're too bright. Put those things away!"

Yu-ning walked right up to the man. "No," she said. "We are not putting them away! This is our power. This is love. More love is more power! There is nothing you can do now; our chain is more powerful than you. There is no more fear and no more darkness."

"Put them away now!" the man screamed again.

"We are not putting them away!" Caspar said, no longer afraid. The man looked shocked to see Caspar stand up to him. Soon all the other children were shaking their heads disapprovingly at the man.

"Put those things away! They are too bright!" The man was furious, trying to grab onto the children. The children collectively backed up and moved forward in unison, throwing the man off balance so that he fell backward. He landed on his back and quickly sat up, aghast. The entire factory was shining brilliantly.

The children were no longer afraid. The lights were expanding outward, brighter and more luminous. Every darkened corner of the factory was cleansed and purified by the light. Yu-ning and the children were laughing as they witnessed the magic flow all around. Yu-ning clapped and started singing a melody. "We all have a heart in our hands. We all have a heart to share. Shining so bright, I see a heart for all to wear, shining so bright in my heart!" Soon all the children were singing and swaying.

Yu-ning was standing next to the man with light streaming all around her. "There is nothing you can do. Please don't cover your eyes; please see our hearts so you can know yours."

The man writhed on the floor in agony, yelling, "It's too bright! I can't open my eyes! Put it out!"

"Just look at us. Your heart will grow bigger and brighter if only you open your eyes to see," Yu-ning persisted. The kids stepped back sadly, watching the man become even more deranged. He was swinging his arms, trying blindly to grab them and hit them. He started to turn away and crawl to the stairs, still shielding his eyes.

Yu-ning walked up to the man and produced a shining pink crystal heart from her pocket. "Please," Yu-ning called out, extending the crystal toward him. "This one is for you. It is made from a single pure heart of love and faith. Can you please try?"

"Get that thing out of my face!" he shouted viciously.

"Fine. If you want us to leave, we will leave, but you must give us the keys to exit this place. You don't see the magic. You don't want the magic. We have to leave you now," Yu-ning said with authority.

"Yes, get out of my sight if you don't want to work! Get those things out of my sight!" the man yelled bitterly, covering his eyes with both hands.

"We need the keys," Yu-ning repeated.

The man crawled up the first thirty steps and paused to reach for the large key ring in his coat pocket. He threw them at Yu-ning and bounded up the final ten stairs, rushing to his chambers. Through the window the children could see him taking a key from around his neck and opening a lock on a small wooden chest. He took out several ingots of gold and hugged them to him, looking back and forth in a state of panic. He rushed to the window and quickly pulled down a shade, closing himself off in darkness. Yu-ning picked up the keys. "He needs the crystal heart the most, but he doesn't want it. Now everything around him will remain dark forever. The light is within him, but he doesn't realize it."

She looked at her friends and held up the keys. "I told you that with our power we would open the doors." The children were still in a circular chain with their hands clasped together. Yu-ning entered the circle and gripped the hands of the child on either side of her, lifting their arms and swinging them with determination. "It's time. Let's go outside."

Yu-ning saw a little boy, no older than four, standing timidly on the end of the circular chain. He was weeping and frightened, and he was the youngest of all the children. Yu-ning knelt down to hug the boy. "What is it?" Yu-ning asked, filled with compassion.

The boy was so tiny, and he was trembling like a leaf. "I'm scared. He's up there watching us with his stick."

"Don't worry, he can't hurt you," Yu-ning said, hugging him again. "And look, his stick is broken!" she said, pointing to the wooden pieces on the floor nearby. "Hold your crystal heart and come with us. It's all right . . . we are all here for you." Yu-ning ushered him into the center of the circle.

Yu-ning waved to the man above. "Goodbye! I'm taking everyone to my Island. Everyone is welcome, and you can come with us if you want."

The man opened his door, still shielding his eyes. He screamed spitefully, "Never! Who cares about an island with rainbows and no gold? I can always get more children!"

Yu-ning looked at him intently, eye to eye, and shook her head. "No. There will be no more children in this lonely place. We are leaving the mountain of crystal hearts here. Anyone who comes here will know only light. You can come with us or be trapped in your dark chambers forever. These are your only choices."

The man's eyes practically bulged out of his head. "No! Take them with you. You said you'd leave with all of those things."

Yu-ning repeated herself slowly and deliberately. "There will be no more children in this place—ever. There will be no more suffering. We all have to go now."

"You have no power over us any longer. There is no power without love," another girl shouted to the man above.

"We will only make toys for ourselves to play with from now on!" a little boy called out.

Yu-ning nodded and smiled with pride. "Yes! Let's go! Let's go to my Island."

All 500 children had their crystal hearts around their necks, glowing pink in unison. Yu-ning led the circle, holding the little boy's hand, as they all moved forward up the stairs toward the door leading to the courtyard. Before they left, they found the kitchen and took large quantities of food as well as a good supply of water—each child carrying a water skin. The children were amazed at the variety of food the man stored in his larders—most of which he had never shared with them.

They left the kitchen and pantry and headed down a corridor toward the exit. They all stopped in front of the foreboding door. It was enormous and heavy. Yu-ning fumbled with the large key ring and worked hard to unlock the bolts. Once it was unlocked, she tried to push the heavy door open, but it wouldn't move. She realized that only an adult could push open a door of this weight.

Yu-ning continued pushing, and then saw Caspar standing next to her, pushing with all his might. Soon several children were pushing the door on either side of Yu-ning and Caspar, and the others were giving them support from behind. Slowly the door swung open, and the children shouted with joy.

Yu-ning felt someone take her hand. It was Caspar, and he was smiling. He reached into his jacket and pulled out the toy rocking horse he was making. "This is for you. We will play with it together on Rainbow Island."

Yu-ning hugged him tightly. "Thank you, Caspar! Thank you."

The children followed Yu-ning and Caspar out the door, across the inner courtyard of the fortress, through the far passage, and out the side door near the main gate. They looked proud, happy, and relieved. All the children were celebrating as they exited the fortress and walked down the path that led toward the beach.

As they passed through the dunes, Yu-ning asked Caspar how he ended up working at the factory. He told her that when he was five, his parents had both died in a flood, and he was left without a home. He was sent away to a boarding school on the island of Malinga. "It was an awful place," said Caspar. "I was only there for a year, but I had a hard time reading, because sometimes the letters get jumbled on the page. The teachers thought I was lazy."

"Oh!" said Yu-ning. "One of the children in my school has the same struggle—our teachers have him make up a story out loud, and they write it down for him. Because he knows the story, it makes it easier for him to read the words on the page, and then write it himself! Our teachers have lots of ways to help children learn."

"They didn't help me like that at the boarding school," Caspar said. "The headmistress told everyone I was better off living with my aunt. But it was a lie. Instead, the headmistress sold me to that man in there, to come work at the

195

factory. One night he came to the school, and many of us were taken away in his boat while everyone else was asleep. Anne was taken then too. All the kids that were sold were orphans—I guess because no one would miss us if we disappeared . . ." Caspar grew silent, just looking up at Yu-ning.

Dumbfounded, Yu-ning asked, "Sold? You were sold as a slave?"

"Yes," said Caspar, with great sadness.

Yu-ning stopped in the midst of the windswept dunes and hugged Caspar. "You will never be a slave again, Caspar," she whispered.

As the afternoon advanced, Suparna and Magic joined the large group of children at the beach. Together, they constructed a makeshift camp nestled against the shelter of the dunes. They used driftwood collected from the beach and tall grass from the dunes to make lean-tos. The children spread blankets inside for sleeping.

But the greatest excitement surrounded Suparna. The children were fascinated by the enormous, rainbow-colored raptor, and begged him for rides around the cove. Suparna spent hours taking groups of children on rides high above the bay. Toward the end of each ride—to the children's delight—he would fly low toward the water and then splash down in the bay, drenching the screaming children in warm salt water.

Anne stood next to Yu-ning watching the younger children laugh and play in the ocean. "Some of us have been here for years, Yu-ning, and this is the first time we have swum in the ocean. I have never seen some of these children smile before," Anne marveled.

"Caspar told me how you both came to be here on Dar-qendia . . . I am so sorry about what has happened to you, Anne," said Yu-ning, squeezing Anne's hand.

"Caspar is like a little brother to me now," Anne said. "We have been through a lot together."

"Are you originally from Malinga Island, near the boarding school?" Yu-ning asked.

"No, I am from Farcara Island, from a village called Caer-a-mor. When I was six, my parents were killed in an avalanche while working in the mountains. My younger sister and I didn't have any known relatives, so the elders of our village thought it wise to send us to boarding school on Malinga. But I doubt they would have sent us away had they known what would happen to me . . ."

"Is your sister here on the beach with us?" asked Yu-ning.

"No, Ariadne is still at the school. She's very smart, which makes the school look good. Smart kids get to stay, I guess . . ." Anne said with a wan smile.

Yu-ning squeezed the girl's hand. "Suparna and the teachers on Rainbow Island will not let this continue, Anne. We will go to Malinga Island and take your sister away from that boarding school. Any adults who would sell children for not getting good enough grades . . ." Yu-ning couldn't say another word, but just choked back her own anger and tears.

"Why are you here on Darqendia, Yu-ning?" asked Anne.

Yu-ning felt a connection with Anne; like Yu-ning, she had lost her parents. And right about now, having a girlfriend her age was a welcome change. Yu-ning explained all the events of the past three weeks. She described Rainbow Island, the attack of the obsidigon, and the stolen crystals. She also told Anne about Lightcaster and that she and Suparna were looking for clues about the missing arrows.

"That's why we came here to this island," Yu-ning said. "We were hoping to find someone who might know more about the Darq Render arrows that used to be made here on Darqendia."

Anne grew keenly interested and said, "My village is at the foot of Snowy Mountain, the tallest peak on Farcara Island. There is a local legend that a mysterious warrior lives near the peak of the mountain, and that he has magic arrows that were once used to kill dragons. It's just a story that I used to hear around the campfire as a young girl, but many of the elders swear it's true."

Yu-ning was skeptical; what were the odds that this mysterious warrior could be Jacob's long lost brother, Joshua? "Did this hunter have a name, Anne?" asked Yu-ning.

"I think his name was Jeremiah," Anne said. "No, wait, it was Joshua. I remember his name because I used to have a cat named Joshua. Funny how I remember that after so many years."

Yu-ning became animated and smiled broadly at Anne. "Thank you, Anne. I think the man on Snowy Mountain might actually be the person we are searching for!" Yu-ning sprinted down the beach in search of Suparna, whom she found splashing in the waves with a large group of children. The kids were climbing up on Suparna's back and jumping and diving into the waves. Suparna was very encouraged to hear the news and told Yu-ning that they would need to make a plan for traveling to Farcara Island.

Once the sun set on that momentous day, the children all pitched in to cook a meal of rice, carrots, and beans, which they had brought from the fortress's pantries. When night fell, it became surprisingly chilly. The children gathered up a large amount of driftwood, and soon a huge bonfire was blazing on the beach in front of the camp. Yu-ning and Suparna stood apart from the warming glow of the flames, discussing what to do with the children.

Suparna would return to Rainbow Island and gather all the pink dolphins he could find to come to the bay, so the children could return to Rainbow Island. At first light, Suparna prepared to head back to Rainbow Island to arrange transportation for the children. He and Yu-ning calculated that he would need to gather a pod of at least fifty pink dolphins, each of whom could carry ten children on its back. "I will see you in two days' time, Yu-ning, assuming the weather remains fair," Suparna said. "Take care of yourself, and make sure the children don't wander away from the beach camp. The desert here is cruel, and a child could easily get lost out there."

"Anne, myself, and the older children will keep a close eye on all the little ones, Suparna," Yu-ning assured her feathered friend. "Safe travels!"

Suparna headed out, flying swiftly southward, as Yu-ning looked on, watching her friend until he was out of sight.

# Eighteen

# Minkaro

TWO DAYS HAD PASSED since Suparna had left for Rainbow Island to gather the pink dolphins. All was well on the beach, as the children were still celebrating their release from the factory and the joy of knowing they would never have to return. Despite all the happiness surrounding her, Yu-ning felt tired and lonely. And though her scar was no longer painful to the touch, it ached at night when the temperature dropped. At both ends of the long beach, the land poked out into the sea—two long fingers that nearly met in the middle, forming a natural cove within. Yu-ning walked to the end of one of these fingers, a rocky peninsula that led her away from the laughter and playful sounds of the children.

At the end of the headland, she found a soft patch of grass growing atop the rocks, which afforded her a full view of both the ocean and the bay. It was hot, but the cool ocean breeze made for a perfect day. She lay down on the grass, wishing she were back on Rainbow Island. For a while she dozed off but was awakened by a wave that crashed against the rocks, hitting her face with sea spray. From the position of the sun, she guessed she had slept for two hours.

She stared up at the perfect blue sky, feeling small and ill-equipped for the task of retrieving the arrows or confronting Hobaling—not to mention the unthinkable prospect of fighting the obsidigon! "One," she whispered. "There are surely others in this world better able to find the sacred crystals than me." The only response was the sound of the wind through the grass and the waves against the rocks. Magic had accompanied her on her walk, and had been hunting for bugs nearby. He brushed up against her leg, and she picked up her sleek green friend and held him in her hand. Yu-ning began to cry, sitting with her knees tucked up against her chest.

"What are these tears about? The little girl I know is more full of laughter than tears," came a voice from behind.

"Metatron!" Yu-ning yelled, as she sprang to her feet and ran into his arms. He was walking heavily, with his staff as a crutch, and nearly fell down from her hug.

"Easy, child, your master teacher is still weak! But when Suparna told me you were here with the children, contemplating a trip to Farcara Island, it seemed to accelerate my recovery," Metatron said. "So I returned with Suparna to see how you are faring."

She hugged him again, more gently this time, understanding that the trip had been difficult for him. She had missed him more than she realized and was encouraged to see how far he had come in his recovery. The afternoon was gone and the sun was ready to set by the time they reached the beach camp. Metatron was delighted to meet all the children, and he told them about their impending journey back to Rainbow Island.

He and Suparna had left Rainbow Island at the same time as the great pod of pink dolphins, but despite how quickly the magnificent mammals could swim, Suparna could fly nearly twice as fast. So the dolphins weren't expected to reach the cove until the next morning. That evening after a simple meal of rice and fish, Yu-ning, Metatron, and Suparna talked around the fire about the plan ahead. Yu-ning relayed all that Balthazar had told her about Hobaling and his grandfather, the strengths and weaknesses of the obsidigons, and the strategies and methods of warlocks.

"As to why Hobaling stole the stones, the answer is not complicated," Metatron offered. "Though the Seven Sacred Crystals have little power of their own, they project the light of love further into the world. In this sense, the stones are like the moon, which reflects the light of the sun—the crystals simply reflect the light of love from our hearts, and project it outward. Those who embrace goodness and love bring the light, and the rainbow sends it further into the world. Hobaling understands this, and by taking the crystals, he reduces the reach of the light. Could he win a war without the crystals? Perhaps. But he knows he needs every advantage he can muster."

Suparna and Metatron informed Yu-ning that darkness was spreading across the ocean—they had seen it in the distance as they flew from Rainbow Island to Darqendia. It looked like a large dark stain, moving across the ocean's surface. As well, several sea friends—including a pod of Tunzai blue whales—reported seeing the darkness coming from Baggul Island, a main nesting site for the last Great Obsidigon

Horde a century earlier. The whales also spotted strange, shadowy creatures racing across the sea, coming from the direction of the dark pool.

"Master Balthazar also believes that Baggul Island is the most likely place for Hobaling to hide," Yu-ning said. "It is where Hobaling's grandfather hid from the royal armies after the Great Obsidigon War."

Metatron smiled with pride at his young student. "Very good, Yu-ning. I see you were listening to old Balthazar's lessons." Yu-ning gave a sheepish grin, and Metatron continued in a more serious tone. "This changes our plans, Yu-ning, as I did not realize that this darkness had spread so far so quickly. Suparna and I will need to bring the children to Rainbow Island as swiftly as possible. I don't know if the ocean lanes are safe, so Suparna and I will stay with the dolphins in case there is trouble. Though I don't like to split up, I believe we will have to: Yu-ning, when the royal pod of dolphins arrives tomorrow, I want you to rendezvous with King Minkaro and travel with him to Farcara Island to see what you can find out about this mysterious man who lives atop Snowy Mountain. With any luck, it is the hunter, Joshua, whom we are seeking."

"But Master, why can't Suparna take me—I would feel so much better if I was going with him," Yu-ning said. Suparna smiled kindly at Yu-ning as Metatron said, "That would be our first choice, Yu-ning, but Suparna is not built to fly in frigid temperatures. Minkaro, on the other hand, is used to swimming in cold waters. There is no other way."

Yu-ning did not want to leave Metatron again so soon. She understood, however, that she needed to be the one to bring Lightcaster to Farcara. Showing Joshua her Darq Render birthmark, along with the great bow, should be sufficient proof to convince Joshua that she was, indeed, the right person to receive the Darq Render arrows.

"But what about the children at the boarding school—Anne's sister, and the other kids who are being mistreated?" Yu-ning said. "We must help them, Metatron!"

"We will, Yu-ning, in due time. But that is of secondary concern to us right now, with Hobaling on the move, and these Darq creatures prowling the waters—coming ever closer to Rainbow Island. We will not forget the children of Malinga Island, but they will have to wait a little longer for relief."

"Metatron, this school is a horrible place, and we must—"

"Yu-ning, you need to trust my judgment in this situation," Metatron insisted. "We have two crises to deal with, and we must handle the larger one first—making sure the obsidigon does not attack Rainbow Island again unawares. Suparna and I must make sure that all the children and the pink dolphins arrive safely back on the Island. We will be about a half day behind you when we arrive on Rainbow Island. But again—do not wait for us. Make all haste for Farcara in search of the arrows. We must unite the arrows again with Lightcaster!"

Yu-ning was silent, sensing that Metatron would not budge from his position. But the thought of those children suffering in the boarding school—it was almost too much for Yu-ning to bear, especially after seeing what had happened to the children in the factory. She had never seen children suffer like that, and it had made her very sad.

So the plan was set: all would travel to Rainbow Island in great haste, with Metatron and Suparna guarding the great dolphin pod and the children. Larger and swifter than his dolphin subjects, King Minkaro would race ahead with Yu-ning, stopping on Rainbow Island only long enough to gather fresh supplies before heading south for Farcara.

"Once Suparna and I finish guiding the dolphin pod and children safely to Rainbow Island, we will depart eastward for Baggul Island, to see if Hobaling has made himself comfortable there," Metatron continued. "With luck, we will find Romeo along with the crystals, and manage his escape. When you have finished your exploration of Farcara Island, I want you and Minkaro to head to the island of Tunzai and meet us at the Imperial Palace."

"Why the Imperial Palace, Metatron?" asked Suparna.

"I must brief the Empress about this foul business with the obsidigon, and seek her council on our forward movements. She knows Hobaling, since he was married to her younger sister. She may know his mind, or what he might be inclined to do with the seven crystals."

In the morning, Yu-ning and Metatron woke early and walked down the beach toward the headland to get a good view of any arriving dolphins. But before they left the beach, several children started yelling excitedly, "Look, the pink dolphins are here! The dolphins are here!" At the mouth of the bay, several pink dolphins could be seen swimming into the cove. More and more kept coming, and as they entered the cove's calm waters, they began to leap into the air, much to the delight of the children.

In all, forty-seven pink dolphins had answered Suparna's call for help, traveling all the previous day and night to come to the aid of their friends. Many dolphins were out patrolling Rainbow Island; otherwise more would have come. All the dolphins were dancing in the cove; some jumped high into

the air, while others performed what looked like a choreographed dance, with timed leaps, flips, and dives. Best of all, the largest animal, a majestic pink dolphin nearly twenty feet in length, skipped across the entire length of the cove on his tail. This was Minkaro, king of the pink dolphins.

The children ran into the ocean to greet the dolphins, and the pink mammals proceeded to give many of the screaming kids short rides around the cove. It was an uplifting scene, and Yu-ning smiled in spite of her concerns about what lay ahead. Minkaro raced through a small wave, riding the breaker high onto the beach, to the very edge of the wet sand.

"Greetings from Rainbow Island," Minkaro called out to the children all around. "It is so nice to see you all, and we are looking forward to bringing you back to your new home on our beautiful Island. You will never have to make another toy in your life—unless you want to!" With this, there was an explosion of cheers and tears of joy from the ecstatic children. Many of the kids surged forward to hug Minkaro.

Metatron, Suparna, and Yu-ning greeted Minkaro and confirmed their plans. Minkaro and Yu-ning would travel south past Rainbow and Malinga Islands, and then due east around the northern coast of Gracia Island, staying out of the icy southern waters as long as possible. Once past Gracia, they would travel southeast, straight on to Farcara Island, home of Snowy Mountain. At the same time, Suparna and Metatron would travel east, in the direction of Baggul Island.

The beach camp was quickly struck, the children scattering the driftwood and sea grass back to where they found it. When they were done, the beach seemed just as they had found it. As preparations were made for departure, Anne approached Yu-ning and asked to speak with her alone. "Yu-ning, please promise me that you will try to rescue my sister from the boarding school on Malinga island."

"Anne, I don't know if we will have time—we must reach Farcara Island as swiftly as possible to find Joshua and recover the lost arrows."

"But you know what the headmistress did to us—she sold us into slavery!" implored Anne. "And she will do the same thing with other students—this is not the only sweat factory in our realm. There is always a market for child slaves. You must promise me that you will try."

"All right, Anne, I promise. I will do what I can for your sister," Yu-ning said. She had no idea how she would convince Minkaro to stop at Malinga Island, but she knew she had to try when the opportunity arose.

The children were organized into groups of ten and eleven and guided onto the backs of the dolphins. It was a wondrous sight to see the long line of pink dolphins beached in the shallow water, with excited children atop their backs, waiting to depart for a new life on Rainbow Island.

One moment it was a loud, raucous celebration, and then, just as the last group of waving children disappeared around the point of the bay, it became very quiet. The only sound was the soft *swoosh* of the waves breaking upon the steep, sandy beach. Yu-ning, Metatron, Suparna, and Minkaro said quiet goodbyes as Yu-ning mounted the dolphin king. Her saddle had been secured around Minkaro, along with her backpack and Lightcaster.

Metatron gave Yu-ning a goose-down jacket, which he had brought with him from Rainbow Island. "Your goose friend, Mary, and her friends donated the feathers, Yu-ning.

It was made especially for you," he said, as he hugged her goodbye. "I venture you will need it in the snowy climes of the southern isles."

Magic tried to hop onto Minkaro's slick back, but kept sliding into the shallow water. "No, Magic, you can't come," Yu-ning said. "If something should happen to us in the open ocean, it would be a very long swim for you!" Magic was downcast, but dutifully hopped into the front pocket of Metatron's robe instead.

Minkaro was a very fast swimmer, and as he and Yu-ning left the beach, it took only a few seconds for him to cross the small bay and head into open water. As they exited the mouth of the cove, the water rapidly turned from an aqua blue to a deep purple. Yu-ning looked over her shoulder just in time to see Suparna take wing, Metatron on his back.

# Nineteen

# School

As Yu-ning and Minkaro, Suparna and Meta-tron raced south, they eventually caught sight of the great pod of dolphins, with the children safe and secure on their backs. Minkaro pulled up alongside the pod as the children cheered and waved at Yu-ning. But this was not a pleasure cruise for Yu-ning and Minkaro; serious business lay ahead for them.

Yu-ning gave one last wave to the children as Minkaro swam ahead of the pod, determined to cross as much open water as possible while they still had the daylight. She looked back and nodded at Metatron, who tipped his large grey hat in her direction as the great pink dolphin put distance between himself and the rest of his pod. As decided earlier, Suparna and the wizard would escort the dolphins and their young passengers back to Rainbow Island, just in case of trouble. From there, Suparna and Metatron would go to Baggul on their rescue mission.

Yu-ning felt as if she was gliding across the sea, as Minkaro was achieving speeds she didn't think possible. They were swimming so fast that Minkaro was actually skimming across the water, bouncing rhythmically over the glassy sea. The fine weather and calm conditions made for easy travel, and the dolphin king was making even better time than he had hoped. Afternoon came and went, and evening fell, a canvas of brilliant stars hanging above the dark floor of the smooth, vast sea.

By the following morning, they had crossed the strait between Darqendia and Rainbow Island and were headed into more familiar waters. "We will only be able to stop on Rainbow Island for a short while, Yu-Ning," Minkaro said. "Just enough time to refresh your water skins and alert everyone that the children are on their way."

Yu-ning was thrilled to hear that they would be stopping, even for just a short while. They entered Rainbow Cove at daybreak, just as the village was beginning to stir. Yu-ning was given a hearty reception, but her friends were sad to hear that the stop would be short. Feeling very homesick, and dreading the thought of leaving again so soon, she asked Minkaro if they could at least wait to make sure the dolphins and children arrived safely.

"I wish we could, Yu-ning, but we must keep moving," Minkaro answered. "The children are now many hours behind us, and we can't afford to spend that much time waiting for them." Yu-ning grew quiet, and Minkaro sensed her sadness. "I know you miss your friends, Yu-ning. But be encouraged—destiny has chosen you for this place at this time, and it is a brave thing that you do."

She nodded and left the beach to search for Cristobel, her trusted friend and instructor. Yu-ning found her in the main room of the school, which now looked like a regular hall again, since the last two patients from the makeshift hospital had been released just the day before.

Yu-ning told Cristobel about the boarding school on Malinga, the trafficking of students as slave labor, and her promise to Anne to try to release her sister, Ariadne, from the school.

"We can't allow any child to stay at a school where they are being mistreated, Cristobel," said Yu-ning. "We must go and find out. When Suparna arrives, tell him to fly to Malinga straight away—I will be at the boarding school this time tomorrow, so he can't waste any time. Tell him it's on the northernmost tip of the island, on a high bluff—Anne says it's impossible to miss. I may need Suparna's help, since Minkaro can't venture from the sea."

Cristobel promised that she would deliver the message to Suparna just as soon as he arrived. "But you mustn't tell Master Metatron. He will try to stop Suparna!"

"I will tell Suparna, but if Metatron inquires, I will have to tell him the truth," Cristobel said.

After stocking up on fresh supplies, she and Minkaro headed out to sea again as the Rainbow Children, Julian, and all Yu-ning's animal friends waved goodbye. The weather still held, and they made excellent time as they ventured south toward Malinga Island. The days and nights started to blend together for Yu-ning, who awoke on the third morning to see land in the distance. "Is that Malinga Island, Minkaro?"

"Yes, it is, Yu-ning. But we won't be stopping there. We are heading east from here, and will travel around the northern end of Gracia Island and then straight on for Farcara. That will allow us to avoid the colder waters for a bit longer."

"I need to stop on Malinga Island for a few hours, Minkaro. There is something I must do there," Yu-ning said, with authority in her voice. "I made a promise to Anne that I would check on her sister."

Minkaro protested and told Yu-ning there wasn't time. "Minkaro, if you don't stop, I will jump off and swim to shore. I made a promise!" Once Yu-ning relayed the story of how the students were being sold into slavery, Minkaro reluctantly agreed to make a brief stop on the island. Minkaro had swum past the island before and had a general idea where the boarding school was located. The shore was rocky, but Minkaro found a small sandy cove, depositing Yu-ning on the soft sand. "Thank you, Minkaro, for understanding," Yu-ning said.

"Well, I am not sure I *do* understand, Yu-ning. But I know you feel strongly about this, so I will let you go. But you must be back here before the sun sets if we are to stay on schedule."

Yu-ning agreed to return on time, and set out north along the beach. At the end of the beach was a rocky bluff, at the foot of which she found a well-trodden path. The path hugged the side of the bluff in a steep ascent before leveling out at the top. From there she made her way swiftly north, toward the boarding school. The path afforded an excellent view of both the sea and the inland hills and forests. Malinga was a lush, green island, and Yu-ning was struggling to reconcile such beauty with the atrocities occurring in the nearby school.

The path led downhill and paralleled the beach for a short distance, and rose again onto a rocky cliff high above the sea. At the top, just a quarter mile further on, was the school. From this distance, it looked peaceful and stately—a finely built school with high white walls and a red terra cotta roof. She picked up her pace, now jogging down the path and working out a plan for what she was going to do when she arrived.

As she approached the school, she took in the beautiful green lawn surrounding the main buildings, as well as the immaculate gardens and well-trimmed trees. She approached the front entrance and walked inside. A guard greeted her at the door, and, perhaps thinking she was a new student, allowed her to proceed. Through the main lobby, two corridors led in opposite directions. She chose the corridor to her right and began to walk down the hallway. There were many rooms on either side of the hall; however, they were dark and closed.

Yu-ning walked toward the room at the end and quietly opened the door. She was standing at the back entrance to a large classroom, with high walls and windows with drawn shades to block out the sun. The space was plain and mono-tone; there was no decoration or color. About thirty students sat quietly at their desks, writing. They were all silent and expressionless; no one was smiling.

Yu-ning saw a woman who looked to be in her late forties, with glasses and a tight bun at the nape of her neck. She was standing at the front of the classroom, writing on the chalkboard. It looked as if her attractive, feminine features had been hardened by a life of strict discipline, control, and rigidity. She was wearing a white blouse buttoned to the collar, and a long blue skirt. She looked stern and severe. On her desk were a jar of pencils sharpened to a perfect point, a yellow-lined notepad, and a long bamboo reed. The sight of it made Yu-ning quiver.

Fear and restraint filled the room. Yu-ning heard the intermittent exhalations from the children who were holding their breath as they worked. An eight-year-old boy with gentle eyes and brown hair sat in the back of the room, next to the windows. He was the only person who looked directly at Yu-ning standing in the doorway. He, like the other children, was wearing the school uniform: white shirt, blue shorts, with navy blue V-neck sweater.

On the right side of his sweater, embroidered in red thread, was the name "Percival." He was writing. Yu-ning, instantly drawn to the boy, tiptoed around the back of the classroom and over to his desk. "Hi," she whispered. "Is your name Percival?" Yu-ning was smiling.

Percival was surprised. He quickly looked up at the teacher, whose back was still toward the students, and around at the other children, who were so immersed in their writing exercise that they didn't notice Yu-ning. He nodded at her and smiled. He held his index finger over his mouth and ducked down to whisper, "Yes, my name is Percival, but people call me Percy. What is your name?" He looked around again to make sure no one noticed them.

"My name is Yu-ning. What are you writing?" Yu-ning saw two piles of papers, one pushed up against the right corner of his desk and the other to the left.

In hushed tones Percy explained, "Well, this stack on the right has all the ideas I *want* to write about, and this stack on the left are the *school* assignments. I have to sneak to write what I want so the teacher won't get angry. If we don't follow the rules, she thrashes us with that bamboo reed on her desk." Percy raised his sleeve to show Yu-ning red welts on his arm.

"What type of rules?" Yu-ning asked curiously.

"I don't know where they come from," Percy said, shrugging his shoulders. "She says they are the rules of tradition and the elders of this school. But I want to write and learn something else. There is new information out there; I know there is," Percy said, looking unhappy.

Yu-ning placed her palm on the right-hand pile and moved it toward Percy. "Then why don't you write something else?" she said. "Write the things that make you smile."

Percy looked at her wistfully and smiled. "I want to, but I can't. I have to follow what everyone else is doing or I'll get in trouble. Everyone must follow the rules here, or you are punished. If I get punished too many times, they call my mother, and it makes her sad. She works two jobs now that my father is gone, and I don't want to make her sad. I can't do what I want to do." His eyes were downcast and forlorn.

"Why don't you tell the teacher what's in your heart?" Yu-ning persisted, filled with empathy.

"No, she won't listen." He spoke with the weight of one too old to be eight. "Who's going to listen to me? I'm eight. I would have to move from here and find another school."

Yu-ning nodded with wide eyes and said, "I know where that is." But Percy just looked at her blankly and then at the blackboard at the front of the room.

The stern teacher whipped around at that moment and lowered her glasses to her nose. She slammed the chalk down, breaking it in two, picked up the bamboo reed, and walked briskly over to them, looking very angry. "Oh no!" Percy said, panic-stricken, as he quickly pulled out his writing assignment.

The teacher hovered over him. "Percy! What is this? No talking! Do your assignment!" She turned to Yu-ning and snapped irritably, "Who are you? Do you have permission to be in this classroom?"

"Hi, Teacher, my name is Yu-ning," she said with innocence. "I'm here to see the classroom, and to bring colors if you allow me."

The teacher scoffed dismissively. "What color are you talking about? Whose class are you in?"

"I'm not from any class, Teacher. Why don't you let Percy write freely?" Yu-ning asked. Percy sank into his chair, trying to disappear.

"No one is allowed to go outside the rules," the teacher said sternly. "Everyone must follow the rules."

"Teacher, where I'm from we don't have rules that force us to be someone we are not," Yu-ning countered politely. "We draw, we play music, we write, we read, we create freely. You don't need to teach the rules, you allow your heart to guide you."

"I don't care where you are from," the teacher snapped. "There is a right way to do things and that is the way *we* do it here, little girl. Now get back to your class! Are you in Fujimura Sensei's class?"

Yu-ning felt quite small standing next to the teacher, yet she didn't flinch. "There are so many other, different ways to do things," she continued. "You can't live your life by rules alone. We are each different and unique, and what we discover within our heart is the best path for each of us."

Percy was completely dumbfounded, watching Yu-ning stand up to the teacher. The other children had stopped writing and were also watching with keen interest, which made the teacher irate. Her eyes on her class, she addressed them as a whole. "Now listen to me, class. We all know that if you don't follow the rules, you will get bad grades. If you get bad grades, you won't be able to beat your peers and you won't be successful in the future. The rules allow you to earn a title, get a superior job, and make money. That is success."

Then she turned back to Yu-ning and said, "I am Genju Sensei. You will address me as Sensei. If you are not in Fujimura Sensei's class, you must be a new student. Therefore, I will allow you this one mistake of challenging our rules, but it must not happen again. Did your parents bring you to the school? Why haven't you checked in first with the headmistress? Never mind, take a seat and we will sort it out at lunch." Sensei pulled out a chair from a desk next to Percy.

Yu-ning nodded as she sat down in the chair. "Yes, Sensei, but where I come from we have no titles. We create freely; we don't compete and we aren't judged or graded. There is no older or younger, bigger or smaller; everyone is the same and has something special to offer, so there is only healthy interaction, which builds us all," Yu-ning explained wholeheartedly.

The teacher was taken aback by Yu-ning's precociousness and intelligence. This vexed her, and she rapped her bamboo reed on Yu-ning's desk with full force. "That's unacceptable. You will follow the rules and the system like your classmates, and you will follow my instructions. Now, no more talking!"

she said in a loud voice as she thwacked the reed again on the desk.

Percy and the other children were stupefied by Yu-ning's audacity and courage to confront the teacher. They murmured among themselves, creating a commotion that was heard in the other classrooms. Percy looked up at the teacher and said softly, "Sensei, Yu-ning is right. You don't need to follow the rules, either."

The teacher threw Percy a wilting look, and through her teeth she said, "All of you, keep writing." Then, in a lower voice for only Yu-ning to hear, she said, "How dare you question me! Everyone must follow the rules. Anyone who breaks the rules will be punished."

Yu-ning was sitting peacefully at her desk, unfazed by the teacher's anger. "But, Teacher, why can't everyone just do what they love?" she questioned forthrightly. "A book holds only the view of its author. We should be free to express different views, especially those that flow from love and light."

Percy looked at Yu-ning with deep respect and appreciation. "Yes, Sensei, can we write our own thoughts and inspirations?"

The teacher glared at Yu-ning and Percy. She looked up to see the whole class watching, as well as many children from other classes gathering in the hallways and looking through the windows in stunned silence. They were whispering to one another and nodding. One twelve-year-old girl said, "Wow, that little girl is so brave, and that boy, too." Her friends nodded.

The teacher, feeling self-conscious, began to lose her resolve. She smoothed out her bun and said calmly and firmly, "Listen, everyone. The rules of this school have been in place for two centuries. They create the rules and laws we follow as a people. As your teacher, I have been trained in these studies and I have mastered them. I have more knowledge and more experience than you. I know what is right. You do what I tell you to do, and then you will not make mistakes. You will do well in life."

The teacher took a deep breath. Yu-ning realized that she wanted the best for the children, and that the teacher believed order and regimentation would guide them on a path of righteousness and success. "If you don't listen to me," repeated the teacher for the whole class to hear, "I will have no choice but to send you to the headmistress's office." She said this while looking straight at Yu-ning. She turned to Percy and said, "And you know what that means for you, Percival. Didn't I overhear you promising your mother better behavior in our last conference, when she was crying?"

"My mother just wants me to be happy, Sensei," said Percy. "She has only ever wanted my happiness. But in this classroom I am not happy. There is no inspiration here. You don't allow us to think for ourselves. How can I be successful if I am not happy?"

"Follow the rules!" the teacher exclaimed bitterly, "You climb professional ladders. You become elite members of society. You gain financial security. You succeed in life. *That* is what makes you happy. And if you don't follow the rules, you will have to leave this classroom at once!"

The teacher pulled down her shirt and smoothed back her bun. "I have to attend a faculty meeting, and I want you all to open your books to page thirty and do lessons one through fifteen five times until I return. All the teachers are meeting with the headmistress now, and you are on the honor system."

She looked at her watch and added, "And I am already late! If you return to your studies immediately, I will not report you. The headmistress is the most powerful person here, and she will make your lives miserable if you do not listen to me this instant!"

She thrust a textbook at Yu-ning and said, "And that goes for you too, young lady. We will sort this out at lunch, upon my return."

# Twenty

# Suparna

**Y**U-NING REMAINED IN HER CHAIR as the teacher returned to the front of the classroom, the eyes of the class following her. From the back of the classroom where Yu-ning was sitting, she had a view of the only window whose shade was not drawn. The only other student with a view of the open window was Percy, who was looking at Yu-ning.

A sudden flash of color drew Yu-ning's attention to the trees outside. As she peered through the window, she saw a familiar sight: Suparna, standing at the edge of a grove of pines. He had arrived in time to get the message from Cristobel, and had obviously made excellent time to arrive at the school just when Yu-ning needed him the most. Suparna was peering at the school, looking for any signs of her. Yu-ning raised her hands and began waving her arms back and forth to get Suparna's attention.

Suparna, however, did not see her. She continued to wave her arms, trying to get him to look in the direction of the window. She saw that Suparna was gazing right at her, but he wasn't able to see her because the sun was reflecting off the window from the outside. She quietly stood up, tiptoed to the window, and with all her effort, tried to pull it open. The window didn't want to budge—it was apparent that it had been closed for quite a time.

Yu-ning felt the window move slightly, which allowed her to slip her fingers under the frame. She pulled with all her might, and to her surprise, the window flew open, making a loud *bang!* as it did. Yu-ning looked toward the tree line and saw that Suparna had heard the noise and was looking in her direction.

"You! What are you doing?" came the angry voice of the teacher from the head of the classroom. Yu-ning continued to wave her arms at Suparna, motioning for him to come to the classroom. Just as she thought Suparna had seen her, she felt a firm hand on her shoulder and was spun around by the teacher.

"I said what are you doing at the window? Students are not allowed to touch the windows," the teacher said, pointing her finger in Yu-ning's face. Then, glancing outside, she added, "And why were you doing exercises?" Yu-ning was hopeful as the teacher peered toward the nearby grove of trees. But no one was there; Suparna had disappeared.

"I . . . I wasn't doing exercises, Sensei. I was trying to get the attention of my friend Suparna," Yu-ning said.

The teacher slammed the window shut, threw down the shade, and told Yu-ning not to move from her seat again until the break. "I don't know who you are, young lady, but you are in big trouble. The headmistress will be very interested in talking to you, I can tell you that!" Yu-ning was crestfallen.

Had Suparna seen her signaling for him to come to the classroom? She just knew if Sensei could meet Suparna, her attitude would change. She decided to appeal to the spark of life she sensed in the teacher, in spite of her stern warnings.

"Teacher, my friend Suparna is one of the most beautiful creatures you will ever see. He comes from light and love, and uses his gifts to help others—not to control them."

"Suparna?" Percy asked quizzically.

Yu-ning nodded emphatically. "Yes, he's here with us today—in the trees at the edge of the grass. He is magnificent, with colorful wings that fill up the sky. He is very powerful, with a vast heart and a noble mind. When Suparna expands his wings, a rainbow of colors shines brilliantly to inspire all people to do their best, because their best comes from the qualities that characterize him! His bright, colorful wings have touched my heart, and they are here today to touch your heart. I'm telling you this because I am hoping he will come today, and this is your chance to let go and surrender." The children were quiet and riveted. Even the teacher was speechless, and just stood there breathing deeply.

"Oh wow, I want to see Suparna!" Percy exclaimed.

"I hope you can see him, too," said Yu-ning. "Each of you needs to believe and you need with teachers to guide you from this path of habitual learning to illumination."

"Nonsense," muttered the teacher. "Stop wasting time imagining impossible things!" But her voice had dropped, and she sounded hesitant.

Yu-ning noticed this instantly and appealed to her. "Sensei, you have been misguided as well. Deep down you know this. You want the best for your students; that is why you have followed the rules. But what if this isn't the best path for them? What if anything is possible, and all you had to do is say, 'Maybe, I don't know for sure'? Can any of us, really without a doubt, know all the mysteries of this beautiful universe?"

The teacher was silent.

At that moment, there was a loud banging noise on the roof of the classroom. For the first time, Yu-ning noticed that the roof had two wide rows of windows that met in the middle—like an old solarium. Though the windows were painted black, there were handles at the ends of the rows, which Yu-ning assumed were for opening them. The windows made a loud popping noise, and dust floated down from above onto the heads of the children. "What is going on here? What kind of trick is this?" the teacher asked, now feeling utterly confused.

Then, with a loud whooshing sound, the windows opened outward, and sunlight poured into the room. As the teacher and all the students gazed up in shock, there, hovering in the sky, was Suparna, who dove down and swooped into the large classroom. It was a spectacular vision. The shining, colorful bird had a smile on his face, and his bright colors illuminated his lustrous wings. The classroom immediately brightened as he appeared, and the light began to disperse, spreading across the entire school grounds.

"Suparna! Oh, you did see me!" Yu-ning was so excited to see him again. She waved and bowed reverently. He smiled broadly at everyone and stood in the middle of the classroom, the children having scrambled out of the way to give him space.

Suparna didn't say a word but simply nodded at Yu-ning and then at the stunned teacher. "Hello, miss. I assume you are the teacher here. Don't be afraid—I am not here to harm you, nor is Yu-ning. Listen to her wisdom, and know that her heart is true." Then, turning to Yu-ning, he said, "I will be waiting for you outside, Yu-ning. You know what to do!" In a matter of seconds, he darted back into the sky and disappeared over the roof of the school. Slowly the colors faded.

"Oh my," Percy said, astounded. "That is him, that is Suparna! It's true! Everything Yu-ning said is true!" He followed Yu-ning's example and bowed. Soon, with their teachers attending the board meeting, all the students had left their classrooms and congregated in the hallways outside Yu-ning's classroom. They were also bowing together.

Sensei gasped and brought her hands to her mouth. Her face was pale as her eyes remained fixed on the exact place where Suparna had vanished. She collected herself and walked slowly to the front of the room to sit at her desk. She sat there for a long time, staring at the class and Yu-ning and Percy. She smiled and nodded gently at them. Percy understood instantly that she was telling the children to do as they pleased.

Percy was beaming. "Yu-ning, I don't know how you did it, but you transformed Sensei! It's a miracle!" Percy shouted joyfully.

"You did it too, Percy, you did it. You told her what's in your heart; you said what you feel in your heart!" Yu-ning replied.

Sensei invited all the children into her classroom. Thirteen classes of twenty students from kindergarten through twelfth grade were assembled. In all, 262 children wedged into the classroom with Yu-ning and Sensei. Yu-ning walked over to a shelf and removed several stacks of white paper and several cases of colorful pencils. She brought them over to her desk and started handing several pages out to each student.

Percy was looking at the pristine white paper with wide eyes. After she distributed the paper, Yu-ning gave a simple instruction: "Whatever inspires you." She sat down next to Percy at his desk. There was a frenzy of commotion in the classroom, but the spirit was joyful and reflective. Some children were working together in groups, others in pairs. The creative energy was powerful and flowing throughout the room.

"Percy, here," Yu-ning said enthusiastically. "Do you want to draw with me?"

Percy nodded cheerfully. "Sure! I love to draw!"

"We'll each draw," Yu-ning said, picking up a pencil. "I can show you my picture and you can show me yours!" Yu-ning was excited as she quickly drew a small circle and leaned over the table to pick out another colored pencil.

"All right!" Percy agreed. They were both giddy with excitement, delighted to be drawing freely. As they drew they talked, laughed, and shared their work together.

Sensei rose from her desk, turned off the ceiling lights, and walked over to the windows, opening each shade. Bright sun streamed in. She stood there astonished by the colorful transformation of her once dismal and cheerless classroom. She was standing in the front next to the eraser board, looking amazed and staggered by the events of the day. She smiled and waved tentatively to Yu-ning and Percy across the room. They waved vigorously.

"Sensei, thank you for allowing us to create from our hearts," Percy said.

"Yes, Sensei, I'm drawing a picture for you," Yu-ning added. "I'm drawing Rainbow Island for you. It is beautiful and colorful." Yu-ning smiled joyfully.

"Rainbow Island. I want to go to Rainbow Island," Percy said to Yu-ning.

Yu-ning smiled and nodded. "Suparna and I will take you there. We're taking everyone there who wants to go—even Sensei."

In the midst of the joy, a stern-looking woman dressed in a white blouse, black pants, and black jacket stormed into the classroom. "What is going on here?" she said in a loud voice, her face growing red. "What are all of you doing out of your regular classrooms? And Sensei, I've come to get you for our faculty meeting, and this is what I find?"

Percy clutched Yu-ning's arm and whispered, "That is the headmistress, Mugoi Sensei."

Sensei stood up and looked the headmistress square in the eyes. "Hello, Headmistress. I understand your concern; however, you need to know that I am in control of my class and have directed this session in free drawing."

"This is unacceptable, Genju Sensei. You will get back to the daily curriculum as scheduled, and you will do it now. Then, I need you in the conference room immediately." The headmistress turned to leave, signaling to Genju Sensei that the issue was settled.

"I am sorry, but no—I will not be teaching from the curriculum today—" Sensei stopped, lowered her head, and placed her hands on her hips, as if gathering her thoughts. Then she raised her head slowly and looked at the headmistress with fresh resolve. "You know that I have always abided by the rules of this academy and instructed the lessons rigorously. However, these children taught me today that I was wrong. The academy is wrong," she said firmly.

"What are you saying? This is not acceptable, Genju Sensei! I don't want to have this conversation in front of your class, but I feel as if you have given me no choice: I hired you, and I can fire you. You dare insinuate yourself into the teaching of your colleagues by accepting their students into your classroom? You must tell them to disperse at once and return to their proper classrooms. Do your job, or you won't have one." This time the headmistress did leave, without giving Sensei the chance to respond.

A stunned silence fell over the classroom as the headmistress left. Yu-ning placed her hand on Sensei's arm and asked, "Why is she so angry?"

Sensei touched Yu-ning's cheek affectionately and said, "Because we aren't following the school rules. When we don't follow the rules, she feels helpless, and that makes her try to prove her strength through anger. She was my headmistress too, when I was a student here. I have followed her rules my whole life. But now, I'm done." She turned to Yu-ning and Percy and said, "I'm so very proud of you both. You showed her what it means to speak your heart and mind, and you showed me how to do this too. Bravo. Thank you."

Sensei turned to all the students. "Children, you learned a lifetime of education here in this classroom today. Learn from Yu-ning. Find your inner power and light and shine from there." Children from five to eighteen were beaming and nodding with wide eyes. Sensei fiddled with her buttons nervously. "Now," she said pensively, "the question is, what to do? How do we proceed?" The academy was a boarding school and all the children and some of the teachers lived on campus. Sensei was trying to figure out the logistics to liberate all of them. She could think of no solution.

Percy sighed happily and looked at Yu-ning. "What do we do now, Yu-ning?" he asked.

"Let's go outside and see if we can find Suparna," Yu-ning said excitedly.

The children all began to cheer, and Sensei nodded. "Good idea. We could all use some fresh air."

They exited the classroom, talking and laughing happily. The entire school had gathered, almost every person either having seen Yu-ning's visit and the appearance of the "rainbow bird," or heard about it from someone who had. Once out of the positive energy of the classroom, however, it was as if each person had been programmed to walk the halls with fear and trepidation. Yu-ning tried to lighten the mood. "It's all right, everyone. You don't need to stay in this school if you don't want to. You have choices, and you can come outside where the air is fresh and the sun is warm. Don't worry!"

As they continued quietly down the hall, Percy pointed to a dark room. "All the teachers are gathered in a meeting in there. This is where they discuss how to enforce the rules and create different forms of punishment," Percy continued, with panic in his eyes.

"We better hurry and get out of here," a five-year-old boy said.

A senior student holding the boy's hand added, "Yeah, let's just go. Don't go in there, Yu-ning."

Another older girl spoke up and said, "I think we need to confront the headmistress about—well, *you all know.*"

"What do you mean, Ariadne?" asked the girl who was holding the boy's hand.

"My sister, Anne. And Caspar. All the other orphans who have . . . *disappeared!*" When Ariadne said this, the children all became very quiet. It was obvious this was a taboo subject that few ever spoke of.

The five-year-old boy said, "But Headmistress says those kids all went off to a better school."

"Don't believe everything she says," added Ariadne.

"Ariadne!" Yu-ning said. "It was your sister, Anne, who sent me here! I have just come from seeing her. She has been working in a factory far to the north—but she is free now. She is on Rainbow Island, my home!"

"You've seen my sister?" said Ariadne, hardly believing her ears. "Is she all right? Is she safe? I haven't seen her in more than three years." Ariadne was overcome with emotion, and sought comfort in the arms of one of her fellow students.

"This is the reason I am here, everyone—to take away those of you who want to go, who want to leave this school. I have seen enough to convince me that many of you are here against your will. Is that true?" There were nods and whispers of agreement from most of the students. "For those of you who do not wish to leave, you may stay. The choice is yours. But for those who wish to leave, you can come back to Rainbow Island, and attend a school that will never treat you with hatred or abuse."

"But some of us aren't orphans," said Percy. "Our parents won't know where we went, and we will miss them."

"Percy, once you are on Rainbow Island, we can tell your mother where you are now. She will be able to visit you any chance she can, or even come live on our Island if she wishes."

Yu-ning turned to Genju Sensei and said, "There is something I must do, Sensei. I must confront your headmistress

232

about the children she sold into slavery—the children who had to go away to Darqendia Island."

"I had no idea, Yu-ning, that the children were sent away like that," insisted Sensei. "Whenever a child went away, Headmistress always told the faculty that it was to another school, on Gracia Island . . . But sold into slavery?" Sensei began to cry, realizing that those poor children had been suffering in sweatshops all these years.

Yu-ning turned toward the door of the conference room and placed her hand on the knob. She heard One's voice in her head, saying, "Speak your truth. Tell these teachers the truth." Yu-ning nodded quietly to herself. She looked at the whole group of people very gravely and said, "No, I can't leave yet—I need to explain to them why we are leaving. I need to tell them about the missing children."

A twelve-year-old girl spoke up. "But we are only kids, and they will not listen. They think they are always right."

Yu-ning shook her head. "Don't worry. We need to tell the truth. There are more of us, and they cannot control us any longer. They cannot do anything to us."

Sensei said, "Yes, you must tell them just what you have told me, Yu-ning. You must speak from your heart. I have lived in fear all my life until this moment. All that stops now."

Sensei came forward and whispered into Yu-ning's ear. Yu-ning slowly nodded her head in agreement. Sensei turned and walked briskly down the hallway toward the main offices.

"All right," Yu-ning said. "Let's go." Yu-ning lifted her small hand to knock on the door. She paused briefly before she tapped the door three times.

"Enter!" a stern voice boomed.

# Twenty-One

# Confrontation

YU-NING SLOWLY TURNED the knob and opened the door. The room was dimly lit. She stood at the door and saw the headmistress and eleven teachers seated around a large conference table. Yu-ning and Percy stepped inside and stood close to the doorway.

"Why are you children in here? You're not supposed to be in here," a man snapped.

In a gravelly voice the headmistress said, "You are not allowed in here; how dare you disturb us." There was palpable anger and hostility in the room.

Percy and two other students approached. Percy said, "We are done with rules that only hold us down and make us feel ashamed of our true talents. We don't want to learn in this way any longer."

This defiant declaration, spoken in front of her staff, made the headmistress stand and say in a loud voice, "I have had enough of this insolence. This goes beyond a mere disciplinary problem, and I have given you several opportunities, Percival, to right your ship. If you do not return to your classroom at once, I will consider expulsion. And no other school will accept you without letters of recommendation and your grade cards. There are always more students. This is an exclusive academy, and thousands apply every year for only 260 slots. I will mark your transcripts with F's! You will all be janitors! Go!"

Yu-ning looked confused and asked, "I don't understand. Janitors? If they are happy doing their work, then why judge that labor? Janitors work to feed their families. Why wouldn't you respect that work? And you may think this is an exclusive academy and among the best in the world, but you have an entire student body that is miserable. The seniors have spent thirteen wretched years here. How do you find success in unhappiness? Rules aren't always right. Yours have locked down this school and created a prison. You have closed down the hearts and minds of everyone in here, including yourselves. Look at you all. Look at this dark room. Look at your severe expressions and hard faces. You are not happy. How was this working? If one is miserable, how is she successful? Why not try something different?"

"What do you kids want?" said an older male teacher, ignoring Yu-ning's question. "We are in the middle of a meeting. Go back to class, or you will all receive detention and extra assignments for this disobedience!"

"We are gathered here to tell you the truth about your school," Yu-ning said straightforwardly. "My name is Yu-ning, and yes, I am just a little girl. But I am also free, and I know how important freedom is to a child. I am here to tell all of you that your headmistress is not what she says she is. Do you know what really happened to all those children—the orphans—who have been transferred to other schools?"

The teachers were silent, and all looked at the headmistress, who was seething with anger. A male teacher spoke up. "What are you talking about, young lady? We have many students who come and go, and some who transfer to other schools. There is nothing unusual about that."

"Is there nothing unusual about a headmistress who lies to children, tells them they are going to another school, a better school where they will get special attention, only to take them in the night and sell them as child laborers?"

"You are way out of line, miss! Our headmistress would never do such a terrible thing," responded Mayeda Sensei, one of the older women teachers. The headmistress just stood there, saying nothing.

"Ask her yourself, then, where all those children went— Anne, Caspar, and all the others. Isn't it interesting how all the children who were 'transferred' were orphans?" Yu-ning said, with growing emotion. "If they were transferred, then why don't we go visit them? My friend Suparna can take us there right now, Headmistress. Gracia Island is just a short flight from here. And I know the Grey City quite well, we could help you find the school."

The headmistress finally spoke, saying, "Of course, these allegations are outrageous and unfounded. I will not stand here and be accused by an insolent young girl who doesn't know her place. I am going to find the school guard, and then we will see what happens to disrespectful little girls who lie about their superiors!"

"Do you deny it then, Sensei?" asked Yu-ning. "Do you deny selling the orphans?"

With that, the headmistress stormed out of the room and strode down the long corridor. Yu-ning, the teachers, and the students watched her leave, and Yu-ning walked out of the room, moving down the hallway after her. The headmistress removed a key from her pocket, opened an office door, walked inside, and locked the door behind her. Yu-ning arrived just in time to see her grab her satchel and leave through the back door of her office.

Percy was at Yu-ning's shoulder. "She's getting away, Yu-ning! What should we do?"

Yu-ning just smiled at Percy and said, "It's all right, Percy, justice always finds its way. Come, follow me."

Yu-ning threw open the large double doors of the school, followed by the children and even the teachers. She walked around the side of the school and then toward the back of the building. As she turned the corner, she stopped, and waited for all the children and teachers to join her. There in the center of a courtyard behind the school was Suparna, hovering ten feet off the ground. Below him the guard was holding the headmistress's arm, and Genju Sensei was standing by.

The disgraced headmistress had the look of a trapped wild animal. "You don't know what it takes to run a prestigious school like this!" she screamed. "It costs more money than you can imagine, and donations and tuition never cover all the costs. This school has been here for 211 years—who is going to miss a few orphans? They all found gainful employment—the best future for them anyway."

The teachers—and even the children—were stunned. Though their leader had always been a severe, mirthless woman, no one imagined she was capable of such shameful acts. The oldest teacher among them, Mayeda Sensei,

was a distinguished teacher who had been at the school for
thirty-four years and had served as the head of the faculty
board. She broke from the silent crowd and approached the
headmistress.

Though Yu-ning could not hear what Mayeda Sensei
said, it caused the headmistress to hang her head in shame.
Mayeda Sensei turned back toward Yu-ning and the rest of
the children and teachers and said in a commanding voice,
"This is a shocking turn of events. Remain calm, children,
until your teachers and I can decide on a course of action. In
the meantime, you are dismissed for lunch—but do not wander far. We will gather here again in half an hour!"

Mayeda Sensei turned to the guard and said, "Take her to
the magistrate and turn her over to him. Let the courts deal
with her now." She walked over to Yu-ning and said, "How
did the guard and your friend Suparna know to apprehend
her? She owns a boat just down the path there, which leads
to the school's private dock," she added, pointing down a hill
that led to the beach. "She was probably headed there to
make an escape."

"That was Genju Sensei's idea—to alert the guard and
Suparna," said Yu-ning. "She thought the headmistress might
try to escape."

Mayeda Sensei approached the teacher and said, "You
have done a wonderful thing for these children today, Genju
Sensei. You have a promising future at this school and in how
we rebuild the curriculum and our entire approach to learning. If that is what you desire."

"Thank you, Mayeda Sensei. You honor me. I think I
must go, however, and begin a new life on Rainbow Island.
As you know, I have always had a heart for our orphans, and

those children returning from the factory are going to need special attention. I will miss you, though, as you have always been kind and helpful toward me." Genju Sensei bowed deeply before the school's new headmistress and walked back to Yu-ning, who was laughing and playing with Percy and Ariadne.

The teachers were amazed at the sight of Suparna—they had never seen such a beautiful creature, particularly one who talked! The children laughed and played on the beautiful grounds of the school, typically marked "out of bounds" for the students.

As the students continued to celebrate, Genju Sensei, Mayeda Sensei, and Suparna met with the rest of the teachers in the courtyard to discuss what would come next. After the lunch period ended, all the students gathered in the outdoor courtyard. It was completely quiet as Mayeda Sensei rose to address the crowd. "From this day forward, this school will change its ways—it will change the way it teaches, what it teaches, and it will be run by an elected group of teachers who will take turns sitting in the headmaster's chair. No more secrecy, and no more dictatorships!" With this, the children broke out in wild screams and applause, and even some of the teachers were clapping.

She announced that the students would need to seek their parents' permission if they wanted to leave the boarding school for Rainbow Island. However, all orphans wanting to go should be allowed to do so. As the news spread, the children became animated, inquiring of one another as to who was staying and who would be making the journey to Rainbow Island.

Percy would stay and wait to ask his mother whether or not they both wanted to come to Rainbow Island. He said to Yu-ning, "Her life is so hard, Yu-ning, and she deserves a new life. I so want to give that to her!"

Yu-ning hugged her new friend and said, "Soon enough, Percy, you will be with us on Rainbow Island. In the meantime, be well, and remember that you have the light in your heart!"

Of the 260 children at the school, thirty-three were orphans—and twenty-eight of them decided they wanted to return with Suparna to Rainbow Island. Yu-ning and Suparna promised all the children who were remaining at the school that they could come visit any time they wished.

Soon it was time for Yu-ning to return to Minkaro, who would be getting worried about her now that the afternoon shadows were growing long on the grounds of the school. She said her goodbyes to her new friends and climbed onto Suparna's back for the short flight to the cove where she had left Minkaro that morning.

"You have done very well indeed, Yu-ning," said Suparna, as she climbed atop his neck. "I am very proud of you."

"Thank you, Suparna," said Yu-ning. "I only wish that *you* could take me to Farcara Island. It is a long journey, and I will miss you. I will miss Metatron." The majestic bird took wing as the children and teachers waved goodbye from the grounds of the school below.

"How I wish these wings of mine could fly that far south, Yu-ning," Suparna said. "But I am built for milder climes, I am afraid. Minkaro is a noble king, Yu-ning, and you are in good hands with him. He will do everything within his power

241

to protect you, and will make sure that you arrive safely on Farcara."

Yu-ning could see the small cove in the distance and Minkaro's large pink form waiting in the water near the shore. They landed on the gravelly sand, and Minkaro greeted them both. "Minkaro, I trust that you will be taking the eastern route across the north end of Gracia and then turning due south, straight for Farcara, yes?" said Suparna.

"That is the plan, Suparna. With any luck we will be there in four days," said Minkaro. Yu-ning hugged Suparna and climbed on to Minkaro's back, securing the harness. Suparna remained on the beach until the dolphin and girl cleared the cove and headed into deep water. Then he returned to the school to arrange for the transportation of the twenty-eight orphans, plus their instructor, Genju Sensei, who had decided to go with them to Rainbow Island.

The remaining teachers decided to stay, as many had families on Malinga Island. As well, they all wanted to be a part of reforming the school and beginning anew with the remaining students. After a good night's sleep and a quick early-morning farewell on the lawn of the school, Suparna was ready to leave. Ariadne took the first position directly behind his head, while the other children spread out across his back, secured by harnesses that the teachers helped to secure. All the teachers and students gathered on the lawn to say goodbye to their friends. It was a joyous sight.

As Suparna headed north again toward Rainbow Island, the winds were at his back, and he made excellent time. By the same time the following morning, Rainbow Island was within sight. The children, who had been snuggled down, sleeping under Suparna's soft feathers during the night, became excited and started laughing and pointing toward the beautiful green island in the distance.

Pristine, azure blue waters surrounded Rainbow Island's lush green mountains, trees, grasslands, and flower-laden fields. And although the rainbow was gone from the Island, it was still a beautiful, magical place. Suparna was happy to be back. Faster and faster they descended, and as they neared Rainbow Meadow, they could see all the teachers and children running from houses and exiting the school, coming to greet Suparna and the orphans. "This is your new home now," said Suparna to the orphans. "You will always be a part of our community, and you will be able to create and imagine as never before."

He landed in Rainbow Meadow, just across from the main school hall, and all the children scrambled down from his back, with teachers and Rainbow Children coming forward to greet them. Ariadne was the last child to dismount, and she anxiously scanned the crowd for her sister, Anne. There were so many children! Some looked healthy, tanned, and well fed, while others were thin and careworn. But all the children were beaming from ear to ear. Ariadne searched the little faces as she walked through the crowd of laughing children, searching for the sister she had not seen in years.

Ariadne stopped. Standing alone toward the back of the crowd was her sister, Anne. She was staring at Ariadne, and her lower lip began to tremble. The older sister ran forward and scooped up the frail little girl in her arms, kissing her cheeks. "Oh Anne, how I have prayed for this day. It's you, it's really you!"

Genju Sensei approached the girls, and seeing Anne, placed her hands over her mouth, stifling a cry. "My darling little Anne, you are safe!" Sensei threw her arms around both girls, and all three cried—tears of laughter for what was happening this day, and tears of sorrow for what had happened before. "I am sorry, Anne, that I let headmistress take you away," Sensei said. "If I had only known . . ."

"It's all right, Sensei," said Anne. "My sister is here now, and that's all I want. It wasn't your fault." The little girl gently touched Sensei's cheek, bringing a huge smile to the teacher's face.

"It's over now, girls," whispered Sensei. "You will never be apart again. And I will always be here for you."

Suparna had made his way through the crowd and had witnessed the reunion of the sisters. He turned to Genju Sensei and said, "You put these children first, and for that you will be forever rewarded." Suparna swept his wings through the air, making a rainbow of light around everyone. "Go now and celebrate! Welcome to Rainbow Island!"

Ariadne, Anne, Sensei, and many of the children ran down into Rainbow Meadow, which was flashing brilliantly from the colors of the flowers. Suparna darted back and forth in the sky in large sweeping motions, showering light onto the meadow, celebrating along with the children and teachers.

Ariadne whispered, "This is heaven!"

"Yes, this is beyond my dreams," Sensei said, as she reached out to enfold Anne in a loving embrace. Julian, the former beggar from the Tower of Light, was there too, celebrating along with the other children. He introduced himself to Sensei and told her if she needed anything, he was there to help her.

They played for hours in Rainbow Meadow, and Julian took the children to go discover the Great Kapok Tree. They shrieked with delight as the living arms of the tree began to pick them up and pass them quickly upward, limb by limb, all the way to the top of the tree. From the village, where Metatron looked on with warmth in his heart, he could see dozens of children ascending and descending within the limbs of the great tree.

It was not the same, however, without Yu-ning and Romeo. Metatron felt a nagging unease for sending Yu-ning off to Farcara, but knew it was her path. He and Suparna had darker, more dangerous business to attend to. Thus far, the Darq waters and creatures that he and Suparna had spied while traveling to Darqendia had not been seen near Rainbow Island. The pink dolphins had doubled their patrols and were circling the waters of the Island night and day. No creature would slip through unseen—the great pink dolphins would see to that.

"You won't touch this place again, Hobaling," Metatron whispered under his breath as he gazed out at all the children at play. "Oh, you can try, but I won't let you catch us off guard again. No, it is you who should be watchful, warlock. I will find you, and I will not rest until the rainbow shines over our Island once again."

Sensei and a dozen children walked back to the village, toward the beautiful school building. Sensei saw lovely gardens, some fully grown and others newly planted since the obsidigon attack, and beautiful fruit trees by the side of the school.

When they all reached the school, several of the Rainbow Children grabbed Sensei's hand, saying, "Come see our school!

This is our school!" At that moment, five teachers came forward to greet them with warm hugs. They had kind, happy faces, and were dressed in earth-toned linen clothing. "Our teachers! These are our teachers!" the children exclaimed.

Everyone was immersed, focused, and joyful, doing exactly what he or she loved. They were working together in harmony, cooperating and creating wonderful, imaginative arts and crafts. Older and younger children alike played together, while others picked flowers, which they used to make floral garlands for their hair.

One of the teachers asked Sensei, "Would you like to teach with us?"

Tears flowed down Sensei's cheeks as she nodded eagerly. "Yes, thank you. Thank you. I have waited my whole life for this moment."

The teachers led Sensei into the lovely structure. The front doors were wide open. They walked into the beautiful room with floor-to-ceiling white curtains blowing in the breeze and three sets of French doors on each wall. No signs of the makeshift hospital remained. Today, it seemed as if the attack of the obsidigon had merely been a bad dream, hardly a reality.

Joyful children filled the room. The walls were covered with colorful drawings, the blackboard was decorated with paintings, and there were colorful wooden pencils strewn about the wooden desks where the students worked with smiles on their faces. On one side of the room was a soft purple sofa with large plush cushions and a coffee table covered in fairy-tale books. Many children were gathered here, lying on the couch and on the pillows atop a lovely shag wool carpet. Others were playing music in one corner; some were studying art, while others were reciting poetry and rehearsing a play.

Sensei was amazed. She observed other classmates weaving wool on a loom. "We learn through relationships and interaction with each other," said a male teacher. "We treat each other the way we want to be treated. We create everything by ourselves from nature. Everything is handmade. We learn from our inspiration and imagination."

Cristobel approached Sensei and said, "Yes, our children do what their hearts tell them to do. They do what they love and what they are good at. We don't have titles and grades; we help and love each other, and we create magic. We don't need rules; we don't control people here. Because there are no rules, everything and everyone is limitless and infinite, so we can go beyond. This is a school of love. Welcome to your new home, Sensei!"

"Yes—I *am* home," rejoiced Sensei, with a broad smile on her face.

Outside the school, Metatron spied Suparna in the distance and, as quickly as he could, ambled over to him with the aid of his staff. "And you!" he said to Suparna with irritation. "You have cost us precious time—why didn't you tell me you were going to Malinga Island to help Yu-ning?"

"My friend," said Suparna, his eyes shining with deep wisdom to rival the wizard's. "You often say that life is a mysterious book, and all we have is today's page. When Cristobel told me where Yu-ning had gone, I had no choice but to answer her call for help. That, my friend, is what was written on *my* page."

Metatron simply looked at his longtime friend, a twinkle in his eye. He slowly nodded his head, raised his staff to Suparna, and gave a low chuckle as he turned to walk away. "You, Magic, and I leave for Baggul Island in the morning— no matter what words are written in your book *tomorrow!*" Metatron yelled, his back to Suparna.

# Twenty-Two

# Ship

INKARO AND YU-NING traveled through the night, and by the following morning they had crossed the wide channel separating Malinga from Gracia, reaching the northwestern tip of Gracia Island by noon. The coastline looked familiar to Yu-ning as she recalled her previous trip to the Grey City. How long ago had that been? It seemed like a lifetime—so much had happened in the past two weeks.

They followed the north coast of Gracia most of the day before rounding the northeastern tip of the island and turning south. As evening fell, Yu-ning could see the glow of the Tower of Light far in the distance, piercing the sky with its brilliant beams. Though she knew it was only her imagination, she thought she could see Balthazar in his black jacket and green shirt, waving from the top floor of the magical tower.

But with the turn south also came a foul shift in the weather. The skies grew dark, the winds rose, and the sea grew violent and raw. "This weather is not normal, Yu-ning," Minkaro said, as they bounced across the rough seas. "The patterns are very predictable in these waters, and storms of this strength just don't happen at this time of year."

"What do you think is going on, Minkaro?"

"I don't know, Yu-ning, but keep a close eye out, and look for any unusual activity," said Minkaro. As they pressed southward, the weather grew more vicious, and soon the rain was falling so hard that it was difficult to make out where the rain ended and the waves began.

"Minkaro, the water is turning the color of dark ink. What is going on?" asked Yu-ning. Minkaro noticed that the water had grown increasingly dark—subtly at first, but with increasing gradation. The swells grew larger, and began to appear as mountains in front of Minkaro: huge, fifty-foot mounds of water, rising up like giants before them. Up they rose, mounting the huge walls of water, and then down they would race into the dark troughs before beginning the treacherous pattern over again. Yu-ning did her best to keep a sharp eye out, but she was cold, and drenched to the bone.

"What was that?" yelled Yu-ning, above the howling wind. "I think I saw dark shapes in the wave above us," she said, as the two rode from the trough of a swell up the face toward the top.

"What did you see, Yu-ning?" Minkaro shouted. At that moment, Minkaro also saw the shapes, racing down the swell directly toward them—two huge shadows just below the surface of the frothy waves, dorsal fins breaking the surface of the wind-whipped water. He had very little time to react but managed to dodge to his left as the first shark hit him just behind his dorsal fin, nearly knocking Yu-ning off his back.

Minkaro managed to escape the jaws of the first shark while slamming his powerful tail into the second one, sending it, reeling and stunned, into the depths below. Minkaro recovered and accelerated up the wave, leaving the two sharks in his wake. Yu-ning righted herself, grabbing the saddle cinch and tightening it around her waist. The element of surprise now gone, the sharks circled back to pursue the dolphin and the diminutive girl.

"Hang on, Yu-ning!" shouted Minkaro, and just as she tightened her grip on the pommel of the saddle, Minkaro pumped his powerful tail and accelerated with such quickness and strength that Yu-ning was thrown backward—if it weren't for the cinch around her waist, she would have fallen into the stormy waves.

"The Darq creatures!" screamed Minkaro. "These are the sharks that Metatron warned us about! And look, off to your left—there are three more following us now!" Minkaro raced onward, putting distance between him and the sharks. Up and down the great swells they raced, but no matter how swiftly Minkaro swam, he could not widen the gap between himself and the sharks. Before long other fish joined the hunt, all with the same black scales and yellow eyes—including several barracuda—all in fevered pursuit of Yu-ning and Minkaro.

"We need to look for shelter, Yu-ning. Keep your eyes open for somewhere for us to take shelter!" shouted Minkaro. Hours passed, with the distance between the dolphin and the pursuers growing smaller. The exhausted dolphin couldn't keep up the pace much longer. He was desperate to find a cay or atoll where he could at least save Yu-ning, if not himself.

"Look, Minkaro, I think there is a ship ahead!" Yu-ning yelled as they rose to the top of a giant swell. But before Minkaro could spot the ship, he was racing down the steep backside of the wave. He pumped hard as they raced downhill and rose swiftly up the face of the next wave.

"Hold on!" he yelled as he surged forward in his ascent up the giant swell. At the top of the wave, the largest one they had encountered, he accelerated with all his strength, his body completely vertical as he punched through the peak, through spray and wind, and was airborne, high above the apex of the wave. "Where is the boat?" he yelled at Yu-ning, his entire body now twenty feet above the wave.

"There! There, Minkaro, do you see it?" shouted Yu-ning, as she pointed directly south toward a small grey object in the distance.

"Yes, I see it!" said Minkaro, as his body turned a full 360 degrees in the air and then descended nose first toward the violent water below. "Hold on!" he shouted. He entered the water hard; Yu-ning was lying flat against the saddle, trying to make herself small. The impact was enormous and ripped Yu-ning's hands from the saddle. Down they went, into the cold water. She held her breath, closed her eyes, and waited.

Minkaro plummeted downward into the depths, and then turned his body upward; his angle was flat and gradual as he sought to maximize his speed. Yu-ning held her breath for what seemed like an eternity, and just when she began to feel dizzy, Minkaro burst through the surface of the water again. The maneuver had been impressive, and Minkaro had put a bit more distance between himself and his pursuers, who now numbered more than half a dozen.

They raced forward, the grey ship now growing closer. Soon the details of a large vessel became visible—two large smokestacks, a huge mast, and a few lights blinking on deck. Once again, however, the Darq creatures were starting to close the gap—Minkaro just couldn't outrace them with Yu-ning and her gear on his back.

The ship was close now, and Minkaro believed they might have a chance to reach the vessel before they were overtaken. "When we get close, I will pull alongside the boat," shouted Minkaro. "You will need to jump from my back. Look for a ladder or rope on the side of the ship!"

"All right, Minkaro—faster, though, they are almost upon us!" shouted Yu-ning, as two massive barracuda with wicked eyes and long yellow fangs appeared on their right.

"There, Yu-ning! There is a rope ladder hanging down on the starboard side," Minkaro exclaimed. "You will need to jump from my back. Unhitch your belt, grab Lightcaster, but leave your pack lashed to the saddle. Once you are safely on the ship, I will try to lose the creatures and double back for you. Stay on the ship until I can return for you. If I don't return, you will need to get to the nearest land, and find your way to Faruda on your own. Whatever happens, hang onto Lightcaster!"

"You will be safe without me slowing you down, Minkaro! I will see you soon," shouted Yu-ning. The great dolphin closed in on the bow of the ship, veered to the right side, and pulled alongside the vessel. "Go! Now, Yu-ning!"

Holding onto the loose leather straps of the saddle, Yu-ning carefully rose to her knees, then to her feet, with

Lightcaster slung over her shoulder. Just as she gathered herself to jump, one of the barracuda launched itself out of the water, hitting Minkaro just below the center of his body, knocking him sideways. Yu-ning fell and scrambled to grab hold of the saddle. She had the pommel, but it was slick, and she lost her hold. She fell over the saddle and began to slide down the length of Minkaro's body. She grabbed his enormous dorsal fin, but it was slippery, and she feared that she couldn't hold on for very long.

Minkaro peered behind to see Yu-ning's predicament just as the second barracuda flew all the way out of the water, directly toward Minkaro's head. With all his might, he pulled his head away, and then swiftly brought it back, making contact with the barracuda's snout. The fish was not expecting the blow, and Minkaro's massive head sent the fish tumbling end over end as it bounced against the side of the ship and disappeared under the waves. Minkaro could not see the second barracuda, but the two sharks were nearly upon him, and the rest of the Darq creatures were close behind them.

Yu-ning held onto Minkaro's dorsal fin with one hand, trying desperately with the other to grab hold of the leather strap dangling off the back of the saddle. There! She had the strap in her hand and quickly grabbed it with her second hand as well. Slowly she made her way back toward the saddle, hand over hand. She grabbed the saddle and slowly stood again, riding Minkaro, one hand on the leather strap, the other ready to grab hold of the rope ladder dangling down from the ship.

"Now, Yu-ning! GO!" Minkaro shouted, as one of the sharks closed the gap on the giant dolphin and was about to clamp its gaping jaws around his tail. Yu-ning jumped, letting go of the leather strap in midair. She flew across the gap between the dolphin and the ship, desperately trying to grab the rope ladder. She had it—a rung of the ladder was in her hand! The momentum of her jump, however, was greater than she had anticipated, and she lost her grip on the rope. She found herself falling toward the water—upside down. As she braced herself to plunge headfirst into the icy depths, she was jerked upward.

Her foot had caught in the rope ladder, about three feet above the waterline. She bounced against the waves, trying to reach upward and grab the ladder. Lightcaster dangled precariously from her shoulder, and she could feel it slipping over her head. Pain shot through her injured left arm as it slammed against a wave, and with her right arm she lunged upward. She had the rope. Slowly, she was able to raise herself up with her right arm, and as she did, Lightcaster slid safely back around her neck and shoulder. She was hanging on the lowest rung of the ladder. She looked wildly in Minkaro's direction, fearing the worst. The pink dolphin, however, had outmaneuvered the shark, and now that she was no longer weighing him down, he was racing away, beginning to put distance between himself and at least seven dark silhouettes visible just under the surface.

Yu Ning scrambled upward on the rope ladder, out of danger of any remaining Darq creatures. She stopped halfway up the side of the massive ship, in shock, but relatively unharmed. Her arm ached, but the pain was bearable. She was shaking and felt weak as she clutched the rope, waiting for her breathing to slow. As she looked out to sea, she could just make out the pink shape of Minkaro, racing ahead of his Darq pursuers.

Satisfied that Minkaro was safe, she carefully climbed the rest of the way up the rope ladder and swung first one leg, then the other over the wooden railing, landing upon the wet, wind-lashed deck. The ship was larger than she had thought: there must have been at least sixteen decks. The mast looked infinite as it jutted into the dark sky. The entire boat was painted gold—the exterior body as well as the interior walls and deck. The gold had faded, and in some areas the paint was dull and peeling. Was Yu-ning on a ghost ship, void of passengers? It seemed that the ship was cast at sea in the middle of nowhere.

Then, near the bow of the ship, through the wind and rain, she saw a boy who looked to be about sixteen years old. He wore a sailor's uniform and hat and had moved to the very front of the bow, where he was pulling on a rope with all his might.

"Where is everyone?" Yu-ning said to the boy as she approached. "It is so empty here. This is like a ghost ship."

The boy looked at her and nodded. "You are right, little girl, this is a ship of ghosts. People disappear here," he murmured.

"What do you mean, they disappear?" Yu-ning asked.

"You forget who you are here. You forget where you came from. You disappear. I don't know," the boy said, trying to brush her off. He continued, "I don't have answers for you. I don't talk to anyone. They are probably shut in their rooms, or hiding somewhere."

"Do you work on this boat?" Yu-ning asked.

"Yes, but there's no work to do anymore. I used to be a deckhand, but the crew either abandoned ship in the lifeboats, or . . ."

"Or what?" asked Yu-ning.

"The darkness came twenty days ago, and ever since, we have been wandering in this storm. All the passengers keep to their cabins. I haven't seen the captain in days. He's not on the bridge, so he is probably in the engine room—downstairs."

"Yes, I know about the darkness," Yu-ning said. "Did you see the dark creatures as well—the ones with dark scales and yellow eyes?"

"Like the ones that nearly ate you when you jumped from the back of the huge pink dolphin?" asked the young man. "That was impressive." He said this with no emotion.

"Yes, those creatures. Listen, I need your help," said Yu-ning, adjusting Lightcaster on her back. "I must get to Farcara—are you heading in that direction?"

"Farcara Island? No, we are heading for Tunzai, to the imperial capital. At least, that is where we were headed until we lost steam power. The skies turned grey, and they have remained that way ever since." He said curtly, "I don't know why I am talking to you. Leave me alone."

"There is an unnatural darkness creeping across the sea," Yu-ning said. "It feeds off of fear—it sensed fear and sadness on this ship, and it took advantage of it. You must fight it. Everyone on the ship must fight the darkness. You saw those terrible creatures that almost killed my friend and me. We need your help!"

"Yes, of course I saw them—they've been swarming around the boat for days," said the boy. "But still, I don't know what to do. All I know is, the storm is getting worse, I can't raise the captain, and much of the crew is gone. Perhaps the captain will listen to you . . ."

"What is your name?" asked Yu-ning.

"Jonas."

Yu-ning walked over to Jonas and folded her hand into his. He didn't pull away. She looked at him and nodded. "I'll go and see what I can find out." She was about to go search the ship for the captain when she noticed a man and a woman walking up steel stairs onto the long, dark, weathered deck. They walked like ghosts, emotionless and silent. They looked at Jonas and Yu-ning with stoic, frozen expressions. Yu-ning noticed how grey they were. "Why are they grey, Jonas? Their faces and bodies are grey. Look, even their hands are grey. How could that be?"

Yu-ning saw more and more people walking on the deck now. There were dozens of them. They were all grey like the sky, walking like zombies, without life or purpose. Even as the rain drenched their clothing, they didn't seem to notice. Yu-ning was very concerned. "How come I don't feel their spirit? Where is everyone's light?" Yu-ning said, looking at them.

"This is how it is now; this is what I've been trying to tell you, Yu-ning."

"We must get out of this dark storm," Yu-ning said, shaking her head. "That will wake them up. We must move and change the direction of this ship."

A man walked by Yu-ning and Jonas. He was looking down at the deck as he walked. Yu-ning noticed how everyone looked down as they walked; yet no one bumped into anything. Yu-ning approached a group of people drifting in one direction. "Hello. Sir? Ma'am? Hello? Do you hear me?" She gently reached out and tried to touch a few people's sleeves. Yu-ning stepped toward a man as he walked past her; she felt chilled to the bone standing next to him. He didn't respond and continued walking.

"They are all ghosts, Jonas," Yu-ning whispered gravely.

"It's no use. I told you not to bother," Jonas said.

"Look, Jonas, it's getting darker. The storm is growing worse, and I think I know what is causing it. The darkness is getting closer to us. We must navigate the ship out of the storm!" Yu-ning said in distress.

"The captain already has plans," Jonas said with concern. "He sails this ship toward the clouds. That has been his navigation system for many days. He follows the storm clouds."

Yu-ning had an idea. She reached around her neck for the familiar red cord of her crystal heart necklace and pulled the crystal out to show Jonas. It was glowing pink. She cupped it in both hands and looked at the boy. "Place your hands over mine, Jonas."

"What? Why?" he asked. But without waiting for an answer, he slowly placed both of his hands over the pink crystal heart. As he did, he felt a tingling sensation move through his hands and up his arms, and shoot down into his heart. He felt as if the light of a thousand stars had exploded inside, shooting their light down to the tips of his toes and up to the top of his head.

"What is . . . ?" he whispered, closing his eyes as the light continued to bathe him in peace and warmth. As Jonas said this, the light of understanding dawned on him. He opened his eyes, which were now fully alert and locked onto Yu-ning's. "The captain has kept us in this holding pattern, and we have allowed it to happen. We have allowed the darkness to overtake us!" Jonas shouted, clarity flooding his mind and spirit.

Yu-ning nodded and hugged him as he removed his hands from hers. The pink heart necklace continued to glow brightly. "We can't keep on following the dark clouds; we must get out. Where is the captain? I need to tell him to change direction," Yu-ning said urgently.

"The captain is downstairs working on the engines," said Jonas. "But I need to warn you: no one ever goes down to that section of the boat. He has become very dark recently, and he has a violent temper. He keeps the doors locked and bolted, so he will not listen to you."

The clouds were producing an alchemical reaction in the sky; it was pure fury. "I must try, Jonas. I need to tell the captain," Yu-ning said, as she pointed up to the sky. "It looks like three storms are colliding. We need to guide this boat to the light!" Yu-ning said as she started to run down the long deck toward the steel stairs. "Gather as many passengers as you can, Jonas, and tell them we need to sail out of this storm!"

"All right, I will try!" yelled Jonas.

"You have a job again," she said smiling back at him.

He nodded, encouraged, and flashed her a smile as she disappeared into the stairwell.

# Twenty-Three

# Visitor

ROMEO AWAKENED IN A DARK PLACE. After a moment of disorientation, his heart sank: he was still in the lair of the obsidigon on Baggul Island. He remembered that a locked, rusty gate and a four-ton dragon stood between him and freedom, and his mood grew as gloomy as the inky blackness of the cave.

*What was that?* he thought to himself as he heard scuffling sounds in the distance. For the first time, the thought occurred to him that he might not be the only living creature in his cavernous prison. Now fully awake, he strained to hear any unusual noises. As he sat listening, he quietly groped in the dark for a large rock. Just in case.

*There it is again!* he thought, the same soft scuffling noise—like something moving across the cave floor, low to the ground. The unsettling part was that Romeo felt like whatever was out there was circling him; he heard the sound several times, but from different directions. Was he being hunted?

The sound was very close now—no more than ten feet away. He got to his feet in case he had to run; he had a general idea where to go to avoid hitting his head again. He stood crouched like a coiled spring, the heavy rock resting in his hand.

"Romeo, it's me!" said a deep voice, just a couple of feet in front of him. Completely startled, he shuffled backward several feet and almost fell down.

"Who's there?" yelled Romeo, the deep boom of his voice compensating for the fear in his heart.

"It's me," said the voice, just as Romeo felt something land on his right shoulder.

"Ah!" he yelped, startled by the feel of something cold on his body. He swiped at the creature with his hand and fell backward, hitting the hard, rock-strewn ground. He scrambled backward on his hands, trying to get away from whatever was stalking him.

"Romeo, what are you doing? It's me, Magic!"

"Magic? You nearly scared me to death! I thought you were a cave shade here to drag me off to the underworld! Why didn't you announce yourself?"

"Romeo, my night vision is very good, but I can't see in pitch darkness like this," Magic said. "I had to make sure it was you, and I couldn't be sure without getting close. It is so good to find you, Romeo. We have all been so worried about you!"

"It's a relief to see you too, Magic—though you nearly scared me to death," added Romeo, his heart still pounding like a drum in his chest. "But how did you find me? Who told

you I was here?" Romeo was in shock that the little frog could find his way to Baggul Island and discover exactly where on this forsaken rock he was being held.

Magic explained that he had come with Metatron and Suparna, having heard rumors that Hobaling was here. "We flew for two days straight from Darqendia and arrived here around midnight. Suparna circled the island several times, and just when we were about to give up on finding any signs of Hobaling, I spotted a faint light coming from high on a cliff—it was coming from Hobaling's grotto. So Suparna landed along the cliffs about a hundred feet above this cave. I was able to climb down from above and find the cave entrance. First I searched Hobaling's grotto, but I didn't see any signs of you or the Seven Sacred Crystals. Then I looked on the other side of the cave, and after getting past the sleeping obsidigon, I followed the passage until I came to the locked gate. I knew then that I was probably in the right place."

"As great as it is to see you, Magic, it doesn't change the fact that there is no way out of here. I am stuck."

"Have you forgotten the light, Romeo?" Magic asked.

"What do you mean, Magic? There is no light here."

"Do you still have your purple crystal heart? The one Yu-ning gave you that day before you were kidnapped from Rainbow Island?"

Romeo put his hand against his chest and felt the small, round crystal hanging from its silk thread underneath his shirt. "Well, yes, I still have it."

"Then use it, Romeo," urged Magic.

Romeo reached into his shirt and pulled out Yu-ning's purple crystal heart. He had all but forgotten about the crystal since he had been abducted. As he removed it from his shirt, it glowed ever so faintly. This gave him hope, which caused the heart to glow even more.

"Yes, Romeo, that's it. Your belief is making the crystal glow!"

Romeo stood up as the purple crystal illuminated the entire cavern in soft, pulsating purple and lavender light. Romeo smiled at Magic, as if seeing the frog for the very first time.

"You are full of surprises, you crazy frog . . . I have an idea, Magic; follow me."

Romeo walked to the center of the large cavernous chamber, toward the cleft where the stream ran downhill. As they followed the stream deeper into the cave, it began to pick up speed, skipping and bouncing off rocks. The passage here was narrow, and it headed downward at an increasingly sharp angle. As they continued downward, they could hear the sound of rushing water. Not of a stream, but of a river. They picked up their pace as the lights from the purple crystal revealed the path forward.

"There, Magic, do you see it? The stream disappears down there." They approached the place where the stream disappeared, and Romeo had to stop abruptly. Just before him was a gaping hole, across which he could not jump. The stream fell into the chasm, and below him, in the darkness, was the unmistakable sound of running water. He held the purple crystal over the chasm, but he could not see to the bottom.

He picked up a fist-sized rock, dropped it in, and counted out loud—"One pink dolphin, two pink dolphin, three pink dolphin—" until he heard a faint splash. He remembered a lesson from his math instructor: it takes 1.7 seconds to fall

50 feet. Or was it 7.1 seconds to fall 500 feet? He couldn't remember. In either case, he calculated, the drop was far. Should he risk the jump? Though the water was rushing loudly and sounded deep, how could he know for sure? What if he jumped, only to land in a few shallow feet of water? He certainly wouldn't get far on a broken leg—or worse.

He could either spend another night in the cave, or try to make his way down to the underground river. He and Magic backed away from the chasm and decided to go back to the main chamber to discuss their options. As they did, Romeo held the crystal heart aloft, and noticed that they weren't alone. There were bones and old clothes scattered about; he had not been the first prisoner to occupy the cave. The others had been less fortunate, though: as he scanned the cave, he saw several skeletons. Many looked ancient, wearing old clothing from the Third Age some 300 years before.

Immediately he knew what to do. He told Magic to return to Suparna and Metatron: at first light, they were to watch for him along the cliffs, where the rocks met the sea. "I am confident that the river below leads to the ocean. I will find my way down to the river through the chasm, and ride the current to where it leads to the open sea." Sensing concern on Magic's face, he added, "Don't worry, Magic. I am the best swimmer on Rainbow Island—I will be fine." He wished he were as confident as he sounded.

Magic and Romeo walked quietly back toward the exit of the cave, stopping at the turn in the passage, just before the rusty gate. They peered around the corner and didn't see the obsidigon. Magic slipped through the bars and gave a quick wave goodbye as he slinked back down the passage toward the cavern's opening. Romeo waited for a long time, listening for signs of trouble, but heard none. It seemed that Magic had been able to make his escape. By the looks of the light down the passageway, he guessed that dawn was still an hour away. That would give him just enough time to get ready for his big plunge.

He moved back to the main chamber of the cave and scrambled from one skeleton to the next, gathering waistcoats, breeches, shirts, and other items of clothing. He made a large pile, then set to work tying the pieces together, end to end, to make his descent rope. He would take his chances in the chasm and hope that the river headed out to the nearby sea and freedom.

When he had tied together all the garments he could find, he dragged the makeshift rope toward the large hole. He tied one end of the rope around a nearby stalagmite, gathered the rest of the rope, and set it just next to the lip of the chasm. Making sure that his feet were not entangled, he gently pushed the mound of clothing over the edge. It made a quiet whooshing sound as it fell.

Romeo waited for the splash of water. It never came.

What now? He sat on the edge of the chasm, his heart racing, hands sweaty, and mouth dry. He took several deep breaths, wiped his hands on his pants, and gripped the rope tightly.

"Here goes," he said. He wrapped his feet around the rope, just as he had been taught in climbing class on the Emerald Cliffs of Rainbow Island. But this wasn't the Emerald Cliffs, and Romeo wasn't wearing a safety harness. He turned onto his stomach and edged himself over the side of the chasm, gaining purchase with his feet on an outcropping below. He gently swung himself away from the rocks until he was dangling in the air. He began to descend, slowly but surely. It was easier going than he had imagined, but he was in complete darkness and didn't want to bump into the jagged walls. He was wary of removing his crystal heart necklace, as he was afraid it would fall off on the way down.

Hand over hand he descended. Finally, he could feel the large knot he had tied just three feet from the end of the rope, another trick he'd learned in climbing class. The water was louder now, but still a long way off. As he swung there in midair, trying to decide what to do next, his decision was made for him—the friable cloth rope gave out. With an inauspicious snap, Romeo was in free fall and found himself upside down.

He twisted in midair, trying to right himself so his feet hit the water first. He closed his eyes and waited for impact, not wanting to see what might be awaiting him. Just as he righted himself, his feet hit the water hard, and he was engulfed by cold, fresh water. He braced for the jarring impact of hitting bottom, but his feet found no purchase. Down he went, like a stone, tumbling and turning in the turbulent water. He fought to free himself from the heavy weight of his rope, which had felt so light, but which now encircled his waist, heavy and deadly.

Try as he might, Romeo could not untangle himself from the billowing clothing that surrounded him. He could tell that his time was almost up, and he gave one last lunge for the surface. His hand punched the surface of the water, and just as he was about to break the surface for a breath of air, the water-laden cloth rope began to drag him down again.

He kicked with all his might, but he knew that his energy would soon be gone. In that moment, he had the strangest vision: Yu-ning was playing tag with him on the beach. He could almost smell the chalkiness of the dry sand and the salty balm of the water and hear the sound of Yu-ning's feet slapping against the sandy shore, running just out of his reach.

He could see her; she was just in front of him. If only he could touch her! Then he would be able to breathe. As he began to lose consciousness, a soft purple light began to glow all around him, and he thought perhaps he was leaving this world and beginning his journey to the next. And then all became calm, and he wasn't frightened anymore. He was on the beach with Yu-ning, running on the wet sand, a soft, purple light flowing all around him, growing brighter and brighter.

# Twenty-Four

# Vortex

YU-NING RAN DOWN the steel stairs of the old vessel, flight after flight, until she was on the bottom level of the boat. On her way down she passed passenger room after passenger room. Some doors were cracked open, and inside she saw people sitting in darkened, silent rooms.

She ran down a long hallway with dim lights flickering on the walls. She made two right turns and came to a door with a steel plate that said "Engine Room." The compartment was closed, and there was a small round window in the door. She stood on her tiptoes and peered through; the captain was sitting in a chair, holding a cup. He had a white mustache and white curly hair. He was round and heavy.

Yu-ning knocked on the door tentatively, but when there was no answer, she knocked firmly. When there was still no answer, she began to shout through the door. "Captain, we are headed directly into the heart of a treacherous storm. Open the door, Captain!"

"Go away!" the captain finally replied. "No children in the engine room! You know nothing," he yelled angrily.

"Captain, please listen. The ship is drifting toward the eye of a terrible storm; you need to start the engines and navigate the ship in the opposite direction."

The captain kicked back his chair angrily, stomped toward the door, and launched it open with a blast of fuming energy. He stood in the doorway with his hands on his waist and his chest puffed out. "Who do you think you are, banging on my door?"

She bellowed back, "CAPTAIN! THIS SHIP IS HEADED STRAIGHT FOR A TERRIBLE STORM. YOU HAVE TO DO SOMETHING! TURN THIS BOAT AROUND!"

The captain was taken aback by the power of this little girl, and didn't know how to react. "It's not me!" he said, with less anger. "I don't make the decisions; those people up there told me to go this way. I'm only doing what they told me. They paid me and asked me to go this way!"

"But you are the captain!" Yu-ning said in a gentler, more persuasive tone. "You steer this ship, not the passengers."

"Everyone on this boat wants to go this way, so don't talk to me," the captain said, raising his voice again. "You go talk to them on deck and get them to change their destination. Now get out!" With that, he slammed the door violently in her face.

Yu-ning whimpered in frustration. She paused for a second and was about to knock on the door again, but instead quickly ran off, back up all the flights of stairs to the top deck. She was panting and out of breath when she reached the top. She held tight to her necklace, readjusted Lightcaster, and ran toward the center of the deck, calling for everyone to gather, rain lashing against her face.

"Everyone! Please come here. We are heading right toward the worst of the storm, and the ship needs to change direction! The captain won't turn around until he is told to by all of you. Come on, everyone, please tell the captain to turn around. The storm is here!"

"What are you talking about?" a man screamed out. "This is where we want to be. There's nothing in the other direction."

Others listened and nodded. A drone of voices repeated, "We stay where we are."

Yu-ning's frustration was mounting. "It couldn't be any worse than this! Look at all of you. You are all grey and lifeless. This is not natural—there is evil magic at play here. You have to believe me. Don't let your light be stolen away!"

Dead silence greeted Yu-ning when she stopped shouting.

She softened her voice, sensing an opening. "Please trust! The other way is bright and light."

"What do you know?" a man screamed out. "You're just a kid!" He turned around and started down the stairs, mumbling as he left, "Just a stupid kid."

Yu-ning was at the end of her strength. The storm was growing worse, and the swells were now nearly cresting the deck of the ship. Then, to her amazement, she saw a shape in the water, swimming next to the boat. "Yu-ning! It's Minkaro! Can you hear me?" shouted the dolphin king, now directly below her in the water.

"Oh, Minkaro! I am so relieved to see you. Where are the Darq creatures?"

"I dove deep, Yu-ning—deep where the water is icy cold. They stopped following me. I believe they are susceptible to the cold. I then stayed deep, but made a wide circle, leading back here to the ship. But you are running out of time, Yu-ning. The storm is worsening, and the water is strange. This is not a normal storm!"

"I know, Minkaro. But I can't leave all these people—if they stay, I am worried that they are going to be swallowed by the storm!" Yu-ning said.

"Hurry, Yu-ning! We don't have much time. Save as many as you can!"

When she turned back toward the passengers, she noticed that more had followed the man below decks. Yu-ning watched in frustration as a steady flow of people drifted away. Yu-ning looked up at the ominous sky and ran back to the side of the ship.

But Yu-ning was heartened by Minkaro's presence and felt a wave of inspiration flow through her as she darted back toward the center of the ship. She held onto her necklace, calling out as she walked through the crowd, "Wake up! Do you want to be stuck in this storm forever? Tell the captain to go the other way, please!" She felt the chill of their bodies as she moved through to the center. People slowly began to gather around her.

"No, we don't want to go to the unknown," a man said, looking down at his feet, pulling his wife back into the crowd as they both disappeared.

"Please tell the captain to turn the boat around. Let's go tell the captain to change direction; come on, everyone . . . open your heart. You want to believe. I can feel it."

*They want to believe,* Yu-ning thought.

"What do you know?" a woman said. "You are just a child!"

As Yu-ning took the woman's hand, she noticed color subtly returning to the woman's cheeks. Yu-ning's spirits were buoyed. "What is your name?"

"My name is . . . Sarah," the woman said, as if waking from a dream.

"You have stopped believing in hope, and now that hope-lessness has affected all the others," she said to Sarah as she looked to everyone else. "This entire ship has lost heart. But you aren't ghosts. You are alive, but you are not living. Please choose life!"

Sarah was weeping. Yu-ning took off her necklace and placed it in her hand. As she did, color flowed from Sarah's hand, spreading throughout her body. The crowd gasped in shock. Yu-ning saw Jonas approach the woman. He smiled at Yu-ning and reached out to hold Sarah. "You are Jonas's mother!" said Yu-ning, realizing what was happening. The two of them embraced for a long time, and all the while Yu-ning was holding Sarah's hand.

Furniture and belongings were flying everywhere as the wind and rain became more powerful. Over the fury of the storm, a blast of sound emanated from the ocean, louder than the thunder or crashing waves. Everyone was taken aback as they heard the voice bellow from the sea. "Yes! Follow me. Listen to Yu-ning. If you don't leave now, you will forever remain in the eye of the storm." It was the voice of Minkaro, and everyone had heard it.

With the wind and rain slamming against their bodies, about 100 people began to drift toward the rail, following the voice. Yu-ning stared wide-eyed as they began to nod at one another and point to Minkaro. "Did you hear that dolphin? It spoke! Did you hear it?" A murmur passed through the crowd; there was no denying that the large pink dolphin had spoken. Many people in the crowd seemed to awaken from a daze, shaken from their somnolence by the voice of Minkaro.

"Come on, people, let's go tell the captain to follow Minkaro," Yu-ning said urgently. "We must go now, or else we can never get out of this storm. There's no time to save this ship, but we can save ourselves!"

Just as Yu-ning spoke these words, she saw something looming in the darkness on the port side of the vessel. Yu-ning wiped her face, trying to focus her eyes as the rain poured down on her in sheets. She saw it! It was a boat—a shining white boat, smaller than the cruise ship, but solid and stable and holding steady in the storm. It was about 200 yards away. One light at the top of the mast was shining and flashing like a beacon. Yu-ning stared wide-eyed as she saw the passengers slowly begin to point.

The white lights of the boat were shining brightly as it drew closer to the larger vessel, which was noticeably listing toward the stern, taking on water. A voice boomed from the darkness, coming from the direction of the white ship. "We are with the Imperial Navy of Tunzai! We are heading out of the storm—there is only one safe way out. Your vessel is taking on water. You must lower your lifeboats now, and we will rendezvous with you!"

The boat drew closer—as close as it dared in the treacherous conditions of the storm. It was now a mere fifty yards off the port side of the ship, and Yu-ning could see a man in a rain slicker and white captain's hat standing on the deck, holding a megaphone. He had a safety harness clipped to his waist and was having a difficult time staying on his feet as the naval vessel pitched violently in the swells. Even so, it was riding high on the water, as if built for the stormy conditions.

"We can take you out of the storm. Just lower your life vessels, and we will throw you ropes to tow you alongside!"

Yu-ning stood high on the rail at the edge of the deck. "We don't have any lifeboats—they were all taken," Yu-ning yelled in frustration.

"Yu-ning, take the rope ladder—lead the people down the rope ladder!" It was Minkaro, swimming at the top of a swell next to the boat.

"Yes, of course, Minkaro! I will guide them to the ladder, and you can shuttle us to the ship!" Yu-ning didn't wait for a response but darted away from the railing, back toward the haggard group of passengers.

"Our boat will fit everyone who wishes to come," boomed the captain's voice. "Bring them all now—there isn't much time."

"Yes, I will get everyone!" Yu-ning whipped around on the rail, shouting, "Come on, everyone, it's time. We are all going onto the naval boat. It's here to take us out of the storm."

She jumped down onto the deck and ran furiously toward the center of the crowd, shouting and grabbing onto people. "Everyone! There is another boat that has come to save us; they are here to take us out of the storm! Look, over there!" Some craned their necks and tried to peer through the storm. Others stood there in apathy, ignoring Yu-ning. By this time, several hundred others had gathered to see what all the commotion was about.

Jonas and Sarah grabbed people by the shoulders, trying to convince them to abandon ship. Most people shook them off and just walked away, struggling on the pitching deck to make their way back down the stairwells. Yu-ning was frantic. "Please come back! If you don't leave with us now, you will go down with this ship." Yu-ning shook her head frantically. "The captain is following *your* orders! He's waiting for you to tell him what to do."

"That's ridiculous, child," a woman called out. "The captain runs this ship. He steers it and charts the course, as all captains do." Everyone around her nodded.

She darted toward the steel stairs and called back to the people, "The captain doesn't know! He's waiting for you to tell him you want a different course!" Yu-ning disappeared down the steps, jumping four steps onto the landing of each level as she descended. She ran down the hall to the engine room and pounded furiously on the door. "Captain, it is too late for this ship, but a new boat is here to save all of us. Please come with me!"

Slowly the door opened. The defeated captain stood there looking at Yu-ning with sadness and resignation. "Yu-ning, a captain never abandons his ship. You tell everyone to board the naval boat. I can see it through my window. Tell them to save themselves," he said stoically. "I have to stay with my ship. We are more than 700 souls on this boat. Those who stay will need me to steer the ship," he said.

Yu-ning was frantic because she knew time was running out. She composed herself and said with gravity, "Captain, everyone has a choice. You do not have to sacrifice yourself because of others' choices. The decision you make must come from love, not sacrifice. This ship does not need a martyr. Those people who choose to stay are so fast asleep, they won't even know if you're down here or not."

The captain looked with amazement at the little girl standing before him. He felt so very old and tired. But she had sparked something in him—there was now no doubt. He grabbed Yu-ning's hand and said, "I know a shortcut up to the main deck. We have to hurry." He led her through a door at the back of the engine room, and they dashed up the stairs. On the way topside, the captain stopped on all the passenger decks, grabbing the first person he could find on each deck. "We are abandoning ship," he repeated on each deck. "Knock on everyone's door on your deck, and tell them they MUST leave now, or they will sink with the ship!"

Yu-ning and the captain burst onto the front of the boat on the center deck. The ship began to jerk violently from one side to the other, and slowly it began to spin out of control. People were pushing, running, and grabbing onto the deck rails and furniture. Yu-ning pulled the captain's hand and said gravely, "Captain, this is it. Look." She pointed upward to a most unruly configuration of black storm clouds swirling brutally into one another. The blackness was covering the entire sky. There was no longer a pause between the thunder and lightning.

The captain shouted, "We have to move, now!" They ran toward the center of the ship where throngs of people wandered aimlessly. Yu-ning passed a man dragging a heavy metal trunk in one hand and a suitcase in another. He was muttering, "I can't take this off the boat; it is too heavy." Despite Yu-ning's protestations, the man heaved the trunk down a nearby stairwell. She could hear the heavy trunk clanging on each step as the man dragged it down to his doom.

The boat was tilting toward the stern at an alarming angle—it was most certainly sinking, even as it drifted toward the eye of a gigantic waterspout. The enormous black funnel whipped around, with every cycle growing in size and intensity. As each wave reached the bottom of the tornado-like waterspout, the funnel's tip crested and snapped like a whip. Yu-ning and the captain were now both screaming to the others to warn them.

As Yu-ning reached the railing near the rope ladder, she couldn't believe her eyes. Jonas and Sarah had gathered at least 150 people and were organizing them for the descent down the ladder. "Jonas!" Yu-ning called as she ran to him and hugged him tightly around the waist. "All of these people? You did it!"

Jonas hugged her back and said, "Not me, Yu-ning. You! I told them all about you. These are the people you saved! Come on, we don't have any more time," Jonas said as they both eyed the waterspout swirling in the distance, but growing closer to the bow of the ship. The ship's captain grabbed the rope ladder, steadying it in the howling wind. Jonas descended first and, following Minkaro's instructions, latched himself to Yu-ning's saddle. He helped people down from the rope ladder onto the back of the great dolphin.

The captain threw down extra ropes, and Jonas instructed the passengers to tie themselves together, and hold on for dear life. Once Minkaro had about twenty-five passengers on his back, he raced the short distance to the white ship, where crew members waited to help the stunned survivors climb ladders onto the deck of the naval vessel.

In a matter of seven minutes, Minkaro was able to shuttle all the willing passengers to the other ship. It was an amazing feat, aided by the precise actions of both captains working in unison. Sarah and Yu-ning helped each passenger descend the ladder toward the safe haven of the white boat. Yu-ning tried one last time to save anyone who would listen, but everyone was gone. The remaining passengers had all disappeared below decks.

The captain of the ship waved to the captain of the white boat and signaled him that he, Yu-ning, Sarah, and Jonas were the only ones remaining. Minkaro returned for them, and the captain grabbed onto Yu-ning's and Sarah's hands as he helped them climb onto the dolphin's back. Yu-ning noticed tears in the captain's eyes, though he didn't say a word. Yu-ning reached out to the captain and squeezed his hand. "I'm so glad you are here leading us, Captain. You opened your heart," she said.

The captain nodded at her and said, "Thank you for saving us."

From atop Minkaro, Yu-ning tried one last time to reach the other passengers, some of whom were staring blankly over the railing of the ship from above. "Everyone, please. This is your very last chance. If you don't leave now, you will never get out!" Some of the passengers simply stared, while others left the railing, walking away from their last hope for survival. A young man, however, climbed onto the railing and dove into the water. Minkaro reached him quickly, and the captain and Jonas helped him climb onto the dolphin.

Tears streamed down Yu-ning's face as Minkaro tried to comfort her. "Yu-ning, we have to go now. You tried. They chose their journey," he said kindly. "Hold on now. It's time to leave."

Yu-ning nodded wistfully. "It's time."

As Minkaro swam away, they saw the gigantic ship pulled toward the funnel of the waterspout; an enormous whirlpool

circled where the monstrous funnel met the sea. The ship
lurched toward the whirlpool and was sucked into the dark
swirling sinkhole, which was pulling down everything around
it. The ship disappeared into the deep darkness in less than
two minutes. As it sank, Yu-ning thought she could see dark
shadows in the water, circling around the ship.

Minkaro raced away from danger, plunging through the
stormy waters with Yu-ning, Jonas, Sarah, the captain, and
the young man looking on in sadness and silence. Within
less than a minute they arrived at the white boat, and one by
one they climbed aboard as the crew welcomed each person
with a warm blanket. The other passengers were all staring
at the terrible scene—the place where the ship had once
been was now empty, and the whirlpool seemed to be moving away from the naval vessel. They were out of danger, but
their hearts were heavy as they grieved for their lost friends
and loved ones.

As the imperial naval vessel headed east, the storm began
to abate, and within an hour the sea swells were smaller. The
rain kept on, but it too had lessened. The water changed
color too, growing less dark. It seemed they had left the Darq
waters behind.

As much as Yu-ning wished she could stay with the naval
vessel, she knew she had unfinished business away south, on
Farcara Island. After refilling her pack with fresh water skins
and provisions, she climbed down one of the steel ladders,
assisted by Jonas. "You will be safe in the imperial city on
Tunzai, Jonas. Perhaps we will meet again some day!" she said.

Jonas waved goodbye as Yu-ning settled herself in the
saddle, removing Lightcaster from around her shoulder and

tying it securely to the back of the saddle next to her pack. Minkaro pulled away from the white vessel and headed due south. Soon the ship was out of sight, and they were back on course toward their original destination. The farther they traveled, the fairer the weather. Through the night they traveled without incident. The sky was clear, and the stars were out, but there was an increasing chill in the air.

Early the next morning, Yu-ning awoke to find Minkaro swimming with renewed urgency. "They are back, Yu-ning." About a half mile behind them she could see four dark dorsal fins slicing through the smooth waters. "How did they pick up our trail so easily again, Minkaro?" asked Yu-ning, as she turned around to look at their pursuers.

Behind her, though, she found her answer. "Minkaro, look! My pink crystal necklace is leaving a trail of light in the water—maybe that is how they picked up our trail again!" Though the sharks were color-blind, they must indeed have found Yu-ning and Minkaro by the light trail they left in their wake. Yu-ning quickly dropped the necklace under her jacket, which caused the pink lights to stop glowing. But it was too late—the creatures had them in their sights, and no longer needed a light trail.

By midday, the Dark creatures had cut in half the distance to their quarry. They sensed that they were gaining, and increased their speed. Soon, Yu-ning and the pink dolphin could see white shapes ahead. "Icebergs!" shouted Yu-ning.

"Perhaps I can drop you on one of the larger ice floes, Yu-ning, and once again lose those horrible creatures!" As they ventured south, chunks of sea ice increased in number, but none were large enough for Yu-ning to climb upon. The

Darq creatures were now only about a quarter mile behind them.

The ice floes were all around them now, and the air had turned frigid. Yu-ning removed the jacket from her pack—the down jacket Metatron had given her before she left Darqendia—and buttoned it all the way up. She looked around again, fearful that the creatures had gained even more ground. Instead, it seemed that they had fallen behind—the distance had grown between them. "Minkaro, look! They are falling behind!"

It seemed too good to be true, but Minkaro saw that Yu-ning was right. As he looked back, the four fins stopped all together. They were turning around! "Yu-ning! It's the cold—they cannot tolerate the icy waters. Remember how I told you that when I dove deep, they stopped their pursuit? It is the same thing here—they are giving up!"

As the pair surged onward, they saw the four dorsal fins fade in the distance as the creatures swam northward, in the opposite direction. "Thank you, One," Yu-ning whispered as Minkaro glided across the glassy water in the direction of Farcara Island.

# Twenty-Five

# Escape

**D**EEP DOWN, Romeo knew he wasn't on Rainbow Island, running with Yu-ning on the beach. He knew he was drowning. The heavy cloth from his makeshift rope entombed him, the weight dragging him deeper into the churning waters.

Still, the water *was* purple and glowing around him. Then he saw it, bobbing against his chest—his crystal heart necklace was glowing, and a soft purple light was shimmering in the water around him. *But if I am drowning,* thought Romeo, *whose hand is that?*

There! He grabbed Yu-ning's hand, and she was pulling him upward. As he teetered just on the brink of consciousness, his final thought was that it was impossible. *Yu-ning is far away—a world away. She is safe on Rainbow Island, isn't she?* But the hand definitely was grabbing his, and he felt himself surging upward.

He broke the surface, air exploding into his lungs. Suparna was paddling in the water, and Metatron was on his back, leaning low—it was the wizard who had reached down to grab hold of Romeo's hand. Suparna helped push Romeo upward as Metatron pulled the exhausted boy onto Suparna's wing. The bird turned himself around to exit the large sea cave.

Romeo dragged himself onto Suparna's back, wrapping his arms around Metatron as they emerged from the cave into the choppy waters below the cliffs. Magic poked his head out of Metatron's pocket and jumped onto Romeo's shoulder. "I am so happy that you made it, Romeo. Our plan worked!"

"Magic, I hope you are right. Hopefully the warlock and his dragon won't discover I am gone until we are far away from this terrible place!"

Romeo saw that they were directly below the obsidigon's lair. The foreboding cliffs of Baggul Island loomed above them, sending a shiver down Romeo's spine. "Hold on—here we go!" said Suparna as he took flight, heading east toward Tunzai Island, the home of the imperial princess in her floating palace. As they made their way away from the island, Romeo was full of questions. "Metatron, how did you find me?" the boy asked.

"Magic returned to the cliff above the obsidigon's lair just before dawn, and told us your plan about the underground river," said Metatron. "We flew above the island, using the low clouds as cover. We kept circling the island, looking for you along the coast. It was Magic who spotted a very faint purple glow coming from that sea cave. We quickly deduced that it was your purple crystal heart that was causing the light. Thankfully, the cave was large enough for Suparna to enter."

Romeo held the small purple gem in his hands, thankful for its light and for his friends. "Thank you, Magic. Thank you, everyone, for helping me." The small frog jumped into Romeo's pocket, a smile of contentment on his face.

"Romeo, did you see any sign of the Seven Sacred Crystals?" Metatron asked.

"No, Master. I didn't really have a chance to explore, though—they threw me in the cave prison straight away," Romeo said.

"That's all right, Romeo. We will find the crystals. For now, we are off to Tunzai Island, to seek counsel with the Royal Empress. I must give her a full report on everything that is happening."

They flew east as the sun rose before them, warming Romeo's chilled bones and raising the spirits of the small party. Romeo's purple heart crystal rested against his chest, casting its light outward. As they flew across the sky, a vivid purple trail of light could be seen for miles behind them.

As Suparna flew away from Baggul Island, little did he know that the very gem that had saved Romeo's life was also leaving a telltale trail for the enemy to follow. And it didn't take long for the dragon to realize the boy was gone: the obsidigon could no longer smell Romeo's flesh.

Enraged, Hobaling mounted the dragon and set out with terrible speed, heading in the direction of his quarry. The purple path was faint but visible, making easy tracking for the obsidigon and the warlock.

# Twenty-Six

# Farcara

"WE ARE SAFE FOR NOW, Yu-ning, for those creatures won't follow us into the frosty waters around
Farcara Island," Minkaro said. In the distance, a breathtaking
island appeared, with tall, snowcapped peaks rising above the
sea. The pair swam into an immense fjord—a steep ocean
passage with ice and rock jutting up hundreds of feet on
either side. The fjord narrowed and came to an end where a
long, rocky beach met the water. Just beyond the beach was
a village. Here Minkaro and Yu-ning parted ways, the dark-
haired girl removing her pack along with Lightcaster.

"I will come to this spot, Yu-ning, every day at noon to
rendezvous with you once your business is done. Use your
pink crystal to signal me when you return. Best of luck, and
may the light be with you." Yu-ning crossed the rocky beach
and then turned to wave goodbye. Minkaro decided to stay
the night in this protected place—close to the village, in
case Yu-ning needed him.

Yu-ning entered the village and was greeted at the local inn by a kind woman with soft eyes. She glowed with the light of love, and Yu-ning was heartened to be out of the darkness of the ghost ship, in a place where people were kind and friendly. The innkeeper told her that she did, indeed, know of the legend of Joshua, who the village elders believed lived near the top of the island's tallest peak, called Snowy Mountain.

"This is the mining town of Caer-a-mor, young lady. Our livelihood depends on that mountain that towers over our village. We mine basalt, magnesium, and potassium from the mountain." The innkeeper explained that there were daily expeditions up the mountain—treasure hunters seeking their fortune, chasing stories of hidden caves with gold pieces the size of a fist. "You can normally find treasure seekers at the trailhead early in the morning. You could hike to the top with such a group, I would think. But don't get your hopes up, little one. No one really ever finds anything."

She recalled Anne, the girl from the factory on Darqendia, telling her about the village. Yu-ning asked the innkeeper if she remembered the sisters, Anne and Ariadne. "Oh yes, the sweet dears," said the woman. "So sad about their parents, killed in a mining accident. I believe the girls are at school now, on Malinga Island."

Yu-ning was too tired to explain what had actually happened to the girls, so she said, "They are both fine—they live on Rainbow Island now, and attend a different school." The innkeeper was glad to hear news of the orphaned sisters. She showed Yu-ning to her room, where the weary traveler was happy to have a hot bath, a tasty meal, and a full night's sleep in a comfortable bed. She awoke before the sun, refreshed and ready to face Snowy Mountain.

After a simple breakfast, Yu-ning prepared to leave. As she stepped outside, the innkeeper stopped her. "You don't want to climb the mountain unprepared," the innkeeper said, handing Yu-ning a pair of hand-woven gloves and a thick scarf. Yu-ning thanked her and headed out.

She easily found the wide trail behind the inn, which led steadily upward toward the foot of the mountain. During the night it snowed, and a pure white blanket dusted the entire valley. The peak of Snowy Mountain was impressive—it rose majestically above the beach and village, its lower slopes covered in pine, with vast amounts of snow covering the treeless upper peaks. The summit was reflecting the light of the early morning sun, taking on a pinkish hue. It was a breathtaking vision. Yu-ning was amazed as she gazed at the beautiful peaks and valleys leading up to the crest, framed in pure white snow.

It was a brisk morning, and the air was frosty, but she was dressed for it, thanks to Metatron and the jacket he gave to her, as well as her new gloves and scarf. She walked for almost a mile toward the base of the mountain, her leather boots insulating her feet from the cold snow. Yu-ning paused every now and then to rest and look up at the sky. It was a blissful and quiet journey, and before she knew it, she was at the base of the mountain.

At the very foot of the peak was the trailhead, but before she could see it, she heard the voices of a crowd of people. They were not peaceful sounds, and Yu-ning could sense discord. Rounding a bend in the trail, she saw a small group of adults and children standing at the trail's entrance. All the adults seemed to be speaking at once; no one was listening to the other.

Three adults were gathered together looking at a large map laid out on a rough wooden table next to the trailhead sign. Two were standing to the side, shivering and looking miserable; the remaining adults were gathered at a distance, chatting secretively. Yu-ning noticed that when they weren't distracted by their parents' unseemly behavior, the three children had moments when they were overcome by the landscape. They looked up at the tall snow-covered mountain with smiles of innocence and awe. When they refocused their attention on their parents, their faces fell again, and they became solemn. This made Yu-ning's heart sink; she knew she needed to offer help. She walked toward them with a purposeful stride.

The crowd turned toward her and stared with cool suspicion as she approached. "Hi, everyone, why are you all standing here?" she asked, trying to inject an air of friendliness into the crowd. She smiled broadly. The people looking at the map turned back to their survey, annoyed by the interruption.

A man narrowed his focus on her, wondering if she could help them, and broke the silence. "We are studying the mountain. This is the highest mountain on the island, and within it are labyrinths and veins of gold. We are studying the maps so we can decide upon the best route."

The man next to him elbowed him in the ribs as if he had divulged too much information. He and his wife stared at Yu-ning. The woman said, "Do you come from here? Do you know this place?"

Her husband continued, "We are on an expedition, and we hear that there are treasures inside this mysterious mountain."

"Treasures?" Yu-ning asked inquisitively. The adults stayed silent and continued huddling around the map; they looked guarded and tightened their circle. "I don't think there are treasures in this beautiful mountain," Yu-ning remarked. "Not from what I've been told," she added.

One of the children, a boy around nine years old, whispered to Yu-ning, "I heard them say that this mountain has hidden caves full of gold. They want to find the gold, but they don't know if the information is accurate."

"Oh, I see. Well, look at this magnificent mountain—I believe there are treasures waiting for us. What's your name?" Yu-ning asked sweetly.

"James," the boy replied, smiling. Yu-ning held out her hand and James took it.

"Well, James, the only way to find out is to climb up the mountain. I'm sure it holds treasures of a different kind, don't you? Look how magical it is. And what are your names?" asked Yu-ning, gazing at two little girls who looked to be about seven years old.

"My name is Marisol, and this is my sister, Solimar. We are twins. But my sister is deaf, so if you want to talk with her, you need to speak where she can see your face—she reads lips!"

"Oh, but I know some sign language, Marisol. We learned it at my school!" With that, Yu-ning signed to Solimar that she was happy to meet her. Solimar's face lit up when she realized Yu-ning understood sign language, and she started gesturing very rapidly back to Yu-ning.

Yu-ning began to laugh, and said, "Whoa, you are going really fast! I can't follow you. Sorry—I wish my signing was better!"

Solimar started to laugh too and said, "That's all right. I can just read your lips, and talk to you that way." Yu-ning was amazed at how clearly Solimar could speak. She was already feeling a warm kinship with James and the twins.

Yu-ning tried to gather all the adults together and said, "We can go find the treasures together. We can climb this beautiful mountain. I am trying to find a man named Joshua—some say he lives at the top."

A man replied, "She is right, we should start our climb. We've come all this way to make this expedition. Moreover, we've been standing here for hours. I'm not going home empty-handed."

"Yes," another man agreed. "Either we do it now or we turn around."

"Well, we don't even know if there are gem deposits; it may just be a legend," said James's mother. This theory elicited a withering look from another woman in the group.

"Come on, Mom, look at how beautiful it is, just like this girl said," James said, turning toward Yu-ning. "What's your name?"

"Yu-ning," she said cheerfully.

"Just like Yu-ning said. Let's climb it; let's do it!"

Yu-ning removed her pink crystal heart necklace from under her jacket in an attempt to bring more light into the tense situation. A glow of pink mist surrounded the children, but hopeful smiles were lost on the parents, who didn't seem to notice the pink light. They turned back to one another and continued talking about safety measures. The children looked crestfallen.

Yu-ning saw brightness out of the corner of her eye and turned in anticipation. It was One. He appeared at Yu-ning's side dressed in brilliant white clothing, beautiful white light flowing around him, mixing in with the hues of her pink crystal. Yu-ning, James, and the twins saw him and were astounded by his awesome presence and the warmth of his divine light. Yu-ning introduced One as her special friend. Several adults noticed the children's strange behavior and walked over to investigate. The children's eyes were wide and their smiles were broad and beautiful. They were entranced.

James's mother interrupted this reverie. "What are you kids doing?" she said. "James, stop daydreaming; I told you I needed you to help us hold these maps."

James looked at his mother and said softly, "You don't see the man dressed in white, Mom?"

"See what?" she said, with mild irritation. "James, I don't have the patience for your games right now. We have to get moving; it's getting colder." She led James away from the girls, but as she pulled him away his eyes remained fixed on One. The children realized none of the adults could see One, and they knew they were in the midst of something magical and special.

One said, "It is true. There are treasures on top of the mountain; and it's true that Joshua is at the top—that your climb will be rewarded. But you must go quickly and only follow the path of light. Though the Darq creatures were not able to follow you here, Yu-ning, there is still danger here. So never stray from the lighted path. Be strong and follow the light. And help the others find the way. Let love be your guide."

With those powerful words, One vanished into the cold crisp air in a shower of soft lights. The children looked at each other in astonishment. "Did you hear what he said?" Yu-ning asked.

"Yes. And he was so beautiful, Yu-ning! Who is it?" said Marisol.

"That is One—he is a divine protector—like an angel," responded Yu-ning.

Solimar began to sign at Yu-ning, but then smiled and switched to speaking words. "What did he mean about *dark creatures?*"

Yu-ning was amazed that although Solimar was deaf, she could hear One. But then, Yu-ning remembered how One had spoken to her in her cave, though Metatron was unable to hear his voice. "It's a long story," Yu-ning said to Solimar, "but just know that a dark presence is loose in the land, and that is why I need to get to the top. This man, Joshua, may have something that could help us defeat the darkness."

"We will help you!" Solimar said to Yu-ning.

"I never believed that I could see an angel!" exclaimed Marisol.

Yu-ning nodded eagerly. "Yes, always believe. Never let anyone tell you that the magic you see is not real."

Yu-ning pointed at the adults. "Look! Your parents are getting ready to leave. Let's climb up the mountain and lead them to the top. There is a man at the top—perhaps he has gifts for all of us!" Yu-ning was shouting with excitement as she rallied the children, who walked over to join their parents. They gathered together behind the adults, who were whispering to one another and pointing toward several trails that branched off from the main trailhead only a short way up the mountain. One of the parents saw how excited the children were and looked suspicious. "What are you kids talking about?"

"We are going to climb the mountain. There is a kind man waiting for us, and he is going to give every one of us treasures," Marisol answered innocently. Yu-ning and the children nodded intently.

"That's ridiculous," one adult responded. "No one lives at the top of this mountain—that is just a local wives' tale. But maybe there are people there who can lead us to the secret mines, where the gold is located."

"It's true, it's true! One just told Yu-ning it's true," the children exclaimed together.

"Which one? You are not making any sense. I don't have time for your foolishness," an elderly man said.

"Not *which* one. Just One!" yelled James. The man just stared blankly at the boy. "He told Yu-ning that a man lives on top of the mountain and he is going to give us gifts!"

The adults shut the children down. "There is only an old hunter up there, from what I've heard. And he is poor—lives in a shack, folks say," exclaimed one of the men.

"We don't want to be late," Yu-ning continued. "Follow us; we know the way. Hurry and come with us."

"We will lead the way, little girl," said James's father. "You children can walk behind us together, but stay near and obey us." The children looked at one another and shared confused looks. "Father, look at this pink path ahead of us—don't you see it?" Solimar signed to her father, and pointed at the path of light from Yu-ning's crystal necklace. The pink path of light wound up the mountain and onto one of the four trails that branched off just up ahead. Her father signed back to her, telling her to settle down and stay in line.

"Remember One's guidance," Yu-ning said to the three other children. "We must follow the light. That is all we have to do. Don't doubt now before we even begin. We follow the light."

The children looked at her and nodded solemnly. "All right, let's go," said James.

The adults—eight in all—clustered in a mass, moving forward in fits and starts in between arguments and confusion. Their doubts, fears, and skepticism spread like a cacophonous drone. Negative comments swept through the crowd as the children stepped forward.

"Follow the path that is projected by Yu-ning's pink crystal heart," Marisol said to her mother and father.

"What are you talking about, girls?" a woman snapped. "Don't you see how dangerous this is? This mountain is a death trap. We could die climbing it, and if we're lucky enough to make it to the top, we could get lost on the descent."

Of the four paths that split off from the main trail just in front of them, the pink light was directing them to the trail on the far right. Yu-ning said, "It is this way. Follow the light."

A man spoke up at the same time, not realizing he was corroborating Yu-ning's directions. "I have the map right here; it says we should head to the right 40 degrees and continue south. This is the correct route to the top of the mountain."

The adults acted as if they were following his advice, unwilling to acknowledge that Yu-ning had just said the very same thing! Yu-ning just chuckled.

They all began moving up the mountain. And even though they were all going in the same direction, the adults' reservations were slowing the momentum and flow of the four children. They followed behind the adults, looking at one another with exasperation. Yu-ning spoke up, "Just follow the pink path and you will not need your maps; it will take us safely to the top." The adults ignored her and stopped yet again to look at the map and deliberate among themselves.

Yu-ning and the children took the opportunity to move ahead as the adults were busy with the maps. They walked all the way to the front, excited and energized by the beautiful, colorful path. They were now far ahead of their parents, who didn't even realize the children had passed them. The sounds of the children's laughter caused two adults to look up. Irritated, they yelled, "Get back here right now!" But the children were too far ahead to hear them; the adults had no other choice but to continue on in the same direction. One adult was looking at his own map, which said they needed to continue forward at 45 degrees SW; as he looked up, he saw that the children were already moving ahead in that direction. "They are following the exact coordinates the maps and compass indicate. How do they know where to go!"

"Maybe one of them has been here before, and knows where to look," a woman murmured. "We have to catch up. They won't know what to do with gold nuggets if they find them first. Hurry!" The children were now colorful specks in the distance amidst the white landscape. The adults were quickly scrambling upward on the mountain, leaving their maps aside.

One man said, "Those kids know nothing. They are just going to get lost on the mountain—or lead others to the gem deposits." At that moment, the children rounded a huge

301

rocky outcropping and disappeared out of sight. The adults tried to run up the steep trail, but they couldn't catch up. "I can't see them anymore! Where did they go?" It began to snow, first lightly, and then with increasing heaviness. The trail was becoming difficult to see with the new layer of snow. The adults began to wander down a side trail, headed in the wrong direction. Adjacent to them was the true trail, where the children had journeyed on.

The adults continued to climb, fearing for their lives at every turn. The snow was increasing, and it was clear that a large storm was brewing on the horizon, with dark, ominous grey clouds threatening on distant peaks. The winds became more and more violent. Strong gusts blew, and the snow started whipping across their faces. They couldn't see beyond the sheet of snow, and stumbled as the incline grew steeper. The wind chill factor dropped below zero—they were slowing down now, and losing their stamina. All the adults were walking alone, trying their best to navigate the way forward. In the distance, they could hear a distinct echo of the children's sweet singsong voices. Yu-ning and the children were making steady progress. They used their small hands to help one another as they traversed the pink mountain trail.

"I can't go on. I am so tired and cold; we're being led to our grave," one woman wailed.

"I'm turning around and going back down," another man agreed. "It's too cold on this mountain, and I can't see anything. There is nothing here!"

Up ahead, Yu-ning stopped in her tracks and closed her eyes. She was silent for a full minute. "Everyone stop—the adults are in trouble. They have lost their way. They can't see us and don't know which way to go. We have to go back and help them." The children all agreed, and they started back down the mountain toward the adults. The pink light flowed ahead of them as they descended the mountain with dexterity and speed. They found the adults a short way up the side trail, huddling under a snowbank, cold, tired, and shivering.

Some were crying, others were shouting and arguing, until one of the adults looked up and saw the children. "Oh thank goodness, we have found you! Don't you know you could be killed out here? Where have you been?"

Yu-ning spoke up for the children. "We can see the summit up above. We came back to help you and lead you there."

"We're turning around," said one of the men. "Now come, all of you. Follow us; we're going back to the village."

"No, don't go back—we are so close," Yu-ning said. "Keep following the path; we'll get there soon. We've come back to guide you. Follow us."

"Just follow us," said James, appealing to his mother and father. He picked up a stick and drew two lines in the snow on either side of the path. "Walk straight, and don't go beyond these points."

As they walked, the snow began to let up a bit. Several adults stopped in their tracks and noticed a trail heading southeast, along a ridge leading away from the pink path. "That trail looks like it is well traveled, and leads straight up to the summit. Let's go this way!" a man shouted to his wife and a friend who had accompanied the couple. The other two adults nodded and started to follow the man. But the children were concerned: it was off the pink path, and something felt ominous about the trail, which cut across a huge rock scree formation, with a high overhang of snow several hundred yards above. Yu-ning remembered One's firm words and looked at the other children with concern. They called out warnings to the three adults.

The couple and their friend ignored Yu-ning and started across the path. The other adults, however, stayed where they were, silently watching their fellow hikers head off on the other trail. About halfway to the other side, one of the men stopped and turned back toward the hikers looking on. "We will reach the summit before you! Just wait and see who finds the gold first." There was a low rumble as the man shouted across to the hikers.

An older gentleman, whose name was Elliot, stepped next to Yu-ning. He had a look of concern on his face as he stared at the three hikers exposed on the face of the mountain. "He mustn't yell," he said to Yu-ning. Then, in a louder voice, but trying not to yell, he called out to the three other adults, saying, "Keep your voices down. You don't want to—"

The man on the mountain face screamed back, "What? We can't hear you!" in a loud, booming voice.

Elliot made a slicing motion across his throat, trying to get the man to stop yelling. Then there was a second rumble, and everyone turned in the direction of the deep sound. High above, as if in slow motion, the large overhang of snow gave way with a deafening crack, sending a giant wall of snow crashing downslope.

This time, Elliot screamed as loud as he could, "RUN! RUN BACK!" The panic-stricken adults on the face saw the avalanche headed their way and began to move as quickly as they could back toward the horrified adults and children. The woman was closest and had the greatest chance of getting back to safety. The men were close behind, running with every ounce of speed they could manage on the rocky trail.

Yu-ning screamed encouragement to the three adults. "Look at us. Don't look up. You can make it!" The adults were getting closer, but it was uncertain if they could escape the wall of snow racing toward them. The woman reached the nine adults first, falling into Elliot's arms. Her husband was about twenty steps behind, and their friend was behind him. The wave of snow was nearly upon them, and they had only a few seconds to escape its terrible path.

Solimar ran forward, holding a climbing rope she had removed from her pack. She yelled, "Hold me!" to the adults as she threw the rope to the first man. Yu-ning and several adults grabbed the end of the rope, along with Solimar. The rope flew in the air, and just as the first man grabbed it, they could see the second man lunging for the legs of the first man.

The avalanche slammed into the men, and instantly, Solimar was yanked violently downhill. The adults held on with all their might, some gaining a grip on the rope, and others holding Solimar around the waist and shoulders. After a few seconds, the rumble stopped. The snow was still. All was quiet.

"Where are they?" exclaimed James.

"Everyone take a section of the rope and start pulling," yelled Elliot. But it was no use. The weight of the snow made any progress with the rope impossible. "I have another idea," Elliot said, and he started to follow the rope, hand over hand, through the snow down the hill. It was deep, and everyone took hold of one another's belts and jackets, forming a human chain as they followed the rope downhill.

"I think they are here!" yelled Elliot. They had reached the end of the rope and couldn't pull anymore. The rope disappeared straight down into the snow. "Dig!" yelled James. Everyone dug furiously, the soft snow of the avalanche giving way with relative ease.

"There's a hand!" yelled Yu-ning, as a thumb and index finger protruded from the bottom of the hole they had dug. They continued furiously, and soon were able to reach the back of the man's jacket and pull upward. As his head broke through the snow, he gasped, taking in a huge gulp of crisp mountain air.

"Where is Ewan?" the rescued man said, referring to his friend who had grabbed his legs just as he had caught the rope from Solimar. The thirteen hikers dug furiously, but try as they might, they could not find the second man. The morning wore on, and for two hours the group searched. It was Ewan's friend who finally found him, a bit farther down the mountain, a gloved hand poking from the snow. Though they tried to resuscitate the lifeless man, it was to no avail. He was gone.

The couple decided to return to Caer-a-mor to arrange for transportation of the body from the mountain. Though the remaining hikers offered to join them, they insisted that everyone press on. "Ewan would have wanted you all to get to the top. Please don't call off your search for the treasure now." With reluctance, the group voted to continue on. Yu-ning wished she could turn back, but she knew that her mission had meaning beyond this snowy mountain. She had no choice but to press on, in search of Joshua and the elusive quiver of arrows.

# Twenty-Seven

# Mountain

$\mathcal{T}$HE CLIMBERS CONTINUED UPWARD in a somber line, moving in silence. The snow eased even more, and bits of blue sky could be seen through the mass of grey and white clouds swirling around the mountain. No one spoke; all were still very shaken by the sad events of the morning.

Marisol moved up the path to walk just behind Yu-ning. "Why didn't they listen to us, Yu-ning?"

Yu-ning slowly shook her head and said, "I don't know, Marisol. Maybe it's because we are children, and adults aren't used to taking direction from kids. I wish they could see the pink path, but they can't, or won't." Yu-ning was crying, though she swallowed her tears, not wanting to upset the younger girl even more.

She missed Romeo so much right now. Oh, what she would give to be playing music with her best friend from the top of the Great Kapok Tree! The cold seeped into her upper left arm, the familiar dull ache of her wound reminding her of her foe and the tasks before her. She trudged on, though, and took comfort in the twins, James, and James's parents, who had been deeply shaken by the avalanche and the death of the couple's friend, Ewan. It softened them, and they began to warm to Yu-ning as they hiked ever closer to the summit of Snowy Mountain.

The small party stopped to rest in the early afternoon. The storm clouds had cleared, giving way to a brilliant cerulean sky. Though the temperatures were still very low, the warmth from the sun was a very welcome change. The grandeur of the surrounding mountains was awe-inspiring: the massive peaks rose up in all directions, with the picturesque village and deep blue fjord well below them. Yu-ning pretended she could see Minkaro doing flips in the water. She strained to see any sign of his pink body, but she couldn't make out anything at this distance. Beyond the village and the deep fjord, Yu-ning could just make out the shining reflection of the sea in the distance.

"It is beautiful here, isn't it?" James's mother, Lorelei, sat down on a flat rock next to Yu-ning.

"It is very beautiful, yes," Yu-ning replied.

"Are you here alone, Yu-ning? I mean, where is your family—your parents?"

"I am from Rainbow Island, and it is a long way from here. The teachers at the school raised me. I was brought to the Island when I was a baby. I believe my parents were from Darqendia, but I don't know what happened to them. I am here to seek out a man named Joshua. I am hoping he can help me."

"A young girl like you should not be alone in a place like this, Yu-ning!"

"Oh, I am not alone, ma'am. My friend Minkaro is waiting for me near the village." But that's all Yu-ning said. She was too tired to explain to an adult that her friend was a talking pink dolphin, and that she was here to find some magic arrows that could be used to stop a creepy fire-breathing dragon. Instead, she added, "When we reach Joshua, he will be able to help all of us, I think."

"That's fine, Yu-ning. What matters is that we are all together. And don't worry, we won't let any harm come to you," added Lorelei, patting Yu-ning's arm.

"And I won't let any harm come to you either, ma'am!" With this, Lorelei let out an easy laugh, marveling at the precocious nature of this unusual little girl. "Tell me about that pretty necklace of yours," said Lorelei.

Yu-ning beamed. "This is my crystal heart necklace . . ." Yu-ning said, and then paused. "I have an idea. Do you want to play a game?"

Lorelei nodded her head, smiling at Yu-ning. "Close your eyes," Yu-ning said. Lorelei obeyed. "Now hold out your hands. All right, good." Yu-ning placed the glowing pink gem in the woman's hands, and placed her smaller hands on top. "Now think of the one thing in the world that you love more than anything . . . do you have it in your mind?"

"Yes. Yes, I do."

"Open your eyes!" Yu-ning instructed. As Lorelei opened her eyes, the most beautiful, pure light she had ever seen glowed before her. It was flowing all around her in transparent wisps of pink, rose, mauve, puce, fuchsia, and amaranth.

"It . . . it's amazing! It's like heaven! Where did this light come from?" exclaimed Lorelei, taking in the beauty of the colors as they radiated away from Yu-ning, illuminating the trail as it weaved further up the mountain. Yu-ning took her pink crystal heart and placed it next to Lorelei's heart, pressing it against her coat. "From here!" Yu-ning said, with a broad grin on her face. "The light is from your heart—you just needed to see with the eyes of innocence and love. By the way, who were you thinking about?"

Lorelei looked at Yu-ning with a smile, and then turned her head to look at her son, James. He was resting on a nearby rock, stretched out on his back, soaking in the warmth of the sun. Yu-ning just smiled back. As they took to the trail once again, Yu-ning was encouraged that at least one adult could now see the pink path. Yu-ning turned to Lorelei and said in a low voice, "Why don't you take the lead now? I think the other adults will listen to you more than they will to us kids."

Lorelei understood Yu-ning's meaning and nodded her head. "Here, I can take a turn in the lead," she said to Elliot in a louder voice. He smiled and yielded the front position to Lorelei, who turned around and winked at Yu-ning. With Lorelei at the point, the group moved more swiftly. With the pink rays of Yu-ning's necklace leading the way, Lorelei had no trouble covering the last remaining section of trail before the tired, cold group neared the summit. As the afternoon wore on, the shadows on the mountain lengthened, and the temperature began to drop.

"Hurry, everyone, this way!" shouted Lorelei, reading the coordinates on her compass as she pretended to study a thick topographical map. Again she winked at Yu-ning and said, "We are almost at the summit." Talk of gold deposits had dissipated since they had left the tragic scene of the avalanche. However, now that the group had nearly reached the top of the mountain, a few of the adults became more animated, and picked up the discussion of the elusive treasure once again. "The caves are said to be just on the other side of the summit, as you begin your descent down the south face," said Elliot, who was limping from a stiff leg.

"No, that's not right," one of the other women said. "The golden nuggets are said to encrust the walls of a deep crevasse, located *east* of the summit. I heard an old man in my village on Tunzai Island say that when he accidentally stumbled on the hidden crevasse, the nuggets were embedded in the walls like barnacles on the side of a ship. All he had to do was scrape his knife against the ice and rock, and the gold would pop into his hand!" Back and forth they argued, with most of the adults entering the debate. Yu-ning noticed that neither of James's parents, however, was saying a word.

They entered an area of the mountain where the trail was narrow, clinging to the side of the cliff wall, in some places no wider than two feet. "Don't look down," Yu-ning said to James, Solimar, and Marisol, who were all walking single file behind her, doing their best to hug the cold rock wall as much as possible. Not following her own advice, Yu-ning glanced down. She immediately regretted her decision: the cliff fell away more than a thousand feet into grey mist below.

This part of the journey was slow going, and seemed to take an agonizing amount of time. Then the cliff face turned sharply, and around the corner the party could see the trail open up into a broad area of rocks and boulders where the cliff gave way to flatter ground. The children celebrated as the weary travelers decided to stop once again, if only for a moment, and then press on before darkness fell.

Yu-ning wandered a little bit away from the group and noticed that the trail once again broke off in different directions—one trail heading due south, and two other trails heading east and northwest, respectively. As she held up her pink crystal gemstone, its lights illuminated the path heading south. She hurried back to the group to inform the others.

"My husband and I are heading *east*," said the woman who had talked about the hidden crevasse brimming with gold. The husband added, "We will make camp at the head of the icefall, and begin our explorations in the morning."

"I would advise against that," said Elliot. "That route is treacherous. Many never return from those icefalls. The ground is unsteady, and the crevasses are difficult to see— sometimes they are buried under just a few inches of new snow. One false step, and that's it for you. You need ice ladders, crampons, pickaxes . . . and a lot more rope to traverse that part of the mountain. You don't have the proper equipment!"

"We are going," announced the husband, his chin slightly raised in the late-afternoon air. No one else spoke. The couple headed east away from the main group, which set its sights on the southern path. They figured they had about two hours of daylight left and were determined to find a sheltered place where they could spend the night. Lorelei stayed in the front, following the pink light emanating from Yu-ning's necklace, its light floating over and around her as Yu-ning walked just behind.

Ahead of them the trail was visible, even after the day's fresh snowfall, but it was getting harder to follow in the fading light. Here at the summit, the mountain was flat; no vegetation or trees grew here, as they were far above the tree line.

Then something curious happened: though there was only one trail, the pink light broke off from the main path, leading Lorelei across open, rock-strewn terrain.

"Where are we going?" asked an older woman named Caroline, who was unrelated to anyone else in the group. "The trail leads straight on—why are we heading cross-country here?"

It was a reasonable question, but Lorelei lacked a satisfying answer. Yu-ning spoke up. "It's because there are treasures in this direction. I guarantee it."

"How do you know that for sure, little girl?" asked Caroline.

"I just do. You need to trust me."

Caroline gave a cheerless laugh. "Um, no, I don't. I am staying on the path."

Of the ten members left in the group, Yu-ning, James, Solimar, Marisol, and both sets of their parents decided to keep moving cross-country. The woman stood alone on the trail, while the elderly gentlemen, Elliot, stood undecided.

"Come with me, Elliot. We shouldn't veer from the trail," Caroline said.

"Perhaps not, but the first rule of the wilderness is to stay together. I am staying with the group. And you should too." Caroline was furious, but she knew it would be foolish to head off by herself, especially with night nearly upon them.

As they set out again, the pink light led them around enormous boulders that littered the summit of the mountain. It was a labyrinth, weaving in and out, in no easily discernable direction. Then, the pink path dropped steeply into a cleft in the rocks—hidden from above, and only visible if one was standing just in the right place between the two boulders at the entrance.

"It's a secret cave!" exclaimed James. Though technically it was not a cave, but a high-walled slot canyon, the effect was the same. It was dark and cold, with snow piled on ledges above and some scattered on the ground, where it had fallen from the exposed walls above. The hikers followed the natural stone passageway for half an hour, the light ever fading, evening nearly upon them. Just when Yu-ning was beginning to falter in her hope for a good ending, the slot canyon opened up onto a beautiful, flat open ledge. High cliff walls soared above them on three sides; the view in front was open, the mountains and valleys of Farcara stretching away south into the weak, dusky light.

It was a natural tabletop ledge, nearly a perfect square—about a quarter-mile wide and long. In the middle of this flat table of stone stood a handsome cabin made of granite rocks, huge wood timbers, and large, heavy windows. It had a sturdy wooden roof and a tall stone chimney, a thin line of grey smoke floating from the top. It was lovely—and fantastically out of place here at the top of the world.

The ten weary travelers stood for a moment, trying to comprehend this place. As they stood there, just staring at the handsome cabin, the door swung open and a tall man with long dark hair and a dark beard walked onto the porch. He was dressed in a huge wool jacket.

"Don't tell me!" he yelled. "You must be Yu-ning, correct?"

# Twenty-Eight

# Quiver

YU-NING STEPPED FORWARD. "And if I'm not mistaken, you are Joshua."

"That's right. It seems we both expected this meeting!" said the dark-haired man, handsome eyes measuring Yu-ning, a long pipe clamped between straight white teeth. "You are all welcome here," said Joshua to the approaching travelers. "Come in—the night is going to be a cold one, and I'd prefer to keep the heat within my home. Quickly, enter, enter!"

The four children and six adults entered the cabin, stamping the snow from their boots before crossing the large wooden threshold. The cabin was large, rustic, and welcoming. All the furniture was hand-carved from gnarled pine and other woods, presumably gathered on the slopes below the summit. There were tables crafted from slabs of granite and a stairway leading to a second-story loft. The walls were adorned with beautiful charcoal drawings of the mountain, horned sheep, snow leopards, eagles, bears, and hawks.

Lying on a huge, flat-stone table in the center of the room was a large sketch. It was clear that Joshua had been working on the drawing when he heard the visitors approach, as pieces of charcoal were scattered around the edges of the thick paper upon which he was working. Yu-ning was startled to see that the drawing was of an obisidigon, and that Joshua had gotten every detail correct, right down to the hard black scales covering its back.

The others removed their coats and gathered round the huge stone fireplace to warm cold and aching feet and hands. Yu-ning stared at the ominous drawing on the table. "Where did you see this?" she asked, tension creeping into her voice. "Have you seen one of the dragons? Is it here on the mountain?" she inquired with alarm.

Joshua was quick to assure her that she was not in danger. "No, Yu-ning. I saw it—in my dreams. I also saw *you*. For the past seven nights I have had the same dream. A dark-haired girl with intelligent eyes visits me, seeking that which only I know of—save one other in this wide world. In the same dream, I see this—" He removed the pipe and tapped the bowl against the drawing. "I know the creature only through old tales—told long ago by a tall wizard on a colorful island, and before that, at the outer reaches of my memory, by kin now forgotten. But oh yes, I have seen it, for it haunts my dreams."

The other children moved away from the fire, fascinated by the picture of the dragon. "I like your picture," said Marisol. "But it's a little scary."

Joshua smiled at the girl and proceeded to welcome everyone to his home, furtively placing a blank sheet of paper over his obsidigon drawing. "My name is Joshua, and as you can probably guess, I don't get many visitors here on top of the

world. And though I don't mind the solitude of my mountain perch, I also welcome strangers on those rare occasions
when they land upon my doorstep. Welcome to the Porch
of Tranquility!"

On the wall next to the beautiful drawings was something that caught Yu-ning's eye—a beautiful arrow case,
fashioned from rich, dark brown leather. Inside the quiver
were finely crafted arrows—Yu-ning counted a dozen. The
case and the missiles looked as if they were from another
age, a distant time. Intricate designs were etched into the
rich leather. Curiously, the tips of the arrows were rounded,
and shiny.

Joshua noticed Yu-ning's eyes fixed on the arrows and
leaned down to whisper in her ear. "Don't draw attention to
the Quiver of Light or ask me any questions about it tonight.
A person can't be too careful."

James approached Joshua and asked him, "Why do you
call this place the Porch of Tranquility?"

"That is an excellent question, young man. When I first
saw this place, I found it completely by accident. I was a
bit lost, wandering through the boulder field above, and
I stumbled upon the narrow cleft that leads to this ledge.
When I emerged from the passageway, I was overcome with
wonder—the way the cliff walls soar above us on three sides,
the large rock ledge with its flat, smooth surface, and the
sheer cliff, which drops off in front here. It reminded me of
a giant stone porch. And when I sit on this massive porch,
high above the kingdoms of the earth, I feel as if it is the
most tranquil place this side of heaven. The Porch of Tranquility!" Joshua smiled at James, who was pleased with the
tall man's answer.

The company spent a peaceful night at the Porch of Tranquility. Joshua fed them well and gave them soft feather-down blankets, which they heaped upon the ground in mounds. Everyone slept well, the physical and emotional toll of the day driving all to an early bed. In the morning, they gathered round the table for steaming mugs of tea, cream, biscuits, dried fruit, and a wide assortment of nuts. It was common fare, but satisfying, and it tasted wonderful to the visitors.

"You are here for treasure, yes?" said Joshua, his eyes narrow, his pipe perched thoughtfully in his mouth. The question startled the adults; Yu-ning smiled, while James and the twins sat up in their seats at the mention of treasure.

Before anyone could answer his question, Joshua added, "There isn't much gold on Snowy Mountain. Oh, I've looked. I looked for a dozen years. That is what first drew me here— the allure of wealth in the form of a major gold strike. Well, I can tell you with certainty that I have surveyed this entire mountain, roots to peak, and no treasure exists. At least, none that you can trade for money."

"What do you mean?" asked Elliot.

"The treasure of this place is found in its beauty, its *tranquility*. The wealth of the mountain is its grandeur. It commands respect, deserves reverence, and yields to no man or woman seeking to tame or control it. The treasure is here, all around us," Joshua said. He gestured toward the cabin windows, beyond which the guests could see the morning mist blanketing the distant mountains and valleys across the expanse of Farcara. "You just need to look for it," Joshua said, as he rose to refill the teapot.

The children gazed at Joshua, not used to hearing adults talk so forthrightly. James's parents, as well as the twins' mother and father, looked chastened. Elliot smiled thought-fully, and even Caroline seemed at peace. After breakfast, the adults gathered their gear; Joshua volunteered to guide them back to the north face for their descent down the mountain.

Yu-ning was staying, much to the chagrin of Lorelei and the three children. But Joshua insisted, and the adults did not argue. "I promise I will treat her well, and will personally escort her back down the mountain when her visit is over," Joshua assured Lorelei.

With the decision made, the rest of the travelers prepared to leave. Yu-ning hugged them all, and stood apart with Soli-mar, Marisol, and James. "Please come visit me on Rainbow Island," Yu-ning said to them. "You will love it there." Yu-ning removed three rainbow-colored beans from her pack and handed one to each of the children. "These are from Rainbow Island. They glow!" As the children looked at their beans, they began to vibrate and grow in their palms. "When you get lonely, or are in a dark place, they will help you find the light again!"

Solimar used sign language to tell Yu-ning that she would miss her. Yu-ning signed back, saying, "I will miss you, too!" The girls hugged.

Yu-ning remained at the cabin while Joshua escorted the six adults and three children across the summit of the mountain. She was sitting on Joshua's porch upon his return, an hour and a half later. During that day and all the next, Joshua showed her his mountain hideaway, and told her what had happened since he and Jacob parted ways twenty-one years before. After Jacob left the *Paragon* that night on Palova Island, Joshua made his way south to Farcara. There were rumors of a gold strike on Snowy Mountain—gold nuggets the size of a man's fist were being pulled from the crevasses and hidden caves of the peak. At least, that was what Joshua had heard.

Joshua spent a dozen years searching every crease and crevasse for the elusive gold. And while he found a little gold, its worth was barely enough to scratch out a meager existence. Though he built a crude cabin only two miles outside Caera-mor, only a few villagers had ever been inside his home. One or two of the old folks who entered the cabin told the story of a beautiful quiver of arrows that hung on the wall. They said the quiver looked remarkably similar to pictures in dusty books depicting Darq Render warriors—the kind who'd fought in the Great War against the obsidigons a century earlier. Only the oldest villagers had relatives who had fought against the obsidigons. Still, the elders recognized the craftsmanship as the work of Darq Render fletchers.

After a light midday supper, Joshua and Yu-ning took advantage of the cloud-free afternoon, hiking the trails surrounding the Porch of Tranquility, taking in the stunning beauty of endless snowcapped peaks as far as the eye could see, with deep green valleys below. Shining ribbons split the deepest valleys—fast-moving rivers flush with snowmelt from the peaks above. As they walked, Joshua asked Yu-ning many questions about his brother, Jacob, and his life on Palova Island. Yu-ning assured him that Jacob was now in a place of harmony and that he had discovered the light of love.

Joshua was gladdened by the news of his brother and explained that over the years the mountain had slowly changed his own heart—that as he explored its terrain seeking gold, he began to awaken to its true wonders. "Even though Metatron and the teachers of Rainbow Island were kind to Jacob and me, I had to rediscover the light in my own heart, in my own way. Metatron tried to show us the light, but a part of me died that night in Darqendia when my mother was slain by the warlock. He not only stole my mother's light, but mine as well. I had a choice to either stay in that dark sadness, or allow the fire within my heart to be rekindled."

"So how did you ignite the light in your heart again, Joshua?" There was a silence then. Yu-ning could hear the wind moving through the rocks, a low whistling that punctuated the quiet.

"I didn't ignite it myself—I know that," said Joshua. "I rediscovered beauty, Yu-ning. It was this place—and I remember the exact day when it happened, some eight years ago. I had been in the mountains for about two weeks, surveying a new section of the mountain I had never explored before. It was brutally cold, and I became lost. I was high on the western face of the mountain, and as darkness fell, I realized I was in real trouble . . ."

Joshua stared out across the range of mountains below as he recalled the experience. "By morning, I couldn't feel my hands or feet, and I became very sleepy. I knew I had frostbite, and if I didn't move, I would die. As I prepared to leave, I saw a white flash on a rock ledge above me. Yu-ning, it was the largest snow leopard I've ever seen, and it was staring at me. And then, it dipped its head three times, and moved off the ledge. It disappeared for a moment, but then there it was, right in front of me. We locked eyes for a second, and the leopard just closed its eyes slowly, and opened them. It turned slowly, and walked in a direction I had not yet explored. Then it stopped and turned to look at me, as if to say, 'Well, are you coming?'"

Yu-ning laughed, and Joshua, still gazing into the distance, continued. "So I followed it. Every few hundred yards, the snow leopard would stop and turn to make sure I was still following. Seven hours later I met up with the main trail, but when I turned to thank the leopard, it had vanished."

"That is an amazing story, Joshua!" said Yu-ning, as they descended the trail back to the Porch of Tranquility. It was late afternoon, and the sun was casting long shadows across the rock faces above. As they walked inside the cabin, Yu-ning asked Joshua if he ever saw the snow leopard again.

"Oh, you mean Snowheart? Wait here for me." Joshua walked to the cabin door and gave a long whistle. He turned around and smiled at Yu-ning for a moment, then peered back outside. The most beautiful cat Yu-ning had ever seen padded into the cabin and began brushing against Joshua's leg. It was four feet long, with magnificent white fur and dark spots, and was purring loudly as Joshua scratched its fluffy head.

"Yu-ning, meet Snowheart. Snowheart, this is the girl I was telling you about—the girl in my dreams!"

Yu-ning was delighted as Snowheart crossed the cabin and sat next to her chair, allowing Yu-ning to pet him. "Yu-ning, thank you for coming here," said the leopard in a deep, resonant voice, looking up at her with piercing light green eyes. "We know it was hard for you, but we also know that this is a critical task you have undertaken."

"But how do you know who I am?" asked Yu-ning, stunned by the amazing cat.

"In my kingdom, Yu-ning, word travels fast. I was hunting yesterday low on the mountain and saw my friend Gamaliel. He is a grizzly bear who lives on the slopes of the fjord—he likes to fish where the rivers flow strong and full of salmon. Gamaliel told me that he met your friend King Minkaro at the water's edge. He is the one who told the story." Yu-ning was overcome with joy—it was heartening to know that she had friends even here, at the end of the world.

The following day, Joshua removed the Quiver of Light from its place above his mantle and laid it on the large stone table next to Lightcaster. "Do you realize, Yu-ning, that it has been nearly a quarter century since the arrows have been reunited with the bow? Look at the arrow tips, here." With a swift motion Joshua ran his finger along the edge of one of the arrows. "Nothing!" said Joshua, raising his finger and showing it to Yu-ning. She expected to see blood, but his finger was uncut.

"They are dull," Joshua said. "Why? I have studied these arrows for more than twenty years, and have never unlocked the mystery—how can arrows with dull points take down an obsidigon?" Yu-ning had no answer for Joshua, nor did he expect one.

"But there is something else, Yu-ning. Something I have not told you. Before I met Snowheart, I often hunted the animals that live in these mountains. On that expedition when I first met Snowheart, I experienced something I couldn't believe—even now, I don't fully understand it." With this, he looked over at Snowheart, who was stretched out on the hearthrug, enjoying the warmth of Joshua's fire. The snow leopard nodded at Joshua, a peaceful smile upon its face.

Joshua walked to the corner of the room and grabbed an old bow resting against the stone wall. It was dusty and clearly had not been used in a great while. "Follow us," he said, as Snowheart rose and followed Joshua outside. Snowheart trotted about thirty feet away, stopped, and turned to face Joshua. Without saying a word, Joshua nocked one of the magic arrows, raised his old bow, and let loose, the arrow flying directly at Snowheart. It happened so quickly that Yu-ning could not intervene—she watched in horror as the arrow flew directly at the leopard's head. Just before it made impact, however, it stopped in midair. It was as if an invisible hand had grabbed it and was holding it, suspended, an inch from the leopard's face! "What? How did it . . . ?" Yu-ning stared in disbelief.

"I had never hunted with the Darq Render arrows before," said Joshua, lowering the weapon. "I always told myself they were not for hunting—that they were sacred, to be protected. But that winter I was low on ammunition, and so before I left on that mining expedition, I grabbed four of the arrows from the Quiver of Light, just in case I ran out of my own hunting arrows—which I did," Joshua said.

"When Snowheart found me near-frozen that morning, I hadn't eaten in days and was desperate. So, as the leopard stood on the ledge above me, I grabbed one of the Darq Render arrows, raised my bow, and loosed the arrow. But the arrow didn't penetrate Snowheart's fur—it did just as it is doing now! It just stopped, floating in the air."

Yu-ning reached her hand toward the arrow, and as her finger touched the shaft, the arrow immediately fell to the ground. She picked it up; it looked just the same as it had before—yew wood shaft, with a black, dull tip.

"Yu-ning, these arrows are not made for destroying nature's creatures or for harming men. Do you understand? Though I cannot be certain, I believe these arrows are only effective on creatures that are *unnatural*—that have been created *by* evil, *for* evil. Does that make sense?"

"I think so," said Yu-ning.

"The Quiver of Light and the Darq Render arrows are yours now, Yu-ning. I don't understand all that is going on, but in my dreams these past several nights, I was visited by a man surrounded by white light, and he spoke to me," Joshua added.

"That is One! He visits me in my dreams, and sometimes when I'm awake," explained Yu-ning.

"In my dream, this man of light—One, as you say—told me to give the Quiver of Light to you," Joshua continued. "And then I heard these words, which I will never forget: 'What you give is an instrument, not a weapon. What you offer is love, not death. And what will come is light, not darkness.' Do you understand it, Yu-ning?"

"I believe I am beginning to understand," said Yu-ning.

Joshua smiled at her, and she smiled back.

# Twenty-Nine

# Sharks

*E*ARLY THE NEXT MORNING, Yu-ning took Lightcaster, along with the Quiver of Light, and strapped them to her pack as she prepared to leave the Porch of Tranquility. As she rearranged her supplies, she removed the Light of Balthazar, admiring its beauty. For the first time, she noticed that its light shimmered in undulating waves, just like the light pattern of her pink crystal heart necklace. The only difference was the Light of Balthazar cast a yellow light.

Yu-ning informed Joshua that her friend would be meeting her at noon, in the bay in front of Caer-a-mor. Joshua assured her that he would have her there by midday. It was a calm, clear, cloudless day. The air was very cold, but as Yu-ning and Joshua descended the mountain, their brisk pace kept her blood pumping, and she was not cold. For the first three hours, Snowheart traveled alongside Joshua, keeping a watchful eye out for danger.

Though Joshua knew every path and trail on the mountain, Yu-ning's crystal heart necklace was shining brightly upon the path. "You don't really need that, you know," said Joshua, breaking the rhythm of their boots crunching upon the trail.

"What, my crystal heart?" Yu-ning asked.

"Yes. You know I know the way, right?"

"Oh, I didn't know you could see the pink lights, Joshua!"

"Well, of course I can see the lights—look how bright they are, even on a sunny day like this. Who could miss them?"

"Oh, you'd be surprised!" Yu-ning said, giving Joshua a big smile.

They could see Caer-a-mor far below. Here Snowheart said goodbye. "It is too dangerous for me to venture any closer to the village, Yu-ning. I must leave you now. May the light forever caress your heart, and may we meet again someday."

Yu-ning knelt down and wrapped her arms around the leopard's head. "May it be so, Snowheart," she said in return.

She and Joshua reached Caer-a-mor just before noon, having made the descent in five hours—less than half the time it took Yu-ning and the treasure seekers to negotiate the summit three days before. Not wanting to draw attention, Joshua led Yu-ning on a hidden deer trail that circumvented the village and ended at the water's edge on the far side of the cove.

As the deer path exited the fir trees at water's edge, the still blue depths of the bay lay just below them; the beach and village were to their left, a quarter mile away. They heard loud rustling in the bushes beyond, and out stepped the largest bear Yu-ning had ever seen—much larger than Stout or

Madrigal, or the bears of Palova. "Hello, Joshua, you grumpy hermit!" bellowed the huge brown grizzly.

"Gamaliel, my friend—I see you have grown even fatter since the last time I saw you. Have you increased your salmon intake, old bear?" Gamaliel laughed and rose upon his hind legs, walking toward Joshua. The bear was at least ten feet tall! He enveloped Joshua in a stout hug, and then dropped to all fours as he turned toward Yu-ning.

"Hello, young lady. I am Gamaliel, Prince of the Lower Hills of the Great Fjord. Snowheart has told me about the light you have brought to this mountain, and your valiant efforts to bring the light to the gold seekers. I wanted to see you off safely!"

"It is very nice to meet you, Gamaliel," Yu-ning said, bowing low before the great bear. "Thank you for coming." Yu-ning turned toward the water and held her necklace high in the air. The sunlight reflected pink shards of light in all directions. Soon they could see a pink form swimming upward from the depths of the bay. Minkaro's pink nose and head were visible first, and then his entire body as he broke the surface of the water, a loud *phutt!* coming from his blow-hole as a fine spray of water rose into the air.

"Hello again, King Minkaro. I wish you and your little friend here safe travels, and a fruitful journey," said Gamaliel. Minkaro smiled at the enormous grizzly and dipped his head low in respect.

Yu-ning turned to Joshua. "Thank you for everything. You have deeply touched my heart. Remember that Palova Island is not far from my Island. It would warm Metatron's heart to see you and Jacob again. Perhaps it is time for a visit?"

"I will think on it, Yu-ning. If anything could wrest me from the warm hearth of the Porch of Tranquility, it would be the prospect of seeing Jacob again and my friends on Rainbow Island—especially you," said Joshua, bowing before Yu-ning. Joshua hugged her, and watched as she and the great dolphin glided across the still waters of the bay. Yu-ning looked back in time to see Joshua slip quietly into the forest for the long trek back to the Porch of Tranquility.

As Minkaro and Yu-ning left the protective waters of the fjord and entered the open sea, they turned northeast, in the direction of Tunzai Island. Their destination was the Floating Imperial Palace of Tunzai, residence of the Empress. "We should reach the Imperial Palace by dawn tomorrow, Yu-ning, barring any trouble!"

"Look, Minkaro!" Yu-ning exclaimed, pointing to her left. In the distance, slicing through the water, were four pink dorsal fins.

"Yu-ning, they are members of my royal dolphin guard—I would know those fins anywhere!" Minkaro lit out in the direction of the four pink dolphins, amazed to see friendly faces in waters so far south.

"My king, we have come to warn you about the Darq waters," said Molikan, one of Minkaro's most trusted lieutenants. "There are increasing numbers of Darq creatures roaming the oceans, from Rainbow to Tunzai Island."

"How did you know where to find us, Molikan?" asked Minkaro.

"When we returned from our patrols around Rainbow Island, Master Cristobel told us you had gone to Snowy Mountain on Farcara Island."

"Did the Darq creatures stop pursuing you once you hit the ice floes?" Minkaro asked.

"Yes sir, they did, but there are so many now, I am afraid it will be difficult for you to find a safe route to Tunzai. We would have been here sooner, but a dozen Darq creatures followed us. It took some time to lose them in the depths before heading south into safer waters."

"I have an idea," said Yu-ning, which she shared with Minkaro. The five dolphins formed a circle as Minkaro shared the plan for safely transporting Yu-ning to Tunzai Island. The conversation took only several minutes, but all the dolphins knew how critical it was for it to succeed. After making sure every dolphin knew their role in the plan, they split up—one group heading northwest, and the other group heading northeast.

After the sinking of the ghost ships, the Darq sharks had continued to cruise the waters surrounding the wreck, looking for any survivors. There were none, so they decided to swim south again, in hopes of picking up the trail of the large pink dolphin and the girl who rode him. For days they swam back and forth along the northern edge of the ice floes, looking for signs of the pink dolphin.

"Look—back toward the north!" hissed one of the sharks, directing the attention of the rest of the pack to a faint light trail in the water, heading northward. Senses heightened by the thought of picking up the trail of the girl and her dolphin, they turned north again, the glow of the water leaving an easy trail for them to follow. The sharks swam swiftly through the water, the glow growing stronger every mile. After three hours, their search was rewarded: up ahead, they could see movement no more than 300 yards away. They quickened their pace, and all converged on the mass swimming quickly through the water. Though their quarry tried its best to escape, it could not outrace the blood-crazed sharks.

The sharks closed in and finally were on top of their targets. The light was just in front of the sharks, and its rays were painful and blinding. The sharks struggled to see clearly through the bright lights in the water, but descended upon their prey with a vicious fury. Minkaro's first lieutenant, Molikan, burst high out of the water, the Light of Balthazar around his neck—where Yu-ning had tied it just hours before. The beautiful orb projected brilliant lights that reflected off the dolphin's sleek body. The blinding lights of the orb disoriented the sharks and allowed the dolphins to burst forward with great speed—for they had been swimming slowly on purpose, to make sure the sharks followed them away from Yu-ning! They left the confused sharks in their wake, easily outswimming the larger, slower creatures.

Because of their color blindness, the sharks couldn't tell the difference between the yellow glow of the Light of Balthazar and the pink glow of Yu-ning's crystal heart necklace! And once they realized they had been tricked into following the wrong party, the sharks lost resolve. Knowing that Minkaro and the girl were long gone by now, the sharks made their retreat, heading north away from Molikan and his lieutenants. The Light of Balthazar had been the perfect decoy, as its light led the sharks away from Yu-ning and the Dolphin King.

# Thirty

# Tunzai

N O MATTER HOW HARD SUPARNA FLEW, he could not lose the obsidigon.

Suparna, Romeo, Metatron, and Magic had traveled swiftly away from Baggul Island, knowing that sooner rather than later, Romeo's escape would be discovered. And sure enough, within an hour of their departure from the warlock's lair the obsidigon had discovered Romeo's escape. The obsidigon could no longer smell the boy through the bars of the gate—and knew he was gone.

It wasn't difficult to track the escape party—the boy's purple gemstone left a trail of light, and the dragon and his master easily followed it across the sea. Though it was normally a day-and-a-half flight across the Tunzai Strait to the Floating Imperial Palace, Suparna made the crossing in just twenty-four hours. The great bird was exhausted and feared he could not keep up the pace. And no matter how quickly he beat his enormous wings, the obisidigon remained fixed on his tail, no more than half a mile behind.

Dawn broke and the sun rose before them as they made landfall. They flew over a wide beach, which led into low green hills. The obsidigon flew with renewed urgency, sensing the colorful bird was nearing safe refuge. The dragon was now only a few hundred yards behind Suparna.

The first sign of civilization gleamed before Suparna high in the sky—it was the majestic Floating Imperial Palace of Tunzai. It was a few miles in the distance, perched in the clouds, as if anchored there by angels. It was the most beautiful structure Romeo had ever seen, with gleaming walls, elegant buildings, and huge multicolored tiles on its dramatic, arched roofs and towers.

"Make for the Floating Palace!" yelled Romeo.

"There is no time!" shouted Metatron. "The Floating Palace is on the far side of the city—we will need to try for the Western Gate, which is just over this rise!" They flew over the last hill and headed across a wide, sloping plain—a mile in the distance were the high walls of the ancient city of Tunzai. "There, Suparna! Head for the Western Gate—there! If we can make it inside the city, we can seek shelter from the dragon!"

Suparna narrowed his eyes and let out a ferocious cry—the sound of 1,000 eagles pierced the early morning silence. As his cry went forth, Romeo could see men scrambling to the city walls, looking in their direction. "Will they fire on us?" Romeo said with deep concern.

"No, Romeo—I have long been a friend of the Imperial City of Tunzai, as has Suparna," said Metatron. "They know Suparna's colors and his call; they will not harm us."

Suparna redoubled his speed and flew hard for the shelter of the approaching walls. Just as Suparna was about to clear the wall over the enormous Western Gate, a fireball blazed past them. Suparna dodged left, the scorching heat of the fire singeing the tip of his right wing. The fireball erupted against the city wall, sending soldiers scrambling in every direction.

As they cleared the turreted wall, Metatron saw an open area directly below. "Let us down there, Suparna, and make your escape!" The creature alighted in the inner court of the Western Gate; Romeo and Metatron scrambled off and headed for the safety of a nearby guard tower. A dark shadow passed above as the obsidigon and Hobaling crested the tower and hovered above them. The warriors on the wall unleashed a ferocious barrage of arrows, but the missiles simply bounced off the dragon's impenetrable scales.

Suparna took wing from the courtyard and flew directly for the obsidigon from behind. Romeo was helping Metatron reach the archway, the wizard leaning heavily on the boy's shoulder for support, his tall staff in his opposite hand. As they scrambled through the archway, a fireball erupted on the ground just outside, sending flames shooting through the entrance. Romeo pushed Metatron to the ground as the intense heat blew over their heads. Romeo looked back to see the obsidigon reeling end over end through the air—Suparna had hit the dragon hard from behind, taking him by surprise.

Romeo helped Metatron climb the winding stone steps inside the tower, and they emerged into the morning light. Turreted walls ran adjacent to the tower in both directions. Men at arms raced past them as an officer approached. "Metatron, it is good to see you again. But you must get below the city—my lieutenant will take you into our bunkers, where you will be sheltered!"

"Captain Darius, we are expecting a young girl—she will be approaching on foot from the south, and she will most likely be alone. Do everything in your power to protect her. She carries a powerful tool that might help us defeat the obsidigon. Do not let any harm come to her! Do you understand me, Captain?"

"Yes, Master Metatron. I will send out horse patrols to begin the search. We will do all we can to escort her safely into the city. I will alert you immediately with news." Captain Darius saluted and called one of his lieutenants to his side, instructing him to lead the boy and wizard back down the tower stairs. At the bottom of the tower stairs, the lieutenant led them through a small door just behind the staircase, otherwise hidden from the tower entrance.

As they entered through the low door, the air turned cool and damp. Well-worn stone steps led steeply downward between narrow walls just wide enough for Metatron to squeeze through. Wall torches pointed the way down, and at the bottom the passageway split in three directions. "This way," said the lieutenant, veering to the left. The narrow passage broadened and intersected with many other passages, which seemed to converge in a central area under the city. Large rooms could be seen off the corridors, containing sleeping quarters, kitchens, and an underground hospital. It was a military outpost ingeniously placed under the city, completely protected from aerial attack.

The lieutenant led Romeo and Metatron to a simple room containing two beds, a table and chairs, and other basic furnishings. "These are the Captain's quarters," the lieutenant said. "You will be safe here—any of the soldiers in this section will be happy to help you. I am Lieutenant Marcus, and I will bring you news just as soon as I can." The lieutenant saluted and hastily returned to his post.

"Why do we have to stay here, Metatron?" Romeo protested. "I want to go look for Yu-ning. We have to help!"

"In due time, Romeo. The Captain's men are much better equipped to find Yu-ning, my boy. They have horses and armor. This is not the first time the obisidigon has attacked Tunzai. There have been other attacks in the past three weeks, and these men are good at what they do. The best thing we can do, Romeo, is rest, recover our strength, and await word from above. Once it is safe, we will make for the Floating Imperial Palace to seek the council of the Empress."

Though Romeo was not happy to remain underground, he was exhausted from his ordeal on Baggul Island. After a simple but satisfying meal, he curled up under the covers of his bed and was asleep before his head hit the pillow. For the next two days, the wizard and the boy recovered their strength and waited for news from the city above. By the morning of the third day, Romeo was growing restless.

At the same time, Yu-ning and Minkaro were getting ever closer to Tunzai Island. With Yu-ning's pink crystal heart necklace hidden deep in her pack, she and Minkaro left no trail of light, and were able to slip past the Darq patrols along the ice floes north of Farcara Island. After swimming all night without incident, Minkaro could see the coast on the blue horizon. And he thought maybe, just maybe, their dangerous journey had come to a successful end. He looked behind him, relieved to see nothing but empty ocean in every direction.

Yu-ning began to stir after catching a few hours of sleep, and Minkaro greeted her. "I trust you slept a little. I'm glad one of us was able to rest. Look ahead there, Yu-ning. It is the island of Tunzai. We have arrived!" Minkaro and Yu-ning swam into a rocky cove not far from the Southern Gate of the city. Yu-ning dismounted in the shallows and bid Minkaro farewell. "Go now, Yu-ning. As fast as you can, make for the Southern Gate," he instructed her. "The guards will welcome a friend of the great wizard Metatron, who has been an ally of this fair city for many years. Metatron and Suparna will meet you at the Imperial Palace."

The sun was already warm overhead as Yu-ning peeled off her goose-down jacket and stuffed it behind the saddle on Minkaro's back. Her crystal heart necklace glowed as it lay against her tunic. She slung her pack on her back, secured the Quiver of Light and Lightcaster crossways on her shoulders, and negotiated the rocky shingle of the small beach to a low cliff. Scrambling up the cliff and emerging above, she turned and waved down to Minkaro, who nodded to her and turned to begin the long journey back to Rainbow Island, where he was most needed now.

She turned toward the high city gates, which stood in the distance across open and treeless terrain. Over the city she could see flashes of light—red bursts. A creeping fear slipped into her heart—the fire was coming from a dark object flying over the city. As it rose and dove, the sun reflected off its shiny exterior. It was the obsidigon. As much as her head told her legs to move, they seemed to have a mind of their own.

She turned around, searching desperately for Minkaro in the waters of the cove. He was gone. She was alone.

Her legs felt weak; she needed to sit down. She found a large rock nearby and leaned against it. She felt like she was shrinking—fear and terror pressed down upon her head. She stared at the scene before her and thought, *I can't do this. I know I should, and I know I must, but I can't.* She removed her pack and fumbled in the outer pocket for her water skin, her mouth dry.

As she felt for the water, her hand fell upon a small hard object. She removed the seedpod along with her water skin. As she took a long draught from the skin, she stared at the pod. Octavian the owl's words came back to her: *You might be small like these seeds, but you are also mighty like the kapok.*

"Thank you, Octavian," she whispered, tossing the pod in the air and placing it safely back in her backpack. She removed Julian's apple—she had been saving it all these days, and though it was a bit bruised, it tasted heavenly as she bit into the crisp flesh. She finished the apple and hefted her backpack, feeling refreshed from the water and the fruit. She stood, took three deep breaths, and set out for the gates of the city. As she jogged across the plain, the pink glow of her crystal necklace could be seen all the way to the top of the high city gates.

"What is that moving across the plain?" shouted one of the soldiers from atop the turreted wall, just above the Southern Gate.

"It's a girl, running toward the gate. If the dragon sees her, she will be killed! Alert Captain Darius—that might be the girl he is seeking!" The soldier called for a runner and hastily wrote a message for Captain Darius: *girl spotted—approach to southern gate—requesting cavalry patrol.*

The runner grabbed the small scroll and took off along the top of the wall, heading in the direction of the Western Gate. Soldiers scrambled to get out of the runner's way as he flew down the length of the wall. As he sprinted toward the Western Gate, he saw the dragon in the distance, breathing fire down upon the central district of the city. He reached the guard tower above the Western Gate and screamed, "Message for Captain Darius! Where is Captain Darius?"

"Here!" shouted the captain, stepping forward to receive the message. Darius hastily read the scroll and screamed orders to Lieutenant Marcus near the stables below. "Mount up, Lieutenant! A child has been spotted heading for the Southern Gate. Take thirty cavalry archers. Go now!" Within two minutes the massive doors of the Western Gate swung open, and the horsemen thundered out of the city and raced south along the Western Wall in the direction of Yu-ning.

From the center of the city, Hobaling saw the Western Gate open, and could see the dust cloud generated by the horses hoofs. "Something is happening outside the city. Follow them!" shouted Hobaling to the obsidigon. The dragon turned and sped across the rooftops of the city, weaving between turrets and towers. Arrows continued to bounce off his scaled armor like sticks against stone, falling harmlessly into the streets below. As the obsidigon flew over the Western Wall, it banked left in pursuit of the horse archers. Hobaling could see the last of the horses disappear at the end of the wall, heading toward the Southern Gate.

"See there, my pet?" Hobaling whispered into the obsidigon's ear. He was pointing south, at the grassy plain approaching the Southern Gate. "There is the girl! I told you she would come. Now is your time. Kill her light!" The obsidigon opened his massive jaws and let forth a terrible screech that shattered windows in the city and sent the soldiers to the ground, covering their ears in agony.

Lieutenant Marcus turned toward the terrible sound coming from the city walls, and urged his horse archers to increase their speed. Yu-ning ran as fast as she could toward the safety of the horses—she could see the obsidigon flying toward them further in the distance. A quarter mile from the Southern Gate, the horsemen reached the girl and quickly encircled her, falling into a testudo formation—shields above their heads, locked together in a tortoise-like protective covering. Yu-ning crouched under the mane of Marcus's horse, the sun completely blocked by the interlocked shields above her.

As she peered upward, a great blast of fire crashed against the shield wall—the fireball came in low and flat and bounced off the testudo, tumbling across the grass beyond them, leaving a trail of scorched earth. The obsidigon had flown in low and hard—thus its fireball had harmlessly deflected off the horsemen's shields. As the obsidigon turned to make another pass over the soldiers, Hobaling reined up, directing the beast higher into the air, aiming to send fire straight down upon the phalanx.

From under the protection of the archers' shields, Yu-ning removed Lightcaster and extracted an arrow from the Quiver of Light. She locked eyes with Marcus. "This is a Darq Render bow!" she said, thrusting the great bow before him. "These arrows can bring down an obsidigon!" she added, the arrow gripped in her right hand.

Marcus nodded and yelled, "Inner five, spread shields with me!"

As the obsidigon positioned itself to release its fire, six shields in the center of the testudo parted. A small figure emerged, nocking an arrow and aiming directly toward the dragon high above. Yu-ning released the arrow. The moment it left Lightcaster, the arrow lit up with brilliant beams of blinding white light. It streaked upward like a white-hot flame, heading directly for the obsidigon's head.

There was no time for Hobaling to react as the arrow of bright light struck the obsidigon above its eye. As it neared the dragon, the arrow burst into a million bright shards, disintegrating before Yu-ning's eyes. White heat could be seen gleaming above the dragon's eye, a large circle of light glowing upon its dark scales. Though the light missile had not hit the dragon's eye, the creature seemed dazed. It turned and retreated from the field of battle.

"Back to the city!" Marcus commanded his men. They disengaged their shields and prepared to gallop for the Southern Gate of the city.

"No! We must pursue the dragon! It is injured. We must go after it!" Yu-ning urged. Ignoring her, one of the horse archers bent down and grabbed Yu-ning by the collar, swinging her up and behind him in the saddle. "Into the city with us, before he returns," he shouted, spurring his horse toward the gate.

"No! I must pursue the injured dragon!" she shouted. "Now is my best chance!"

"Over my dead body," yelled the soldier. "The Empress will want to have a word with you, I am sure, my little mighty archer!" As they raced back toward the city gate, Yu-ning pushed the archer from his horse. He rolled safely away, but Yu-ning took off in the direction of the dragon and Hobaling. "I'm sorry, sir!" she yelled as she sped away on the soldier's horse.

"Crazy child!" shouted the smarting horseman, a bump already forming on his head.

"You four, come with me after the girl," said Marcus. "The rest of you, report to Captain Darius!" Marcus and the four horsemen spurred their horses in pursuit of the girl as the remaining horse archers returned to the city.

# Thirty-One

# Hobaling

ETATRON AND ROMEO received reports that the dragon had left the city, headed in the direction of the Cliffs of Conundrum along the northern coast of Tunzai Island. They gathered their few belongings and followed Captain Darius up long flights of stairs leading back to the Western Tower. Once aboveground, one of Captain Darius's men was assigned to escort them to the Floating Imperial Palace, where the Empress was waiting to receive them.

"I don't see Suparna!" Romeo said, scanning the skies above the city.

"What we need, Romeo, is a terralight basket," Metatron said, scanning the skies. He explained that on Tunzai, the island's most precious gemstone, called tunzanite, contained propulsion properties that allowed the inhabitants to ride through the air for short distances in large baskets powered by the amazing gems.

As they pondered where to find a terralight basket, a bright flash of color flew overhead—it was Suparna, who landed next to them. Suparna had tried his best to hinder the obsidigon, but soon found that he was no match for the immense dragon. He had sought shelter as best he could, biding his time for a better advantage. Metatron and Romeo thanked Captain Darius for his hospitality and mounted Suparna for the trip to the Floating Imperial Palace.

As they flew over the city in the direction of the palace in the clouds, Suparna told them he had just seen the obsidigon and Hobaling flying away from the city. As they passed over the walled city of Tunzai, the devastation wrought by the dragon was all around—burned buildings, smoldering piles of timber, and people in the streets clearing debris.

Growing closer in the sky, a spectacular structure floated before them. It was an enormous double-eave building set on a gargantuan, single-level white quartz platform that glistened in the sunlight. The sloping triangle roofs featured hundreds of intricate ridges, each decorated with a line of statuettes. The first was of a phoenix, followed by an imperial coiled dragon, a lion, deer, and koi fish. The palatial architecture measured 3,033 feet from north to south, and 2,002 feet from east to west. It was surrounded by a beautiful, crystal clear moat, with a wide wooden bridge leading to the entrance of the palace. The tall, wide, rustic wooden double doors at the entrance held two majestic hanging tablets in red silk, with black calligraphic writing beautifully inscribed onto each. They read, "Love/Peace" and "Power/Wisdom."

Beyond the moat were multiple levels of imperial gardens, descending into an oasis of greenery surrounded by a circular stone wall pierced by four golden gates at the north, east, south, and west points. Flags hung at each of these points, adorned in red with black calligraphy. Romeo read the characters slowly as the red material blew in the wind. "Justice and honor," he whispered, lost in the reverie of this magical empire. Beyond this beautiful bastion were clouds and sky.

Romeo was overcome by the majesty and beauty of the palace and was full of anticipation when Suparna touched down in the courtyard near the entrance. Finely dressed guards approached. "Welcome to the Floating Imperial Palace of the Empress of Tunzai," they said, bowing before the travelers. "Master Metatron, her highness is expecting you and your companions. Please follow us."

They were escorted across a finely built stone bridge that covered the moat, and through the doors of the gate into the grounds of the palace. While the outside of the Floating Palace was grand and spectacular, the inside grounds were lovely, calming, and beautiful. Gardens, fountains, and finely formed statuary ringed the entire grounds directly in front of the enormous palace.

They walked up the beautiful marble stairs in front of the palace. The wooden doors had intricate hand-carved designs laced throughout, painted in the most vivid, striking colors he had ever seen. "As colorful and bright as our rainbow!" he whispered to Metatron, who simply nodded at Romeo.

A tall, elegant man in a flowing robe and shaved head approached them, bowed, and said, "Empress is expecting you. Come now."

"The Empress!" Romeo exclaimed. Together they all followed the tall man through the glorious palace—the ceilings were high, and were also inlaid with delicate, hand-carved designs and patterns, painted in all the colors of the rainbow.

The floor was glistening white marble. High, open windows lined both sides of the long room, as diaphanous white curtains gently swayed in the afternoon breeze. It was lovely and elegant, and its delicate beauty enchanted Romeo and the others. Magic peeked out from Metatron's robe and was about to bound away to explore—Metatron caught him in midair, and whispered, "Not now, Magic. There will be gardens and insects soon enough for you. But right now, you must stay put!"

Two double golden doors opened on the opposite end of the room, and out drifted a breathtakingly beautiful woman. She was elegant and graceful as she swept toward them like a vision. She was the most stunning woman Romeo had ever seen. She had long dark hair, dark angelic eyes, and flawless ivory skin, and she was wearing a long, shining white gown.

Atop her head was a glistening crown covered in crystals and jewels. She was glowing. A stunning, ornately crafted necklace adorned her neck, pulsating pink hues that shined outward in a ten-foot radius. She moved gracefully in her flowing gown, waving and smiling at everyone as her gaze fell tenderly upon Romeo, Metatron, and Suparna. She nodded her head with dignity. "Welcome, all. Welcome to my palace. I know the trials you have endured, my boy, and what your protectors have risked to save you." She gazed at Romeo as she said this. Romeo said nothing but bowed deeply before the Empress.

"And my good friends Metatron and Suparna—thank you for coming to our aid. The kingdom of Tunzai thanks you, and I thank you."

Metatron and Suparna bowed, and Metatron said, "My Empress, the obsidigon was seen flying toward the Cliffs of

Conundrum, but we do not know why. As well, we are awaiting the arrival of our companion—a small girl, eleven years old. Her name is Yu-ning, and she possesses the last known Darq Render bow, Lightcaster. Have you seen her, your highness?"

"We have no knowledge of such a girl, Metatron. Are you sure she has arrived here on Tunzai?" said the Empress.

"No, all we know is that Minkaro, King of the Pink Dolphins, was to escort her here from Farcara Island, where they were on a quest to find the long-lost arrows of Darqendia."

"Ah, Lightcaster and the Quiver of Light, yes? When I was a girl my grandfather, Emperor Ming, used to tell me stories about the great Darq Render bow and quiver of arrows. I didn't believe the stories, but again, I didn't believe there was an obsidigon skull hidden in the catacombs below this palace—until I saw with my own eyes the obsidigon wreaking havoc on the city below," added the Empress. "Hobaling deceived the imperial court, tricked my beloved sister, and stole the obsidigon skull from the catacombs below this very palace! There is no love in his heart, and if he is not stopped, I fear a great darkness will overcome all the islands of our fair realm," she said with increasing emotion.

The doors of the palace swung open, and all heads turned toward the entrance. The tall man entered swiftly, followed by Captain Darius and Lieutenant Marcus. "Your highness, I am sorry to disturb you, but we come with urgent news," said Captain Darius. "We believe the girl these three are looking for has gone in pursuit of the dragon and the warlock. We would have been here sooner, but we had difficulty finding a terralight basket that hadn't been incinerated by the dragon."

"What did this girl look like, Captain?" said Metatron.

"I was with her on the battlefield, Master Metatron," said Marcus, stepping forward. "She shot a single light rod at the dragon, and it seemed to startle the creature, which fled the battlefield."

"What do you mean, she shot a light rod at the dragon?" asked Metatron.

"She nocked a normal arrow, but when she loosed the missile, it transformed into a blinding yellow light rod—it was the brightest light I have ever seen. It stunned the creature, which made its retreat. The girl took one of our horses and rode in the direction of the obsidigon. We pursued her as far as the Cliffs of Conundrum, where she abandoned the horse and entered the cliffs on foot. Soon the trail went cold. We returned as swiftly as we could to report the news to you."

Metatron had a mind to scold the lieutenant for allowing an eleven-year-old girl to outsmart him. But then again, this was Yu-ning, and she was no ordinary girl. Yu-ning was well skilled in the art of tracking—she had Metatron and the instructors of Rainbow Island to thank for that!

"We must make haste, Empress! Suparna, Romeo, and I must pursue Yu-ning! She is in grave danger and needs our assistance!"

"Of course, Metatron! Go quickly—my prayers are with you all!"

Metatron, Suparna, and Romeo raced from the palace and swiftly took flight in the direction of the Cliffs of Conundrum, just northwest of the Floating Palace of Tunzai.

# Thirty-Two

# Butterflies

*I*T WAS RELATIVELY EASY for Yu-ning to lose the soldiers in the twisted labyrinth of rocks and boulders along the sea cliffs. She had pursued Hobaling and the dragon across the plain, and had seen the beast fly over the cliffs and disappear behind a rock formation that resembled a finger pointing toward the sky. As she reached the rock outcroppings near the coast, she found herself staring at a maze of gigantic rocks and boulders that stretched in both directions as far as she could see. It would be easy to get lost in those rocks, and that was her plan.

She glanced behind her to see the five horsemen approaching swiftly. Dismounting her horse, she took off on foot, Lightcaster in one hand, the Quiver of Light slung over her right shoulder. She darted into a narrow opening between two massive boulders, barely able to squeeze through the narrow passage, which continued for about 100 feet before opening onto a wider passage. She knew the larger soldiers would not be able to negotiate the passage, but she found some tall, dried grass nearby and erased her tracks, just to be safe.

She knew her only chance to get close enough to the obsidigon was by using her small size and stealth. And she knew she would be more effective alone, without the soldiers in tow. The larger passage wove around the rocks until it emerged at the cliff face, which dropped hundreds of feet to the rocky shoreline below. Here the passage gave way to a narrow path that hugged the side of the cliff that led in both directions. She remembered seeing the finger rock to her right, so she set off in that direction. Behind her she could hear the shouts of the horse archers, searching for a sign of her trail. She quickened her pace, using the tall finger rock as a point of reference. She was getting closer. The cliff trail, however, ended abruptly at a huge rock. No way around. What now?

"I must have missed something," she whispered, as she retraced her steps along the trail she had just walked down. About fifty feet back, she saw an enormous slab of rock that had fallen from above and was now leaning against the side of the cliff. She'd barely given the rock any notice as she'd slipped past it a minute before.

Now, however, she could see faint light coming from behind the large rock. She peered inside—there was a slim opening that had been blocked when the slab fell onto the trail. It was very narrow, and she had to remove her backpack to squeeze through. Once on the other side, the going was very slow, as the walls of the cliffs were barely a foot apart. As small as Yu-ning was, she had to turn sideways to inch her way along the passageway, dragging her pack and Lightcaster at her side. As she peered down the narrow space, she could see daylight—and a rock formation in the shape of a long finger.

She smelled the obsidigon before she saw it. She inched toward the end of the narrow passage and peered around the edge. The passageway opened onto a rock ledge, with cliffs rising all around. In front of her the ledge dropped off to the plains far below—the Imperial Palace of Tunzai floated serenely in the distance. The dragon and the warlock had their backs to her, about thirty feet away. It looked as if Hobaling was trying to calm the wounded dragon, having brought it to rest on the exposed ledge after they fled the battlefield.

As quietly as she could, Yu-ning removed an arrow from the Quiver of Light and nocked it into place. She stood still at the end of the passage, still hidden from the view of the dragon. She closed her eyes, took a deep breath, and exhaled. She had to step out onto the ledge to have room to fire the arrow. She knew this was risky, but in the tight confines of the passage, it would be impossible for her to maneuver a shot. She stealthily stepped out onto the ledge, brought the weapon to her shoulder, and pulled back hard on the bowstring.

A memory flashed through her mind. During an archery lesson given by her instructor, Cristobel, back on Rainbow Island, Cristobel had said, "Clear your mind before you let fly the arrow. Take a cleansing breath, and hold it—and gently let go of the bowstring. Do not *shoot* the arrow, but *release* the arrow—set it free." Yu-ning narrowed her left eye, aimed the arrow at the dragon, and let fly. As before, the instant the arrow left the string, it flared into a brilliant yellow rod, trailing blinding light as it streaked toward the dragon's head.

Hobaling cried out, just in time for the dragon to swing its head out of the path of the flashing arrow. Yu-ning knew she had now lost the element of surprise, and she frantically fumbled for another arrow. As she lowered it into place, she saw that Hobaling was almost upon her. He had raced across the ledge faster than she could have imagined, and she had little time to react. She let the arrow fly, but it banged harmlessly against the cliff wall in a cloud of sparks. She turned to make her retreat down the passageway, hoping the space would be too narrow for Hobaling to follow.

Wedging her body sideways, she moved away as quickly as she could. She took two steps—and was yanked backward. She lost her footing and fell hard on her tender left shoulder, red-hot pain shooting up her arm and into her body. The warlock pulled her back as she tried to grab hold of the cliff wall. Her hand found a rock hold, and she pulled with all her might, kicking at Hobaling. She scrambled away, crawling deeper into the passage, out of reach of Hobaling's grasping hands. She was free!

But her heart sank as she realized that in the chaos, Lightcaster had slipped out of her hands and was lying on the ground near the entrance to the ledge. Hobaling had seen it too, and was stretching his hand toward it. It was just out of his reach. Yu-ning turned to flee, but paused, looking back at Lightcaster. Making a split-second decision, she lunged for the bow just as Hobaling's bony fingers curled around the wooden frame. She grabbed Lightcaster from the opposite end and pulled. But Hobaling had ferocious strength, and he heaved the bow backward, grabbing Yu-ning's wrist with his free hand.

She was lifted off the ground, pulled through the passage and onto the rock ledge. They both hit the ground hard as Lightcaster fell from Hobaling's hands. Yu-ning scrambled away, lunged for Lightcaster, and pulled it toward her. Hobaling stood and advanced toward her as the obisidigon rose up behind the warlock. Yu-ning saw a swirling circle of fire forming in the dragon's mouth, but the warlock was between them, causing the dragon to hold back. Yu-ning rolled away from the warlock and scrambled toward the tall, fingerlike rock formation.

"Now!" screamed Hobaling at the dragon. Yu-ning made herself small behind the large rock formation just as the fireball exploded against the outer side of the rock, sending flames past her face. She had one last chance, and she knew it. Swiftly she removed another arrow from the quiver and nocked it in place.

"Did you really think you could defeat me?" hissed Hobaling, moving toward the finger rock. "That you could stop me from spreading this darkness? From here, I will spread the darkness to the rest of the world—especially now that I have your precious sacred crystals!"

Yu-ning glanced around the rock, gauging the distance to the dragon. She leaned out from behind the rock, seeing her chance: the dragon lowered his head, the soft spot on the back of its neck momentarily exposed. Everything moved as if in slow motion as Hobaling appeared before her, diving to tackle her just as she readied herself to loose the arrow.

Sensing danger, the obsidigon raised his head high and gave a loud cry. As Hobaling's weight crashed into her, Yu-ning released the bowstring—but the arrow was heading for the front of the obsidigon's head. As she hit the ground, she looked back as the dragon swatted at the arrow, pushing the light missile off course so that it smashed against the cliff behind the creature.

The obsidigon was above Yu-ning now, preparing to release its fire upon her head. Hobaling, however, rose to his feet close by—too close for the dragon to release its fire. Instead, the obsidigon raised its razor-sharp talon high into the air, ready to bring destruction upon the girl's head.

At that moment there was a terrible crash, and Yu-ning and Hobaling were knocked sideways. Yu-ning looked up and saw that the obsidigon had been thrown against the rock wall, boulders and loose stones crashing down from above. Hobaling, too, had been knocked against the rocks, and lay still on the ground. Suparna landed in the middle of the fight, with Metatron and Romeo on his back. The dragon recovered, and swiped at Suparna with his tail, knocking him sideways and sending Romeo sprawling across the rocky ground. Romeo's head hit hard against the stones. He lay motionless next to Hobaling.

"Yu-ning, to me!" yelled Metatron, reaching a hand out to the little girl, who was still clutching her bow and a single arrow. The Quiver of Light was empty of its missiles; the remaining arrows had been strewn across the ledge during the battle. She grabbed Metatron's hand, and he pulled her onto Suparna's back. As the great bird took wing, the obsidigon's tail crashed down on the rocks, missing them by inches.

The dragon was pacing, his head swinging between Suparna, suspended above him in the air, and Romeo, who lay unconscious next to Hobaling. Now hovering above the dragon, Suparna was considering his next move. The dragon

drew back and unleashed a molten fireball. Suparna anticipated the flames, however, and dodged the fiery missile. The
dragon roared in frustration. Swiveling his jaundiced eyes
back to Romeo, the dragon crossed toward the unmoving
boy, who lay a dozen feet away.

Suparna and Metatron saw what was happening, but
realized they were too far above the scene to reach Romeo
in time. Yu-ning froze, realizing that Romeo was about to die.
A love she had never known flooded her heart as she stared
down at her best friend in the world. She remembered that
she still held the last arrow, and her bow. With a fierceness in
her heart, she recalled what Balthazar told her in the Tower
of Light: *The arc of the bow is like the curve of the rainbow—as
the arrow of light shoots forth into the world, it tears the darkness,
and brings its love with it.*

The dragon looked up at her with malice in its eyes. With
resolve in her mind, and love in her heart for Romeo, she
narrowed her sights, nocked the final arrow, and aimed at
the creature that stood directly over Romeo now. The dragon
swung his head upward at Yu-ning, a dark gleam in his eye. Yu-
ning resisted the urge to loose her arrow—it was not yet time.
She waited for the obsidigon to turn its head back toward
Romeo, the arrow poised and ready. As the dragon swung its
head down and raised a talon above the boy, Yu-ning knew it
was time—she loosed the arrow directly toward the back of
the obisidigon's neck. The arrow became infused with blinding, swirling yellow light as it raced toward its target.

The arrow stopped in midair just before it reached the
dragon's neck. The barren spot on the obsidigon's neck was
glowing—a vivid circle of yellow light. The dragon froze,
as if unable to move as the arrow floated just an inch from

the creature—just as it had when Joshua had fired the arrow at Snowheart. As the arrow hovered there, the light grew brighter, and flowed toward the exposed circle of light on the creature. The beautiful yellow beam streamed directly toward the barren circle on the dragon's neck and entered into the dragon. The obsidigon slowly rose from the ledge—its massive body floated upward into the air, as the lights from the arrow flowed into the dragon, filling it with clean, pure light.

In a flash, the yellow, swirling display exploded, sending streams of light in every direction. Yu-ning and Metatron had to shield their eyes from the intensity of the explosion. "Look, everyone," whispered Yu-ning, in deep reverence. The dragon's body had changed—the light had infused it, and the dragon was becoming transparent. Small individual points of light began to form, and these sprouted wings—vivid wings adorned with the seven colors of the rainbow! Thousands of beautiful, multicolored butterflies appeared, still holding the shape of the dragon. The light of the arrow had penetrated the soft spot on the dragon's neck and invaded the hulking creature with the light of love. The anger and malice of the dragon was gone, and in its place thousands of delicate butterflies hovered close together, in the form of the dragon.

"Butterflies, just like during the Great Obsidigon War . . ." marveled Metatron, as he finally understood the old mystery. "That is why, after every battle, waves of butterflies would follow the Darq Renders home."

Metatron raised his staff, and spoke toward the dragon-shaped mass of winged creatures. "Be free, and fly!" The colorful creatures fluttered their wings and took off in every direction. As they flew away in the afternoon light, the only thing that remained of the obsidigon was its skull. Clean, white, ancient—it was as if all the hatred and malice that Hobaling had poured into his creation had died, replaced by the arc of light extending from Lightcaster—and the love it represented.

Suparna landed on the ledge, and Yu-ning scrambled down to check on Romeo. He lay by himself where he had fallen—Hobaling was nowhere in sight.

There was no movement or sign of life. Tears began to roll down Yu-ning's cheeks as she whispered, "Oh, Romeo." She knelt down, hugging his still body, weeping quietly. Metatron and Suparna exchanged pained looks as they observed the sad scene, Metatron resting his hand upon the grief-stricken girl's delicate shoulder.

Yu-ning rested her head on Romeo's chest and felt something under his shirt—it was his purple crystal heart necklace, which was void of light. She gently picked up the violet-colored heart in both of her hands and closed her eyes, tears continuing to roll down her cheeks. She gently set the heart down again on Romeo's chest, rose, and walked back into Metatron's waiting arms. She was sobbing now.

"Yu-ning, look," said Metatron, pointing at Romeo behind her. Yu-ning turned around and was stunned to see the purple crystal heart begin to glow, a soft purple speck of light pulsing from the very center of the crystal. The light was growing stronger! She rushed back to Romeo, who opened his eyes wide and took a deep, sharp breath.

"He's alive, Metatron!" Yu-ning exclaimed.

Romeo's eyes fluttered and opened, and he stared up into his friend's large brown eyes. "What happened? And why are you crying, Yu-ning?" She just laughed, and gave Romeo a big hug.

"Where is the dragon? And what happened to the warlock?" Romeo inquired, a bit wobbly on his feet as Yu-ning and Metatron helped him up.

"The dragon is gone," said Metatron, leaning on his staff. "The power of Lightcaster has torn the darkness, and broken Hobaling's curse. The obsidigon is no more."

"You mean, you killed it?" asked Romeo.

"No, not killed. Transformed. Yu-ning's arrow filled it with light, breaking the Darq curse that created it."

"And what of Hobaling?" Romeo asked.

"He is gone—he slipped away during the battle, I am afraid," said Metatron, concern etching his brow. "But he cannot run far." Metatron took a blanket from behind the saddle on Suparna's back and carefully wrapped the obsidigon skull within it. He stowed the grim trophy behind the saddle and urged everyone to climb aboard. "This is indeed a great day, my friends. Quickly, to the Floating Palace to inform the Empress of today's fair tidings!"

Yu-ning was about to climb atop Suparna, but then jumped off his wing. "Where are you going?" asked Romeo.

"I traveled far to find these—they are treasures worth keeping," said Yu-ning. She retrieved ten arrows and placed them in the Quiver of Light. "All right, let's go!" she said as she scrambled onto Suparna's back.

As Suparna took flight from the ledge high above the Cliffs of Conundrum and turned toward the Floating Imperial Palace, hundreds of tiny, rainbow-colored butterflies gathered around him and the three passengers, joining them in their flight into the clouds. The butterflies fluttered in and out among the riders, as if celebrating with them, brushing delicate wings against their smiling faces.

# Thirty-Three

# Empress

YU-NING AWOKE IN A BEAUTIFUL BED in a royal-looking bedroom. Colorful trogons, mot-mots, quetzals, and other bright tropical birds flitted in the trees just outside her window, searching for their morning's breakfast. Their birdsongs were mellifluous, welcoming her to the Floating Palace.

She wandered outside to find Romeo standing on the porch of the room next door. The scene before them was breathtaking: an enchanting sanctuary of temples, gardens, streams, and forest glades. They dressed and were greeted by benevolent imperial ambassadors, attendants, and masters, who were there to give them a tour of the serene grounds. As they prepared to depart, Metatron and Magic joined them. "I have seen these grounds many times, but I never tire of seeing them again!" Metatron smiled as he stood between Romeo and Yu-ning, squeezing the children's shoulders.

Magic jumped into Yu-ning's arms, grateful to see his master whole and fit.

"Welcome to the Imperial Palace," a group of temple teachers, leaders, and students, known as brothers, chanted simultaneously while bowing. Metatron and the children were awestruck by the startling sight before them, and Yu-ning was deeply moved. Every last ounce of fear, weariness, and trauma from the previous day's events evaporated the moment their gaze took in the miraculous sight before them.

One of the brothers stepped forward to greet them. His head was shaved, and he was wearing a beautiful, long, azure blue robe with woven bamboo sandals. The crystal beaded malas around his neck and wrists glistened in the sunlight. "Welcome, welcome. Come, come," he said, bowing with a smile that lit up his entire face. "My name is Yeshe, and I welcome you." In a quiet and humble tone, he led the three visitors on a tour along a beautiful garden pathway through the imperial grounds. Slowly and methodically he announced the sights with wonder and reverence, as if he himself were seeing the kingdom for the first time. "There are eight sections of the grounds, which occupy over 100,000 acres of pristine rain forest, gardens, and meadows. We have the outer court, inner court, front and center, and the main palace where our divine Empress resides. We have meditation gardens, temples, museums, libraries, and parks. There is a school that all the children in the community attend. But there is so much more. Let me lead you."

The trio stood in awe, taking in every detail that Yeshe was sharing. He continued, "Toward the center of the imperial grounds stand the tallest and largest buildings. This is the Imperial Palace, where the Empress resides. It is the only building not made out of wood, but is composed of carved stone, marble, and crystal. It is gold-framed, with yellow stone walls, speckled throughout with citrine crystals. The gabled brick roof is covered in gold vermillion shingles."

The travelers continued to follow Yeshe toward one of the green gardens. The group stood in a grove of orange trees, smelling the intoxicating sweetness of the neroli blossoms and the ripe fruit. "This garden is where everyone plays and gathers. Over there behind the apricot trees is the green teahouse. You are all welcome to come to this garden and have tea anytime," Yeshe said, pointing at a small green wooden house in front of them.

With serene gestures he guided them toward a set of red buildings. "This way," he said softly. "These red buildings are for ceremonies and celebrations. The pink buildings at the rear right are used for special ceremonies, meetings, and observances for the Empress. The middle white buildings to the right are all the creative buildings where artists come to think, meditate, and create. The orange buildings toward the front in the middle are where everyone works, and this ancient bridge here takes you to the tallest tower that oversees the lands for meditation, prayer, and worship.

"The blue structures on the left are the sacred temples for the masters and teachers. These wisdom temples and meditation temples encircle numerous libraries and museums, so that our knowledge and appreciation of beauty is blessed with pure intention. The large yellow building to the right of the Imperial Palace houses relatives of the imperial family.

"I am going to the temple now, and all of you are welcome," he said, standing in a serene pose as he bowed his head. Eager nods received his invitation, and everyone ventured down the garden path together toward the blue temples. As they approached the magical circle of temples sweeping across the land in multiple shades of blue, Yu-ning was struck by the beauty and peacefulness of the space.

The shades of blue were the colors of a tropical lagoon, surrounded by an array of blue blossoms: lilies, violets, hyacinths, and more. As the threesome pondered the breath-taking sights before them, Yeshe whispered, "Enjoy, and know your way. I will leave you now to your walking." He smiled, bowed, and stepped backward very slowly.

"Thank you, Yeshe," Yu-ning added, waving enthusias-tically. Yeshe looked at her and everyone else and smiled broadly. He placed his hands together at his heart and turned to leave. Yu-ning and the others looked all around. The site was heavenly and calming. They saw many masters walking slowly, looking very peaceful and kind. They bowed, smiling at Yu-ning and the others as they walked past. On a beauti-ful, long cobalt porch in front of a sapphire and cerulean blue temple, they saw a brother sitting meditatively with a bowl of rice and chopsticks.

He nodded at them, smiling ear to ear. Others came to join him with their bowls, and together they sat in a circle on indigo cushions. The masters all wore beautiful azure blue robes and crystal malas like Yeshe. Yu-ning saw the clusters of amethyst, tanzanite, calcite, lapis lazuli, and aquamarine catching the light and sighed at the beauty.

As they continued on to the main temple, which was the largest of them all and flanked by smaller buildings, the three slowed to a stop, waiting to move forward beyond the entrance. A brother approached them, bowed his head, and said, "Please, come into the temple. The master teacher would like to meet you. He is the leader of all masters. His name is Master Tenzin."

Yu-ning exclaimed in a whisper, "Oh, he is expecting us!" The brother led the group inside the temple and down toward the center of the structure, forward to the altar. They walked inside the sacred sanctuary, which was bright, open, and serene. The fragrance of sage and incense wafted through the air. The main room was simply adorned. The cypress-wood roof and walls were warm and rustic. There were bamboo and rice paper sliding doors and straw *tatami* mats on the floors. There was a long wooden bench and table on one side of the room. In the center of an elevated platform, the master sat cross-legged on a red silk padded seat. A breathtaking array of crystals was displayed, as well as candles and bowls of beautiful fruit and blossoms. The master was smiling blissfully, eyes closed.

Metatron and Romeo followed Yu-ning and stood quietly behind her at the entrance of the altar space. At that precise moment, the master opened his eyes and looked softly, but intently, at each of them. "Come, sit," he said kindly. Yu-ning knelt down reverently next to him, and the others followed suit.

"Welcome to the Imperial Palace. I am happy you are here with us. I have a gift for you." Smiling, the master took out a large wooden box from behind his sweeping, deep sapphire blue robe and set it in front of them. He gestured down to them to open it.

Wide-eyed, everyone smiled, but no one moved toward the box except Yu-ning. She nodded at the master graciously and reached to touch the top of the box. She gasped. "Light is shining from within!"

The master smiled at Yu-ning and nodded. "Yes, know what you feel." As Yu-ning opened the box, a flood of light burst out from inside it. Inside on a bed of beautiful, dark blue velvet was a single amethyst crystal mala in the length of a necklace. The master took out the gleaming strand and held it in front of Yu-ning. Closing his eyes in prayer, he placed the mala over her head and bowed. Yu-ning was so moved she didn't know what to say. She gasped and looked down, holding the necklace with both hands and bowing down.

As she rose, her voice was in a whisper. "It is beautiful." She looked at the beautiful purple roundel beads. They were perfect. "Thank you, Master," she said. "Thank you from the bottom of my heart." She lifted the necklace to kiss it, and turned to the others to show them.

The master bowed his head, acknowledging her heartfelt gratitude. He looked to Metatron and Romeo and said, "Yu-ning is the embodiment of love, and this necklace will guide and honor her from that place." As he said this, he lifted the velvet in the box to reveal two more malas just like Yu-ning's.

Yu-ning was surprised. She shouted out in glee, "You have a mala for all of us!"

The master smiled and said, "Of course." One at a time, he lifted a mala and placed it over each one's head, saying a blessing. "Wear it, hold onto it, and remember to do everything with integrity and love. Follow your intuition, and be open to learning the wisdom."

Sunlight streamed through shingles on the roof above, causing the necklaces to shimmer. As they rose to leave, the master rose too. He guided them to the door, and they all bowed to him once more before walking outside the altar space. He bowed back and said with tenderness, "Live a righteous path."

As they exited the main temple, they stepped onto the beautiful pathway that led to the other temples. Yu-ning paused at one temple whose door was wide open. Hung above the door was a wooden sign with the words "Sincerity and Openness" painted in black calligraphy ink.

Yu-ning nodded. "We must go inside here." The others followed her onto a short pebble-stone walkway and up the long, shallow steps of the temple. The three interior walls were covered from floor to ceiling in one-foot by one-foot cubes that contained twenty rolled-up paper scrolls in each.

In the center of the room, an elderly, bespectacled scholar-teacher was holding an open scroll. As the threesome walked inside, the old teacher looked at each of them with the deep wisdom of a sage, and nodded. He paused then and smiled with his eyes. "Welcome to the Temple of Eternal Wisdom. My name is Lobsang." Yu-ning discerned that he was the pre-eminent scholar of the community.

Yu-ning was excited; she walked to the center wall and reached high up over her head, taking out one of the scrolls from one of the niches in the wall. As she carried it down, it was glowing pink. The scroll was thick and heavy, with many sheets rolled inside. It looked old and had a musky smell. The edges of the paper were tinged sepia.

"The Scripture of Love," Yu-ning read as she opened the scroll. The others looked at her, nodding. Lobsang approached her and reached for another scroll. He handed it to Romeo, who opened it. "Wisdom," he read.

Lobsang moved back and forth along the walls with elegant, sweeping gestures as he retrieved scroll after scroll with fluidity and grace, handing them to the three visitors. They took turns reading aloud: "Magnanimity"; "Integrity"; "Mindfulness"; "Valor"; "Generosity"; "Gratitude"; "Humility"; "Forgiveness"; "Peace"; "Stillness."

At that moment, Lobsang became very still and quiet. "Read these words," he began solemnly. "Hold them close to you. The wisdom will always stay with you."

The group was called out of their reverie by the deep, resonant gong of an ancient bell, which rang three times. A young brother walked into the temple quietly; he bowed to Lobsang and turned to Yu-ning and the adults. "Please follow me. Her royal highness, the Imperial Empress, awaits."

They all bowed and said goodbye. "Thank you, Lobsang," Yu-ning said, holding her scrolls to her chest. Lobsang smiled and bid farewell to his three guests. They walked back through the circle of temples to the grand entrance of the main palace, where they had first met the Empress. As they entered, a hush fell over them as the Empress walked toward them from the end of the main aisle.

"Welcome, all. It is wonderful to see you looking so refreshed! I trust your walk throughout the palace grounds has been pleasant?" All three bowed before the beautiful Empress, who was wearing a flowing, cream-colored gown imbedded with small gemstones of sky blue. "You have all done a great service for the Kingdom of Tunzai, and we are forever indebted to you for your courage and bravery. As a small token of my appreciation, a small celebration has been prepared. Would you care to follow me?" asked the Empress.

The three nodded again and followed the Empress toward wide double doors off an adjacent corridor. As they reached the ornately carved white doors, they could hear beautiful music playing from inside. The Empress nodded, and, swaying like a willow in a spring breeze, she escorted the group through the doors into her royal chambers. Once through the doors, Yu-ning and the others were so dazzled by their surroundings that they came to an abrupt stop. They were speechless. This was a part of the palace that Metatron had never seen before.

The room was enormous. Every square inch of the space was richly adorned with fine furnishings and artwork. The fifty-foot vaulted ceilings were painted from one end to the other with angelic figures. Though the figures were painted onto the ceiling, it was possible to see beyond the ceiling, into the clear blue skies punctuated by cotton white clouds. The angelic figures appeared to be flying in the air above them. Everything in the room was white, accented by soft shades of pink, lavender, sage green, and soft blues.

There were chandeliers adorning the ceiling, altars on each wall of the room, and heated floors of pristine white and grey marble. The white walls were covered with glazed tiles painted with figures of goats, bulls, fish, lions, seahorses, cranes, horses, elephants, and tortoises.

In the center of the room was a long red velvet carpet leading to three long white steps up to the Empress's throne, which rested on a platform. The chair was large and white with plush, light pink velvet cushions on each side. The throne shined with a soft pink glow from the beautiful jewels and crystals encrusted on the arms and high back of the chair.

The Empress walked slowly up the red carpet and settled comfortably onto her throne, smiling peacefully at the group. At that moment, all the side walls retracted from the middle to reveal hidden screens that opened onto the larger palace grounds. The Empress's staff members pulled back the doors as servants entered the royal chamber with trays of food and drink. There were six tables covered in beautiful lavender velvet, holding an array of fruits, pastries, cakes, chocolates, and cookies. "Welcome, are you hungry?" A woman handed Yu-ning a colorful fruit.

"Thank you," Yu-ning said with appreciation and wonder. Joyous, lively music began to play, as eleven musicians entered the room carrying a multitude of exotic instruments. The Empress laughed and stood, descending from her throne to dance with everyone. Yu-ning was overjoyed, absorbing the spirit of excitement, love, and celebration. The Empress was standing next to Yu-ning, clapping and dancing, her beautiful shining gown swaying to the music.

A handsome man entered the chamber—he was dressed in an elegant robe and held an enormous bouquet of red, yellow, and orange tulips. He saw the Empress and smiled broadly as he approached her, nodding to greet the court of dancers and musicians. He handed the flowers to the Empress and said in a soft voice, "I picked each of these flowers for you, my love."

"Thank you, my Emperor," she said, with affection in her eyes. She leaned down to Yu-ning and whispered, "He is my Emperor."

"An emperor!" Romeo said in wonder, standing next to Yu-ning. Throughout the space people bowed and smiled happily at the Empress. She and her Emperor greeted everyone politely and lovingly. As the Empress took Yu-ning through the cheerful crowd, she noticed a square indigo blue box resting on a table nearby. The Empress leaned down to her and said, "This is a gift for you; you can open it. You see, when you trust and have faith, when you choose love, you receive many gifts and blessings. Open it!"

Yu-ning received the box and looked up to see Metatron standing in the circle, clapping and smiling. "We are all here for you, Yu-ning. This is your celebration," he exclaimed. Yu-ning smiled with tears in her eyes, and opened the box. Inside was a large, clear crystal orb, which began to spin when she touched it with her index finger. Yu-ning leaned in to see the scene play out within the ball. She saw fast-changing images of herself from the very beginning of her journey—from Rainbow Island to this very moment, as she celebrated in the palace. "This is very special—I will always treasure it," Yu-ning said, as the Empress embraced her sweetly.

The Empress reached for Yu-ning's hand and escorted her down the red carpet to her throne. The palace was filled with a spirit of celebration, warmth, and love. Beautiful lights shined from the chandeliers, which reflected the beautiful smiles of everyone in the room. People continued to sing, dance, and celebrate as the musicians played on. The Empress and Yu-ning enjoyed the revelry, standing at the edge of the dancers. A young brother approached and handed Yu-ning a huge slice of strawberry cake. The Empress laughed and placed her hand lovingly on Yu-ning's cheek. "Darling Yu-ning, always remember to live in your true spirit, even when you grow up. Treat everybody with kindness. Use your power with integrity. Heal others with your love."

Yu-ning had just put a huge forkful of cake into her mouth, making the Empress laugh again. But she had not taken her eyes off the Empress, and nodded in acknowledgment. The Empress was filled with affection as she watched Yu-ning.

"Come, you can sit with me; it's a big chair," she said. "We are going to watch a beautiful performance right now. Do you like music and dance?" she asked, as Yu-ning sidled comfortably next to the Empress.

Yu-ning balanced her plate of cake on her lap as her legs dangled off the edge of the throne, swinging back and forth. "I like music and dancing!" she exclaimed with excitement. "Will we see more performers?" Yu-ning queried.

"Yes, my darling," the Empress smiled. "Your heart's desire."

For the next hour, jugglers, acrobats, dancers, and singers entertained the ebullient crowd. It was a joyous affair. As the festivities began to wind down, the Empress put a hand on Yu-ning's shoulder and whispered, "Come, Yu-ning, let me show you my private sleeping chamber." She stood up and extended her hand toward Yu-ning.

"Yes, please!" Yu-ning exclaimed as she reached for her hand.

The Empress stood to face everyone and said aloud, "Thank you all for this delightful performance and celebration. Yu-ning and I will now retreat to my private quarters. Please continue the celebration. Enjoy!" Romeo raised his glass to Yu-ning, and Metatron winked at her and smiled warmly as she exited the celebration with the Empress. Magic poked his head from Metatron's pocket; whipped cream and strawberry sauce could be seen on his mouth. Yu-ning winked at him as she left with the Empress.

They walked down a hallway featuring golden statues of dragons, phoenixes, lions, monkeys, elephants, and other fanciful animals sitting atop pillars. Beautiful paintings lined the walls. They came to a shining pink door, on either side of which stood tall ceramic pots filled with delicate flowers and striking green ferns. Yu-ning noticed that the ceiling was open to the sky, and there were colorful parrots and glimmering blue morpho butterflies flying in and out of the atrium. It was like a dream.

The Empress opened her door, and the lovely aroma of fresh flowers greeted Yu-ning. The walls and ceiling were pink, and the ambiance was feminine and whimsical. Elegant landscape paintings covered the walls, adorned with delicate white frames. Vases of lilies, tulips, and orchids were spread throughout the room, along with beautifully framed photos of the Empress and Emperor and their family and court. One entire wall was covered by a violet bookshelf stuffed with books from floor to ceiling. There was a light blue piano, a sage green desk covered with white paper, an elegant brush pen and black ink plate, and a white wardrobe leading into a vast walk-in closet filled with beautiful gowns and shoes.

Inside this lovely oasis was a beautiful vanity table with a white oval mirror and a plush white chair covered in silk. On the table were approximately thirty strands of crystal malas in rose quartz, amethyst, citrine, aquamarine, rutilated quartz, jade, pearl, pink tourmaline, and prehnite.

"Oh, it's so beautiful! It's just like my magical cave, Empress! My chairs and tables are also painted different colors like yours! Do you read and study too?" Yu-ning asked with excitement, looking around the room.

"Yes, my dearest. I love art and music. I play piano and flute. I practice calligraphy, I read, I study; I am always learning." Yu-ning looked at her with deep admiration. "Be the example you want others to be," Empress continued. "I do the things I like to do, just as I did when I was your age. I have not changed. I follow my truth and I allow bliss and wonderment to guide me. Wait, I have a special gift for you," the Empress said, walking gracefully to her vanity table.

"Another?" Yu-ning said in disbelief.

The Empress held a jewelry box in her hand and extended it to Yu-ning. "Here, open it," she said.

Yu-ning opened the delicate box with awe and gratitude. "Oh, it so beautiful," she exclaimed. She lifted the lid to reveal a gorgeous pink silk scarf. "Oh, it is so soft." The scarf was glimmering soft pink and lavender lights.

The Empress reached for the scarf and placed it around Yu-ning's neck. "Wear this and honor yourself. Honor our gifts to you, and remind everyone on the outside that they deserve all the gifts we give to them, too. Please tell them not to doubt, but to always believe and have faith like you do. You have done so much, and there is so much more love to give," the Empress said.

Yu-ning was pensive. Solemnly she answered, "I understand, and I will. Thank you, Empress." Yu-ning gently touched the silky fabric draped around her neck.

"There's more inside. Keep looking," the Empress encouraged with a smile.

Yu-ning looked in the box and saw another, smaller jewelry box inside. "Yes, open it," the Empress said lovingly. Inside on pale pink velvet lay a large pink diamond ring, and a golden band. Yu-ning was overwhelmed. "This stone is perfect and precious," she said softly.

"This is the ring of power and the ring of leadership," whispered the Empress. "They are for you. Wear them, and conduct yourself and everything you do from your highest place of integrity and love. You rule from love and lead from love. We love everyone, great or small, rich or poor, human or animal," the Empress said.

"Yes, I will always do everything with love," Yu-ning repeated in awe.

"It is time for you to see my favorite place," the Empress said sweetly. Yu-ning nodded enthusiastically. They walked out of her private chamber and exited the back of the palace. There to meet them for their late-afternoon walk were Metatron, Romeo, Suparna, and the Emperor.

The Empress and Emperor joined hands and guided the small group to a smooth dirt path that wound through a lush, spectacular forest. It was if they had crossed a primeval threshold as they walked through primary rain forest, with old-growth trees towering above. Suparna glided overhead, quietly flying between the enormous trees, taking in the serenity and peace of the forest glade.

Yu-ning saw the forest open up to her right, revealing a hidden clearing, surrounded on all sides by a riotous wall of green fecundity. She stopped and sighed with excitement. "Yes, that is a secret forest glade. I go there often," the Empress said, smiling. After a long while, the rain forest gave way to a colorful garden with green manicured grass and colorful tropical flowers. "This is my garden," she said to the group. Then, turning to the Emperor, she said, "Let's walk that way—to the left." The Empress and Emperor walked slightly ahead as the Empress gently touched the blossoms along the path.

Ahead Yu-ning saw a crystal-clear pond and an arc-shaped bridge made of cypress wood. The pond reflected a rainbow of colors as the slanting rays of the late-afternoon sun shined off the water. "It's so beautiful!" Yu-ning cried, as she dashed toward the bridge and quickly walked to the middle. She leaned over the wooden railing, admiring the water. Yu-ning felt like she was soaring as she leaned out over the bridge, gazing with joy into the colorful pond below. She crouched down and with her right arm outstretched, swept her fingers across the water, creating a magnificent ripple of color and movement.

It was very quiet and tranquil. Romeo and Metatron joined Yu-ning, along with the Emperor and Empress, along the railing of the bridge. Magic left Metatron's pocket, lured to the pond's banks by the buzzing of insects. Suparna landed quietly nearby and stood taking in the beautiful bridge and peaceful pond. The only sounds were those of birds, insects, and water gurgling in a small rivulet that flowed out of the forest into the pond.

Large orange and white koi darted back and forth. Their scales shined through the water in a rainbow of colors— orange, red, yellow, green, blue, and purple. As they swam they blended into the water, which surprised Yu-ning and made the Empress laugh.

"Seeing these beautiful fish reminds me of what is still missing: the Seven Sacred Crystals," said Yu-ning. "How will we ever find them again?"

"All of us, together, will reclaim the crystals, Yu-ning," said the Empress, looking alternately at Yu-ning, Romeo, Metatron, and Suparna. "And even though the Seven Sacred Crystals are gone, we all have the light and colors within us, don't we Yu-ning?" said the Empress. "Never forget the colors of hope and love are always within you."

Yu-ning lunged to hug the Empress around her waist. As she looked up and smiled into the Empress's eyes, she said, "I will, Empress. I will." The Empress leaned down to kiss her forehead. Tears filled their eyes.

Yu-ning looked up at the Empress and said, "Empress, this place is so colorful and beautiful. It is just like Rainbow Island! It's as if we were in the same place."

The Empress nodded, smiling at Yu-ning. She looked at the kind wizard, whose eyes were shining like diamonds. Yu-ning and Romeo ran down the bridge, searching for Magic in the reeds along the edge of the pond.

The Empress sighed joyfully, with emotion filling her heart. Tears welled in her eyes as she looked at Metatron. "Is she ready to hear the truth, Metatron?"

"Not yet, your Highness. She has been through so much, and has only just discovered her identity as a Dalq Render. I do not think now is the time. But soon—very soon."

"But you know that her destiny is tied to mine, and mine to hers . . . Should she know that she is the future Empress, and that I am . . ." The Empress stopped in mid-sentence as Yu-ning ran back onto the bridge, holding Magic in the palm of her hand.

"This is so wonderful!" exclaimed Yu-ning. "I feel as if I could stay here forever. Metatron, can we stay here for a while?"

Metatron knelt down, so that he was even with the young girl's eyes. "Yu-ning, this will not be our last visit to the Floating Palace . . . I promise we will return to visit with the Empress very soon."

"Yes," said the Empress, who stood nearby. "I will see you again, my dear. My prayer is that the world will know love again through you, Yu-ning, and through Romeo. All you need to do is trust—live your story, Yu-ning, and live it in love."

Romeo joined Yu-ning at the center of the bridge as they gazed at the tranquil scene before them. At the end of the bridge, a flash of bright light caught everyone's attention—as the group turned toward the beautiful light, One materialized before the group. Though he shared no words with Yu-ning— or anyone else—a pure love flowed from him, filling Yu-ning's heart with an overwhelming joy. A moment later One transformed back into a brilliant orb of light, floated above the bridge, and was gone in a bright flash.

Metatron smiled and nodded his head as he turned back to his friends. "At week's end, my friends, we depart. First we rest, and then it will be time for us to journey to Rainbow Island."

The small group gazed across the pond, down the sloping descent of the green meadows—and out beyond the enchanted walls of the Floating Palace. In the distance, across the western sea, the sun was a fading disc on the far horizon, bathing the bridge in a soft, shimmering pink glow.

# Thirty-Four

# Nest

*I*T WAS DUSK and the sky was dark.

Across stormy waters the lone island was bathed in rain and swirling cloud. Enormous sea swells battered the cliffs, the whiteness of the crashing waves in stark contrast to the dark grey granite rocks jutting from the turbulent sea. High above—higher than the lair of the warlock, or the cavernous jail that once held a small boy—was the highest point on the island. It was an enormous spur of rock that jutted above all others, reaching high into the sky—a dark tower looming over the desolation of the isolated island of rock.

Just below the summit of the craggy peak, a lone climber inched closer to the summit. Though the rain and wind buffeted him, his long, thin fingers held fast as he climbed hand over hand. Hobaling stopped, his feet resting on a small ledge, as he took in the scene all around him. Overhead a shadow passed, followed by a loud screech that pierced the sounds of the storm.

Hobaling continued to climb and grabbed hold of the last rock in his ascent, pulling himself up onto the top ledge. Nestled in a round cleft in the rocks, hidden from below, was a nest. Lying in the nest were seven large crystals. They were void of any life or light, and rain pelted them from above.

The warlock rubbed his hands across the stones, and stopped—his hand was poised in midair as the large dark shadow once again passed overhead. He looked up and shouted, "There were *two* skulls, weren't there, my dear?"

As he turned back toward the nest, his hand continued past the seven stones and fell upon three darker, larger objects. The black eggs had a polished, smooth surface—like hard obsidian rock.

As night fell, the warlock remained on the ledge, admiring his trophies. Darkness came quickly, and the storm grew more violent. Thunder clapped, followed a moment later by lightning that illuminated the hidden nest. The flash of light revealed all ten objects lying side by side, indistinguishable one from the other, as the rain pelted down from the black sky above.

# About the Author

CHRISTIE HSIAO is founder of Serenity Media Group, a global entertainment company devoted to creating high quality film, TV, and digital media projects. It is her vision to create positive entertainment that is uplifting, international in scope, and that catalyzes change. Christie believes in the unique power of story to raise awareness and to compel societal transformation. Originally from Taiwan, she holds a BA from UCLA in East Asian Studies and an MBA from Pepperdine University. Christie went on to study film in New York City, where she wrote, directed, and produced several well-received films. This is her first novel.

# Play the
## *Journey to*
## *Rainbow Island*
## Video Game!

*Available at the*
## Apple App Store,

## Google Play,

## *and* Facebook.

TWITTER
http://twitter.com/j2rainbowisland

FACEBOOK
www.facebook.com/pages/Journey-To-Rainbow-Island/604810816215432